Five Fingers

Māra Zālīte

FIVE FINGERS

Translated from the Latvian by Margita Gailitis

DALKEY ARCHIVE PRESS

Originally published in Latvian by Mansards Publishing House as *Pieci Pirksti* in 2013.

Copyright © 2013 by Māra Zālīte
Translation copyright © 2017 by Margita Gailitis
First Dalkey Archive edition, 2017

Library of Congress Cataloging-in-Publication Data
Identifiers: ISBN 9781628971699
LC Record Available at http://catalog.loc.gov/

RAKSTNIEKU MĀJA DUBULTOS

Kultūras ministrija

Supported by the Latvian Writers Union and the Ministry of Culture of the Republic of Latvia.

Partially funded by a grant by the Illinois Arts Council, a state agency.

www.dalkeyarchive.com
Victoria, TX / McLean, IL / Dublin

Dalkey Archive Press publications are, in part, made possible through the support of the University of Houston-Victoria and its programs in creative writing, publishing, and translation.

Printed on permanent/durable acid-free paper

Translator's Introduction

An introduction to the biographical novel *Five Fingers* by Māra Zālīte requires a brief description of the historical context to provide perspective—to position it as not only the story of the novel's protagonist Laura and her young parents returning to Latvia from Siberia, but also the story of thousands of such deportees.

At the beginning of World War II, the USSR and Germany signed the secret Molotov-Ribbentrop Pact, agreeing to divide Eastern Europe by giving control of the three Baltic States—Estonia, Latvia and Lithuania—as well as part of Poland and Eastern Germany, to the Soviets. In 1940, the Soviet Union forcibly annexed the small Baltic countries, subsequently subjecting their populations to severe repressions. Among the most egregious of these were mass deportations of people, including children, to Siberia. Stalin used this form of brutal social engineering in the hope of eliminating all sections of society that could threaten to undermine the Soviet dictatorship.

In Latvia, the first large-scale deportation was perpetrated on June 14, 1941, when 15,443 Latvian residents were forcibly deported, among them 3,741 children under the age of sixteen. The second, even more massive deportation was executed on March 25, 1949 with 42,125 persons deported, including 10,987 children.

Those selected for deportation were woken in the night and given less than one hour to prepare for the journey. They could take with them only what they could carry. They were herded into cattle or freight railway cars. Many, especially infants, the sick, and the elderly died on the way to their destination. Men were separated from their families and sent to hard labor camps, where many died. Women and children were taken to so-called "administrative settlements" in remote Siberian areas with harsh climate conditions, there to suffer freezing temperatures often registering at minus forty degrees Centigrade. Many fell ill or starved to death, those who survived had to endure inhumane conditions.

Many of the more than 15,000 children deported from Latvia to Siberia did not survive the horrendous circumstances of the Gulag. All the children, even infants, like their parents, were classified as "enemies of the people." The children who managed to stay alive in Siberia received limited, if any, education, which was provided in Russian. Thus those of the young deportees who did return to Latvia after years spent in Siberia, being more fluent in Russian, spoke their native Latvian poorly, and had to compensate for their poor education. All returning deportees continued to be on a "blacklist" and often had trouble obtaining employment.

The terror of the Soviet totalitarian regime exacted a heavy human toll, destroying lives and halting the economic growth enjoyed by Latvia during its brief first period of independence. The Soviet occupation in June 1940 ended Latvia's sovereignty and began a fifty-one-year period of foreign and in many cases brutal subjugation.

Māra Zālīte's *Five Fingers* is an account of the return in the 1960s—after seventeen years spent in Siberia—of two such deported children, Anda and Jānis, now young married adults coming home with their child Laura, who was born in Siberia. The main protagonist and spokesperson for the story is five-year-old Laura. Thus the Soviet-occupied Latvia of the 1960s is seen and described as filtered through her innocent, rarely judgmental eyes. For Laura this is not a return home, Latvia never having been her home, but her arrival in a fantasy land, the utopia dreamt about and described by her parents during their forced exile. She is an infinitely curious and observant child, constantly exploring and often getting into trouble, thus the book is peppered with many funny, sometimes dangerous escapades. Thus, for example, in innocent response to Soviet propaganda, Laura gathers scrap metal to build a boat to send food to starving children in America, and while trying to bring water to tethered horses in a distant field, falls into an abandoned well.

There is much that she does not understand—words she calls

"empty"—empty of meaning, leading to comical misunderstandings. For example "Amelioration" for Laura becomes a nasty woman, who has wrecked some fields. But there also are misunderstandings that metaphorically can be interpreted as any sane person's lack of comprehension of many of the horrendous or absurd elements of the Soviet regime. Laura's observations provide brief glimpses of the devastation of homes, lack of employment, corruption, alcohol abuse, risk of being black-listed and again deported, and the censorship and propaganda, which add up to create as background the harsh reality of Soviet-occupied Latvia. But while Laura witnesses, for example, her mother's shock at seeing the devastated home of her grandparents upon her return, the "great room" turned into a stable now storing manure, trees hewed, and gardens destroyed, nothing can dampen Laura's spirit nor her joy at discovery—the tadpoles in a pond or a garden full of fallen sweet plums.

For Laura the Soviets are the distant dog-faced monsters of fairytales, never assuming real shape.

Briefly awakened childish memories in Laura of Siberia and the people she knew there do reveal how many nationalities were deported—starting with some Russians themselves, Latvians, Lithuanians, Jews (a Jewess, an opera singer, in Laura's barrack is accused of being a British spy by the Soviets, and has all five fingers of each hand broken during questioning), Ukrainians, Romanians, and so on. But these memories also include happy moments of generosity, courage, and community spirit among the deportees.

Laura is five years old at the beginning of the book and still five at its conclusion. There is no happy ending to *Five Fingers* as the harsh reality of life under a brutal foreign power continues for Laura's family. The only bright light at the end of the book is Laura's still undiminished childish innocence and joy in life.

Māra Zālīte, the author of *Five Fingers*, like her heroine Laura, was born in Siberia to parents deported as children. And like Laura she returned to Latvia at the age of five. But the well-known and award-winning poet and playwright, in her fictionalized account of her childhood, also reflects the fate of thousands of Latvians, as well as other Eastern Bloc individuals from Soviet-annexed satellite countries who suffered the horrors of occupation and deportation. Many of the thousands who fled to the West to escape this occupation have family members who suffered similarly.

Most Latvian families have a relative who was deported, who died in Siberia, or if they returned after deportation, had their lives dramatically altered forever.

I, Margita Gailitis, the translator into English of *Five Fingers*, fled Latvia at four years of age with my mother, two sisters, and paternal grandparents, and after spending some time in displaced persons camps, emigrated with my family to Canada. But my father was deported to Siberia and died there. One of my missions in life, therefore, has been to inform English readers through translation, as much as I am able to do, about the horrors of occupation and deportation.

While several books have now been written about the deportation of Latvians to Siberia—for example, thanks to Dalkey Archive, *With Dance Shoes in Siberian Snow* by Sandra Kalniete in my translation, and the current best-seller *Between Shades of Gray* by Ruta Sepetys—very little has been offered in fictionalized form regarding the hardships encountered by deportees returning to their still Soviet-occupied homelands. *Five Fingers* therefore offers a fresh insight into this heartrending experience that's still relevant to many. In addition, recent events in the Ukraine, and the accompanying political saber-rattling by Russia's President Vladimir Putin, have once again raised the specter of new imperial ambitions with all that implies for small nations like the Baltics.

Margita Gailitis
poet and translator

Five Fingers

Everyone is also someone else
and no one is only one's self.

—someone else

The Train

LAURA HAS BEEN RIDING the train her entire life. Perhaps even longer. A train is not something good. More likely it's something evil. Like a gigantic dragon blowing rage from its nostrils. Dreadful anger at the entire world, which the dragon every now and then vents in the form of a hissing mist.

"What was that?"

Papa thinks that the train lets off steam and that it wouldn't harm Laura to do the same. What? Let off some steam? Laura? Yes, then she'd fidget less. How can Papa compare her to a train, how can he? Laura sulks.

The dragon howls, whistles and chokes, and whips its tail. Laura with her mama and papa are riding the train in its very tail. Hence the dragon flings them about like old fools. Laura has no faith in the train, not even a smidgeon of faith. Maybe the train is insane. Maybe the train has no mind whatsoever. How can a person know in what direction this nutty pile of iron is dragging them? A person may think that it's to Latvia, but who knows for sure? How can one be certain?

The train can't do anything on its own, Mama tries to comfort her. The train has to ride straight along the tracks, not to the right or to the left. The tracks control this steed like reins would. Laura can calm down, because the tracks lead directly to Latvia. One more bend and then the town of Ikšķile. Papa laughs. Laura doesn't want to explain all the words she's just uttered. Another time she would, but right now Laura doesn't want any part of such talks ...

Laura can't bear it any longer, can't stand it anymore! Can't and doesn't want to, and that's all! Can't bear any longer the constant jolting, shunting, and rattling, from which Laura feels ill and has to vomit. She doesn't want to smell the sharp odor

of coal and metal. She doesn't want to stomach the sweat and
smelly feet of other people when they take their boots off to lie
down on the compartment's sleeping bunks. Many don't have
socks but rather rags wrapped around their feet. She doesn't
want the fumes of alcohol or Russian cigarettes in the train cor-
ridors, doesn't want the tea in metal containers, because soon
after drinking it she has to go to the train's toilet and pee. Laura
always tries to hold on until the very last minute.

The WC? Let's go to the WC. Laura had trusted Mama. But
what she's seen there… It makes Laura want to vomit, she doesn't
dare even think about it. The most dreadful part of the train is
the WC. A small child can fall into the toilet bowl and drop out
through the open hole! It's the most horrendous thing that Laura
can imagine. The toilet hole moves and disappears, you can't aim
into it, through it you can see flashing railroad ties and threatening, vengeful earth between the ties. In the middle of the tracks
the soil is like a furrow, where people sow their poo. A small child
can only close her eyes and yell. Laura doesn't want the smell, the
jolting, or for her tummy to hurt. She's made up her mind. Laura
will get off the train and never again ride on such a smelly dragon.
She'll think of a different way to get to Latvia. She'll collect her
things. Mama is reading a book, her head bent. Let her read, she'll
raise her head, but Laura will already be gone.

"Laura! Where are you off to?" Papa seems cheerful.

Just wait, wait until Laura gets off. You'll see then if Papa is
still cheerful.

"Laura won't go by train! Laura will go by boat! Laura is
going to get off!"

"Climb up on the baggage rack and don't talk nonsense! You
won't get off, it won't happen! Pull, just keep pulling at that
door. The attendant will come and throw you out!" Mama has
raised her head from the book and is angry.

"Laura's going to go by boat!"

"Where are you going to get such a boat? No boats go to
Latvia."

"Why don't they?"

"Because boats don't have legs."

"Why don't they?"

"Figure it out yourself."

Laura doesn't want to figure out anything. Laura doesn't want to have any reasons for going by train, especially because of Madame Attendant, who can throw children off a moving train.

Their trip had started with a ship. With a big, white ship. With a big ship and with great jubilation. It was no shabby slipper. Why did Papa have to talk like that? It was a big, white ship. On a ship you could go out to get fresh air, look at the blue sky, let the sun warm up hurting knees and elbows, and you could breathe in the big river. A river could be trusted. A river is alive. A river is wise. Not like the tracks that have neither a heart nor a mind. A river smells of fresh fish. Breathing in ever so deeply, you can breathe in some sweet fish. Some totally tiny fish, not the big ones, of course.

Laura draws breaths full of very tiny, the tiniest of fish. So tiny, that you can't see them with your eyes, only sense how the tiny fish begin to play joyfully in her heart. How did they get there?

The fish help Laura feel more alive.

Laura doesn't have seasickness, not even a bit. Some people are ill with it. How can you be seasick on a river? Papa and Mama aren't ill either. They stand embracing by the edge of the ship called the portside and silently sing a Latvian song: "Blow ye winds, drive my boat, drive me on to Courland." Not a little boat, but a ship. Laura objects on behalf of the ship, but they just gaze into each other's eyes. They don't notice the child at all.

Laura understands that there's freedom on the ship that sails along the river. That's what the talk has been about, what the talk is about all the time. At least she begins to sense this. At least something like it. The water and the sky. The wind and the sun. Joy that she has the tiny fish in her heart. The ship that calmly sails there, where you, a person, most avidly yearn to be. When you, the person, can make a deal with the wind for it to help you. Drive me on to Courland or Kurzeme, as they call it in Latvia.

Kurzeme is the same as Latvia.

A Russian Babushka and Eggs

"Mama, how long still?" Laura asks and questions, begs and pleads again and again, already for the umpteenth time. Laura knows, however, that it's useless.

Still a bit longer, it can't be helped. Be patient.

Be patient, don't fidget, don't grumble, whimper, whine, wail, don't be silly!—all of it Laura has heard many times before. Laura can recite it all like a ditty. Even when she's woken up at night.

"Papa, will it be long now?" Just in case, if after all, miracles do happen, if by the least chance, Papa knows better.

"Still a while. Calm down."

Once more the verse. Be calm, quiet down, be well-behaved and obedient, smart, be a big girl and clever. What more can they think of that Laura must be? Oh, yes. Laura also has to be happy because she's going home. But how much longer? What does longer mean? How long is longer? What if it's for all of life?

"Why still a while longer? Mama?"

"Because Latvia is far."

"Why is Latvia far? Papa?"

"Because it's not near."

"Why isn't it near?"

"Because why ends with a y! *Vsyo*—that's it! I'm up to my *dofiga*! I'm going for a smoke."

That too is nothing new.

For quite a while now the three of them have been alone in their train compartment.

Now and then there's a fourth person. He or she enters the compartment, rides for a day or a night and once more leaves. Or two nights, but then also—leaves. Everyone rides for a while and then gets off. Only Laura with her mama and papa ride and ride and ride. What if they have long ago driven by Latvia?

Laura can't forget the skinny Russian babushka.

On seeing her, Laura falls ill. A person is healthy, healthy and here at once—falls ill. An illness seizes one. She sees the babushka and falls ill. Fever, aching knees and elbows that swell, growing pink like peonies. Laura is convinced that it's connected to the Russian babushka. She has a bag.

When did the babushka appear here? Did she enter through the walls? Maybe she's an old snake hag? Maybe there are snakes in her bag? It's suspicious because she holds the bag an arm's length away. She's not a good person, certainly not, you can sense that. Evil oozes from babushka. Like the cold. Like the smell of old age. The smell of old age is when you pee in your pants but don't wash them, an old age smell is when food goes bad.

What if she's a ghost? She's sitting silently, stiffly, so very stiffly and not moving. What if she's a corpse? A corpse, a corpse, she's not alive. Maybe carried in and placed here? A gray fleecy shawl covers her face, from which looms only a pointed and withered chin with a few long, sparse hairs.

Laura wants to, but can't forget her.

Is she mute? Or deaf? Around the old woman's neck is hung a sign with the address where she's headed. She hasn't responded with even half a word, or a glance either to Mama or to Papa, although they've just wanted to help.

A dead corpse, which someone has brought in and propped up in the corner of the compartment. This is what Laura has decided.

But no such thing. Babushka just pretends to be dead. Like a fox, well that fox that the fisherman found on the road. That fisherman who'd caught a whole wagon-full of fish and going home also found a dead fox on the road. What luck! The fisherman was delighted—his wife would have the best of collars. But the fox quietly threw all the fish out of the wagon and in the end fled, so there! Animals do this to fool someone, to escape. Pretend to be dead. But do people?

A fly lands on babushka's nose. If she were a corpse, she wouldn't have raised her hand, wouldn't have swatted and killed the fly, but, if she had tried to kill it, wouldn't have.

She's alive after all and crafty.

Laura doesn't sleep the whole night because babushka also doesn't sleep, just pretends to. Mama and Papa already are snoring, when babushka totally comes to life in the dark and begins to busy herself. Hastily she sets to checking if any of her eggs have cracked. Those are snake eggs. Laura has seen in the boreal forest how a snake lays, no, releases eggs from itself. A whole string of them. They're held together by a transparent membrane. When the membrane dries out, tiny snakelets crawl out of the eggs. Well, at the beginning the snakelets are the size of fat worms. Just black, not rosy like worms. Just quick, not slow like worms. The minute they're out of the eggs, they hurry away in all directions like swift flowing rivulets. What will they do now, if in the compartment snakelets should hatch? The emergency stop lever will have to be pulled. Laura will pull it! The train will have to stop, it won't be able to continue moving being full of snakes!

Each one of the eggs is wrapped separately in newspaper. Babushka carefully unwraps each egg, then makes sure the egg isn't broken, and wraps it up again. Now and then the old woman turns the egg this way and that, clicking her tongue with pleasure—oh, what a lovely egg! Then she wraps it up again, all the time mumbling, grumbling something to herself. The eggs do, however, look much like hens' eggs. Too big to be snake eggs. But what if they're the eggs of a big boa constrictor? It's good that Laura knows where the emergency stop lever is; good that Papa has shown it to her. But if the stop lever is pulled for no good reason, then she'd be in lots of trouble. Then she could be put off the train and asked to pay a fine and she wouldn't get to Latvia! No, Laura will wait for a while yet to pull the stop lever; Laura won't pull the lever at all, then, better that the train be full of boa constrictors! The rustling of the newspapers and the mumbling has prevented Laura from falling asleep. From the upper baggage rack she covertly watches babushka, maybe after all she is a ghost. Maybe she is?

Suddenly their eyes meet. Laura shrinks back in embarrassment, because it's not good to lurk about like this and look covertly at someone.

In babushka's eyes fear and hatred appear. Great, great, dreadful fear. Great, great, dreadful hatred. Laura freezes. Fear of Laura? Hatred of Laura? Why? What for?

The old woman draws the bag of eggs to her gaunt chest and presses it close. Laura hears the fragile egg shells crack. Hens' eggs. Hens. Snake eggs wouldn't crack like that.

"Don't squeeze the eggs like that, they'll break!" Laura whispers and realizes that she's speaking in Latvian.

Maybe she should have whispered in Russian because babushka now grows more afraid, presses the bag of eggs even closer to her chest, the eggshells cracking even more audibly. Babushka keeps crossing herself, as if Laura was the devil himself, and groans so furiously, furiously groans, casts an evil eye at her, and maybe curses her, the old witch?

No way, snake hag! Laura will stand firm. It's not for nothing that the Barrack's Madalina knew such things. In thought you had to draw around yourself a kind of gold hoop, erect a sort of strong wall. In thought. But what was most important, Madalina always urged—that when you're being cursed, you shouldn't be afraid! Never ever! Otherwise you would indeed be cursed. Fear is like a hole in the wall, like a break in the gold hoop. But if you're not afraid then the curse boomerangs back to the person cursing you. In addition it increases ten times in its power.

Laura draws the hoop around herself, erects a wall and is not afraid. With all her strength. A gold hoop, a strong wall. And she's not afraid. Why should Laura be afraid? If there's no ghost or corpse? If the eggs are not snake eggs? Why should Laura be afraid if around her is the gold hoop and the strong wall? They're there.

It's a pity though that the old woman is crushing all the eggs. Lovely brown and white hens' eggs. Hens have hatched them, tried their best, babushka has saved and wrapped them, brought them for somebody, and now she takes and crushes them. Some of the eggs babushka has saved too long and now they're broken and, ugh, how they smell!

But she herself is to blame. Why hate? Why curse? Why be afraid? Why put old eggs in a bag? What reasonable person ever puts eggs in a bag? Could she not have brought a basket?

Laura turns away, doesn't look anymore, gets sleepy because Laura is dreadfully tired from having drawn the hoop, erected a wall, and fought her fear. Also babushka has again become still and is silent. There's nothing more to look at there. The eggs smell. Laura draws a white sheet over her head. She feels illness in her elbows and knees. In the dark she can't see them, but she knows they're swollen and rosy like peonies.

In the morning babushka, as mysteriously as she had arrived, has disappeared. There's not even a whiff of babushka. That's just a saying. In fact the smell has remained, but the illness has passed. Laura is no longer feverish. The peonies in her knees are no longer blooming. Maybe babushka had been a ghost or a corpse after all? Was or wasn't a corpse, was or wasn't a ghost, but the tiny fish that Laura had breathed in on the ship, babushka has tossed from the wagon like the crafty fox. The tiny fish no longer play in Laura's heart.

Laura hasn't rested at all during her sleep. Laughing Child was racing all night along the narrow wagon corridor. The laughter of Laughing Child was loud. Madame Attendant tried to catch the child, caught him and threw him out of the window, but after a while Laughing Child was back again and once more raced along the narrow wagon corridor and giggled, and Madame Attendant again tried to catch him and throw him out of the window, and so on, many more times.

And what's more, Laura also experienced her own birth and that was altogether terrible, because Laura was inside an egg. Inside an egg wanting to get out, because Laura had to be born, but the egg didn't have a crackable, thin shell, which Laura could have broken easily. The egg was soft-shelled, and Laura had to press with all her might against soft and glutinous rubber, against the strong and unyielding casing with all her strength, until she got out. Laura had nearly smothered in that egg, that soft-shell egg, and besides, it was terrible not knowing what kind of an egg it was and what Laura would be when she got out.

When Laura was born

When Laura was born, no one held her among sweet pea blossoms for her to grow up beautiful.

When Laura was born, no one swaddled her in a tablecloth so in her life she'd always be at a bounteous table.

When Laura was born, no one heated up water with linden wood.

When Laura was born, no one smeared honey on her lips so she, when grown, would have many suitors.

All these ancient Latvian customs ensuring good fortune didn't ease Laura's entry into this world.

When Laura was born, it was a freezing fifty degrees below zero.

When Laura was born, she was born before full-term.

Mama didn't have milk in her breasts.

For Mama to have milk in her breasts, these words should have been spoken: my milk comes from Jelgava, my milk comes from Liepāja, my milk comes from Riga, my milk comes from all the lakes, my milk comes from all the rivers, from all the springs, from all around.

When Laura was born, no one said such words because the Barrack in Siberia was too far from the Latvian cities of Jelgava, Liepāja and Riga, too far were the lakes, rivers, and springs.

Mama's breasts were dry.

When Laura was born, she was meant to die.

When Laura was born, she was not yet Laura.

Then the Barrack came to life.

Three Lithuanian women insisted that the infant was not allowed to die without being christened because without a christening no one can enter God's kingdom, no one can receive His mercy and salvation.

Three Lithuanian women—Maria, Laima, and Laura—created an altar, decorating it with the straw from their beds and with cedar cones.

Maria gave up her white embroidered blouse and that became the altar cloth.

Laima gave her brightest little *ploshka*—a candle made of dripped wax with a string inserted as wick—which then served as the christening candle.

Laura melted some snow in a bowl, and that was the holy water.

I baptize you in the name of the Father, the Son, and the Holy Ghost. Amen.

And although I'm neither a bishop nor a priest and not even a deacon, my rights and duties as a Catholic woman are to baptize you.

Not asking for consent, you, who have been given a frail and failing life of the flesh, thus, not asking for consent, I give you eternal life in Jesus Christ. Amen.

In the name of the most holy Trinity I make the sign of the cross on your forehead. And although I'm neither a bishop nor a priest and not even a deacon, by my rights and duties as a Catholic woman I make the sign of the cross on your forehead.

Thus spoke all—Maria, Laima, and Laura—one after the other.

"A name! What name for the child? We have to give her a name," whispered Jukka the Finn from Karelia. From the Kalevala lands, he always used to proudly add.

"Maybe there's no need? You do understand," quietly protested the Ukrainian Oleksander.

His parents at one time were veterinarians in Rivna, a town near Lviva. They had no objections to animal meat in their diet, live or dead, big or small. All of it is just protein, they taught Oleksander, and he had survived eating his own lice.

A leftover, I'm a leftover, he laughed.

In the Barrack all were leftovers.

"Why no need? Of course there's a need!" exclaimed Ciganka Moldovanka loudly, in her accustomed manner.

She was neither a gypsy nor a Moldavian. Hers was just a nickname. Madalina was a Romanian. She knew how to tell fortunes with cards.

"It must be done quickly," urged Kima.

Kima herself was not enthusiastic about her name because it was formed from *Komunistchesky Internacional Molodiozi*, but such and similar word combinations were frowned upon in the Barrack. Nonetheless it was Kima's only memento left by her parents. They were Russian engineers and created the plans for submarines in Leningrad. Dog-faced monsters shot them already before the war even though they were *chistiye,* that is, pure Russians and committed Communists. Kima had ceased growing at seven years of age, and the Barrack people had trouble dealing with her as an adult.

Mama was weak, she reached out for her little girl, whom the Lithuanian women were now holding and baptizing in the Pope's faith, "But we're Lutherans," she whispered soundlessly, "but we're Lutherans." But she was reaching out in her mind only, also screaming and weeping only in her mind, because in reality she lay there silent and unmoving.

Was she in her mind screaming and crying from happiness that the child conceived in love had been born?

Was she screaming and weeping from sorrow that she didn't have milk in her breasts, didn't have sustenance for the child, because her breasts were empty and she, in giving life, would also be the death of her child?

Guilt broke Mama's heart and crushed her with helplessness as heavy as the ice the length of a river.

Mama lost consciousness.

Mrs. Austrums was the oldest person in the Barrack, and this wasn't at all the first birth that she, who had once been the Lamme's district postmistress in Latvia, had to assist with in Siberia.

But this was almost like her own child.

Why almost? She and Lilia, the newborn's grandmother, had been driven to Siberia in the same cattle car from one and the same rural district, torn from the same soil like strips of raw flesh, from Latvia.

Their husbands had been friends from elementary school times and eleven years before had been shot and killed on the same day in Riga, in the cellars of the KGB building, in ancient beautiful Riga! They had shared everything equally, even a nut kernel. Mrs. Austrums would never have grandchildren because she was the only one remaining of her vast family.

Lilia's first grandchild had by now been washed and swaddled; everything had been done as it had to be done. Lilia herself didn't yet know that the little one had arrived. She, just like Mrs. Austrums, lived in the adjacent Barrack since Anda had married Jānis. That's why Lilia's knitted little hats and booties weren't here. They could do without them for a while. Mrs. Austrums knew that Lilia had not only sewn little shirts but also crocheted around the edges of the cloth diapers, but who could have foreseen this premature birth?

Lilia had been called away to the city.

It was fortunate that these were no longer the insane years, when you didn't know with what to swaddle a baby. Men in those times had to give away the rags in which they wrapped their feet, their last rags. If the child died, the men could get their foot wrappings back. Usually they did get them back.

This child could live if only her sucking instinct had developed. Mrs. Austrums anxiously placed the child at her mother's breast.

The instinct had developed, but there was no milk in the mother's breast.

In such instances one had to think of the mother. First of all about the mother. Let the child fend as it might. The mother had to be saved. The mother who herself was no more than a child, not even twenty years old. With luck, she'd have other children.

Mrs. Austrums washed Mama's groin with alcohol and camphor oil, and she collected the afterbirth from the sheet. It looked as if it had been ejected nicely, they'd throw it out later, for now it wasn't good to open and shut the door, she was happy that the bleeding had almost stopped. The child was small so there were no tears. Only the weakness.

Papa, stunned and confused, was stroking Mama's face and looking around in a daze. What is happening here? What are the Barrack people doing? What kind of a theater have they staged here? At a time when he was perhaps going to lose both—his daughter and wife, his only precious, live souls? What salvation, what mercy? What eternal life?

Papa didn't believe in either a Catholic or a Lutheran God, or in a devil, or Allah, or cards, or Muhammad. Not one of them. In nothing.

Now and then Papa hurried to add firewood to the cast iron stove. To boil more water. One more tea kettle, one more. Fire up the stove, again and again. Only thus could he help his firstborn. His beloved wife! By not letting in the cold from outside, the freezing minus fifty.

"Give the child a name! She should be called after one of the godmothers. Maybe—Maria?" proposed the Tatar Ibrahim.

He came from an ancient and famous Crimean merchant family and his God was Allah, and His Prophet Muhammad. He had carved an arrow in a Barrack's log. It pointed in the direction of Mecca.

"Or else Laima? That's both a Lithuanian and a Latvian word meaning happiness and good fortune," said Jukka.

"Laima sounds too gentle. The name needs harshness and power," said Asya.

Asya was a Jewess from London, an opera singer with perfect pitch, and she was an English spy. The latter she had denied despite extensive torture.

That's why she had broken fingers; one by one the Cheka dog-faced monsters had broken all of Asya's fingers. Five fingers of her right hand and five fingers of her left hand. Now her hands tenderly touched the child's head.

"Laura?"

"Laura," said Maria.

"Laura," said Laima.

"Laura," whispered Laura. "Jesus Maria," she continued, crossing herself and shivering in superstitious fear.

At that moment little Laura began to cry. Maria, holding the child close to her breast, blushed like a rose, because the little one plainly was turning her mouth to Maria's breast, but Maria was still a young girl.

"She wants to eat." Maria was frightened and embarrassed.

"Maybe Anda, the baby's mama, will still have milk. She needs protein. I've got some bear's meat buried. It just needs to be unfrozen." Oleksander headed for the door and ran into the

Georgian woman Maya.

Mrs. Austrums had brought Maya from the adjacent Barrack, remembering, thanks be to God, thank God, remembering that nine months ago she had brought little Levan into this world! If the Barrack's floor was not so cold, the boy would already be crawling.

"Too soon you mourn that child! Give her here!" Maya said and drew out her large milk-filled breast from her floral flannel blouse. Maya stuck her nipple in Laura's mouth. The crying ceased. From Maya's crown of abundant and black hair dripped melting frost. Bare-headed she had hurried here.

Silence fell in the Barrack.

If the child would take to the breast, she would live. If not …

Mama regained consciousness. As if through a shifting mist she gazed at Maya's large, milk-filled breast and at her little one, who restlessly fidgeted and moaned.

Papa standing at the open stove door holding firewood froze.

Jukka's round face turned rosy.

Maria, Laima, and Laura, in whose name the child now was called, were praying.

Hail Mary, full of grace.

Madalina hastily laid out some cards.

Ibrahim gazed in the direction of Mecca.

Kima repeatedly crossed herself, like the Greek Orthodox do.

Asya firmly grasped her broken fingers.

Maya squirted a stream of milk into the little one's mouth.

The little one choked and sneezed.

Everyone waited.

Maya, her movements assured, once more placed her nipple as brown and firm as a bud, into the child's tiny mouth.

Laura began to avidly suck.

"*Chame, chame, deda genazvalos,*" Maya, smiling, urged the baby to suck in Georgian. "Levan will be your milk brother. I'll have enough for both of you," Maya added proudly.

"A crazy life. The cards show a crazy life. Crazy. But the main thing is that she's alive."

Madalina had finally laid out the cards.

The Major and the Candy

ON THE RIM OF A WELL sits a tailor
Mending his tailcoat
Pretty Laura passes by
Wants to splash him with water!

Mama sings and rocks Laura on her knee. Mama is trying; it isn't as if Mama isn't trying. The next verse is the one Laura likes the most, the bit where Mama, in a different voice, shakes her.

Lass have you lost your mind?
My tailcoat will get ruined!
I must go to church tomorrow!
What shall I wear then?

The tailor is dreadfully angry. Dreadfully! But all Laura wants to do is laugh. The tailor is hilarious after all! Laura laughs as if she were being tickled. But if Mama actually tickles her, then it's even more ticklish. Where Laura is most ticklish is under her chin. A person can be tickled to death because Papa has told Laura that the Chinese tickle all their naughty ones until they're as dead as doornails.

"Up-sy-dai-sy, up-si-dai-sy, Laura's going home by train! Up-si-dai-sy, tra-la-la—Laura's going home la-la! Laura's going to Avoti upsi-la! Up-si-dai-sy, upsi-la, boozy, woozy, splat!"

Now and then Papa also tries; he rocks Laura on his knee, grasping her under her armpits throws her up in the air, until she tires, and both, out of breath, end up laughing. That's when Papa is happy. When Mama is happy. Those are the good moments. But when Laura has been whining nonstop for half the day, then Papa usually exclaims—*dofiga*—enough is enough! And takes off to have a smoke.

17

At some train stop Madame Attendant opens the compartment door.

"Here you are. There's no other place, Comrade Major," Madame Attendant tries to make excuses for the compartment.

Today she's dressed to the nines; painted her lips a fiery red, drawn-on black eyebrow arches, and is squeezed into a tight-fitting dress.

"It will do, Puss" the Major says as he slaps her soft behind.

Madame Attendant takes no offence. As the door closes after her, she leaves in the compartment a pungent and cloyingly sweet smell of lily of the valley combined with her own body odor.

"May I?" the Major asks, not waiting for a response. He takes off and hangs his army hat. It's a beautiful hat, blue on top. This can be seen well from above. His hair is graying. His face broad and brown like a cedar nut. Mama and Papa exchange worried glances. Why? But Laura is delighted at the appearance of the Major, at least something is happening.

"Where are you young people off to?" After a while the Major begins a conversation.

"To Moscow," Papa's response is abrupt.

Laura is hiding on the compartment's top baggage rack. Where the luggage should be. She's still debating if she should show herself to the Major.

"To Moscow. Yes, yes. *V Moskvu. Da. Da.*" Attempting to correct Papa's abruptness, Mama confirms kindly.

To Moscow? Laura freezes. What Moscow? What are they talking about? Isn't Laura going to Latvia? Have Papa and Mama been telling tales? They're talking in Russian and Laura understands Russian well, but sometimes when grown-ups talk nothing can be understood in any language.

"To study? Are you students?" The Major wants to know.

"No, no!" Papa and Mama are not talkative.

"Have some." The Major hospitably offers, putting out half a loaf of a brick-shaped bread, hard-boiled eggs, streaky bacon, and pickles.

Laura is disappointed because they have the same sort of food themselves.

Always the same. That's why Laura is constipated, that's why her tummy hurts.

The Major busies himself, with a host's gesture of largesse he places a bottle on the table, tears off the green metal strip and pours into the cut tea glasses almost all of the bottle's contents. Three glasses but one of these is Laura's glass! No way will Laura drink the Major's vodka!

"Comrades! What now? We've got *zakuskas* to munch on, glasses we've got, vodka we have, and a reason to drink can always be found! What do you suggest?"

It seems that Papa and Mama don't know what to suggest.

"Let's toast our youth, comrades! To our splendid Soviet youth! A great future is yours, young people! The Party is leading you there! A toast to the Party! To you! To the future!" The Major, elated, empties his glass in one fell swoop, shakes himself, and avidly takes a whiff of the brick-shaped bread.

He smells the bread to be certain that Germans haven't pooed in the rye and contaminated it, Laura knows! Laura knows!

Papa drinks half his glass while Mama only raises the glass to touch her lips. Just a taste, the tiniest of sips. Laura wonders which young people the Major is talking about. Which young people are here? Only Mama and Papa. The major hasn't seen Laura yet. Maybe he does see her after all?

"And you? Also to Moscow?" Papa has become more talkative.

"Only as far as the Urals. That's my usual route. To Sluzba! The enemy never sleeps. But what are you up to in Moscow? I didn't get an answer."

"Laura isn't going to Moscow!" Laura yells from above.

"Now, what have we here? And I was wondering where the third passenger could be? There she is! Ah, I see, I see. Hiding, talking in a strange language, probably a *shpion*—a spy! Hey! *Shpionka, diversantka*—spy, saboteur! I have something for you!" The Major smiles and hands Laura a candy.

Wrapped in a light blue paper, the candy is beautiful. Even more beautiful than the blue hat. And big! There's a picture in color on the wrapper. Two small bears romping among felled trees, while a third watches.

"What do you say?"

Laura herself knows what she must say.

What is most precious is the light blue wrapper. Because that can be saved. The paper wrapper serves as undeniable proof. Otherwise no one will believe that Laura has had such a candy, that Laura has eaten such a candy.

"Laura is going to Latvia!" she says on purpose forcefully, on purpose loudly and on purpose sassily. Not so much for the sake of the Major, no, more so for Mama and Papa, so they may know. That Laura won't go to any Moscow! Laura will get off! If they want to they can go on their own, because Laura won't go to Moscow! And that's not being naughty!

"From Moscow we'll continue further to Latvia," Mama adds, because what else can she do now.

"Home. After fifteen years," Papa explains, immediately regretting what he has said.

He empties his glass to the very bottom, and afterward, pours the contents of Mama's glass into his. Mama looks at him reproachfully.

Mama's afraid that Papa when drunk may talk too much.

"To Tallinn? I was there during the war. In the town of Paldiski. Do you know it? No, you're too young. Besides, the facility was secret!" The Major begins vigorously, but quickly falls silent and seems to be contemplating something.

He pours the remaining vodka into his glass and drinks it in one go. Doesn't even shake himself as he did before, maybe has forgotten to shake himself, doesn't smell the bread anymore because why should he do it twice.

"No, Tallinn is in Estonia. We're going to Riga," Mama clarifies.

"Ah, yes! I still confuse that *Pribaltika*—the Baltics. Latvia. Lithuania. Estonia. Then you must be Lithuanians?"

"No, Latvians." Mama has to be the one to speak, because Papa has grown glum.

"Yes, yes. Latvians. The Communist politician and Latvian writer Vilis Lācis—his book *Sin ribaka* about the fisherman's son. Right? The Latvian Riflemen! Right? How so—after fifteen years?" The Major doesn't let anything slip by.

"That's how it has turned out," Mama is frightened. Laura senses this with every cell of her body how very much Mama is afraid.

"How old are you then, girl?" the Major asks Mama, but Laura thinks she's the one who's been asked. Where, after all, would there be another girl here?

"Laura is five. And she'll be six," she announces.

"My wife Anda is twenty-four," Papa says and, in a protective move, draws Mama closer to him.

"And you, young man?"

"The same."

"Well, well, what a preschool bunch we have here, what more can I say! So I've been plying virtual underage ones with vodka!" The Major pulls out another bottle of vodka.

"Laura, Anda. Aha. And what is your name? Hans? Fritz? Fine, fine, I'm just joking. *Da*. Sit down! Sit! What the hell … ? Sit down. I already said, I was just joking, besides it was stupid, I know, I know, I'm sorry." The Major holds out his hand to Papa.

"Jānis," Papa replies, not noticing the Major's hand.

"Aleksandr Ivanovich. You *pribalti*, don't use your father's name, I know, I know. But it's foolish, *zrya*—a shame, because a father's name is important. Ah, that's why from the very beginning you seemed so odd to me! I enter and see—two young people sitting here. But where is that spark of Soviet youth, where the fire in the eyes? Pale, stiff. Frightened. I think, maybe I've caught them making love? No such thing—*Nye figa*. The fruit of their love wails from above, just look, how big a kid she is, legs right to the floor! Good for you, you started early. Early. Oh me, oh my—*Yomayo*! Deportees? Going home? Freed! Happy! Betrayers of the people? *Kulaks*—rich farmers? Bourgeois nationalists? Children and grandchildren of the enemies of the people?" The Major now totally animated mocks, and once more fills the glasses.

"We've been rehabilitated—you could say exonerated." Papa tries to remain calm.

Mama again is frightened. Mama is always afraid that they may be sent back to Siberia.

"Johnny, Johnny," quietly she whispers a warning. But the Major has heard her.

"*Prekratyity*—That's enough! What kind of a name is that—Johnny? John? What kind of an *amerikanskiy, burzhuasniy, imperialisticheskiy* outrage is this? Is a Soviet person, even if you are Latvian, allowed to call himself by that name? John! *Prekratyity!*" the Major is commanding an invisible army.

"That's just a nickname, just a nickname … just a nickname!" Mama begins to cry.

"A nickname? Aha, maybe a *klichka podpolnaya*—a code-name? Latvians! You can't be trusted at all. *Vot*—see now how you've revealed your true, rotten Western nature!" Having uncovered their nature, the Major calms down. Time to have a drink. The Major no longer offers drinks to the others. He turns to Mama.

"Anda, tell me your father's name," the Major insists.

"Edmundovna," Mama, sobbing, whispers.

"Anda Edmundovna! Are you afraid of my epaulets? Yes, you're afraid. But don't be afraid! You're a beautiful woman!"

"Leave my wife alone!" Papa jumps to his feet.

"Sit down, wimp! Anda Edmundovna! Are you afraid of my medals? They're not decorations, although I deserve them, no, they're just shit medals! I see how afraid you are. Don't be afraid! But under the medals I have, do you know what? Can't you guess? A heart! I've got a heart there! Let's drink! Let's drink this *charka*—a shot to toast Maima! Maima was my Estonian girlfriend. Fifteen years ago. Listen, Anda Edmundovna! Mai–ma! Mai–ma! Like a wolf I howled for her—Mai-ma! But I don't know her father's name and didn't know it then; I couldn't find her on the list of people to be deported to cross it out! I had the opportunity but I could not, see here, that's what happens when you don't use your father's name. That's why I say a father's name is important. Maybe Maima is also returning home? Rehabilitated?" The Major asks Mama.

He clutches Mama's arm. How should Mama know? Laura

also doesn't know, how should Laura know?

"Of course, she's also returning, and she too has some son of a bitch beside her, some John, *yebitvayumaty*—motherfuck, *da* I wouldn't even call a dog by that name! And also he's produced similar brats and hellions with her! Let her return, I don't begrudge it, let her return, the bitch—*blyad*, let her return. Mai-ma! Mai-ma!" the major howls like a wolf and pounds his chest so that the medals clang and jingle.

"Hey you!" The Major turns to Papa. "Let's drink to beautiful women! Drink John Adolfovich, drink Fritz Hansovich, ha, ha, ha! A kick to your ribs! Anda Edmundovna, you too have a drink, *davai, davai*! Reap while there's still dew! Eh!" The major empties his glass in one gulp.

Papa also empties his glass. Mama too empties a glass. Right down to the bottom. What will Laura do with three drunken people?

"Rehabilitated, bastards, rehabilitated. Rehabilitated, scum, all of you rehabilitated! Innocent as lambs? Free as birds? Happy as pigs? Just think. Going home, the little shits! Is that just? Is that honorable? When will I, when will I go home? Who's going to rehabilitate me? Who'll rehabilitate me? Who? When will I return home? When?" The Major, head bent, talks to the floor. He sobs, moans, with snot flying in the air, screams at the ceiling, tries to get to his feet, still wants to say something to Papa and Mama, to Laura and to Maima, tries to pull his revolver out of the holster but fails, finally his body limply slides down on the seat.

"Thank God! He could have killed us!" Mama is still trembling.

"Killed us?" Laura questions in disbelief.

"No, no, he gave you a candy, after all." Mama takes her words back. How can words be taken back, Laura wonders.

"Could I, stupid me, not hold my tongue, did I have to tell about the fifteen years? A KGB Major is the right one to unburden my heart to! Anda, I'm an idiot! Forgive me! It's my fault. Why did I even have to talk? He's got a Nagant revolver. Maybe we should take it from him?" Papa staggers.

"No, no. Are you insane? He's drunk as a pig. Johnny, he'll sleep now like a dead man and won't remember anything either in the morning or at night. He'll get off at the Uralskaya station. Please, please just calm down."

When Laura wakes, the Major is no longer in the compartment. Laura's tummy hurts because she hasn't had a poo the whole time on the train. Laura wants to poo, but then she'd have to go to the toilet, so Laura will try to restrain herself.

"We're past the Urals," Mama is overcome with joy.

"We're in Europe, Laura," Papa says proudly.

For Laura these are strange and empty words. Some kind of Urals, some kind of Europe. The same as Moscow, some kind of Moscow. For Laura many words are empty. Words that only have an outside, and nothing inside. A word that has an outside, a word that has a taste and a fragrance, a word that has color and fullness, such a word for Laura is Latvia.

"Is Latvia still far?"

"Now it's nearer."

"How much nearer?"

"Much nearer"

"How much?" As usual Laura persists and right away also backs off.

Fine, alright fine. Laura has something to do. Laura will eat the candy the Major gave her and afterward will carefully fold up the wrapper. She'll eat the candy slowly, very slowly, and also very slowly fold the wrapper. Where's the candy? Has Laura in her excitement not noticed that she's eaten it? It's nowhere. Laura searches her crumpled sheets, until shame like a great heat wave scalds her, shame! Shame tumbles over Laura like rocks from a mountain, shame! The sheets are soiled brown. Laura has pooed in her bed. Horrid, horrid! The sheets are covered with stains, darker and lighter brown. Laura has shit herself, the big girl; humiliation drives Laura in horror into a black corner. What will Madame Attendant say? She's going to yell it all over the train. Laura will die from shame, just die! Her despair escapes from her mouth as a scream.

"Mama!" Laura, terrified, sobs, and Mama reads her thoughts.

"Child, it's only chocolate! Laurie, it's the candy! Just melted, spread out in the warmth, look, the wrapping paper also torn into little bits. It's alright, it's nothing, calm yourself, now, now. It's just a candy! Honey! My poor little one! It's the melted candy, just the candy. Smell it! Well, do you see it now, are you calm now?"

"We'll buy another one in Latvia. Many, many more. We'll buy lots in Latvia. We'll buy lots of candies, better ones, so don't cry for the sake of one measly candy. We shouldn't have taken anything from that bullshit Major!" Papa tries to pacify Laura.

Papa doesn't understand anything! Because of a measly candy? Laura isn't crying because of a measly candy! It's fine that he doesn't understand. It's true that the sheets don't smell of poo, the sheets smell of chocolate. There is a difference after all.

Calming down Laura notices that the Major has forgotten his hat. Where he hung it, there it still hangs. She could bring that to Grandpa! Grandpa surely doesn't have a hat like that! The blue color is beautiful. Grandpa would like it. Does Papa want the hat for himself? No, he throws it out of the window. Why?

Madame Attendant enters looking grumpy. The red lipstick has disappeared, the eyebrow arcs have faded, her eyes are puffy.

"Has Comrade Major left his *furazhka* in the compartment?

"I really don't know, but you can have a look," Papa urges.

"I don't know what *furazhka* you mean." Mama appears surprised.

"What is that—*furazhka*?" Laura asks.

Madame Attendant angrily slams the compartment door.

"Sourpuss," Mama says.

"For sure," Papa says.

The Platform

SOON, VERY SOON LAURA will get off the train. Never again will she have to travel by train. The three of them are standing in the narrow corridor at the train's exit door. Mama and Papa, pale and happy, are sweating from anxiety.

"Laurie, we'll be home very soon! Do you understand?" Mama whispers through tears.

"Johnny, look, there is the *Upītes* farm! Look, there!" Mama points through the window to Papa.

"Where? Where?" Papa hasn't seen it, although he's bent to the window and the train has reduced its travelling speed. The train slowly comes to a halt.

"Johnny, honey, are we really home?" Mama can't believe it, she just can't.

"Yes." Papa is quiet and overcome with emotion, he too can't believe it, just can't.

"Yes! Yes! Yes! Home!" Laura yells out loud because she can believe it, she can!

No one hushes her. The train attendant silently raises something like a lid covering the steps so they can deboard. Steps to home.

"Happy homecoming!" the train attendant says quietly and sincerely.

She's got tears in her eyes. The train attendant knows from where they're returning. She knows what a long way they've come. How much Laura's tummy has hurt.

Laura has announced it to the whole world. Mama is angry because she thinks one shouldn't blurt it out like that to the whole world, but Laura can't do otherwise than trumpet to the world!

They're already on the platform! Laura feels a fresh breeze, warm sunny air, which enfolds Laura from head to toe, lifts her upward, downright unbelievable—the breeze lifts Laura into the air!

Laura wants to laugh and to abandon herself because this is Latvia's air, she wants to slide into the lap of Latvia's air. Her knees begin to tremble, she grows dizzy, stumbles, but all is fine, it's ok, it's air, simply air—it can't hold up someone as heavy as Laura. The air couldn't have known that Laura would be so big. She feels how gentle Latvia's air is with Laura, how good the breeze. The air knows Laura. Just like the green grass, like the blue sky, just like the platform. They all know Laura.

The earth is steaming after the rain and Laura senses a great love in its warm vapors. Laura wants to respond to so great a love, she has an answer, but again it grows dark before her eyes. Not for long, however. The little black dog running toward her, it too is so precious. He wags his tail and smiles. Even the little black dog knows Laura!

"Don't be afraid, child! That's Ripsis!" says Mīma through tears. Mīma is precious like the green grass, like the fragrant earth.

"Ripsi! Ripsi! Leave the girl alone!" Grandpa growls. Grandpa is precious like the warm air, like the blue sky.

Everything around Laura seems precious and familiar to her. For some strange reason her knees give way. And once more it grows dark in front of her eyes. Laura's heart begins to ache. Papa lifts Laura up on his shoulders.

"That's from the long-awaited. That's from the long-dreamt-about. It'll pass. Get a hold of yourself now!" Mama tousles Laura's hair.

No, no, it isn't only because of what Laura was waiting for, what Laura dreamt about. It's not only Laura's heart that now aches from happiness. No, Laura knows that it's also the hearts of all the people in the Barrack, full of dreams about home, full of yearning for their homeland. In Laura they were saved over and over like in a piggy bank. The hopes and dreams of Buka, Asya, Maya, Levan, Jukka, Madalina—of all of them. The piggy bank is heavy because it's full. That's why Laura's legs are buckling. That's why it grows dark in front of her eyes. But most of all because of the news that Laura's heart is receiving. It's being sent by the platform.

"You, Laura, will never have to fight for my love, you won't have to beg, won't have to ask, because you already have it—my love."

The platform is saying this, who else! The platform is made of stone, of cobblestones shining after the rain. The platform of colored cobbles with green grass fringes is the first bit of Latvia on which Laura now firmly sets her foot. Laura doesn't just firmly set her foot. Laura places her foot tenderly as if caressing the platform.

"The sun will shine its love on you, the earth will exhale it, the trees and the grass will offer it to you, and the sky will gift it to you. You'll be able to come and play on the platform. Like your mama used to come, as did your grandpa Edmunds, as once Mīma came to play." Laura smiles, imagining how Mīma played on the platform.

Laura feels as if she's been given the greatest prize from the world's largest well of fortune. But at the same time as if she has sunk into debt. When a person receives something expensive and much wished for from the well of fortune, then that person is happy. But that person also can't forget that he or she has borrowed much, to get the winning ticket. Has borrowed much, dreadfully much. Not money, but a loan of sorts nonetheless. Fortune, fortune, why can't you be absolute? How will Laura be able to repay this debt, all of this great debt?

Mīma and Grandpa

"Child, this is Mīma and Grandpa!" Mama grasps and shakes Laura's shoulder.

Mīma is Mama's grandmother. Grandpa, of course, is her grandfather. That's how Mama, when she was small, had come to call them, and that's what she calls them now.

Laura opens her eyes. What's this? Mīma and Grandpa are dreadfully old! Laura had already known that they'd be old. She'd been warned. But surely not this old! Laura has never seen people as old as this. In Siberia there aren't any people this old.

"Oh my God! Oh my God! Oh my God!" Mīma is crying as she hugs all of them, one after the other.

"Ripsi, Ripsi!" Laura hugs the little dog.

"Well, welcome, welcome home!" Grandpa's voice and hands are trembling. Also the cane on which Grandpa is leaning shakes.

Laura notices something totally odd. That such old people can have so many white, lovely teeth! In Siberia everyone's teeth have fallen out. Many, many much younger people than Grandpa and Mīma have no teeth in Siberia. Those who can, get metal teeth put in. Laura has even seen gold teeth, a whole mouthful. One person in Siberia had them. Some kind of *nachalnik*—commander. But Laura hasn't seen such lovely, white teeth. Besides, on the train Laura had noticed that one of her front teeth was jiggling. What if Laura also has scurvy?

"Why do you have so many teeth?" Laura turns to ask both Mīma and Grandpa.

Both of them smile shyly. Why do they smile with such narrowed mouths, with such teeth they could smile much more openly.

"We managed to get them put in during President Ulmanis's time," Mīma tries to explain.

"Just before the Russians arrived," Grandpa clarifies.

"Laura!" Mama doesn't allow Laura to question them further about their teeth.

"This is my husband, Jānis," Mama introduces Papa, who shyly and politely bows.

"Goodness, how tall you are, son. But so thin," Mīma exclaims, examining Papa from all angles.

"Just wait, he'll soon put some weight on," Grandpa comforts her. "We've been eagerly waiting to meet you, son. You no longer have any other family, do you?

"You'll just have to make do with us," Mama pats Papa's hand.

"You too don't have a son anymore. I'm so sorry," Papa awkwardly comments.

"But we're still waiting," Grandpa says quietly.

Papa, now even more confused, is silent. Mīma too is silent. Maybe Mīma doesn't know that she doesn't have a son?

"Where is your luggage then?" Mīma looks around.

"Here. This suitcase," Papa says.

"Ripsi! Ripsi!" Laura has revived and for the whole way home wants to play with the little black dog. But chubby Ripsis soon tires and then, out of breath, lies down. His long tongue helps him catch his breath. Ripsis, with this tongue, draws in air, as much as he can manage. Laura too tries.

"Laurie, Ripsis is very old. See how gray his beard is," Mīma feels sorry for Ripsis.

"Very old," Grandpa also makes excuses for Ripsis.

Laura doesn't see any beard on the little dog. Just a smooth, gray nose. A feeling of anxiety sneaks up on Laura. What if in Latvia everyone is as old as Mīma, Grandpa, and Ripsis.

"Anda, dear, you do already know that the Avoti farm is not the same as before," Mīma mentions halfway home.

"Yes, I know. You wrote. It doesn't matter." Mama is not at all upset. Not a bit.

Mama is full of happiness like a basketful of first strawberries. A good old woman friend had brought one like it to the train in Riga. Why old? That friend didn't seem so old to Laura. In comparison.

Mama is holding on to one of Papa's hands, while with the

other hand she carries the wooden suitcase, and while walking, they jostle each other like a couple of naughty kids, gazing into each other's eyes, not looking where they step at all. They'll trip and fall, that'll show them!

Laura isn't holding anyone's hand, even though Mīma and Grandpa have invited her to do so. Laura can't do that right away. Right away hold hands. Is that freedom? Laura has come here to be free.

Also, she's a bit ashamed of the old ones, ashamed of their dreadful old age. So old! So very old! And how they're dressed! Mīma is wearing a brown skirt. The brown skirt would be alright, but Mīma's skirt is also long, right down to the ground! A long skirt to the ground, a light-colored blouse with polka dots, a gray knitted vest, and a totally white apron? Without any polka dots. So she won't dirty her clothes when working. But why white? That in itself must be taken care not to be soiled. She's wearing a just as white kerchief tied around her head. That too can be easily soiled. Odd.

In Siberia no one dressed like this. There every one had *pufaikas, kerzovicki,* and *valenki*—padded coats, rubber and felt boots. Maybe right now there's no need for the felt *valenki*, it's not winter. Will Mama and Laura have to dress like this in Latvia? In long skirts with white aprons? Laura won't dress like that!

Grandpa too has dressed up very oddly. He's wearing a *kostyum*—that's Russian. A suit. Laura remembers what the word is in Latvian—*uzvalks.* Papa, getting ready to return to Latvia, dreadfully wanted to buy a suit. Even though it would be only from the *komisyonka*—the commissary shop. A suit is something sewn from the same cloth, both the jacket and the pants. Papa constantly dreamt about a suit in Siberia. When he'd have enough money saved. Probably he never saved enough because Papa doesn't have a suit. But Grandpa has one. The pants and the jacket are made of the same cloth. And Grandpa also has a white shirt. But that doesn't help much. Even a suit doesn't help much when you're that dreadfully old. Grandpa is big in size, somewhat thick-set, but stooped like an old mushroom, his face pale like the moon. His hands too are pale and chubby; they tremble even when hidden in his pockets, even when holding his cane.

Mīma is exactly the opposite, her face and hands are dark, tanned from the sun, and she's skinny like a twig. Maybe Mīma doesn't have anything to eat?

They both look totally feeble. Dreadful. Laura's afraid that Mīma and Grandpa may even die on the way home. Despite their good teeth.

The Avoti farm, it turns out, isn't far from the train station. Not far at all but close. Ripsis is already turning into the road leading into Avoti. Mama stops as if frozen.

The Avoti Farm

"Where is the big linden tree? Where are the two old maples?" Mama cries out.

"Oh, my God, Mīma, where is our garden? Who has done this?" Mama wrings her hands in despair.

"It's because of the land amelioration. I already told you, child, that Avoti isn't what it used to be."

"This is not Avoti! Mīma! This isn't Avoti!" Mama yells. "Where are the old pear trees? Where the birch grove? Where the oaks? Grandpa!"

Mama is behaving like a young child, exactly the same as Laura, when she has a tantrum. Mama is a real crybaby.

"We'll plant everything anew. This isn't worth worrying about, it's trivial." Papa tries to calm her.

"As it is, the trees were already half dead, at the end of their lifespan. The pear trees were two hundred years old, if not more. The amelioration has affected everything," Grandpa tends to nod off when he has to talk for a longer time.

Laura is very angry at Amelioration! What a name they've given her. That's why she's grown up to be such a monster. Amelioration! Maybe she's walking right around here somewhere. With a scythe.

"Ance, dear, do be a grown-up. The most important thing is that you've returned home alive. Isn't that the most important, my dear child?" Mīma pleads.

"Yes, but . . ." Mama can't control herself.

So whiny!

"Your brother won't ever come back home. Your father won't return! The old man Avots won't return. Our own Reinis won't. Do you want me to name all who won't return? But you've returned alive and back home!" There are tears and iron in Mīma's voice.

"Yes, that's most important." Mama agrees.

"Finally!"

"And I have Jānis. Johnny!" Mamma clasps Papa around the neck like someone drowning, almost strangling him.

Poor Papa.

"You also have Laura," Laura reminds her.

Everyone has forgotten her, but in the meantime Amelioration is strolling about. Laura snuggles up to Papa. Because he stands the closest to her. Laura's afraid to make a false move. Laura feels Papa trembling. He too is afraid of Amelioration.

"You've got a roof over your heads. Don't look for what was here before, child," Grandpa says.

He calls Mama—child. Strange.

On entering Avoti, Mīma still hasn't let go of her sternness because she sees that Mama is walking around the house as if she's lost.

Mama doesn't listen to either Mīma or Grandpa and instead still looks for, looks again for what was there before but can't find it. No buffet nor dresser, no round table nor the fringed table-cloth, not even the wall clock, nothing. Mama looks for books, which her father at one time had bound so beautifully in leather, where are those books? Where are the books? Grandpa shrinks at every word uttered by Mama as if he were hit. Mīma's face has a hard expression and downcast eyes. Mama looks and looks.

Laura and Papa don't look for what was earlier but no longer is. *Prichom*—why would they? They're in Avoti for the first time in their lives. They're happy about what is. Freedom, their homeland, and their own home.

"Laura will have her own room! Isn't that so Papa? There are two rooms here, two big rooms! Mama!" Laura is happy and runs from one room to the other. So much space! Ripsis hobbles after her.

The rooms are half empty. In one there's a wide bed.

"Ance! Look! What more do we need?" Papa takes Mama in his lap and rocks her, Mama tries to wriggle free, but Papa holds her in a strong grasp and carries her to the bed.

"A pull-out couch. Totally new! Where did you get it?"

Mama stretches out on the bed and extends her arms. The bed is wide and comforting.

Mama's joy returns, some part of the joy, a crumb of it. From that immeasurable joy, which was in Mama but which vanished on seeing Avoti.

"Everything will be totally new!" Papa is convinced.

"Come sit down at the table." When has Mīma managed to set the table?

All of Mīma's sternness has vanished. Mīma is happy. She's moving about, as if she weren't dreadfully, so dreadfully old.

Four chairs. Laura knows how to count. Why only four?

"Where is Laura going to sit? Laura wants to sit on a chair!"

But Laura will have to sit in Papa's lap. There aren't any more seats. No, Laura wants to sit on a chair, and that's all! She's finally home and she won't have a chair! What a horrendous insult. Laura's tears fall like beans. There's no way to stop her crying, just the opposite—the tears multiply, they flow as if from a fountain, which Laura has seen in some sort of Moscow or somewhere.

"Wait Laura! You'll have your own chair! Sit," Papa goes into the room with the pull-out couch and carries out a low nightstand.

"I'm going to sit on a *tumbochka*—a nightstand. See? Are you fine now?"

Papa can sit nicely on the low nightstand because he's tall and now he's fine.

On the table there are boiled potatoes and Laura also recognizes green peas with carrots, which she's eaten once in nursery school.

"What's that?" Laura asks, pointing to a bowl.

"It's a roasted chicken. Eat, eat, child, eat," Mīma urges.

"A bit of meat," Mama explains.

"Dig in!" Papa says, becoming more animated.

Laura again senses lovingness. It hits her in the chest like a warm and gentle breeze. Once again like a gentle breeze. It wafts up together with the steam from the potatoes, and is it any wonder, for do potatoes not come from the earth? Vapors from the same precious earth, now mingling with the desire to sleep, with the aroma of the roast chicken, a new aroma, but already precious. And the chicken itself also precious. Will it still be able to lay eggs?

For dessert there's a berry compote with whipped cream. Dear whipped cream, even though Laura doesn't know what it is. Something good, totally opposite to Amelioration! Laura falls asleep in her chair, missing the whipped cream, however, in her dream Amelioration chases Laura, but Laura escapes her, rises up in the air and flies away.

"Eat, eat, child, eat," Mīma somewhere from below whispers.

"*Chame, chame deda genazvalos,*" Laura murmurs in her sleep.

But

ALREADY YESTERDAY Mama had noticed the smell, but how could one discuss such a thing at the table! She also hadn't wanted to upset the old folks. Mīma had tried so hard. As had poor Grandpa. But also Mama, for God's sake, had tried not to show that her joy at returning had been smashed like a clay pot.

Papa tries to divert Mama's thoughts in a different direction and asks, if sleeping on the new bed has not made her happy? Papa won't ever forget his first night in Latvia, that's for sure. Never, kitten.

Mama won't forget either, but.

And isn't the fact that Laura has finally done number two something to be happy about?

Yes, that's something to be happy about, but.

And does Mama not understand that all that insanity is now in the past, finished and that's it, and is that not the greatest reason for happiness?

It is, yes, it is Johnny, but.

Mama is sweet to Papa, and kisses Laura, but.

That's how it is, but.

Mama agrees with everything Papa says, but.

The morning sun is not as merciful as the muted sun of dusk. The second day is not like the first.

All is ruined by Mama's big but.

Madness, madness! Mama walks around muttering. The house without surrounding trees is bare and Mama just like the house, bare. Bare in front of everyone, undressed and robbed! The land around the house has been ploughed almost to the threshold. Do they lack land?

Only two rooms are somewhat usable in the Avoti farmhouse. The other half of the house has been turned into a barn. It's full of cattle manure. Cows have been kept there until quite recently, as witnessed by the smell. The slurry splashes virtually at the doorstep. The cow dung hasn't yet dried out.

Mama weeps.

In Siberia, yes, there humans lived together with beasts, but that was in Siberia! The beasts kept the humans warm and the people kept the beasts warm. They all together thus survived the harsh winter. But in Latvia, but in the summer, but in the Avoti great room, with the white Dutch-tiled hearth and velvet wall-paper? A barn? Piles of manure up to the windowsills? Mama had been ready for anything but not this!

It's like a backward world! Shit everywhere, *hlami*—trash, *barohlo*—junk, a total dung heap! What are those idiotic huts erected everywhere? For hens and rabbits, yes, but why right on the flower beds? On the roses and the lilies.

"No, just have a look Johnny, what a lovely sight!"

Laura also looks. An enormous tractor tire is lying right in the middle of the yard, painted in a bright blue color.

That now is supposed to be the flower bed! That's what their taste is like! Here, in the place where before stood a flagpole? Everything has been befouled! It's all a pigsty, everything has been destroyed!

Papa thinks Mama is raving too much. Well, damn it, after all! Who cares! In Siberia flower beds were also made inside tires, there too the tires were painted bright blue. Russians like blue, this chamber-pot blue. What can one do about it? Nobody has died from that color, except for maybe flies. How can Mama carry on so about nonsense and drag it out so.

Such talk for Mama is like setting fire to flax waste. So that's it, Papa is defending the Russians now? She didn't expect that from a man whose whole family was murdered by the Russians! Papa yells for Mama to think before she speaks! Mama yells that Papa himself should think before he speaks!

Papa should come and have a look in the barn. In the lovely Avoti barn. The roof has caved in, Papa himself sees that. Yes, but why has it collapsed? Just look. Yes, it truly is the height of stupidity, Papa agrees. The supporting beams have been sawed

off for firewood. Everything that in the barn was made of wood
has been torn out and burned. That's why the cattle had to be
housed in the great room. And Grandpa had proudly even called
it a dancehall. What a laugh!

Why cry if it's such a laugh? Laura is running around joyfully.
And laughing. Laura finds a mirror shard and flashes sun rabbits
on the house walls, on the idiotic huts, on the piles of manure,
and laughs. The rabbits hop around, just the way Laura wants
them to. She can make them twitch fast and make them glide
slowly. Laura trains the rabbits, but she could also train lions. If
it were needed. She really could in these calm winds! Laura has
courage to spare.

Laura couldn't tell you why she's happy. About everything!
About the green vastness all around. That's the vastness of Latvia,
yes, Latvia! Latvia—in itself means jubilation and happiness.
How far one can see! Joy sits in Laura's breast like a white and
loving pigeon, flaps its wings and coos with tenderness and power.

"Johnny! Are these people human? It's not the amelioration
but these dog-headed monsters who have sawed down the old
linden! And the ancient maples! And the pear trees, which have
been here since the time of Moses! Look, there's the linden!"

Mamma points to a gigantic round stump of wood, very like
the millstone at the threshold, it's just not made of stone but of
wood. Mama pats it and once more weeps.

Mama's behavior frightens the loving pigeon in Laura's breast.
Scares the sun rabbits. Mama is ruining Laura's life, she can't
stand it anymore and goes to complain to Papa.

Papa wants to have a serious talk with her.

Like with an adult. Under four eyes.

How will that be? Under four eyes? Who has four eyes?
Why under, why below? Who will look from above with four
eyes while Laura talks to Papa? Papa isn't going to lead his child
into danger, is he? Laura trusts he won't. But what are those
four eyes?

Krishka and *Zavals*

"You mustn't be angry at Mama! We both must not be angry at Mama."

"Why?"

"You see, Laura, it's altogether different for Mama than it is for you and me."

"Why different? Why is Mama crying?"

"See Laura, for Mama the Avoti farm is her father's home. Her grandfather's home. And probably also her great-grandfather's home. She grew up here. Everything is very dear here for her."

"Very, very?"

"Very, very. When Mamma thought about Latvia in Siberia, she thought about Avoti. Thought and dreamt about it."

"Why didn't you think about it?"

"We're talking about Mama now! See Laura, Mama dreamt about the Avoti farm as it was before, but as it was before, it turns out, it no longer is. You and I have the luck of fools! We don't know how it was before, so it's easier for us!"

"How was it earlier?"

"Earlier it was as it had to be. Don't interrupt!"

Why does she remember? But Laura doesn't remember.

"You see Mama had already once returned from Siberia. In secret."

"How is that—in secret?"

"That means illegally."

This word doesn't clarify anything for Laura, but she says: "Oh."

"Then Avoti had not yet been ravaged."

For Laura this is something altogether new. Why didn't Mama stay in Latvia then, why return to Siberia? Laura wouldn't have returned. Where was Laura then?

"You weren't born yet. Those dog-headed ogres, those crazy *svolochi*—scoundrels caught Mama and sent her back. Took her from her school bench."

"Why?"

"Transported her back in stages. Laura, I'm talking to you like to a grown-up. Is that clear?"

That's clear. She can't ask what "in stages" means.

In stages. Until this word Papa talks through gritted teeth, but calmly. But now calm is gone with the wind. Laura is suddenly afraid. Papa is exploding! Papa grasps his head.

"In stages! Stages, Laura, so you'll know, no, it's better that you don't know! How shall I explain it—stages, that's, that's...

Papa jumps to his feet and yells at Stages. Maybe Stages has four eyes? Maybe it's now Papa's turn too to yell and holler?

"Stages, that is *krishka*—the end, *hana*—finish, it's *zavals*—the absolute end. For months on end, shunted from prison to prison. Do you understand? Mama, a young and beautiful girl. Together with criminals, all sorts of *zeki*—jailbirds. With whores and murderers! Mama doesn't talk about it, not even to me, but I can imagine. I know. That's why she screams at night. I'm not so stupid to think that they didn't touch her!

"Did they touch Mama with words or with their hands?" Laura asks, but Papa doesn't hear.

"But see, Laura, how it turns out in life. Shush! Could you for once not interrupt, simply listen?"

In general Laura is incapable of not interrupting. But there are exceptions.

"If Mama hadn't been sent back to Siberia then I wouldn't have met her. Understand? If I hadn't met Mama, then you wouldn't be either. And maybe I also wouldn't be. Yes, I wouldn't be, I tell you, Laura, for sure—I wouldn't be! *Nafig*—damned if I would be! Damn! Neither you nor I would be! But see, here we are. Just because Mama is. Right now she's in shock. Understand? But that will pass. If you once more complain to me about Mama, if you're going to make all those faces... *Vsjo!*"

Papa turns away, he no longer wants to talk. He's talked himself empty and he deflates like a pierced balloon. It's enough also, enough is enough. As it is Laura's head is turning and in her tummy guilt is thickening heavily. No, Laura will no longer show her nasty faces to Mama, Mommy, dear Mommy, never again! If she'd known that Mama, Mommy, dear Mommy, was in shock, she wouldn't have shown them. But what is this shock? Whatever it is, the main thing is that it will pass.

Never yet has Papa talked like this to Laura. Like with a grown-up! Laura appreciates this, Laura is proud.

How is that—then Laura wouldn't be? How—wouldn't be? Would die? How is it—not to be?

But a big person can't ask what each word means—why, why, what is that, what does it mean?

If a big person is asked, do you understand, then she has to pretend that she understands. That's why Laura has been nodding her head in understanding throughout this. If one says *vsjo,* then it is—*vsjo*! That's all.

Papa searches for a long time in his pockets, until he finds the matches and his cigarettes, then he leans against the wall, squats and smokes. Squats and smokes. Only the ones who have been to Siberia squat like that. The ones who have lived in a Barrack. Who have gotten used to not having anything to sit on. Laura notices such things.

After a while Laura opens her mouth to ask a question because she already has forgotten that she's a big person. Papa gives her such a look. As if he had four eyes.

Better Laura should leave and chew on a rhubarb stalk.

Mrs. Teacher

Laura hears Mama's happy voice. Finally happy!

"Thanks dear teacher! A poet's narcissus! You're our first visitor. We're sort of confused, not knowing what to begin to do, what not. Laurie, don't hide! Come, this is my dear teacher. Teacher, this is Laura!

"Hello, Laura! What lovely braids you have! Your mama also had braids like these. Like wheat at sunset. You apparently are five years old, isn't that so?" Mrs. Teacher has a kind voice. She has a kind face, kind eyes, kind movements. She's got beautiful gray hair, styled—also to look kind. Laura can't find another word. She's wearing a black, shiny satin smock with a big, white collar. Laura likes the teacher. How can an old person have so young and lovely a voice?

"Laura, answer the teacher! How old are you?"

Why does Mama ask like that? Mrs. Teacher already knows! She herself just now said it! Well, fine.

"Laura is five years old."

"You speak Latvian so well!" Mrs. Teacher smiles. Could it be that she's laughing at Laura?

"Laura is shy," Mama makes excuses as Laura hides behind her back.

"That's good. I like shy children. Are you already learning to recognize letters?"

"Laura's not learning to recognize letters!"

"Never mind. In the fall you're going to be going to kindergarten, you'll learn then, isn't that so?

"Laura is not going to go to kindergarten! Laura's going to go to school! Laura has known how to read already for a long time!"

Mrs. Teacher likes shy children. Mrs. Teacher likes Laura. Laura very much wants to be liked even more by Mrs. Teacher.

43

"Laura knows how to read in Latvian and in Russian! And besides that knows many other languages—English, Italian, and Lithuanian! And Georgian!" Laura announces.

Mrs. Teacher in surprise claps her hands. Now, isn't that something!

Mama thinks Laura is exaggerating a bit. Even though it's true that the Barrack was an absolute Babel, with all sorts of languages, children of course learn quickly.

Mrs. Teacher understands all.

Laura sulks. That's not so good. Laura doesn't want Mrs. Teacher to understand all. For example, bragging.

Mrs. Teacher gives Mama a gift of a nicely wrapped package. Mama unwraps the gift. It's a book. Mama hugs Mrs. Teacher and starts crying. Fricis Bārda! He had been Anda's best-loved poet while she was in school, and this collection of poems has just been published. Laura doesn't like any Fritzes or Bārdas— which in Latvian means beard.

Bārda had been a prohibited author but now maybe he no longer is prohibited. Does Laura like poetry? Yes? Maybe Laura can recite some poem? Recite? Yes, well say it aloud from memory. The one she loves the most.

On the rim of a well sits a tailor
Mending his tailcoat!
Pretty Laura passes by…

Laura can not only recite this but also sing it in a loud voice! Mama thinks that it's enough, that she need not continue, enough, hush! It's not as if Laura only knows stupid ditties, Mama once more makes excuses for Laura to Mrs. Teacher.

"You too have a good voice! When you're a bit older will you come and be in my choir?"

Laura doesn't know, she hasn't got a clue what a choir is, but she'll go. Even to the end of the world because Mrs. Teacher has something Laura yearns for, but she doesn't know what it is precisely. A kind way of speaking, a white collar or so young a voice for an old person. She'd like to tell Mrs. Teacher this but how can she tell her if she doesn't know exactly what she wants to say.

What Mrs. Teacher says flows out brightly and calmly. Like a big river, it occurs to Laura. Laura again can breathe in those small, invisible fishes.

Mrs. Teacher is so happy that Anda has returned. Mrs. Teacher radiates kindness, the laugh lines at the corner of her eyes are full of joy like garden rows of marigolds. Surely all the sorrows will pass, surely there will be a new start in life. It's not suffering that is the measure of a human being, but the capacity to survive it. Anda should definitely continue her schooling, it's not, not too late, Anda has such a bright intellect. It won't be the same as before ever, of course, Anda shouldn't deceive herself, but a person can always retain their humanity regardless of circumstances. And nothing is forever, Mrs. Teacher's voice changes to a whisper.

No, Anda, child. The teacher no longer lives in *Pičiņas* homestead, because a bomb was dropped on *Pičiņas* during the war, directly on it, her old mama had been in her bed then, and had remained there. Now it's an empty place, only the well and some apple trees still remain.

The teacher now lives in *Sila Balceri,* which has been turned into a *kolkhoz,* where she's been given a room, small but warm. About her neighbors the teacher would rather not comment.

The teacher is now looking after the kolkhoz's sheep. No, she's no longer working in the school; she's only allowed to conduct the choir, which is wonderful. There are many Russian children, but all the children are adorable. Children, of course, aren't guilty of anything. Music and books, those are the most important thing. Yes, it's a miracle, but they were saved in the attic. The woman who had owned Sila Balceri was a great reader.

Hopefully she had managed to board a ship. Seemingly she's in America.

Mama talks for a long time with Mrs. Teacher, who hasn't changed one bit, and then it seems to Mama that the old times have returned, that once more it's like it was before and everything that has happened in the interim is just a bad dream, a dreadful nightmare, and besides that, there's this book of poetry.

"Forgive me, teacher, I'm so ashamed that everything here

is in such a state that I can't invite you to come in, and, besides that, this horrible smell," Mama in saying good-bye apologizes through tears.

"Smell? Anda, dear child, what smell are you talking about? I just sense a sweet fragrance. The narcissus fragrance. Soon the lilacs will waft their fragrance, afterward the jasmines. Followed by the fragrance of lindens."

The teacher on leaving smiles kindly at Laura.

The tiny fishes joyfully play in Laura's heart and it could perhaps happen that one of them is a golden fish. Laura can make a wish. Three times. What should she wish for? Not a sausage, of course. Then Mama would say: "May that sausage hang from your nose!" But Papa would wish that that devil of a sausage fall off. So all the three wishes would have been used. Laura has to think this through carefully and only then make the wish. Because the greatest wish has been fulfilled already. Laura is in Latvia. Home.

Why Avoti are Avoti

MAMA IS WRESTLING WITH weeds because she wants to create a garden. To grow some things. Some lettuce or dill. Laura sees that she's pulling out goosefoot and nettles.

"What are we going to eat if we have a famine?" Laura is very upset. Her question becomes a yell, not intentional, but a yell nonetheless.

Mama straightens her back and stares at Laura. As if wanting to say something, as if not. Mama looks in silence, just her face changes expression, which can't be interpreted. As if a change-able breath of wind has crossed a field, leafing through the grass. Either the grass or memories. As if Mama's teeth had suddenly ached, all of them at the same time. Dark sludge surfaces in Mama's eyes and once more vanishes. Expressions like ripples on a river change one after another. What Mama is thinking can't be understood, the waves one after the other interfere. From where will this breath of wind blow next?

"Laurie, there won't be any famine anymore, ever. In Latvia there won't be starvation. Nettles and goosefoot are weeds in Latvia, just as creeping thistles and also this damned couch grass. All to be torn out! Better come and help."

Mama has tamed the river ripples.

Laura doesn't want to. Laura doesn't like to weed. Laura has other things to do. One more ripple of anger, however, breaks from Mama.

"What kind of nonsense of yours, little toad, is this! You've never even seen real starvation! What right have you to talk of famine! What do you, damn it, know of famine! And of everything!" Mama throws down her hoe and yells.

Laura now feels guilty that she hasn't seen real starvation? Why is Mama hollering? What is she accusing Laura of? Of everything in general.

Yes, by the time Laura was born in Siberia, the real famine
had ended. But semi-famine still remained. And eternal hunger
still remained. Just as the fear of starvation and memories of
it remained. The famine could return, could happen any day.
Laura hasn't seen starvation but has been impregnated with stories about the famine like the moss with dark marsh waters in a
bog, with other people's memories, with the weeping and wail-
ing for the ones who have died. About Mama's little brother,
about great-grandfather—the old proprietor of the Avoti farm.
Everything doesn't have to be seen with one's own eyes in order
to be known. Everything doesn't have to be experienced oneself
to be felt. Does Mama not know that? Laura doesn't like it that
Mama is throwing away the goosefoot and nettles like some
repulsive snakes. Laura will get up during the night and pull
them out of the heap. Because they are edible, that's food, and
food must be honored, one shouldn't do this to food, what if
the famine returns?

"Will we no longer gather birch buds?" Laura always had to
help, she had to gather at least a tin cupful.

"Don't you see that the birches are already in leaf? Don't
you?"

"And bird-cherry berries?"

"No."

"And we won't dig up *cheremsha*—wild garlic?"

"*Cheremsha* doesn't grow in Latvia. Here we have real, proper
garlic."

"Laura wants cedar nuts."

"Just wait, in the fall hazel trees will be full of nuts.
Navolam—full."

"Laura wants cedar nuts!"

"Then go to Siberia for them!"

"Laura's hungry!"

"We just ate a while ago, chew on a rhubarb stalk. In the
evening we'll boil up some potatoes, alright? Just don't eat those
green apples anymore, honey, remember, what happened with
your tummy?" Laura can sense that Mama regrets her yelling.

What happened? Bad things happened. She got the runs. She

had a leaky stomach. Not that her stomach sprang a leak but everything that she ate ran right through her.

Papa hasn't yet managed to build a new outhouse. He still has to get boards, there aren't any nails either, and why would you dig a hole if there aren't any boards or nails yet? Laura has to go to the old outhouse. But the old one is full right up to the top. Papa calls the toilet "*brille*." Laura doesn't want to remember, but she can't forget.

How did Laura sit on the *brille*—the outhouse toilet. Laura squats, balancing with both her arms—to make sure not to fall in. Her runs very soon are finished, and Laura reaches for newspaper torn into little pieces. Laura herself had to fold and tear it into pieces along the folds. Accidentally her behind sinks lower and … Laura doesn't want to remember. Repulsive! Laura feels the poo with her bum. This is human poo, why is it the most disgusting? Horse manure, cow manure, that's nothing, but human? In disgust she tries to pull away, her hands slip, and Laura's bum sinks even deeper into the *brille*. Laura feels old, dried-up excrement, some sort of sharp thing pierces her in that place, the girl's place, it's very, very painful. Aee! Laura in disgust and fear scrambles away, away, away, away, out of there!

Laura feels sick, she feels humiliated, dirty, and a great shame makes Laura feel like vomiting. How to wash herself, how to clean herself up? Laura plucks grass and wipes herself, tears off thistle leaves to clean herself. There's water only in the well but the water sprite is also there, and Laura isn't allowed to go there. Laura can't go to the farmyard because Papa will be there, no, in such a state Laura can't approach even Mama.

Laura runs into the field, following her nose wherever it will lead, Laura won't come back, Laura isn't the same as she was before, her legs get entangled in the long grass, thistles pierce and nettles sting, as Laura runs through the field, fleeing from human shit, fleeing from what is disgusting, runs, falls, gets up, and runs again.

Laura will stay sleeping under a bush, because she no longer has the strength to run.

Laura notices that she smells because Laura has wiped her

hands in her dress to be able to wipe away her tears. Her dress stinks, her face stinks! Laura stinks! Where can Laura find shelter?

What's that? There's a bench by the bush. It's hidden by the bush, but Laura sees it. Then she sees a spring. She senses the spring! First senses it, then sees it.

From a wooden trough in the meadow flows a continuous trickle of water. The trough is covered with a green slime, but the water is clean and fragrant. The dripping water from the spring over time has overflowed into the field. The water isn't deep, it doesn't prevent the long grass from growing. The grass hides the water. Water! Laura dashes toward the water, as if it were a savior.

Water will happily save Laura, why not?

Come you sorry little thing, come tiny bug, little froglet, come, come, don't be shy, the water encourages her. That's why I'm here. I'll tell you something. You'll have to learn to distinguish earth from fire and air from water, and the fine from the coarse, and the beautiful from what is repulsive. With great care. With great care, Water warns. Come!

Laura wallows in the clean spring water like a dog. Flaps about like a duck. Rubs herself all over with grass, not only the dirty, horrendously dirty parts. That place, that girl's place, smarts. The water in the meadow has spread far. Laura goes from one washing place to another. Then again to another, a clean and fresh one. She pulls off all her clothes, and moves to yet another place, a clean and fresh one. She lies down in the springwater, gazing at the glistening water drops on the blades of grass and tips of bulrushes.

She moves to another place, a clean and fresh one. Rubs herself down with grasses. From their fragrance she recognizes valerian, as well as sweet flag and peppermint.

Busily bubbling flows the spring water, the sun is shining, while tiny birds twitter, and grasshoppers susurrate. The water flows from mysterious depths, flows clean. Clean, clean flows the water toward the dirt.

Laura rubs herself clean and scrubs her dress and underpants She moves to another place, yet another clean and fresh one.

She lies down in blue and white forget-me-nots. Blue sky and white clouds.

Now Laura knows why her home is called Avoti—the Latvian word for springs.

Grown into the bush is an old bench. The very same one! She's returned to where she was in the beginning. Not a sign is left here of Laura wallowing like a dog, flapping like a duck. The grass again is standing upright, the grass doesn't want to remind Laura of anything. The grass pretends that it has forgotten how Laura has brawled here, the grass will be silent.

The bench is gray, in spots overgrown with lichen, warmed by the sun, a warm, dear silver bench. Laura sits down. The sun warms her cold behind. Only now Laura realizes that her teeth are chattering and how she can't control this, and beside that, these dreadful goose bumps! They won't ever disappear! But Laura is again clean. Laura has been saved. The spring, water, grass, and the forget-me-nots have saved her.

On the bush a light breeze is drying Laura's dress and underpants. Blow gentle wind!

The lady's mantle with bright eyes is gazing at the sky. Would the dew drops be that lady's mantle tea Mama had asked her to gather? How can it be gathered, if the tea spills the minute she touches it? It drips like mercury from a broken thermometer.

From the trough Laura scrapes away last year's leaves and other rubbish that has collected there, rubs off the green slime. The water begins to flow with more force. What did Water say as it saved Laura? That she'd have to learn. But what?

"You'll have to learn to separate earth from fire and air from water. The fine from the coarse and the beautiful from the repulsive," Water is happy to repeat the advice: "With great care. With great care," Water advises her again.

Laura nonetheless doesn't understand, but she doesn't want to upset Water.

The Blue Tire

TODAY THEY'LL BURN ALL THIS dreadful *barohlo*—junk. Away with it. Down to the bare ground. All those hovels, all that useless crap into the fire! Papa won't leave any of it to be used as firewood. Firewood needs to be white and clean. Papa will take care to get it. Lovely birch firewood. There's also a need for aspen wood. Aspen cleans the tar left by birch wood from the chimney.

Papa works energetically. It's good that he has a *lomik*—a crow bar. Papa found it in the grass. Where he also found a scythe. It's a wonder that no one had stepped on it, pierced out their eyes. He'll be able to cut down the nettles. Mama thinks that we should start with the blue tire, the big blue tire should be burned first. So dreadfully she detests that tire. Papa says that all the wood, all the shit to be burned needs to be piled on top of the tire, so—so those hovels hiss and go up in smoke. Mama breaks out in a smile!

The hovels are hissing, truly hissing. Papa breaks up the misshapen, crooked hutches with all their rabbit droppings, with their hen shit and straw and throws them into the fire, they burn like crazy but the tire isn't yet hissing.

The flames have fired up everyone.

Mama is burning with a passion to clean up the farmyard. First the large stuff, then they'll be able to rake and pick up all the glass shards, tins, old rubber galoshes, triangular-shaped vinegar bottles—did they drink vinegar in place of water?—rotted bags with last year's beets, all the small rubbish, all the junk. Dog shit, metal bowls, pieces of broken flowerpots, old newspapers, everything.

"Now see, Ance! Slowly it's getting tidied up. All will be fine. What lovely stone, beautiful craftsmanship. True castle ruins!"

Papa pats the stone wall of the cattle barn.

Once the huts have been knocked down, the stone wall is finally visible. The colors and grandness of its large, chiseled stones are a wonder to behold.

"This is the work of a true master. I take my hat off to him. What chiseling! Well yes, the rich Zemgale region," Papa remarks admiringly.

What if they're jewels, Laura wonders. The rosy ones somewhat hazy, the gray glittering, the black ones with an azure tint. The black ones for sure must be jewels. The black ones are gold-veined, maybe they might even have gold inside.

Papa is feeding the fire again and again. It seems like Papa himself has a fire inside. Laura sees that Mama likes this fiery Papa.

"Laura, just don't go close! Your braids will get singed!" Mama shoots off sparks.

Laura has already crept up close, Mama just hasn't noticed, but she won't creep any closer. Laura doesn't like how singed hair smells. Laura has already rubbed the singed hair off her forehead. Crumpled up, it has blown away like the gray flakes of ashes.

"Guess my riddle, Laura! Who eats without teeth?" Papa calls from across the yard.

"Fire! Fire!"

Laura already knew that, but now she sees it. The fire consumes without any teeth! The fire consumes everything. Laura senses the fire's ferocious power and lack of discrimination. It's good that the fire is on their side. The fire is a friend and a helpmate. But what if it weren't? It's idiotic to think how it would be if it weren't.

The air is vibrating from the heat. Looking through the fire it looks as if Papa and Mamma are trembling and being twisted like a strand of worsted in the wind. Their bodies billow out seemingly floating in the air.

"Johnny, isn't this too much?" Mama, alarmed, from behind the fire, calls out to Papa.

"Fine, let it die down," Papa, ready to wind down, responds.

The fire has no intention to die down. Not by a long shot. Finally the flames have bit into the tire. Sssss! The fire hisses anew. Black smoke like a tower rises upward. The tire is building a castle for the dog-faced monsters up there! Black smoke strikes Laura's face. It's the tire that strikes her, it's the tire! The smell of rubber chokes her, bites her throat. Through the black cloud, Laura can't see anyone or anything. Mama! Papa!

The tire vomits black, wants to vanquish the rosy and orange light of the fire. Laura understands that the hour of decision has struck. The blue tire is no rabbit hutch that will allow the fire to consume it without a word. The tire will show how to roar, how to smell, how to throw black smoke in your face. Let everyone beware who dares to stand up against the blue tire. They'll be smothered, they'll be smoked out. They'll be covered with gray flakes of ash from head to foot, to walk around thus for the rest of their life, tearing off the flakes of ash. Along with their skin. They'll be poisoned! The fire won't help!

"Mama!" Laura screams, because it's totally clear who is most under threat.

Who was the person most set against the blue tire? Who wanted to burn the blue tire first? It was Mama! The tire will take revenge against Mama. Horrendously take revenge! She must be saved! The tire is biting Laura's eyes, blinding her, making her dizzy, burning her throat and not allowing her to save her dear Mama! Dear, dear Mama!

"Papa, go save Mama! Papa, save Mama!" The blue tire with a huge roar takes her breath away, makes her collapse in a coughing, retching fit, and her words leave her to vanish like the gray flakes of ash.

"Laura, why are you standing there frozen right in the midst of the smoke! Can you not step further away?" Mama grabbing Laura's hand draws her away. Why so roughly? "Directly where the wind is blowing! That smoke is poisonous! Don't you understand? Where is your head?" Mama is annoyed.

Papa calmly pokes at the tire with a long pole. It's no longer blue, also the smoke is dying down.

"The tire! Mama!" Laura sobs.

"Are you sorry for that disgusting blue tire?"

"No! Yes!" Laura would like to hit Mama.

Children can't hit their mamas.

Polliwogs

THE LITTLE POND HASN'T YET been cleaned. Papa's waiting for the water to warm up. Then he'll dredge out all the junk that's been tossed in and maybe dig it deeper so that in hot weather one can splash around in it to one's heart's content.

The polliwogs are pitch black and shiny like new rubber boots. They're the young of green frogs, and the pond has dozens of them. No, more than twice a dozen, even more than three times that. Totally swarming with polliwogs. Teeming. So playful, loveable, the polliwogs like to hang out in groups. They look happy, wiggling their tiny tails, smiling. Why not be happy, the sun is shining, the water in the shallows is warm.

The polliwogs frolic like groats in a kettle. It's fun to watch how they prance and dance around each other. Laura doesn't understand how from such a black polliwog a big green frog can emerge. But that's how it is, so Laura has no reason to disbelieve it. She likes the gaiety of the polliwogs, she feels the polliwogs' joy for life. Laura scoops a handful from the teeming pond. Deftly, the little devils scatter to all sides.

Only two remain in her palm. Now she can examine them more closely. When the water has trickled away through her fingers, the polliwogs for a moment still twitch, then grow weary. Then they're just slimy tiny blobs of black. As they dry they lose their shine, shrink, seem to age in front of Laura's eyes, even some wrinkles appear. What's inside a polliwog? It's not so easy to squash it, it's springy. As luck would have it, they don't squeak, squeal, or yell. If they did, it would be even more difficult to squash them. Laura crushes one of the polliwogs, but there's nothing inside, neither blood, nor intestines, no bones, not even flesh, nothing. A black splat, a wet place. Where did the joy for life go, where life itself? It was just there, and suddenly is no more.

The other polliwogs don't care one bit for their poor brother, don't even notice that one is missing. The frogs also have no intention of attacking Laura in protest, or at least yelling at her, reprimanding her, shouldn't they defend their offspring? Frogs don't give a hoot about their young, Laura sulks. The frogs don't give a damn about their babies.

Laura will go and pick some larkspur. To put in a vase. She won't pick anything for tea; let Mama not expect it, because too much is needed for tea. Laura doesn't have the patience. Doesn't have it, that's all there is to it, so what can Laura do about it?

But what's that? A short stretch away from the pond, among the larkspur, bird's eye primroses, and forget-me-nots, there's a big puddle. There the polliwogs are like peas in a pod, squeezed tight together. The edges of the puddle have dried out and the polliwogs have too little room. Here there's no more frolicking, here there's fear and danger. The dried-out place is as if sown with inert polliwogs. They're already dead. They need more water! If the frogs themselves don't care, doing absolutely nothing, then someone else has to save the polliwogs.

Laura after a few moments returns with an old pail, it's the first thing she's come across, for she must hurry. Laura scoops water from the pond and carries it to the puddle. The pail drips water but not to worry. The polliwogs grow more lively. Laura senses them regaining hope. They put all their hope in Laura, understanding that Laura is trying to save them.

Laura carries more and more water from the pond. The pail has a hole in it and is leaking. When Laura, exhausted, kneels down by the polliwog puddle, she sees that the polliwogs are again cavorting around and smiling. Once more there's enough room for them to move their tiny tails. Now the polliwogs are wiggling their tails in gratitude, like puppies, they're smiling just for Laura. Laura smiles back at them and everyone is very happy. She'll carry a couple more pails from the pond. To counter that leak. Later she'll come back to check the puddle, to feel delighted about her good deed.

Laura comes back after two, maybe three or four days. She couldn't come earlier, she had no time. How dreadful! All the water has dried out. Nothing indicates that there had been a large puddle there, an enormous puddle, just the grass is paler, laid back and in places covered with a black film. Laura imagines that...

No, that can't be! In the pond the polliwogs continue to be lively and happy. Somewhat plumper, more satisfied with life. The frogs are croaking cheerfully. When they get carried away with a song then white bubbles appear at their mouths. It looks like the frogs are blowing up balloons. There's real festivity in the pond. No mundane stuff is bothering any of them. All are blowing up balloons. All the frog-mamas are happy. All their children are together again.

Have the puddle polliwogs moved to the pond? Somehow they've managed to get there, because the frogs have finally taken action, seeing that Laura is saving their little ones, the frogs have been shamed, have become reasonable. No matter what, it's been done. The polliwogs have been saved. But how did they get to the pond? Maybe through some underground passage? Oh, she won't trouble her mind so much, Laura wants to be happy too like a polliwog.

Heavy Clothes

"One, two, three, let it rip faster! One, two, three, let it rip faster! One, two, three, let it rip faster!" Laura recites and hops around, thinking about what everyone will say and how everyone will compliment her, when she wears the new dress. When are we going?

"Where?"

What do you mean—where? Has Mama forgotten? Laura thinks about it from morning till late at night. At midnight and in the middle of the night! Why—where? To have a dress sewn! A new dress! To *Vāvere* "Not to Vāvere, not to 'squirrel,' but to Mrs. Vēvere. We'll go of course. Now it's the new moon," Mīma says, "we can't go when it's the new moon."

"Why?"

Laura suspects that Mama is just making excuses, doesn't want to go and that's all. And Mīma also is just fibbing with her new moon. What difference does the moon make? What has the moon up there to do with Laura's new dress? Mama simply doesn't want Laura to have a new dress. She wants Laura to walk around in her old Siberian rags all summer.

"Shame on you! Old Siberian rags! They're English clothes! Just like the sandals! It's good that they're second-hand! Railway Annie already asked me."

"Asked you what?"

"If all children in Siberia have as lovely clothes as Laura?"

"What did you answer?" Papa asks raising his head from the book he's reading. Couldn't tear himself away before, but look how he does so now.

"No, not everyone has, but we lucked out by having a good seamstress. Something like that. Since when are you interested in girls' dresses?"

"I'm not interested in your dresses, but your safety. Only that. It's a question of safety. Laura must have normal Soviet clothes sewn for her," Papa defends Laura.

"But clothes should be sewn during the old moon. Ones sewn under a new moon are heavy on the wearer. And when washed they soon shrink."

"Mīma's wisdom!" Papa smirks and Mama is annoyed at that.

"That's common wisdom! It's a hundred and a thousand times tried and tested. It's a folk adage."

"One can't always believe these sayings." Papa has no intention of giving in. Mama doesn't either. Laura knows the outcome.

"You'd be better off if you looked at the woodstove!"

Laura has guessed it. Well yes, that there stove. Well yes, once again there will be quarreling.

Well then, Laura will go rummage through the package. It's an opportune moment. While they quarrel, while they make up. Meanwhile Laura can feel happy and feel hurt at the same time.

Feel hurt and be happy about her clothes.

There's a new dress for Laura in the package. But it's too beautiful. Green with purple pockets. Laura can't wear it because everyone will immediately see that it's from abroad.

In the package there's also a dark blue taffeta skirt with straps. Seemingly dark blue, but when you turn it this way and that, then it shimmers and changes color like the Aurora Borealis in Siberia. Now blue, now green, then rosy. How marvelously lovely the skirt is! Laura's heart skips a beat, wrenches—she can't wear it, because everyone will know it's from abroad.

In the package there's also a blouse for Laura. One that goes with the skirt. The material is soft and silky, its color light blue. But it's the buttons that are the loveliest. They're smoky bright and round like pearls. Laura will never, ever be able to wear it, because then everyone would immediately know that the blouse is from abroad.

No one is supposed to have clothes from abroad! Because then right away it's obvious that the person has connections abroad. But connections—they're very bad. Very, very bad. Communication with abroad is not allowed! The dog-faced monsters don't like anything to do with abroad. A person is immediately put on a black list. And because Laura with her Mama and Papa are already on one black list then to be put on a second black list would be the same as to put your head under… Laura has forgotten the word that Papa used. It's not so important.

Laura wonders about the black list. Is it on black paper with white ink the same as the Black Book, which the devil himself has written? With this Black Book all kinds of evil spirits can be summoned and then enslaved to do evil deeds. No, no, Laura doesn't need this Black Book.

Guillotine! Laura remembers the word Papa used. To get on another black list would be the same as putting your head under a guillotine. That's what he said. As luck would have it the package has come from Siberia. Those the post office doesn't tear open. The ones from abroad, those they tear open, but Siberia is not abroad, and what if anything can be sent from Siberia? In the village of Lamme no one needs to know that the package in reality has been sent from London. London is in England and England is abroad.

The package has been sent to Siberia by Asya's seven brothers. In her letters Asya tells her seven brothers every time to not send anything too luxurious and the seven brothers respond that, of course, they won't send anything fancy, only the most basic and most needed. The seven brothers would like to send Laura, their only sister's dear goddaughter, some gift, for example, a gold watch, but Asya has had a talk with Buka and has replied to her brothers that there's no need, because in Siberia a gold watch is a very common thing. Everyone has a gold watch. It would be better for the brothers to send some aspirin and some cream of wheat.

Laura's mind wanders. She's been waiting for Buka and Asya for such a long time. A year from now, they'll come, a year from now. When will that be? Still a long time away. Laura keeps hoping. Just hoping—a whole year long—still a whole year's worth of hoping.

Laura takes out and caresses her lovely clothes, which no one else is allowed to see. Mīma must be right. The clothes are heavy. Probably sewn under the new moon. For sure. In England, of course, no one knows Latvian folk beliefs.

The Store. Don't speak badly of Latvia!

Laura is going to the store with her Mama! Laura has never in her life been to a store. In Siberia there was a *lavka*—a kiosk, a small store, but it was far away and she was never taken along. But here it's Latvia, and Laura is going to a store. Both of them have dressed up, as much as they can, Mama has put on lipstick, just in case they meet some acquaintance. Laura has been warned to say hello to everyone they meet along the way. Regardless if the person is someone known or unknown. That's customary in Latvia. She doesn't have to always curtsey, just, if the adults shake hands. But they don't meet anyone. A pity!

There's a counter and shelves in the store. On the counter there's a scale and an abacus. Stacked on the shelves sit large tins. In addition there's a shelf with bottles. *Kochiņi, polshiņi*—quarter-liters and half-liters of booze, bottles of ale, whatever they're called. There's also a shelf with small cans, red and blue ones.

"What's in those cans?" Laura likes the glued-on colored papers.

"Sprats in an herbed brine and brislings in a tomato sauce." Laura is startled, because she's asked the question of Mama, but a strange woman answers in a hoarse voice.

"Do you want some? How many?" The strange woman is in a hurry, although there are no other customers in the store.

Laura figures out that this surely is the storekeeper, who else.

"Two of the sprats and one of the brislings. I meant—the cans." Mama smiles.

"What else?" The storekeeper hurries them and doesn't attempt to smile in return.

"Two brick breads and three white loaves. Is that butter?" Mama points at the show-case.

"That's *kombinzhir*–a fat-mix. A loaf—the last one," the

shopkeeper fishes a flattened loaf of white bread from below the counter.

"And two brick breads, please." Mama reminds her.

"What time is it?" the storekeeper asks Mama, straightening up and sticking out her substantial bosom.

Mama wonders why the storekeeper is asking this. She's got a clock behind her. On the wall. Laura too wonders, but she can't wonder too long. If the shopkeeper should ask Laura, she'll have to confess that she doesn't know yet how to tell the time on a clock. Neither a clock, nor a calendar. Laura can't understand how it's possible to take time that flows like a river, and divide it into small bits.

"Ten after twelve," Mama says.

"Well then. So, you want some brick bread. You have to then come at eight in the morning, when they're delivered. You mustn't sleep so long. You must stand in line like every other decent person. The bricks are sold out in an hour," the storekeeper boasts.

"What's in the big tins?" Mama asks, barely hiding her annoyance.

"*Povidla*. Do you want some?"

"What's *povidla*?" Laura whispers in Mama's ear so the storekeeper won't hear.

"*Povidla* is *povidla*," the storekeeper snaps; she hears everything.

"Then I'll have some of that *kombinzhir*, half a kilo, please," Mama probably is ashamed to ask what *povidla* is.

The storekeeper takes the big slab out from the showcase and with a knife attempts to slice off a piece. The *kombinzhir* is as tough as flint. The shopkeeper struggles in silence. Having hacked off a piece, she wraps it in brown, heavy paper and throws it on the scale. The shopkeeper doesn't attempt to hide how tough it is for her to lift the *kombinzhir*, how hard to cut with a knife such a slab is, and who is responsible for all this hard work.

"Seven hundred grams," she pronounces and Mama doesn't object.

"And a sweet for the child," Mama no longer can stand Laura's fidgeting.

"Pear lemonade."

"No, no, thanks, not lemonade."

"There isn't anything else. The delivery will be on Wednesday. Take the *povidla*."

The shopkeeper probably sees how downcast Laura has become.

"Fine. About 200 grams," Mama resolutely agrees, and Laura is proud of Mama, who is ready to head into the unknown.

The shopkeeper groaning heaves a large, corrugated metal tin from the shelf, she's got to do all this work for a measly 200 grams! *Povidla* turns out to be a brown, oily apple puree.

The shopkeeper vigorously pushes the abacus beads along. From the right side they shift to the left. Mama's eyes worriedly follow along. If she doesn't have enough money, she'll feel shame.

On the floor are piled sacks full of barley and dried peas. Mama wants a kilo of each. While the shopkeeper moves in slow motion, weighing and pouring, with each movement letting it be known what a great nuisance these two buyers are for her, Laura has a moment to look around. In a large bowl are salted mushrooms, in a barrel—herring in brine. Further in semi-darkness can be seen fabric in fat bolts, some sort of wooden poles, and some kind of iron things. There's not much more to be seen, but just the same it's a lot. Laura is satisfied, they'll have something to eat, yes, they will.

"Is that all?" the storekeeper asks.

It's not clear whether they have bought too much or too little.

"That's all," Mama responds.

The storekeeper instantly disappears.

"Thank you! Good-bye," Mama says, but no one responds.

"And that's a so-called store? A real hovel, not a store! And that's what stores are like in Latvia? And what kind of service is that? Laura, did you notice how dirty the saleswoman's apron was? How that old biddy talked to us? What kind of service is that? In Latvia?" Mama on the way home is totally indignant. Laura wonders if doing her hair up in tiny braids was worth it. "Child, if you only knew what kind of a store we once had! This same one, yes. Mr. Goldstein was so decent. Mrs. Goldstein so kind! There was everything in the store! Absolutely everything! The grown-ups were offered coffee, children were given lemonade."

"We were also offered lemonade! Pear," Laura wants to be fair.

"Yes, to buy! But Mr. and Mrs. Goldstein used to treat us. Chatted with everyone. Such good people," Mama gets carried away through tears.

"Where are they now?" Laura suddenly very much wants to have Mrs. Goldstein's lemonade.

"A German, the dog-faced monster, shot and killed them!" Mama exclaims with a moan, she shouldn't have, shouldn't tell a child things like this, but it's too late.

"Why a dog-faced monster, the German? Why shot?"

"They were Jews."

"Like Asya?"

"Yes, like Asya."

"Were they also English spies? Why did the dog-faced monster German shoot them?"

"Let it be! You don't understand any of it!" Mama snaps, seething with anger.

Laura knows Mama's anger, but more so the tiny angers, this is a major one.

"Why are you so terribly angry with Laura?" Laura starts to cry.

"I'm not angry with you, honey! Little idiot, of course I'm not angry with you!" Mama draws Laura close and kisses her.

"With whom then?"

Mama shakes her head but doesn't answer; probably she has other things to think about.

"We forgot salt and sugar! We have to go back" Mama turns back, but then stops and hesitates. She blows her nose. "No we're not going. Not to that *vedma*—witch, I won't go to her anymore!" Mama has decided.

"And this is what Latvia is like now? And this is what Latvia is?" Mama grumbles all the way home, she can't calm down, just can't. Laura finally has had enough!

"Don't talk badly about Latvia!" Laura stops and yells at Mama. Laura too can lose patience. Laura too can feel great anger. "Is Latvia to blame for the storekeeper having a dirty apron? Is Latvia to blame that the storekeeper is a *vedma*?"

Mama in surprise stops. Probably mute in astonishment that Laura has something to say.

Mama gazes at her in silence, it's not a good sign that she doesn't yell back at her. Laura waits for her to yell, but no such thing happens. It's too late to back off, and Laura has no intention of doing so.

"Don't talk badly about Latvia!" Laura hollers once more and stamps her foot.

Laura has to be stern, very stern, because someone has to defend Latvia after all. In Siberia no one talked badly about Latvia. Just to get back there! Just to be in Latvia! Latvia was so beautiful; Latvia was so precious. People were almost dying without their Latvia. But now? Laura has to be firm, but she just can't stop the tears, Mama also can't.

"You're right, child, you're a hundred percent right. Forgive me! Forgive me, Laurie."

What percent? Why a hundred? Laura would like Mama to explain. As a punishment she should right now, immediately, explain, what is a percent and why the hundred! Mama doesn't like numbers. Let her explain! And forgiveness should be asked of Latvia! Laura doesn't need it! But Mama's lipstick has got smeared, black mascara is collecting around her eyes, a tear looking like a black polliwog slides down her cheek, some bobby pins come undone, and Laura senses how Mama's heart hurts.

"Forgive me, Mommy!"

Mama bends down and hugs Laura. Laura wraps her arms around Mama's neck and holds her tight. Mama lifts Laura, presses her to her breast and rocks her. The bag of peas has ripped, now the peas are falling out, let them fall! Tears don't fall neither like beans nor peas, this time peas fall like tears. Cheeks pressed together, their tears mingle. Which tears are Mama's, which Laura's? Which tears are Laura's, which Mama's?

Mīma's Goodies

"CALM DOWN!" Mīma gently entreats the horse and the horse bows her head. It looks like a conversation between the two, Mīma tells the horse to stay put, and the horse agrees. Mīma clambers out of the wagon. It's good that the wagon has a foot-board otherwise Mīma wouldn't get out. She tosses the reins over the mare's back, pats her brown withers a couple of times. In horse language it means that everything is fine, she just needs to stand quietly for a short while, it won't be long and Mīma will return the favor of course. The horse's name is Daira.

Laura remembers the verse repeated again and again from the train. Be calm, be quiet, be well-behaved and obedient, smart, be a big girl and clever. Now the horse has to do the same. Daira has to be like that. Why does the horse have a girl's name?

"Where's the doggy?" a disappointed Laura wonders. She would have liked to romp around a bit.

"Ripsis is Grandpa's dog. He doesn't go anywhere without Grandpa."

"Where is Grandpa? Why didn't Grandpa come with us?" Mama wants to know.

"You know how it is with Grandpa," Mīma says quietly.

It had seemed to Mama that he was better now, he had come to meet them at the station after all, talked and all. Yes, the homecoming, such an event, such happiness, Grandpa pulled himself together, but now again. Yes, once more he's lost heart. No, Ginter Manor had not helped any, and when Grandpa had tried to do himself in at Ginter Manor... Only home would do. Grandpa can only be in his own home. He can't, just can't manage to have the heart to live. Lies in bed and stares at the ceiling and doesn't talk to anyone, no, not even to Mīma.

Can Laura go and see Grandpa! What's it like when one

doesn't have the heart to live? Laura wants to see that. Mama worries that Laura may upset him, maybe impose on him too much. Never you mind, the girl can come to the Upītes farm whenever she wants. Just as long as Papa and Mama let her. It's not far at all, only across the field. Past the spring. Maybe it's grown over. Mīma hasn't been there for a long time.

But Laura has already been there, but she won't tell.

As long as the girl isn't bored by the two old people, let her come. Let her come, but tomorrow is Sunday and all of them are going to Upītes for dinner. Mīma will slaughter the old rooster. Can't put up with him anymore! He's turned nasty, like a wild beast, attacks people. Jumped on Mīma's head, it's a good thing that he didn't peck out her eyes. Laura can't show herself at Upītes farm while the rooster is still alive.

Mīma has brought along a few things for them. She needs Jānis to help with them. Papa arrives, sweaty from working and flushed from the sun. He tans easily.

"Take those taters," Mīma starts to give out orders. Papa looks in the wagon but can't find the taters.

"Look there, in that sack!"

"Ah so? I didn't know potatoes were called taters."

That's not yet all that Mīma has in the wagon.

Peas. Has Ance lost her mind buying peas at the store? She's just thrown money away because there are still two chests full of peas at Upītes farm. No need to buy pearl-barley either at the store. The White Negro transports the grain to the mill and it's ground whenever needed. The White Negro? No time to ask.

Beans. They've been poured into cloth bags, tied with a string. Broad beans, fava beans, string beans, butter beans—Mīma recites. Mīma has saved them for a long time, waited and saved, it's not as if all of this has materialized in one day. The beans need to be thoroughly soaked before being cooked. Maybe even for a couple of days, maybe a pinch of soda should be added.

Be careful, eggs! A whole basketful! What kind of eggs? Laurie, child, hens' eggs, what else could they be? Mīma can't complain about her hens, this year they're laying well, probably they know that there will be more people eating.

Pickles in a clay crock. Mīma with difficulty has drawn the pickles out of the well. From the well? Yes, during the autumn a milk churn with cucumbers is lowered into the well where it stands until Jāṇi—the Latvian Midsummer.

Salted mushrooms. Last autumn at the edge of the moor the white peppery milk caps alone almost needed to be mowed down with a scythe, there were so many.

Jams! Cherry, black currant, red currant, gooseberry, maybe even a plum jam among them, Mīma hasn't made the latter the last few years because no one really eats it. If any happen to have a bit of mold on top, small matter, take the mold off and eat the rest. All of it from the garden, all, Mīma no longer has the strength nor the inclination to go into the woods. For the bilberries or cranberries. In the moor there are cranberries without end, Anda will be able to pick them herself in the autumn. But just at the edge of the moor. And God forbid, let her not venture deep into the woods! The ķeme is not any kind of fancy jam, but maybe it will be good enough. Ķeme? What's that? God preserve us, apple sauce, Ance, have you forgotten? Mama had forgotten what ķeme was, but just now she remembered, yes, no one knows how to make it better than Mīma. With cloves. It's good that Mīma doesn't know anything about what was bought at the store and about the *povidla*, which smells like petroleum.

Mīma feels fortunate to be the one giving. She's shining with happiness.

And besides all the rest there's the shoulder joint. Laura can sense that in Mīma's eyes the shoulder joint is the most valuable thing she's brought. Laura doesn't let it show that she doesn't know what a shoulder joint is. Mīma points out that the shoulder joint has been smoked long and slowly, hence it should be well-smoked, but it still needs to be kept in a cool place. One has to watch out that it doesn't start to go bad from inside out. It happens that by the bone the meat remains raw, no matter if the joint is smoked till kingdom come.

"Mīma, that's totally insane! So much!" Mama is proud because this is absolute proof for what she's been saying, that there's nothing lacking in Latvia. That starvation is not a threat.

Mīma is Mama's dear grandmother, Mīma is so good at running her house! The same as Buka, Mama's mama and Mīma's daughter.

"It's not as if we ourselves had nothing," Papa doesn't know what he should be feeling, after all he seemingly is the head of the family and the breadwinner.

"You fending for yourselves alone? Who are we then? And Grandpa? Strangers? No, dear Jāni, we all are in this together, and it can't even be otherwise."

Mama thinks exactly as Mīma does, Laura thinks the same as Mama. She just can't grasp the riches, these great riches! And she's happy that Papa doesn't know what taters are, but Mama has forgotten what ķeme is. Laura isn't the only one who doesn't know all words.

The Garden

THE UPĪTES FARM IS A MARVEL! In Upītes there are large trees. Oaks, lindens, and maples, and chestnuts. And ash trees, and all the trees are enormous, enormously big. Laura can understand how grass and flowers can grow from soil, but how can such gigantic trees grow? Where does the size of the enormous trees come from? From what? From nothing? How does the soil give the tree so incredibly much nourishment, it's not to be understood, it can only be admired. To wrap one's arms around the gnarled trunks, to gaze upward at the thick branches. A look climbs up the branches as if climbing up stairs. Laura tilts her head back, but the treetops are still far above, in the blue of the sky and her head grows dizzy.

In Upītes there's no blue tire. In the Upites flower bed roses grow. The bed is round. In the middle are the roses, but edged all around are tiny white flowers with yellow centers. And around the bed there's banked sod. But that's not all! In a semicircle around the round bed like a large horseshoe curves another bed. With the same sort of edging with sod and the same kind of tiny white flowers with yellow centers. But these are only around the edge of the horseshoe. Inside the horseshoe all kinds of blue and rosy flowers bloom. Laura doesn't recognize what they are yet. Large bushes with sweeping branches proudly decorate the ends of the horseshoe. And that's especially well planned, because if it weren't would the sweeping branches of the bushes grow exactly opposite each other as they do.

And what's this? The crunch of gravel under Laura's feet. Gravel- covered paths, gravel paths. Buka had mentioned them in Siberia. Buka had created this flower bed! Buka! Chamomile around the edges. Buka had said so. The white flowers are called chamomile! The great branched bushes are peonies! Why hasn't

Buka returned home for such a long time? Where will Buka live when she comes? Will it be here, where she was born and grew up, or on the Avoti farm where she was married out to Edmunds and where Mama was born? Maybe Buka won't even be allowed to live here either in Upītes or in Avoti? What if Buka is never allowed to return to Latvia?

Mīma calls Laura to come in.

No, Laura can't go in yet because she has to look over the garden.

In the garden Laura doesn't know where to put her feet. As soon as she takes a step, she's up to her ankles in yellow plums.

All the plums from the old, half-dried-out trees are on the ground. It's quite odd to tramp among the plums like this. Laura doesn't really believe it's happening to her, that it can even be like this, doesn't understand, if it's the way it should be. Is it good—to trample the plums? To step on edible things. Is it right that Laura alone should have so many plums?

The ones lying at the bottom have rotted, these squish under Laura's feet, but the ones above scatter on top of her sandals like the beads of a large amber necklace. Mīma had such a necklace at one time, but God knows where it is now. The rotten plums emit a strong fragrance, like Kagor wine, like a jam that has started to ferment. She can feel that they've already gotten into her sandals, they ooze between her toes like slimy mud, gluing them together. Like yellow mud.

Laura is in the garden. The garden is a marvel. The garden is a world unto itself. She needs time to grasp it. Laura wants to be in and stay in the garden for an eternity and to marvel at it. When Mīma calls, she'll quickly run to eat some old rooster, or a soup, or sweet bread, and then quickly back again into the garden, back to marveling, marveling and being happy with an intense joy. Laura has never before seen as many apples, in fact she hasn't ever seen apples before. Neither apples, nor pears, nor cherries, never mind plums. Only in Latvia are there such marvelous things. In Siberia there aren't any of these.

In the future Laura will no longer tell anyone that.

For example, that she's never seen an apple. She told Rita this, but she didn't believe her. Rita is the only child that Laura has met up to now. Rita herself had come, her mama had sent her, to see what really was happening at the Avoti farm. What are they doing there, in those Avoti?

She mustn't say anything about Siberia; no one will believe her anyway! They'll think that we're not normal! That's what Papa said and it turns out he was right.

Rita said exactly that—you're not normal! You're lying!

Such riches! Such plenty, plenteousness, plentitude, plentiness. Laura doesn't know which word is the best. The plum is so beautiful. Plentifully beautiful. And absolutely everything is plentiful for Laura alone! Just for her—is that good?

No, it isn't good. Laura remembers the Barrack children. Also recalls Kima, she too is a big child.

Laura picks up a plum round like an egg. It's split open, under the plum skin is sweet, tender, webbed flesh. The skin peels easily, the plum as if by itself divides in half. Rosy tendrils color the fruit like a tearing eye. The plum now appears vulnerable to Laura, skinless, she can't leave it, it must be eaten.

The pit lies in the plum's lobe as if in a cradle. The pit can't be eaten! It's poisonous. There's a blue acid inside, from it a person can die right on the spot. If one doesn't bite into it then it's alright, just a tummy ache, and it passes through. Or, what's even worse, in a tummy a tree can grow from this pit. It does happen that one grows. Then a person is again finished because as it grows a tree tears a person in half.

A person needs to be careful with plum pits. One must show respect for them. The plum tree has thought it all out well, planned ahead.

It's wise, that plum tree. Eat the soft flesh of my plums, people, eat as much as you can stuff yourselves with, please, I don't begrudge it. But leave the pit alone! Inside it is my child, the next tree. If you eat my future tree, then you'll just see what happens! Then, I'll show you! Then you'll die and will be finished forever!

Laura totally agrees with the plum tree. She throws the pit away as far as she can, outside the thicket, so the plum baby will have more space.

In the beginning Laura eats the plums with all their skin. In the beginning the skin didn't seem sour, now it does. The skin is sour. Laura peels it off.

Wasps! One, striped like a tiger, almost stings her. Laura sees the wasp land on her upper arm and attach itself with its sharp little legs very much like firemen's hooks, now she can examine it well. Close up she can see its fine hair, tiny horns, slim middle, fat behind.

A wasp stings with her bum, which is funny. Not like flies. Or bees, Laura doesn't know anyone else that stings with their bum. Why does it sting with its bum? It tickles Laura, she can't keep still for so long.

The wasp positions itself to sting. A quick swipe swats the wasp from her arm. Knocks it down to the ground. Take that! Where did it go?

If she looks carefully, there are wasps galore. They seem furious. And why not? Since forever they alone have eaten here, fed and feasted, probably are upset that someone else might also get some. Laura again is sorry that others can't have any. All the plums are for Laura alone. If she only could call all the children from the Barrack in Siberia. From neighboring barracks. There are a lot of barracks in Siberia.

Laura picks up another plum. Its juice has squeezed out like a tear. No, Laura can't eat anymore. She gathers a handful. Plums are falling from her hand; she squeezes the plums until she can feel the hard graininess of the pit. She places the squashed plums on her face. She wants to press them into herself, so they never again are lost. She breathes through the sweet plums. Through the plums looks at the sun, at the world.

The wasps show ever more interest in Laura, she's covered in plums, her legs, hands, shins, and mouth. She herself is a plum. At least it seems so to the wasps. Maybe she too inside herself has a pit?

No way! Laura will not let the wasps sting her. She'll just head back. Will no longer pay attention where she's stepping. Her sandals are already totally soaked in plum juice. Laura wades through the plums as if through the Yellow Sea.

She wants to pee. Laura squats in the long grass and hears a hiss. How is that? She hasn't yet begun to pee, when there's a hiss. A hiss like the sound of peeing. Laura glances around. An arm's length away there's a snake. Curled up with its head protruding, it's looking straight at Laura and hisses. The snake is saying something, but what? Laura doesn't move. What is dreadful is that the snake is flicking its tongue in and out. If the snake should flick its tongue into Laura, then Laura will be done for.

The tongue doesn't reach Laura.

Nonetheless it's breathtaking to look at the snake close up, Laura can't pull herself away. Mīma had already warned her that there may be a grass snake in the garden, Laura shouldn't be afraid. That's easy to say. Aren't grass snakes snakes? A snake is a snake. Maybe the snake doesn't want to do any harm but how is one to know? Maybe the snake just doesn't want anyone to pee on her. Who would want that?

Laura wavers between fear and curiosity. What should she do? The snake is the first to decide. She uncoils herself and slithers away.

Francis and Riga's Lilacs

FRANCIS IS ONCE AGAIN at the Avoti farm! He drives in from the town of Tukums in a make-do car every second day or so. Francis is always spiffed up, he smells of cologne. Of Shipra. Always looks like he's just been to a barber, maybe the barber has such a last name—Shipra. Laura really doesn't know. Francis always arrives with gifts. And Francis always brings a cake! This time he's brought a pink rabbit made of rubber for Laura. For Mama he brings perfumes. Riga's Lilacs. Francis kisses Mama's hand, as if Mama were some sort of lady.

Laura can't stop raving about the box in which the perfume bottle lies. It's purple velvet, and is a marvel of yet unseen beauty. The interior of the box is lined with silk, also purple, just a lighter shade and soft. So coordinated! And in a special slot the perfume bottle itself. Like a cluster of lilacs. With all the leaves. How can something like that be made? Laura forgets about the rabbit, even though it's made from rubber itself, and can't pull her eyes away even for a moment from the perfume box. Laura would like to have the box for herself but her pleading doesn't help. Mama places the Riga's Lilacs box on the *etagerska*, right at the very top. Where already two such boxes have been placed.

Mama isn't as happy as she was the first few times when Francis arrived with the make-do car, but she has to appear happy to be hospitable. Mama tries because Francis is Papa's best friend from Siberia. Almost like a brother. Both have smelled the same stench of death. Laura thinks that maybe because of that death smell Francis likes perfumes so much—not only Riga's Lilacs but also that Shipra cologne, maybe because of that.

Francis has a slight, but nimble and lithe build like a cat, red curly hair, and a spotted face. The spots are summer freckles but they don't disappear even in winter. Even Francis's eyebrows and the hair on his arms are red. Francis has earned a lot of money mining nickel up North where the white bears are. Nickel-schmickel, no matter because he's rich and he isn't stingy. If Papa had remained up North he too would have a lot of money. But Papa didn't stay because he met and married Mama. Francis would have married Mama himself if she weren't his best friend's wife. He won't marry anyone else, if he can't have her, then there's nothing more to be done. And what he doesn't have, he doesn't need to have!

Mama wouldn't have married Francis even if she hadn't met Papa, well no, because Francis is a *loder*—a laggard and a big blabber mouth. Laura doesn't know why Mama doesn't like laggards and big-mouths, because Laura likes them.

He has brought a small suitcase full of booze, a *polsh* of vodka. The best brand, not just any old horse swill. Laura never knew that horses too have their own vodka.

Just for Mama Francis has brought Kagor. Kagor is a horrendously good wine, it's very healthy, and it isn't any kind of cheap fusel. You can get Kagor only by paying with what the grown-ups call *b-lati*. It's some sort of special money which not everyone has. Others have rubles and kapeikas, before they used lati, but Francis has b-lati, many b-lati. Apparently they're given under the table, on the sly, Laura wants to see what these b-lati look like, but Francis doesn't show her.

There will be partying again at Avoti! Laura knows what Mama thinks of this. The garbage won't be taken out, the manure won't be mucked out nor the woodstove fixed. But Francis is Papa's best friend. The best and the only one. Only with Francis can Papa really talk about things that matter to him. It's only Francis whom Papa can trust. The only one in the world, because they have the same issues.

"Ance, bring some *zakuskas!*" Papa is happy, so happy about Francis.

Laura likes a happy Papa. Then he's more handsome than usual, then he forgets that he's too tall, forgets that he has to walk a bit stooped. Papa's blonde hair then takes on a shiny golden hue. Then he forgets that all of his family has been murdered.

Francis too forgets that all his family has been murdered, that he is all alone in this world like an orphan.

Do they cry because of this? No, they sing, as loud as can be. Johnny's family is now also Francis's family, that's what he says. Life is beautiful! Francis laughs, he has two gold teeth. Live fast and die young! Francis bullshits nonstop. So what? But Laura is a princess for Francis.

"Laura, you'll have to scoot off to Mīma's to have her give you a hunk of smoked meat." Mama begins to contemplate what to put on the table.

Mīma's goodies have already been finished off. Laura doesn't want to scoot over to Mīma's. Laura is a princess. Do princesses have to run for smoked meat? Laura hopefully turns to Francis. Francis is thinking, he knits his freckled brow until it's deeply wrinkled, taps with his fingers on the table. Laura waits for the judgment.

"Well, yes, you'll have to run. If Mama is a queen then princesses have to run, that's how it is! That's the bitter truth, princess."

"Johnny, we have no bread," Mama says.

"How can that be? Yesterday we bought two bricks."

"Finished," Mama shrugs her shoulders helplessly.

"As Marie Antoinette, the queen, said, among other things: 'If the people don't have bread, let them eat cake!'" Francis opens the cake box.

Green and pink flowers bloom on the cake like in a flower bed.

And at such a moment Laura is to run for some sort of meat? Leave the cake and all the joy and excitement? In protest Laura starts to malinger, her leg starts to hurt. Where does it hurt? Just at that moment Laura can't come up with where.

How you talk!

Mīma, slicing the smoked meat in the pantry, is cross and crotchety. Probably she's gotten out of bed on the wrong foot. Grandpa can't be seen anywhere. Grandpa most of the time is not to be seen. "Tell your parents that it's the last piece I'm slicing. And that too shall be eaten by someone else who's not one of the family."

"Francis is not someone else. He's Papa's best friend."

Mīma doesn't notice that Laura is talking back to her, but that's fine, let her carp and fuss while she quickly slices the meat, Laura is in a hurry.

"You tell your parents that this smoked meat is not given but lent!"

"What does lent mean?"

"Lent is not given but borrowed. Borrowed is what needs to be given back!"

Back? Laura wonders if she should tell her that this piece of meat Mīma won't get back. Because it will be eaten. As it is Mīma is seething with resentment.

"I'm not going to feed all the drunks who hang around Avoti. Like at a pub! Soon people will begin to talk. This partying has to stop once and for all! Why doesn't Jānis look for work?"

"Papa is looking!"

"He's looking half-heartedly if he hasn't found it!" Mīma gripes.

Mīma is unfair! Laura has to defend Papa.

"Papa is not at fault! He went to the *kochegarka*—the central heating plant, but Papa wasn't hired. Because the *kochegarka* is an important object. And they don't hire people who've been deported to Siberia. Maybe Papa will become a *gruzchik* or maybe get on a *stroika* or drive a *benzovozha,* but maybe—work

78

on a *betonameshalka*. But maybe he'll work part-time. The part-time work isn't at such important objects, where Papa isn't allowed to work," Laura, heated up, says and is happy because at the last moment she's remembered this important word—object. While listening Mīma's eyes grow wider and wider.

"How you talk? My God, child, what kind of language is that? I don't understand a word!" Mīma sits down on the wide kitchen bench in despair.

Laura is confused. How does she talk? It's clear that in Latvian. That's the Latvian language! Mīma doesn't understand? How can that be?

Laura tries so hard, tries to learn, hangs onto each new word, tries to understand what's inside the word. Laura gets lost among words like in a dense, strange forest, but she doesn't give up, parts branch by branch, bush by bush, through the wide leaves and feels joy when words reveal themselves like a suddenly discovered wild strawberry patch. Laura absorbs words like a blotter sucks up ink, blotters that are in each school child's notebook. Laura has such a notebook, even though Laura is not a pupil, not yet.

How does Laura talk? Like everyone! What does Mīma not like? Everybody else praises Laura. Everyone else marvels. Laurie speaks so well! Laurie's vocabulary grows with each day! And now—Mīma doesn't understand? Laura is mad at Mīma. Because when Laura doesn't understand a word that Mīma has used, then Laura doesn't show it and doesn't reproach her. Laura is a tactful person. She doesn't say—what kind of a language is that? Laura feels great bitterness against Mīma.

"What was wrong with the farm brigade for Jānis? He only worked a week if that. To disgrace himself so? Shame!"

"Doggone it! Papa wasn't suited for the farm brigade. Papa doesn't like that sluggard sweatshop! Papa had an issue and he and the supervisor came to loggerheads! That's that and amen! Papa won't do a senseless job! He won't shovel that Chile-crap fertilizer all day in the sun! Just because some idiot left the Chile-crap out in the rain and it became as hard as a rock. Papa won't have anything to do with idiots! That kolkhoz will go down the drain even without Papa! Finished!" Laura snaps back. She'll show Mīma that Laura knows how to talk, and not only like this!

At the last moment Laura begins to feel sorry for Mīma, Laura decides to spare Mīma and to keep the rude Russian mother so-and-so words to herself after all.

Mīma has become speechless and mutely just shakes her head. Mīma is totally deflated, but nonetheless she slowly wraps the meat in a grease-proof paper and takes two last jars from the shelf. Black currant jam and some other stewed mess.

"That stewed mess you, child, don't eat, I shot in too much spice, it's too hot. It can burn out your stomach. But for those drunks it will be just right." Mīma isn't particularly worried about the stomachs of drunks.

"Do you have any bottles?" It occurs to Laura to ask at the same time.

"What? What more now!"

Mīma misunderstands dreadfully. Now it's total hell. Mīma probably thinks that Laura is asking for moonshine. Mīma knows how to make moonshine with bowls, somehow, Laura doesn't know how, but that's not what Laura is talking about.

"No, no, empty ones, do you have empty bottles, empty?" Laura explains, while Mīma hasn't yet fainted.

For each empty bottle you can get 12 kapeikas in the store. For three empty bottles you can get a small tin of *mon pensé*. Mīma doesn't know what *mon pensé* is? Well they're sweets, rock candies, although they're not as lovely as the words *mon pensé*. *Mon pensé*!

Does Laura bring empty bottles to the store, do Mama and Papa make her do it? Laura sees that in Mīma's eyes there is fear. Accidentally Mīma turns over the salt shaker, oh dear God, that means quarreling, all that salt over the table. Fear. Mīma is afraid. Of what?

"Laurie, let's have a talk," Mīma clasps her rough hands in her lap and invites Laura to sit down beside her.

"Laura doesn't have the time! Francis brought a cake!" Laura is already halfway out of the door.

Mīma slowly takes a feathered goose wing from the hearth's mantel and begins to sweep together the spilled salt.

The wing of the white, nasty gander, so like the wing of a

small innocent angel.

Salt so like sugar.

Mīma's hands so like the bark of an old tree trunk.

The hands move slowly, but Mīma is not conscious of this movement. Mīma's hands have for a long time now been used to moving on their own.

Mīma recites a prayer, she talks only in her heart and even though her lips move, her voice cannot be heard.

Her sighs are without number, and her heart is weary. When will she be able to let go of her great sorrow and the sadness in her heart? In the adjacent room Grandpa clears his throat.

When?

Neighbor Liepa

LIEPA, THE NEIGHBOR CLOSEST to the Avoti farm, is visiting. The Liepa farm is just a boot's throw away. In fact this isn't true, Laura has tested it, but let them think it's so.

"A man like an oak, last name—Liepa." This is his usual greeting when he meets someone, but "liepa" in Latvian means linden which in folklore is a feminine tree whereas as the oak is considered the manly tree.

He's brought a hunting knife with a horn handle for Papa. Papa has to pay at least one kapeika for it, because according to a folk belief it's bad luck to accept a knife as a gift without payment. Papa gets out a two-kapeika coin. Now the knife has been legally bought. May it serve its owner well. From Mama Liepa doesn't ask payment for a wooden spoon. Will Liepa ask for money for the green ball and if he does where will Laura get it? Papa and Mama don't have any more. Luckily, Liepa doesn't ask payment for the green ball. For the *polsh* of vodka he doesn't ask either. Nor for the eelpouts.

The eelpouts turn out to be fish, although they don't look like fish at all.

Liepa has the seaside full of fishermen relatives, and he can get eelpouts enough to gorge oneself with. Papa and Laura have never ever seen such eelpouts, but Mama has and she shows them how to eat the eelpouts correctly. They have to be held by the tail and the side fins have to be pulled off downward. Then they have to be divided in half, the green fishbone removed and only then eaten.

"So that your stomach may marvel. The skin though must not be eaten, otherwise it will cause heartburn," Liepa adds.

But it's precisely the skin that Laura likes the best! And she won't get any heartburn!

"Anda, when I start to sneeze then chase me home," Liepa pronounces after his third glass.

Mama laughs heartily, for she recalls Liepa's sneezes. From her childhood, when Liepa had a drink with Mama's father Edmunds and grandfather Jūlijs. During Easter or Whitsuntide. Never mind Jāņi—Midsummer's Eve. Liepa's sneezing is the same as it was before, and for Mama everything that's the same as before is precious. Liepa, a man like an oak, is the same as he was before, just gray-haired like an old apple tree.

"Zelma will come another day. She sends her greetings, thinks a lot about you. She keeps waiting, Anda, for your mama Lilia. It's today precisely that Zelma had to go to the artificial bull, yes, well yes, that's what they now call Švāns. One of her cows has not taken."

A sense of empty words again overtakes Laura. When she seemingly understands but doesn't understand. Laura tries to picture the artificial bull. She isn't able to, all sorts of hobgoblins appear but not the artificial bull. But now it's clear for Laura where artificial fertilizer originates. From the artificial bull. Laura wouldn't like to meet up with him.

"Zelma would like to see Lilia's first grandchild of course! This lovely young miss with the long braids! But most of all you, Anda dear, and, of course Lilia's new son-in-law. Now then, Jāni, have another one."

Laura would be that first grandchild? Would Papa be Lilia's son-in-law? Lilija would be Buka. But what is a son-in-law? Laura is afraid—what if it's something bad.

"And now—to those who haven't returned and who shall never return," Liepa stands up with glass in hand, stands much too long, as if he had forgotten what he wanted to do, finally he remembers and downs his drink.

"Anda, when I begin to sneeze, chase me home."

"You already said it once!" Laura reminds him.

Mama shushes Laura. She shouldn't be so familiar.

"One need not be formal with good old neighbors. What do you think about that, Miss Laura? Shall we drink to neighborly familiarity?"

Laura agrees with Liepa. Liepa laughs.

"How many of us locals are left anymore in the village of Lamme? All have either gone abroad or wolves are chewing their bones in Siberia. You've been lucky, that you could get back on your farm. Don't say anything, Anda, no matter how devastated it is, it still is your ancestral home. Is it the first time that you have to start all over again? No, Anda, don't spit God in the face, not everyone who has been in Siberia is able to return to their own farm. It's good that you have someone like Mīma."

Does Anda not even know that Mīma has bought back Avoti from the kolkhoz? Yes, by paying in installments. Mama had thought it was just given back to them.

"Given back? Given back? Damn! Holy simplemindedness! Anda, dear heart, who's going to give you something for nothing? Mīma bought it, I take my hat off to her!"

It's a surprise for Anda. Also a surprise for Papa. Where did Mīma get such money?

Liepa doesn't know where Mīma got the money, but the chairman of the kolkhoz had an old debt owing to Mīma. Not in terms of money. No! Mīma, during the time of the German occupation, had hidden the chairman. Where? Liepa doesn't know where, but it did happen. On retreating a German had burned down Mīma's house, the Soviet dog-faced monster had sniffed out something, who knows. Maybe he didn't have time to get to the bottom of it, for the Russians came back in force. Tumins is a party man, a Lithuanian, but a decent person. He arranged that Mīma could buy the Avoti farm. Liepa has to spend substantial time in the kolkhoz office, when he has to obtain a *naryad*—a formal work order, hand in a report, arrange some papers—*bumagi* now and then, and during such times he overhears all sorts of things. Liepa is a brigadier.

Tumins had allotted a different place to live for the Russians who had taken over the Avoti farm. What do you think, a better one, damn, of course a better one! Otherwise they'd cause a furor! The Russians get all the best deported people's homes, with all their furnishings and all their worldly goods, including all the old jars of jam in the basement, that's how it happens.

That's why the Latvians were deported so that Russians could be put in their place, damn, that's how it is.

Mama doesn't know if she needs to feel happy or not that Mīma has bought back the farm. Has she done the right thing? It turns out that they once more have a privately-owned property. What if because of this they're sent again to Siberia?

No, no, nothing to be frightened about, the mustached Stalin is dead and buried already, Now the dog-faced monsters themselves, the jackals, have started to kick that dead lion. All that is finished. I feel sorry for our men who are still in the forests, our partisans still are, one or two of them. But they senselessly are ruining their lives, their comrades, the 'enemies of the people' have been liquidated.

Collectivization has happened!

The farming bourgeoisie has been destroyed!

The ethnic structure has been changed!

As they say, all the ducks have been lined up, per the full program, the dogfaces have got what they wanted. Now communism needs to be put in place! Soviet power plus electrification!

Laura doesn't understand if Liepa is talking seriously or if he's joking. Laura is hearing too many empty words, sleep is overcoming her, but Mama and Liepa are passionately talking.

Laura sees that also Papa's attention has wandered, he isn't listening at all, Papa in his thoughts is somewhere else, his eyes grown red from the smoke. Papa's cigarette pack is already empty. A tin full of butts. Laura understands. She snuggles up to Papa but he doesn't even notice. Laura understands that everything that Mama and Liepa are talking about is foreign to Papa. All the relatives, neighbors and friends here Papa doesn't know, never has seen, hence never mentions. Papa's close relatives and friends aren't close to anyone here. Now they no longer are, but were! His mama, papa, and sisters.

Papa's home is in the region of Vidzeme, yes, Papa is from a totally different land! That's nothing, Papa must surely have in his heart the same... What? Something the same as Mama's "like before." Papa is silent about it.

Liepa keeps talking. It's too much for Laura. The artificial bull and *naryads* and brigadiers, and more of all those words. The bottle is nearing empty. Papa puts a new one on the table. It's a matter of honor. He opens a new package of cigarettes. Kazbek. With a picture of a horseman racing toward a mountain peak. Liepa begins to sneeze. To sneeze and sneeze.

"Anda, what did I say you had to do?" Liepa gasps through his sneezing. "Let that stay as a nest egg," Liepa adds, getting up heavily from the table and pointing at the bottle.

"A bottle remains, uncorked, not drunk! There'll be hell to pay anyway!" Liepa sings on leaving.

Mama goes to accompany Liepa up to the farm's boundary. This has always been done at Avoti, a neighbor needs to be accompanied to the boundary. Even though there no longer is a boundary.

"Papa what is a nest egg?"

"What nest egg?" Papa startles as if he had just woken.

"Go to bed! Right now!" The words are scolding words, but the voice is tired and quiet, the voice doesn't scold.

Nest egg. Such a word even Papa doesn't know. He opens the bottle.

Oranges in the Field

"Where were you all day?"

"All day? At the old railway crossing." It seems to Laura, however, that she had been there only for a short while.

"At the old crossing! So. We searched for you everywhere! We were worried! What could you do for such a long time at the old crossing?"

"Wait for the train to go off the tracks."

"What more can I say!"

Also Laura has nothing more to add, she thinks that the essence of the situation she has expressed quite clearly. Mama waves her hands in frustration and repeats the same thing three times. It's odd that on doing that Mama looks like Mīma.

"What more can I say?! I have nothing to say! No, I have nothing to say. Just listen to this, Johnny!"

"Laura, where were you all day?" Papa is happy that Laura has been found. Laura repeats what she said before. Papa laughs.

"Why are you laughing? The girl is ready to pull the train down off the tracks! Can you comprehend such a thing? The train! And you think that's funny? Do you hear what I'm saying? The train! Off the tracks! Boys might be that crazy? But Laura, you? Being a girl!"

Laura doesn't intend to pull anything. Laura is just waiting to see if it will itself go off the tracks. There at the big bend.

"What kind of nonsense is this!" Mama doesn't give in.

Papa only laughs. Next time, though, Laura must tell them where she's going. So Mama doesn't worry.

"But such ideas! One day she'll go and pull it off! I'm the one who has to worry about the child of course! You don't care!"

Mama can't, just can't calm down. The pulling of a train off the tracks is the most horrendous thing that can be. In Siberia someone was shot down right on the spot. Just for being suspected of this. And even being suspected wasn't necessary. Shot, and that's all!

Mama is moving pots and pans around noisily and absolutely needlessly. One has to cover one's ears. Papa puts a warning finger to his lips. He lets Laura understand how great the fear, how uncontrollable the fear, the unsubstantiated fear, that has found a home in Mama's heart, and nothing can be done about it. This time Mama is expressing this fear with the noise of clanging pots.

"What did you really want?" Papa asks, kneeling, looking at Laura eye to eye.

Did Papa himself not hear what Liepa, a man like an oak, said?

"What did Liepa, a man like an oak, say?" Papa doesn't remember.

"That once a train had gone off the tracks at the big bend."

Right. He did say that. Now Papa remembers. It's true of course that only the last wagon derailed, but Papa understands that this isn't so important.

Laura had asked at that time what was being transported in those wagons. And didn't Liepa, a man like an oak, not say that it was oranges? That the train was transporting oranges! Liepa had said—China's apples, and had explained that these were oranges.

Papa says—fine, that's clear. And laughs. It looks like Papa doesn't really believe Liepa, a man like an oak. Papa unwinds his tall build to its full height. He has to go and construct a ladder. He has to see what's in the attic. Maybe the woodstove problem is there.

The pots and pans no longer yell Mama's fear as loudly.

From the moment when Laura heard what Liepa said, she's been seeing a field full of oranges in her dreams.

Laura sees that somehow, by chance, she is close by when the train is catapulting at a crazy speed, not even noticing the big bend and then—as one might expect—the last wagon, which can't handle the crazy speed, tips and lurches, and bounces, and gets unhooked, and goes off the track! Yes! It remains leaning on the high embankment. The train is so long that it doesn't even notice its last wagon. For such a long train it's a small detail. It winds away like a lizard, leaving its tail behind.

The wagon tilts in the direction of the field ... Tilts, tilts, tilts, and ... the oranges start to tumble out into the field like sugar beets from a dump truck. Round, orange, juicy. Probably also fragrant, but Laura doesn't know how oranges smell, can't imagine it. The field is full of oranges like enormous rowan berries right up to the horizon. But they keep falling from the wagon more and more. Only Laura sees this. It's likely midday, because no one else is there.

Laura now has the green, green field, white flowers, and oranges up to the horizon all to herself. What happiness! Laura wants to run, gather a lapful, smell, taste, but—what's that?—she can't. Her legs are as if turned to stone. They don't budge a centimeter, as if they were disconnected, grown stiff and immoveable.

It's been like that before. When legs are petrified as if turned to stone. What she wants is so close, all she has to do is take a tiny step toward it, but she can't—her legs are like stone.

All at once Laura understands in her dream that she's dreaming. How sad. A dream understands that it's a dream. Laura cries. Not about the oranges but about the fact that she understands that the dream understands that it's a dream. Just for a short moment, as short as a matchstick.

But who can swear that a train, well fine—a last wagon, that has already once derailed—will never again derail in real life?

And if on that train they're transporting oranges, then who can swear that they're not precisely in the last wagon? And by the big bend ...

It can happen. It can happen. What has happened once, can happen a second time. As Francis once said—everything that is has already been and everything will be that also has been! Of course, he as always was laughing and as always added—on behalf of that joke it wouldn't hurt to have a glass of lemonade!

Laura will wait at the old railway crossing until she gets what she's waited for.

Visitors

MAMA IS ONCE MORE FRETTING. She had hoped so much that all would be like it was before, but it's not. Nothing gets better. Papa says that he'll settle everything as soon as he gets a bit of money. Mama thinks that it can't be just got but must be earned and that manure can also be mucked out without money.

But Papa doesn't have the time, because visitors keep coming. Shouldn't they celebrate their return after all? The fact that life has finally begun! Do Mama and Laura lack anything? See now, Papa has even found a bed for Laura. So what if it was found discarded among nettles? Has it not been scrubbed clean and white? So what if it's a bit too short?

Nothing is amiss, nothing is lacking. And if they should run short of something, Mīma will give it to them, grumbling a bit, but still give it. Money for bread can be borrowed from Liepa. When they get some, then they'll give it back. Liepa himself has offered. And when they have some, they'll repay him.

What's to be done if the dog-faced monsters, and they also have people who help them, don't want to hire Papa to do any work? An enemy of the people. Offspring of the bourgeoisie. So what if he's considered a free man, so what if he's considered exonerated. Nonetheless, nonetheless. There's no smoke without fire, there isn't. Can one trust such an ex-hard-labor-camp deportee with the kolkhoz's machinery, tractors, and dump trucks? Can he be allowed near pedigreed cattle, entrusted with granary keys? A tiger can't change its stripes.

Despite everything, Papa had never thought or hoped that in Lamme there would be so many generous and sincere people. That so many people would come to visit. That in Latvia the nights would be so long and so light and so warm! And a man can't do without sleeping either, be it during the day even, but an hour or so must be grabbed here and there.

The round woodstove is smoking so badly that all three of them have to flee outside so as not to suffocate. Once they even had to stand outside in the rain. Mama reminds Papa of this. Stop *pilyit*—beefing about it, it's not a problem to sometimes stand in the rain also, it's almost like an adventure, a trek or an excursion, Papa defending himself says.

Mama thinks that the woodstove can be repaired also without money, maybe some brick has fallen into the chimney, or maybe the chimney needs to be cleaned.

Papa has no time to look, because visitors come again and again and one needs to have some pleasure in life finally. To forget everything even for one night! The visitors always bring a pint of vodka, either store-bought or a home brew, every day there's a chance to nip a drop or two to celebrate meeting once more.

An empty glass shows a full heart
Bottoms up!
To bright eyes.
Drink my pal, a swig of booze
While you're still young
This ale is ours.

Mama thinks that all Lamme's village drunks simply are taking advantage of them. No. Papa doesn't think so. Visitors come to be introduced to Lilia's son-in-law. To Anda's husband. To a new neighbor. To the new master of Avoti farm as it should be!

Papa is happy and gratified that the Lamme villagers accept him as a *svoyak*—one of their own. Papa won't talk out of turn, let Anda not be afraid. Even if he were to get drunk. Papa has a block in his brain. It's *zhelezno*—iron-strong.

Let Mama herself not chatter so much. With whom? With the teacher? With Liepa? Can one trust them? No you can't! Can't trust anyone, let Mama not be such a simpleton!

The visitors want to know. When will Lilia herself return? Ah, maybe only a year from now? They're not handing back her passport? They don't let her leave her work? Too valuable a worker? Well, that could be. Sounds exactly like Lilia.

But maybe it's something else altogether, what do you

say? Maybe some old guy has latched onto her, a Russian or a Mongolian, is that it? Maybe that's what isn't letting Lilija return? And Juris? How sad! Yes, we had heard, but it's hard to believe it.

"If it's so hard, then don't believe it! Don't torment yourself!" Mama yells.

"Anda, dear! Why are you like this? We meant well."

"Do you not remember me?" One of the visitors wants to know. It's Fredis. "Well, yes, you were young then of course."

Laura hears relief in his voice. That Mama doesn't remember. The Russians have arrived, and all sorts of riffraff, he complains.

"But see how you've returned, Anda, dear! Let's drink to that! Many probably won't return? Let's drink to that also!"

Is it true that old Avots died of starvation?

But how can you not know?

That's what everyone has been saying. Just think! Lamme's civil parish elder for so many years, an honorable man. How can one like him die of starvation?

Don't you know?

Let's drink to old Avots!

Well, but Edmunds? Thousands have been tortured to death in those hard labor camps.

The visitors start to talk in whispers.

You don't know?

Yes, no one really knows anything, it's possible that it's all only hearsay: Yankee propaganda. Americans especially tend to bullshit, just to malign the Soviet regime. Why isn't there a word on this in the press then? Why is nothing reported on the radio? Maybe it's just rumors, gossip only. Evil people's tongue-flapping, bourgeois, imperialist fabrication. What is the real truth?

Don't you know?

Maybe Edis is still alive? No notices have been sent after all. Maybe Edis was lucky?

Don't you know?

Maybe Edis is in America, living there in clover? Maybe he's in Australia, there are Latvians even there. Let's drink to Edis!

If Edis is really dead, wouldn't Lilia have managed to get a new husband during those fifteen years, she's still a woman in her prime. When she was deported was she not about thirty? Then she's not even fifty yet. Well, it can't be that there hasn't been anyone else. No? Then she's still unattached? For someone like Lilia there would be takers in the village of Lamme. No lack of people wanting to marry her. Where are they? We ourselves could be suitors, the ones to woo her. We could hit on her! Nothing wrong with us, we're still full of beans. It still stands up for us, the old men laugh. Let her just come home!

Are the suitors talking about Buka? Laura feels sick to her stomach about such talk. Laura sees that Mama too feels sick.

Laura sees how smart Mama is. And how stupid the visitors. Mama almost doesn't talk about anything except about the beautiful flowers that grow in Siberia, about the taiga where berries abound and about the mushroom places that aren't here in Lamme, aren't and never will be, but the visitors think that Mama reveals a lot.

The visitors leave satisfied that they've learned so much about Siberia.

Laura clearly knows what Mama is not telling. The real story.

Papa also doesn't talk about it, he only rambles on about all sorts of trivial things about hunts, squirrels, bears, and chipmunks, makes people laugh with his jokes, but it's not the real story about Siberia.

To the visitors it seems as if it is.

The visitors are curious and they also question Laura, but Laura knows that she mustn't talk about Siberia. Knows and that's all. She isn't permitted to talk about Siberia—never, nowhere, and to no one! Because no one will believe anyway, Papa had explained. Because a normal person can't even understand it. They'll think that it's us who aren't normal, explained Mama.

But most importantly—because of the dog-faced monsters. Laura has to bear it in mind and know this fact like her five fingers. The fact that the dog faces don't want anyone to talk about Siberia. The dog-faced monster wants to hide Siberia like a cat his own shit. The dog faces have eyes and ears everywhere. If she was to talk about Siberia, then the dog faces would catch her and send her back. Does Laura understand this?

Laura understands.

This fiddle wasn't twiddled by Stradivari

ALL THE CELEBRATING TILL NOW had been just a vulgar drinking binge, a doleful waste of time. Now with the arrival of Krazy Kārlis with his fiddle it's a totally different matter. May the devil turn into a door jamb! Kārlis draws everyone into boisterous fun! The violin strings get snapping. Kārlis's craziness is as infectious as chicken pox. Everyone gets carried away by his songs:

"Here, where pine forests sway!
Long ago by River Venta in blossom time!
The summer then was so iridescent!"

"Shush, are you mad, that's a prohibited song!" The visitors shout, but they've drunk enough to join in passionately.

"I remember that kerchief blue!" The visitors link arms and sway along with the tune.

Nafig—so what if it's prohibited! To hell with them, and that prohibition! What after all isn't prohibited? Everything is prohibited! But what's not prohibited is obligatory! Play, Kārli!

"Neither idling, nor rotting away
May a proud song sound for thee, free Latvia."

"No, that's too insane! Kārli, dear! I truly beg you! Give it a rest! Let's talk. How are you?" Mama anxiously asks.

Mama stuffs Kārlis's mouth shut with a pickle, a potato, and then a marinated mushroom. Mama is scared. She keeps looking at Papa. Laura understands what Mama is wordlessly saying to Papa. For such crazy singing the dog faces could send all of them directly to Siberia. Papa without saying a word responds that he understands but doesn't know what to do.

Kārlis allows himself to be fed, he's terribly hungry but when he plays then Kārlis forgets his hunger. At the Riga railway station buffet this morning he made a round of all the tables. One must do so there before all the emptied plates are taken away. To

leave a bit on the plate is considered in fine taste nowadays. The
Russian officers always leave something. A bitten-into fine pastry
or a *belash*, or a turnover. However, sausages are never left, that's
for sure, but fine pastries are left quite frequently. Fine pastries!
Kārlis likes fine things. He's been raised to appreciate fine things.

Eat, Kārli, don't talk so much, Mama shoves one more potato
into Kārlis's mouth and makes him wash it down with water
sweetened with black currant jam.

Ah, a woman's divine hands! Kārlis can't remember when last a
young and lovely woman's hands had offered him food. Maybe never.

"A woman's hands, oh, such rapture, such torture!" Kārlis recites.
"Just because of you, lovely ladies, because of you!
In Ķemeri hamlet, in a tiny hut!"
The singing starts up again full force.

Kārlis has come by train from Riga, playing and singing all the
way, delighting the passengers and being happy himself that he
hasn't been thrown off the train en route. Look, he's even earned
a few kapeikas, to be able to buy a ticket for another train ride.

Yes, I and my fiddle travelled the world!
"Travelling the world, I lost my fiddle!"
Kārlis has not so much lost fiddles as they've been taken
away from him. Not only fiddles but also a mandolin was once
removed from Kārlis on the train, as well as a banjo and also a
cymbal. But when a zither was confiscated, Kārlis was very upset.
The very last memento he had of his father! Then Kārlis had
wanted to jump in the River Daugava. But on the bridge he had
seen Riga's castle engulfed in flames. As a reflection in the River
Daugava. So moving a sight! It had seemed that the president
himself had returned again to his castle. Kārlis had forgotten
right there on the spot that he'd wanted to jump into the River
Daugava. My throat, my instrument! Kārlis had remembered—
my throat, my instrument and had sung the anthem. Which
one? What kind of a question is that? Of course the real national
one. The real and only one! Then he'd been dragged to the precinct. How many times Kārlis has been lugged to the precinct!

Who dragged him there? The militia, who else.

Kārlis hides from the militia like a partisan hides in a forest, but when a militia man is dressed in civilian clothes then he looks like an everyday person. But what can anyone do to Kārlis? Drive him to the precinct, tell him off, beat him up, rough him up, jail him? Lock him up overnight? Threaten him? Damn it, so what! He just whistles about it! Yes, they take away the instrument. Which is the worst they can do to Kārlis. That's the greatest punishment.

Well, and that's it. That's all. Nothing else can be taken away from Kārlis because he doesn't have anything else.

Kārlis is on a list of the insane, but Tvaika Street, where the asylum is, no longer will admit him because he's not crazy enough to be committed, there are no beds either, besides that he's classed as an invalid due to his poor eyesight. Others are even crazier, and then there are those whom the doctors have to certify as insane. Well, those who've been blabbermouths, who've had the truth on their tongues. With them they've got the most difficult time until they've medicated them enough. Well, up to the point where they can't even recognize their own mothers. Kārlis isn't important enough. What now? They have to let Krazy Kārlis loose once more.

Kārlis scrounges up some money and again buys a train ticket. He doesn't care where the train is headed. Kārlis has no need to head for somewhere nor to arrive there. No, Kārlis doesn't need that.

Kārlis has need of an audience.

Kārlis sings and plays on the train. That's the only thing that Kārlis needs.

And just a short while ago once again! Once again? Once again they took away his fiddle. No, this time it wasn't the militia, but a young, respectable-looking man. Maybe he thought that the fiddle was worth something.

"My dear man, this fiddle wasn't twiddled by Stradivari! What are you going to do with it?"

Kārlis tried to persuade the young, respectable man, but he hadn't listened.

"Did the others on the train not say anything? They just stood by when he took your instrument?" the visitors question.

They hadn't said anything, had let it happen. But Kārlis doesn't hold a grudge against these people. Such are the times. No one wants any trouble.

Kārlis will get another at the flea market! No matter what kind. Kārlis knows how to play all instruments. Kārlis even knows how to play on a saw. On a comb with tissue paper.

The train is Kārlis's concert hall.

When he sings and plays *Ave Maria* then the train is also Kārlis's church.

The passengers snigger, point their fingers at their temples, now and then Kārlis is beat up, but, overall, the train has the very best audience in the world for Kārlis! Restrained but sincere, as Latvians tend to be. Except for the Jūrmala train heading to the seaside. There the passengers are foreigners, not locals, a new breed. And the conductors recognize Kārlis from a distance already, as does the militia.

No, Kārlis has not come to Avoti to talk about himself. That's all! Leave him alone! All of you, leave him alone!

Kārlis has come to welcome and hail his dear relatives, dear deportees returning from *katorga*—penal servitude, who have come home after so many years of pain and exile. He'll do his singing and playing. A song will be Kārlis's lapful of flowers and the playing will be Kārlis's strewn roses under the dear returning people's feet.

Kārlis has come to mourn the people who have been unduly dealt a martyr's death and to shout his scorn of their executioners. He'll do this by singing and playing. A song will be Kārlis's lament, but he won't be a man who shall die of sorrow having the lyre of moans in his hand, no, let no one expect that. Kārlis's song will hew the Devil's head in nine pieces! Made of steel will be his soul, when he with a song will face off against evil and the darkness of the dog-faced monsters.

Kārlis has come to extol the ones who have endured the heavy burden of suffering and to honor those who were unable to survive it. What man can't survive. Kārlis swallows the lump in his throat. May God nurture their souls.

Kārlis has come to be happy for the ones who are alive because the day will come, and Kārlis doesn't doubt it, when

Latvia will again be free and a proud nation like it was before. Kārlis in a song will attest to his belief.

The visitors fall silent and lower their eyes. Simpleton! Such talk! Madman! Crazy! Brain-dead! A total psycho! Some of the visitors go outside to have a smoke, but they don't return.

Kārlis has come to speak to God through his song and to pray—God bless Latvia!

Laura listens agog and as if she was intoxicated. By Kārlis's words that are so true and beautiful. Laura could listen to him on and on. Why is Mama shushing Kārlis? Why is Papa pulling him to sit down on the bench and not letting him stand up again? Kārlis wants to stand! To stand up and sing.

Fine, alright, fine, Kārlis says. He finds it hard to express what he has to say in ordinary words, that's why Kārlis has written a poem and as soon as he finds his glasses in his bag he'll read it.

"Anda, dear, hand over that there bag of mine!" Kārlis says to Mama but looks at Laura.

"Kārli, I'm Anda. But that's my little daughter Laura."

"You don't say? I thought you were Lilia. You're Anda? And that's your daughter Laura?"

"Yes, Kārli."

"Laura? Laura! Beautiful, divine rose with eternity's scent! Oh, come but hither, come! Step lightly as a dove! Don't be afraid! That's a poem. That's Petrarch's sonnet to Laura. Do you know what a sonnet is?" Karlis leans forward and gazes directly into Laura's eyes. He doesn't even ask about Petrarch. This probably every fool should know.

Laura doesn't want to be a fool and a know-nothing in Kārlis's eyes, from which, in addition, shines goodness of heart and hope. Hope for Laura. That she'll know what a sonnet is.

If hope should die in Kārlis's eyes, in its place will be sadness and sorrow.

Laura will be responsible, but as Latvians say, lies again would have short legs—they wouldn't get her far before being uncovered. Kārlis gazes at her in expectation. She has to say something in response.

"Don't hope and don't be sad!" Laura says the first thing

that springs to mind.

"Don't hope and don't be sad? That child says don't hope and don't be sad! Did you hear that? Don't hope and don't be sad! Incredible! Incredible!" Kārlis enthuses. He places the fiddle under his chin and plays.

A spring wind rises. A violin cries mournfully along with the wind. The violinist plays as he once did when he was younger, not as old as Kārlis. His heart was then full of love. Well, that is, that violinist or was it maybe Kārlis himself had a girl he wanted to marry. But then another man came along. He had much money, while Kārlis or that violinist—had none. He couldn't compete. The girl chose the rich man. And Kārlis also isn't handsome. Had he only dressed better. That's why he sounds so sad. Laura is very sorry for the fiddle, the poor fiddler and Kārlis, who sobs along with the fiddle and the song. He's begging the fiddle to tell the girl that he loves her. That he'll never forget her.

Laura would understand the words better, if everyone around the table would stop yelling along with Kārlis, but the thought is clear. What will Kārlis do now, so sorrowful is his heart.

Kārlis finishes, with a high flourish removing the bow. The visitors applaud, Kārlis bows and smiles happily. How can he forget so soon that he had just grieved and wept?

"Don't hope and don't be sad! Laura, that will from now on be my motto!"

Laura manages to sneak outside, because she's afraid that Kārlis will ask her what a "motto" is. Laura just knows what lotto is.

Kārlis it seems has found his glasses. Laura from outside hears him reciting a poem. In the beginning everyone listens, but then they start mumbling. The poem is long. As soon as they start to sing again, Laura wants to go back in. To look at Papa and Mama how they're singing, to feel that energy that a song creates within people and the enchanted circle, when people return the energy back to the song. It seems to Laura that a song becomes more lovely and gains in strength each time it's sung. They've begun:

"*Blow ye winds, drive my boat, drive me on to Courland.*"

Courland is the same as Kurzeme.

The fiddle cries along with the wind.

Dispatch

Liepa has sped into the yard on his emku. The Emku is a motorcycle.

"Where is that damned Kārlis?" Liepa, man like an oak, is mad.

"He left on the morning train. Couldn't be persuaded to stay and visit for a while longer."

"Where did he take the train to?"

"Seemingly to the town of Tukums, but maybe to the very end of the line—to Ventspils. One never knows with Kārlis. Kārlis goes where he wants and does what he wants."

"And says what he wants! What happened here yesterday?"

"Why, what happened then?"

"It's what I'm asking you, Anda!"

"What kind of inquisition is this?"

"No, this isn't an inquisition yet, but it could happen that it will be. If that swine of a man had dared to go further! Where's your common sense or don't you have any?" Liepa rages. Papa doesn't understand what the discussion is about. Laura too doesn't understand. What man? What swine? Where would he have gone? Mama is scared, probably she understands.

"Krazy Kārlis maybe can afford to talk like that, but who can afford to listen to it?"

"But to what?" Mama is wringing her hands.

"Anti-Soviet talk, anti-regime propaganda and agitation! That's the sixty-fifth paragraph without question! Do you want to be fingered for it? Everything that's written there?"

Liepa waves a torn-out page from a graph-paper notebook. Laura notices how carefully the edge has been cut off.

"The propagation of fabricated lies! Slandering the Soviet regime and system!" Liepa reads.

"Singing of bourgeois songs and dissemination of literary work of a nationalistic nature!" Liepa recites.

"The concealment of ideologically harmful literature!"

What language is Liepa speaking in? It's not Latvian nor Russian, nor is it Italian. Laura doesn't understand.

"That's not true! The poet Fricis Bārda no longer is considered ideologically harmful. And am I concealing it?" Mama yells grabbing the book.

"Who wrote this?" Papa yells.

"Fricis Bārda!" Laura explains, but no one is listening.

"What difference does it make if it's not true? What difference does it make who wrote it? You have to be more careful! It's a genuine *klyauza*—complaint! You must understand! You're behaving like children! Good and fine. You must calm down. You have to cool it. That complaint stays with me, amen and not a word more about it." Liepa is tired of yelling.

"Who submitted it?" Papa doesn't let it go.

"I'm not going to tell you, so you don't cook up more shit. Anda, make some coffee!" Liepa sits down heavily at the table. It, as luck would have it, has been cleared, Mama hasn't been lazy.

"We've only got tea," Mama worries.

Liepa won't say no also to tea. Here's the story. This morning Liepa as usual went into his office for the *naryadi*—work orders. He had as usual kibitzed a bit with the ladies in bookkeeping, and was prepared to leave. He then saw standing at the door of the *partorg*—the party secretary, well, That Person. What does such a lush want with the *partorg*? Very interesting. Liepa asks Lush—Laura understands it as a last name, "Why isn't he at work?" Liepa is a brigadier, Liepa is entitled to ask, he has such rights. Apparently his business is with comrade *partorg*, but comrade *partorg* hasn't yet arrived. Liepa sees some sort of a dispatch in Lush's hand, look here, this same bit of paper. Liepa has a bad premonition. A scoundrel of a man at the door of the *partorg*. Liepa goes up to him and asks if he's going to join the party, or what? He needs a recommendation perhaps?

No, no. But a dog knows what he's done. He appears to fawn, be a bit ashamed. Give it here, show me what you've written, otherwise on the report day I won't put you on the list! He doesn't want to show the paper. Liepa yanks the paper from Lush's hand, and look now what's on it!

Son of a bitch!

Thanks for the vigilance, Liepa says, but don't you now become the idiot! How so? Lush asks.

Who doesn't know that Kārlis is mentally deficient, but you're seeing him as accountable. That's one thing. You've sung the songs along with the rest. That's the second thing.

You're the one who regularly steals the *kombikorm*—a mish-mash of fodders from the kolkhoz's barn, and I can prove it. That's the third thing.

How many broads do you have in this civil parish? An amoral lifestyle. That's the fourth thing. Liepa had listed five more things.

If you won't drop this, I'm going to report what you did when you were with the Germans. That's the last thing.

"What did he do?"

"Do you remember Mr. and Mrs. Goldstein, the shopkeepers? And their daughter who was twelve years old?"

"Yes, that was madness!"

"That Person was there."

"But it was the Germans, the dog-faced monsters, who did the shooting!" Mama starts to wail pitifully and angrily like a she-wolf.

"Mommy, what's wrong?" Laura, frightened, starts to cry.

"I don't know who precisely was the one to shoot, but he was with them. And he was also there like a stuck bent nail when the deportations took place."

"Oh my God, my God, and such a man was at our table? And what if he doesn't drop it?"

"Who is it? I'm going to kill him," Papa says gloomily.

"He's going to forget it. You too forget it, Jāni."

"Does your woodstove still work well, Anda? That's good."

Liepa tears up the graph paper with the writing and throws it into the maw of the stove.

"What should be done now?" Mama is still trembling.

"There's nothing to be done. All Judases hang themselves."

The Emku starts up with a roar and is gone.

"It's good after all, Johnny, that we don't know who it was," Mama tries to disperse the thunderous clouds, which have covered them all.

"No, it's not good. Now we suspect everyone. That's much worse. Did you notice what Liepa said about a recommendation? You didn't hear? He had asked if That Person wanted to join the party, if that person needed a recommendation?"

"Yes, so what?"

"A recommendation can only be given by a party member. Besides, one who has length of service."

"Liepa in the party? Never!" Mama protests.

Mama breaks glasses

MAMA NO LONGER WANTS to see any visitors, not even a glimpse of one. Mama loathes the visitors. Even Francis with his perfumes and cakes Mama no longer likes. Mama no longer wants Kagor wine, no matter how healthy it is.

But Francis is again here.

Just for fun it wouldn't hurt to drink a glass of lemonade.

Mama is chasing Francis away. She opens the door wide and yells for him to go back to Tukums. Papa insists that Francis stay. He won't go anywhere. Why is Anda not ashamed to chase away Papa's best buddy, almost like a brother!

"Yes, his boozing buddy!"

"Shitty brother, Ance, you forgot, shitty brother. And skunky brother! *'I'll be damned but I love you! Can't live without you!'*" Francis sings. "And don't want to either! Anda! Don't want to!"

Francis has no intention of taking Mama's anger seriously. He gives Papa his small suitcase and unpacks a cake. Bending and bowing, Francis hands Mama the customary box of Riga's Lilacs perfume. Mama tears off the lid of the box, grabs the beautiful bottle, which doesn't immediately give way, doesn't come out of its specially-made depression.

Mama tears out the lovely silk lining, tosses it in the corner with the firewood, throws also the wonderful velvet box there, unscrews the bottle cap and pours the perfume on the floor.

"Idiot! Clown!" Mama yells at Francis.

"Calm down!" Papa yells at Mama.

Mama tears out of the room, Papa and Francis run after her, Laura also. Madwoman, what is she going to do?

Mama runs with the perfume bottle to the other end of the house, yanks back the propped up door and begins to sprinkle the expensive perfume on the manure piled up there and not yet removed. Mama has to shake firmly the bottle that looks like a lilac cluster for the perfume to spill out. Mama shakes and shakes the bottle to all sides.

"Take that! Take that! Avoti farm's manure! So you can smell like Riga's Lilacs, and not smell of manure! Don't smell! No! Smell even more horridly, because I detest these perfumes! Francis, I feel sick to my stomach from the smell of these Riga's Lilacs! For once, I've had enough! I'm not going to let you turn my husband into a lush!"

When the bottle has been emptied, Mama tosses it into the puddle of slurry. Laura thinks she could fish it out later. Mama runs back to the living room. There are two more perfume boxes.

But Mama doesn't touch those.

Mama breaks all the glasses. She takes a glass from the table and smashes it against the wall in the corner where the wood-stove sits, takes another from the table and—against the wall! And on and on against the wall! Mama is raving mad. Mama is in full sail. Papa tries to save a glass or two, but Mama has begun to enjoy how the glasses smash to small bits. She's ecstatic.

"That's enough now," Papa gets a hold of Mama's elbow.

She pulls away from him like a she-cat. Now she starts on the plates. One plate is finished, then a second.

"Please, Ance, please, Anda, please, stop! Those are Mīma's plates."

"Yes! Porcelain! Kuznetsov porcelain! Yes, Buka's wedding service! Yes! My mother's porcelain! Let it all go to ruin, let it!"

Francis has fallen down on his knees.

"Dearest!"

"I'm no dearest of yours! You can call your broads that! Hands off! Don't manhandle me!"

But Mama doesn't smash the third plate. She delays in smashing it. Francis in the meantime places another plate, a more common, cheap one, in Mama's hands. Better that she smash that one. They're *raboche krestyanskiye*—working man's plates, he says.

"My good one, beautiful one, incredible one! And dearest! Forgive me or else kill me! Here's something to stab me with! A tragedy is after all the most superior of genres," Francis hands

Mama a fork from the table.

"Fool!" Mama calms down a bit. Then she summons her strength once more, gets a second wind, grabs the *polsh* of vodka, which Papa has already managed to set on the table, and sloshes its contents into a slop pail. She dribbles a bit, then throws it into the slops. Gurgling, the slops flow through the narrow neck to fill the bottle.

"Just not that," exclaims Francis, "Johnny, let's get down on our knees."

Francis and Papa falling down on their knees, beg Mama, for God's sake, not to smash more dishes. Where will they get new ones, on what will the child eat?

Francis won't come so often anymore, tomorrow between the two of them they'll muck out the manure, it was such a good idea—to make it more fragrant beforehand. Everything will turn out for the best, they hadn't expected such a lightning storm from Ance. But it doesn't matter. Papa likes such a storm, such a whirlwind, such a wife. For Francis Ance appears even more lovely. When women are angry then they become just simply more lovely. Although! Anda shouldn't try so hard to be angry, as it is there's no other woman who is or will be in this whole world as beautiful as her. After a lightning storm the sun appears. The world becomes fresher. Oxygen conquers nitrogen. Ozone, that's very healthy, healthier than Kagor. What does Laura think of that? Laura is sorry about the perfume boxes and the little bottles that Mama has thrown into the manure. Let Laura not feel bad about them, in the future Francis will bring Riga's Lilacs to Laura.

When it seems that there's once more peace at home, when one more glass is found to be intact, when Francis, talking endlessly and promising not to bring Riga's Lilacs anymore for Mama but to bring them for Laura, while for Mama he'll bring Red Moscow perfume, when Francis gets ready to slice the cake, for Laura a piece with tiny flowers, of course for a princess the best, then Mama lifts the cake up high in the air and with a flourish shoves it straight into Francis's face. Francis manages to catch with both hands the cake shoved in his face. He stands still for a moment and then carefully separates the cake from his face and places it on the table.

The cake has almost not been ruined, just the little flowers have stayed on Francis's face, but on the cake, an impression of his face itself—his forehead, cheeks, chin, and nose. The nose most deeply impressed in the cake.

"Lovely," Francis is delighted.

The flowers one after the other fall off his face. Francis gazes at the cake.

"It's my after-death mask," he says.

Manure and Gold Dust

FRANCIS ISN'T AMONG THOSE who don't do what they promise. The morning after he gets up first and looks for a pitchfork. Laura's eyes too are open, and yes, she can show him where the pitchforks are. Francis is whistling. He's going to muck out that wonderful manure, which Mama has anointed with perfumes and myrrh. Anda's blessed manure. It's going to be a blast of joy and a boar's roar.

Let Johnny and Ance sleep in.

Francis is together with Laura and that's definitely a powerful duo! Where's a wheelbarrow of sorts? What's a wheelbarrow?

Where's a pushcart? What's a pushcart?

Princess, how can you not know? Well a sort of *tarataika, drandoleta*—a worn-out old thing, with which to transport the manure. There's neither a wheelbarrow nor a pushcart at Avoti, nor is there a *tarataika*. There isn't even a *drandoleta*. The two of them have done a thorough search. But instead there's an old tin tub with rusted-through holes. It will have to do. Eagle-eyed Francis spots a long cotton stocking hiding in the nettles. They can tie it to the tub to be able to drag it. Women's stockings are a fine thing. Francis likes women's stockings.

Isn't there an old coat lying around somewhere? There isn't one, all the old, unclaimed coats have been burned together with the blue tire. Never mind, Francis says, if there isn't one so be it. If the nanny goat has no milk, then lift her tail and pour some back into her. Manure won't harm good clothes, while poor ones need not be saved. Francis just takes off his shoes but not his fancy suit pants nor his white shirt.

Where do you think we could pile up the manure? Where pull it to? To the field? No, Laura, we won't give away this gold to the kolkhoz. They've got enough shit. Let's drag it there behind the outhouse. Laura, remembering the outhouse, begins to retch. It's because the princess hasn't had any breakfast, Francis thinks.

Let him think that. Yes, she hasn't had any breakfast so Laura will go inside to eat. Francis will slowly get started on the Augean stables. That's a saying, Laura, go, go on. No. Francis doesn't need breakfast. Francis has managed without eating for fifteen years. Francis knows how to get food through his skin like India's yogi. Francis will describe this more precisely to Laura later. Now Laura needs to eat her breakfast.

Mama is frying up some eggs. Papa is clearing away yesterday's glass and plate shards.

"Where's Francis? Call Francis to come in for breakfast."

"Francis doesn't need breakfast. Francis is going to eat through his skin. Like ..." Laura can't remember like who ...

" ... India's yogi. Of course." Mama finishes.

"What's Francis doing?" Papa asks.

"Francis is moving manure in the tub."

Damn! Papa rushes out. He's just remembered what he promised yesterday. Papa too isn't one of those who forget what they've promised.

Mama likes that the men are working. Mama can't stop sneaking a look through the window how the two of them are almost killing themselves but Mama doesn't go outside, she has to maintain her cool. Laura eats a fried egg and leaves. She's finished eating just in time, because it's starting to smell. If you shift shit, then it smells. That's a saying. Now Laura understands it.

Laura stands leaning on the doorjamb and breathes through her mouth. She's pinched her nose tight with her fingers. Francis suggests she take a clothes peg to pinch her nose closed, but that's painful. Bit by bit Laura gets used to it and is no longer aware of the smell. Slowly but surely the manure pile in the great room diminishes. Papa and Francis keep at it talking about their own things.

"What are you talking about?" Laura asks.

Our own stuff. Our own stuff. Our own stuff.

Laura doesn't need to listen. Laura could go and help Mama. Nevertheless Laura listens from behind a corner. For a while.

How long can she listen if she doesn't understand anything. But she can surmise, sense some of it. To sense is worse than to understand.

It was in Berlag?

No, where did you get that! Sevvostolag.

In the beginning about two hundred thousand. At the end you could count who remained on five fingers.

Dalstroy? Well, right there. Twelve months of the year—winter. The rest—summer.

Minus fifty was nothing.

Minus seventy, *vot*, that's death! To survive, *nepolozheno*—not planned.

But we who were underground in the mine shafts, what a great fortune, compared to Tashkent. Such pig's luck. Well such a lucky fluke! We crawled out but everyone else had croaked.

Some one hundred thirty thousand. About. Who can count the stars? The bone road.

M56.

The bones made good fertilizer. If one man weighed, let's say fifty kilos, no one weighed much more, then, imagine what two hundred thousand weighed. Sometime in the future everything there will grow like mad.

Corn!

Ha, ha, ha!

The Japanese had burnt that Sergey Lazo in their locomotive furnace. That incredible hero. In revenge. The Japanese weren't human. We none of us were, but the Japanese especially. Once we had to construct a bridge over a gorge. The Japanese are smaller in build, lighter; they were tied to ropes like toddlers, lowered, to weld or something there. And then the prison guards decided to have some fun. They slashed the ropes in half and the Japanese dropped like beans into the gorge. The *ohranniki*—guards guffawed and sniggered like crazy. Those buggers had the fun of their lives.

Yes.

Yes.

In the mines? Nickel and tin ore.

Cassiterite.

In fact uranium. That's the thing Johnny, there a man dies twice. The raw material for the atomic bomb.

No, us. The raw material, us.

Do you know that joke?

Well?

The women working there were told that they were making sewing machines. The ladies carried out part after part stuffed in their brassieres. They wanted to put together a sewing machine. When they did assemble the parts, they turned out to be machine guns.

Ha! Ha! Ha!

Let's have a smoke break.

Do you know where I managed to scrounge my first bit of gold? On the plane. We prisoners, three political and one criminal, were being flown to another mine. Did we know where? The Kolyma gold circle. The direction—Yakutsa. We were sitting on the floor, and suddenly—*yobtvaimatj*—fuck?! My hands were covered with gold dust, my clothes as well, everything.

The plane was shaking like a rattle trap, the air was thick with gold dust, my lungs full. All the corners were full, we crept along, *blyad*—what a bitch, like stunned flies, gold dust in the air, all the grooves, the depressions full.

It was gold dust that was being transported. We grabbed a few coarse-as-sand handfuls. The criminal type from happiness shouted just one word—*ohuyety*—fuck me!

A hundred times! No other word.

Couldn't put it in our pockets, *shmons*—a prisoner inspection was scheduled, where to shove the gold? In our *valenki*—felt boots. We couldn't drag our feet as it was without that gold, and now it became really tough.

How I dragged myself around with that gold in my felt boots! As if pulling invisible heavy chains, it was hilarious.

And the criminal type just kept yelling—*ohuyety*!

That simpleton had lost his mind with that gold.

I'm still amazed that in the prisoner inspection they didn't find the gold.

Dreadful monkeying about.

Dreadful.

It was a time of deathly starvation. You can't bake bread from dust, even if it's gold dust. I exchanged it for about four rations of grub. It was the only time that I had bread enough to stuff myself.

Seimchan.

Magadan.

Now then, *davai*, come on, let's tackle the manure.

For a long time I still coughed and spit up that gold dust. And that criminal type just kept yelling over and over—*ohuyety*! That says it all.

Hilarious.

A hundred times and no other word!

You could die laughing.

Yes.

Yes. Why don't they laugh? Laura doesn't hear them laughing.

Books

"Gentlemen, lunch is ready!" Mama calls across the yard. The yard is finally clean and raked.

She's prepared potato soup with pearl barley. On a pan she's fried up Mīma's streaky bacon and it smells inviting. She's sliced a brick bread. Papa always eats bread with soup. Also with potatoes Papa eats bread. Otherwise Papa can't satisfy his hunger nor enjoy his meal.

Laura is there right away but the gentlemen don't come. Gentlemen! The gentlemen don't come, but Laura wants to laugh. They were gentlemen before. Now they're comrades. Comrades, lunch is ready! That's funnier still.

"Don't make faces at the table!" Mama remembers that she has to after all teach manners to her child.

Laura isn't making faces, forgets to make faces, because she's a good eater. Just not carrots. The only thing in this world that Laura can't stand is the taste of boiled carrots. Mama doesn't like that. Mama doesn't want to understand the words—can't stand the taste. Mama has never used these words! Neither in Siberia nor now.

"Gentlemen!" Mama yells across the yard again.

Thanks, but the gentlemen can't eat lunch yet. The gentlemen are in shit up to their ears and they can't come like that to the table. Besides, only one corner is left to muck out. They'll finish and then. God knows if their clothes will come clean, Francis's white shirt will really—*tochna* have to be thrown out. And also his *maika*—undershirt. Ance should fill the big kettle with water and put it on to boil and find some soap as well. Just as long as she herself doesn't start to boil, Francis adds. Mama smiles.

"Eat, eat, child, eat." Mama sits down beside Laura and looks on as she eats.

Francis shoves the pitchfork into the manure, but the tines hit something hard. What the devil is that? Papa drives his pitchfork into the manure and he too hits against the same. Rocks? Bricks? Bloody hell! Now what is it?! They're books. Francis pulls a thick volume out of the manure.

"Look, Johnny, it's leather-bound!"

"Look, Francis, here's more!"

The books in the manure, besides being leather-bound, bewilder both of them. There are more books than manure, says Papa.

Now they're mucking out the manure with their hands. Seemingly not to ruin the books. But they already are ruined. Still they're books and they can't use pitchforks.

These are Anda's father's books about which she wailed so. Anda wailed? Yes, cried dreadfully. Francis blazes in anger. Francis could accept even that independent Latvia's books would be burned, but this whorish thing Francis can't accept. Papa could even understand that they would be shredded, but this, no, it's maddening. Books in manure! That's somewhat like, like … shaming of the human species, Francis finishes his sentence. If it still is capable of being further shamed, he adds.

The Latvian writer and playwright Rūdolfs Blaumanis's *Collected Works*. The poet and writer Jānis Poruks's *Collected Works*. The poet and playwright Rainis's *Collected Works*.

Papa and Francis dredge from memory what they've read:

Swamp Wader, Papa says.

In Death's Shadow, says Francis.

White Snow Falls on Fir Needles, says Francis.

The Mama-Cat Had Kittens, says Papa.

Yes, they're from Rainis, says Francis. He won't ever pass up the opportunity to make a joke.

Laura has finished eating and is looking and listening to them from behind the door. Once more she can't understand anything. Totally incoherent talking. Like a competition—who can be more incoherent.

Hamsun, says Papa, lifting up a rosy volume. *Victoria.*

Hunger, reads Francis. That Hamsun should have been deported to Siberia so he could see real hunger.

Latvian *Dainas*—folksongs. Even though the book is soaked totally with slurry, Papa is able to read its title. Francis, a swastika! On Latvian *Dainas*—a German swastika? What kind of aberration is that?

"That's no German swastika, that's a fire cross! Swastika! Idiot fritzes! They screwed up a good and very ancient sign!" Francis is furious.

"How do you know everything? You're a hell of an intellishit," Papa marvels.

"How old were you when we were loaded into the wagons?"

"Nine and my sisters…" Papa grows silent.

"But I was twelve. I had read almost all of this except for the *Dainas*. That old typography can kill you, those versions and that poetry, for me, well are so-so."

"Latvian fairytales and legends! Yes, they need not be bound. They're beautiful as is. Look, more and more. Brown with gold. My old folks also had ones like these," Francis caresses the book.

Fairytales! Laura rushes to them. Fairytales are for children.

"Laura wants fairytales!"

Only up close she can see what the manure has done to the books. Not so much the manure as the slurry. That smelly liquid has soaked into the book pages, crawled in, crept in, and they're brown and stuck together. The covers have grown moldy and it seems to Laura that they've grown old and gray. Who did this, who turned all the Avoti books into shit? Books that have to be respected and honored, books of spiritual beauty and wisdom. Books, wherein is love, books wherein like in a green precious coffer are hidden the human heart's riches!

When Laura hadn't understood the Latvian saying: 'The stomach is not a book,' then Papa had explained it to her. A stomach is not as fine a thing as a book is. A book is a fine and a precious thing, which can't be compared to a stomach. A book is like an inheritance. A person who reads books can feel like he's inherited riches.

Laura can't feel like a rich heir, no, not at all, because grandfather Jūlijs's blue books with the black corners and grandfather Edmunds's lovely leather-bound books, all of which Laura should read, are soaking in dung! Laura feels like the poorest of paupers! Laura has been robbed. Who did this, who? Who besmirched wisdom, which Laura had to acquire, who tarnished the dreams, which Laura was to dream along with the books? Who stole the beauty that Laura had to sense? Who took away the love, which books were supposed to give Laura? Who swindled Laura of her inheritance? The dog-faced monsters! Dogfaces! Laura can't imagine that it could be anyone else.

Laura sees how unhappy the books are. More unhappy even than Laura herself.

Look, Johnny, they're laid down like a parquet floor. Elegant. Such a floor I've never seen in a pigsty. I've never seen one like it! Each day brings one more surprise!

Maybe the books can be washed? Laura remembers the spring in the field. And afterward they could be dried out by a light breeze.

In the meantime Papa and Francis dig around among the poor ridiculed books. Maybe some, even only one little book is still alive, but no, none are. All have drowned in the slurry, all have suffocated in the manure. Also Laura is suffocating like a book under the dung, feeling that the slurry is laughing in her mouth, spilling from her eyes, and her nose. She has to flee!

"I wouldn't want Anda to see this," Francis says.

"We have to dig a pit," Papa replies.

"That's it. We have to get some spades. We'll have to dig a grave."

"No use hiding this. Laura will blab about it no matter what." Papa decides. Anda has to be charmed with words. Diverted in a different direction. Otherwise she'll have another outburst.

Ance, there's something. Do you remember the dispatch, that bit of paper, well that *klyauza*—that order which Liepa showed us? Besides everything else in it there was also listed—the concealment of ideologically harmful literature. Do you remember?

Mama remembers, and so what? That was nonsense!

You hid those books well, Francis tries to joke again, but this time it doesn't work.

These books here, Ance, all of it is prohibited literature. Thank God that it's so, Papa is delighted.

Mama doesn't understand.

If those books were intact and sat on a shelf, we would maybe be on our way back to Siberia, Papa explains.

Mama still doesn't understand.

Now we'll destroy this harmful literature like a species, Francis says. We'll bury it. There will be no trace left.

Mama is confused. She's beginning to understand. But at least she's not crying or going crazy.

Therefore That Person knew about the books in the manure. That means he was present. Papa consolidates another direction.

We'll get our hands on him and...

... tie him to an anthill, Laura suggests.

"We'll..."

"... tickle him to his death like a Chinaman," Laura puts a period to what Papa began.

The thought of such justified revenge calms them all down a bit.

Papa's got work!

PAPA FINALLY HAS GOT SOME WORK! Mama and Laura are happy as is Papa. After all, Laura has heard somewhere "He who doesn't work, won't eat." Maybe that's written in Mīma's bible, she doesn't know. Papa thinks this work will be tailor-made for him. At least for the time being. Naturally, for the time being. Papa has no intention of looking at a horse's ass for the rest of his life. Yes, the kolkhoz will give Papa a horse and wagon and empty barrels and cans. No, this horse isn't from the Upītes farm. What's he like? Well, a horse like a horse. His name? Papa doesn't know the horse's name yet. How much he'll be paid, he doesn't know either.

Papa will have to drive to the depot and fill up the empty barrels and the cans. He'll have to drive them to the fields where the tractors are working. Either mowing green forage or plowing the potato furrows, whichever. Whatever they've been ordered to do, they're doing. In the kolkhoz no one has to think on their own what to do. Everyone has been told what to do in advance. Papa will have to deliver the full containers to the tractor drivers, but sometimes also to the person in charge of the coupler, and then take away the empties. A coupler? Laura giggles. That word sounds very funny! What does he couple, to what does he couple? A coupler—a hooker on! What's funny about this, the coupler is the tractor driver's helper, stop, Laura, stop it!

So, to continue the story. Then once more with the empty containers to the fuel depot, to be refilled and again transported. Sometimes he'll have to drive a short distance, but sometimes far. Papa will definitely prefer to go far because then he can properly see Lamme and its surroundings. The main thing is that he'll be on his own. He alone. Not like a farm brigade, where you alone work like a dog, while the rest are dawdling, doing zilch, but the

118

pay at the end is the same for all. He's going to sit in the wagon like an emperor. Papa is happily explaining, not even noticing that he, while talking, has eaten all the five eggs. Not three, as he was meant to do.

Laura desperately wants to accompany Papa. Please, please, Papa! Laura also wants to properly see Lamme and to learn the horse's name. Papa resists. No, no, those lubricants and oils, all those what-cha-ma-call-its, nigrols, autols, and solidols, and those dirty diesel barrels, those aren't for a girl like Laura. All in all they aren't for girls! Please, Papa, please!

No! At least not on the first day, we'll see later on. No, but Laura wants to go along on the first day! Laura wraps her arms around Papa's neck. Papa stands up but Laura doesn't let go and hangs from his neck like a bag, Laura will be Papa's coupler! Laura couples and wheedles, until she does indeed succeed in the coupling and wheedling and Papa agrees. Well, fine.

Laura sits in the wagon beside Papa.

The oil-slick board on which they've perched themselves is right by the horse's tail, because the wagon is full up with two big barrels against which they can rest their backs, as well as many cans and canisters, big and small. All of them empty.

"Just take care, Johnny, that that child doesn't fall out. And doesn't soil her clothes!" Mama admonishes.

"Clothes? Not on your life!" Papa promises and winks at Laura.

The horse is called Wintry.

"A lovely mare. Young, but let's hope, calm."

Laura doesn't like that girl horses are called mares. There's something disparaging about it. It's bad. Laura has heard that it's bad.

Wintry! Even Laura couldn't think of a better name. The horse is darkly white like a blizzard. Bluish like a snowdrift. Like a cloud. Like the teacher's gray hair! The mane and the tail, that's flicking back and forth, is a bit darker. Like an overcast sky. And the lashes! They're long and white like snow!

"Whoa!" Papa exclaims, and Laura nearly falls under Wintry's tail. "Now you must stay at a distance. But don't go too far either. Here all the ground is slick with oil. Soaked full like a sponge. And here you can't smoke," Papa warns her, as if Laura was just getting ready to smoke. Papa understands and the two of them laugh.

Papa takes out the smallest cans and canisters from the wagon and carries them into the gray concrete building. It has only one small window, and it itself is high up and barred.

"What's that building?" Laura frets, what if it's a prison.

"It's the fuel depot."

"Depot?"

"Yes, depot. Full stop!" Papa has no patience for questions. He has to work. On the building there's a sign, but in Russian letters: *GSM*

"What's *GSM*?"

"*Goryuche smazochniye materiali.*"

Aha, so! That's clear. Laura pretends that she understands. A coupler probably understands.

Papa positions a wide board at a slant against the back of the wagon and rolls down the large barrels. Papa doesn't want Laura to go inside that *GSM*, but Laura wants to and goes in. The odor of gas envelops them as they enter, but it's not the only smell. There are also others. Heavier, darker.

"A devil of a smell. That's from the tar—it has sulfur mixed with it."

Laura's not bothered by the smell. It's not the smell of people or manure. It doesn't matter that it stings one's eyes. Papa places a funnel on the big barrels and using a pail fills them one after the other to the top. It really doesn't happen that quickly. Papa pours and pours. And when they're full, he rolls them up the slanted board back into the wagon. Laura wants to help, because she can see how hard it is for Papa, but Papa yells at her—go away! Laura gets sulky and goes back into the depot. In a container she sees some wonderfully lovely colors. Beside it is a wooden dowel, with which one can do some mixing. The substance is as thick as honey. It glitters, now black, then green, now blue, then lights up suddenly very like a rainbow. Laura gazes as if bewitched. Stirring the thick rainbow, she's overtaken by a sleep-inducing pleasure. Laura mixes together the black sky with a green earth. Maybe God has at one point mixed it like that. Mixed and mixed until the world was created. What will it turn out to be for Laura?

"That's nigrol. Do you like it?"

"Yes."

"And this is autol. That there—solidol."

"Yes."

"That one there on the shelf is motor oil. Here's gas, do you see? Here A66, but there—72. But that's only for cars. We have to fill some liter bottles to be able to start up the tractors. Yes."

"Yes."

"Well and *solyarka*. That's intended for tractors. Diesel fuel. But everyone calls it *solyarka.*"

"Yes."

Papa is pleasantly surprised that Laura, who after all isn't a boy, likes all those lubricants and oils, and *solyarkas*, and motors and tar canisters, and, therefore, he explains and shows her, while he fills all the tubs full. It truly is lovely that the child is interested in her father's occupation.

"Laura! What's the matter?" Papa suddenly notices.

"Nothing." Laura as if bewitched stirs the dark night and green grass and the blue yonder and smiles.

"Quick outside!" Papa grabs Laura and carries her on his hip outside *GSM*. Outside the depot.

"I don't want to! I've got to stir some more." Laura is trying to wriggle free. Her head is spinning, but that's so pleasant. To be like God and to stir up the world, until something develops.

But Papa doesn't allow her to do it. The wagon is full and he can't delay anymore. The tractors are waiting on the field. Without fuel they don't move an inch. Only now Laura notices that there are rainbows in all the puddles. Even in the deep ruts left by driven-in tractors. Laura likes rainbows. But there isn't any longer that lovely smell. Just ordinary air. Too ordinary. The smile that had unawares crept into her face, vanishes somehow.

"Can you sit up? Girl, you're totally woozy from those devil smells!"

"Those weren't devil smells; that was the scent from mixing the world," Laura says slowly but enthusiastically.

A bit of the well-being still remains.

When Laura once more sees Wintry, the bewitchment passes. The wagon now is heavy, but Wintry has to pull it. Everyone has to do what they're ordered to do in the kolkhoz. The horse looks over her shoulder to see if Laura can manage to sit up, and invitingly flutters its long, snow-white lashes.

"Papa, Laura can't sit, it's too hard for Laura. Laura wants to sit on Wintry's back."

"Of course! Who wouldn't want to ride a white horse? That would be the last straw, wouldn't it! Are you going to sit or not, or I'll drive you home?"

What's that about home! The work day has just begun! Of what importance is the horse's color, after all! She'll sit, yes sit, Laura will sit up of course. What are these homesteads called? Why are there so many decrepit houses on all the farms? Why so many castle ruins? What tree is that? Laura has soiled her dress! Did you know that man? Why did he say hello to you? Why is there such a deep ditch there? A tank ditch? Can one wade through it only with tanks? Why are those boots called tanks? Why doesn't Wintry have an oat bag hanging from her neck like Mīma's horse Daira? What are we going to eat for lunch? And for supper?

Papa tells her to stop babbling for a moment.

For a moment she can.

But what was the name of that green lubricant? Validol? Why solidol? Is the world ready yet, or is God still mixing it up? Papa, Papa, look! What are those birds? Why ravens? What are those posts? Electricity? Why don't we have electricity? Laura wants electricity! Will it be installed? What does that mean—installed? Will it be with a tractor? What's that *gorodok*—town? A bird farm? What kind of birds are there? Are they ravens? Maybe storks? What kind of birds, Papa? Papa! Well, what kind? Like peacocks? Like eagles? Like the white owls that were in Siberia? Papa, a barrel is about to fall out! Papa climbs out and fastens the barrel. Be quiet now, Papa wants to think. About what? Please be quiet!

Laura is quiet. The wagon swings to and fro. Wintry

continues pulling.

Laura notices that Laughing Child whom she saw on the train coming home to Latvia is sitting on Wintry's back. Like Laura just now wanted to sit! He's hanging onto Wintry's mane, which is bluish like an overcast sky, he's laughing and throws a victorious glance back at Laura. Papa doesn't even notice Laughing Child. He's allowed to do what he wants! He digs his bare heels into Wintry's flanks, which are darkly white like a blizzard, and laughs. He presses his head of golden curls to Wintry's mane, which is like Mrs. Teacher's gray hair, and laughs. Laura knows that she has to put up with Laughing Child. He gets on everyone's nerves, but everyone tolerates him. There's nothing to be done about it.

Laughing Child hangs onto Wintry's tail and swings, and laughs. Right in front of Papa's and Laura's eyes. Wintry reproachfully shakes her head and in confusion blinks her long lashes, which are white as snow. Laughing Child throws himself back on Wintry's nape. He can sit on a white horse but Laura is not allowed to. Why? Papa doesn't answer. Wintry doesn't know that Laughing Child must be tolerated, that's why she begins to cock her ears and becomes skittish. Wintry starts to shiver and tries to get rid of Laughing Child. She kicks with her hind leg! She clips the rim of the wagon with her horseshoe and that frightens her even more. Wintry startles.

"Whoa! Stand still!" Papa yells at the horse and draws in the reins.

The mouth iron presses in deeply and painfully.

"What now? What is this? What kind of a horse has the kolkhoz given me? Totally unbroken!"

Laughing Child has disappeared.

Blood

IT'S PAPA'S FIRST PAYDAY, and already at the office cashier's window some people have invited themselves over. The first payday must be celebrated! How thoughtful of them. Papa knows full well that Mama no longer likes visitors, but a first payday really must be celebrated, Papa can't refuse, and would it be better if Papa were to celebrate in the ditch by the store, where on paydays all the drunks fall and lie like soldiers after a battle? No, better that Papa invite them to Avoti. There at least is a proper table, moreover made by Papa himself.

The next morning after the celebration it's already light, Laura wakes because of Papa's dreadful snoring and Laura needs to pee. Laura steps quietly. It does happen that the visitors sometimes upchuck here and there. The visitors didn't leave the night before because it was already too late and now they're still sleeping at the table because it's too early.

All the visitors are dreadfully good friends, although Mama doesn't know many of them. For example, the ones at the table. She knows none of the four. All of them are asleep, their heads resting on the table, one right on a plate. A head on a plate! Almost as if placed on a tray. Marinated beets were on that plate. The visitor's cheek looks bloody. That's from the beet juice. Laura understands that it's from the beet juice, but the cheek looks bloodied. Laura doesn't like blood, even though it's only beet juice.

It's odd that all of the visitors are bald. That's funny. Laura wants it to be funnier still. She takes the beet jar, which has been emptied of beets but in which the juice still remains. Laura pours a bit of juice on one of the bald pates, then on a second, but the visitors don't even move. Pours some on the third pate and the fourth, to make sure everyone gets some.

The thick, red juice dribbles into their sparse hair and doesn't stay on their pates. Laura wants particularly that their bald heads should color, so she pours a bit more on each of the visitors. There's no point in saving the juice, so Laura pours out all that remains in the jar, including the caraway seeds. But the beet juice doesn't want to stay on the round pates, it stubbornly trickles downward. One of the visitors wipes his face.

Laura gets scared. His face is bloody! The juice also trickles on shirt after shirt. The visitor once more wipes at his face with his hand and with difficulty opens his eyes and looks at his palm. Blood! The visitor stares glassy-eyed, blinks several times, but seemingly feels relieved to discover that he's alive. The rest sleep the sleep of the dead. Now there's going to be fun, Laura hides behind the woodstove.

"Egon!" The visitor yells and pulls up by the hair the head of the man sleeping beside him. The man's head falls back with a wet splat. Bloody and horrendous: "Laimon! Fred!"

No one moves. The visitor gazes around with unfocused eyes, probably thinking that in his drunken stupor he's slaughtered the others. Probably looking for the bloody knife or sword, or maybe the axe, with which he's done everyone in and finished them off, all dead and bloodied. Probably he's afraid that he'll have to sit in the slammer to cool off. In the joint! In chains!

Laura looks on from behind the stove. The visitor is breathing heavily, grabbing his head, moaning, not knowing where to begin, what to do now, what not. Laura wants to pee. Laura doesn't like blood. How to sneak away without being seen from this vipers' nest of murderers? From this bloodbath?

That's what happens when one drinks too much! Drinks until one drinks away one's mind, boozing and binging, until one gets the heebie-jeebies, until one starts to squabble and fight, and look, now all are dead! Having killed one another like pirates. All of them corpses. A sea of blood! They deserve what's coming to them! They won't get on any honor roll anymore. The only one who's still alive, he too has nothing to be happy about, the militia will come, then he'll get it! The one called Laimonis raises his head.

"Fuck! Zhani, who did this to you? I didn't! Wait, I don't remember anything. Hell!"

Zhanis notices his own and everyone else's bloodied state. Faces, hair, all of their heads, even shirts are soaked in blood.

"Shit! Egons, are you alive?" Zhanis asks.

Can't you see, he's not alive, he's dead? Covered in blood, your Egons is lying there and not moving! As well as Fredis. Laura feels sick to her stomach.

"It's all a blur. Maybe let's get out of here?" Zhanis gets up from the table.

"Mother of God! I don't understand anything. *Davai*, let's get lost for God's sake, we've got to hightail it," Laimonis also gets up from the table.

Creeping out he accidentally pushes into Egons or Fredis, Laura doesn't know which corpse is which. Whoever-he-is limply slides off his chair but doesn't wake.

"Wait, Fredis is still seemingly warm," Laimonis reaches out to touch Fredis.

"Better let's scram. My old lady will kill me," suddenly nasty thoughts about the future occur to Zhanis.

At this point Laura would like to stop what's happening, but it's not possible. Mīma appears in the doorway.

"So. What's going on here?" Mīma isn't concerned about the visitors, she heads for the sofa bed in the room. Mama and Papa are asleep. "I'm asking what's going on here?"

"Mīma, nothing's going on, we're still sleeping," Mama crossly mumbles.

Trying to keep upright by leaning against the doorjamb, Zhanis appears. Mama screams. Papa wakes up with a start. Papa can't believe his eyes. Blood! In his house? A fight? Murder? Then a bloodied Laimonis appears. Mama screams. Hurriedly Papa tries to pull on his pants, but in his agitated state, stumbles and collapses on the floor.

"Drunks! Lushes! Wimps, not soldiers! Like swine!" Veins stand out on Mīma's neck, on her old, wrinkled neck. Mīma is dreadfully angry. "Does a child have to see this? A child shouldn't have to see this! Live as you want, booze away and kill one another, but the child will come with me! The child will live at Upītes until you come to your senses! Out, you alkies!" Mīma yells at Egons, Zhanis, and Laimons.

They obey her without a word.

Mīma looks at Fredis.

"And you aren't ashamed to come here?" There's darkness in Mīma's voice. Fredis wipes the blood from his face and tries to creep away.

"Come, child, let's go," Mīma tries to take Laura's hand to lead her away.

Only now Laura notices her palms. She can't give a bloody hand to Mīma! That damned beet juice! Mama too notices Laura's blood-covered hands, jumps out of bed, clasps her in her arms, what's happened, where do you hurt, did you cut yourself, has someone harmed you, oh my God, what is it?

"Beet juice!" Laura shouldn't say, but she tells her.

Laura isn't any kind of monster, she doesn't want to cause worry for Mama and make Papa, while pulling on his pants, fall down. She's cooked up all this. Laura wants to get away without unnecessary explanations, that's why she lets Mīma hustle her helter-skelter away with her. Out the door, across the threshold, into a horse-drawn wagon, into Daira's wagon, to Upītes farm.

The Hedgehog's Coat

THE UPĪTES'S GARDEN IS AS enormous as the world. Laura hasn't yet seen all of it. It can't be done that quickly. As it is she spends almost a whole day with the hedgehogs. Laura knows the hedgehogs from a fairytale book. The book likes hedgehogs, which one can tell from how the book describes them. Kind of lovingly. The hedgehog's coat. How two hedgehogs have tricked a hare. How God gave the hedgehog quills. It's an interesting story.

But God didn't go and give the hedgehog quills right away, He didn't! First of all, He gave him a golden coat. The hedgehog had done some good deed for God. Had given Him something. Ah yes, Laura remembers—the hedgehog had given God good advice! Figured out how to make the world smaller. God had become very sad thinking that the world had turned out to be too big, that He, God by Himself, couldn't grasp it, nor hold it in His hand, no way. What should He do? The hedgehog had said that the world should be pleated. Pleated? God had been surprised that this hadn't occurred to Him Himself. What a good idea! Not only earth became smaller, but thus mountains were created.

God, of course, would not leave a debt unpaid. No! For this advice God gifted the hedgehog with a golden coat. In the beginning—it was alright, it was very good in fact, everyone admired the hedgehog and the hedgehog was overjoyed, happy, smiling like a piglet lazing in the sun. But, only in the beginning. Soon everyone else started to hunt and push around, and try to catch the hedgehog, in order to get even a tuft of his golden coat, some small strip of gold, a gold fold, and eventually—oh, horror of horrors! Rob him of his whole golden coat! In fact—pull off his whole coat over his head!

Laura is filled with dreadful indignation about this. God gave the coat to the hedgehog, after all, God did! The hedgehog had a God-given golden coat! It was God's gift! How is it that the others couldn't appreciate this, how could they take it away! Had they turned into idiots or what? It was good that the hedgehog had recounted all this to God. He had tried to keep it to himself, until he couldn't stand it anymore and told Him. It wasn't any kind of complaining, just simply told Him, and that was all!

And then God gave the hedgehog a coat of quills. "Now no one will be able harm you," He added.

Now here he is—the hedgehog. Laura has to begin with just one, even though under the briar rose bush there are hedgehogs enough to make a colony. Laura chooses the biggest one, it looks kind of sensible. Laura doesn't show that she's a bit afraid of the hedgehog, they after all are total strangers. The hedgehog angrily grumbles, curls into a ball, pierces with his quills, when Laura rolls it up into her hands. The hedgehog knows how to project his quills as well as draw them in. Very like a cat does with his claws. The hedgehog knows how to flatten his quills against his body, as well as shoot them straight up in the air. And even to leap up when he's furiously angry and wants to pierce!

Laura explains to the hedgehog that the thought of harming him hasn't even occurred to her. Laura wants to be friends with the hedgehog, place him in her apron, and take him to Māra's Church. Laura wants the hedgehog to sense how loveable and nice a creature he is in this world! Laura wants the hedgehog to show himself, to trust her, and to rely on her. Not to draw himself into a quilly ball. They'll have to live together in one and the same garden after all. Laura isn't stingy with good words, showers the hedgehog with all sorts of compliments—how nice it is to meet you, you haven't changed at all, you're just as lovely as you were before, please, I thank you.

Slowly the hedgehog comes to believe her. Understands that Laura is telling the truth. That she's no coat-thief. The hedgehog no longer is afraid to poke out his tiny snout and paws. He allows Laura to tickle his soft tummy. Minces along like a little puppy, no longer being shy at all. The only drawback is that the hedgehog all the time wants to sneak back into the briar rose thicket. No, no, not there! Laura pulls the hedgehog back out.

Once more he's shrunk into a ball!

It's such a lovely day today, what's the hurry, the sun is walking on the surface of the earth, maybe there'll be rain? The hedgehog pokes out his tiny snout. No it won't rain, and once more he curls into a quilly ball.

Friendship requires time.

Ruski

THAT WHITE NEGRO HAS SHOWN UP. He has a broad nose, a big mouth with fat, very fat lips and light, frizzy hair. Truly, if his face was smeared black, for example, with soot, and his hair was dyed black, for example with wagon grease, he'd look precisely like a Negro. Like in pictures. The only thing missing is an earring in his ear. Mīma calls him Arnolds.

Arnolds is tipsy more often than sober. Arnolds is no piece of gold, of course he isn't. He's a lazybones, that he is, Mīma explains to Grandpa. He's also not the best of workers—a master of his trade, as the Latvians are accustomed to saying, it's true, very true, but Mīma can't get anyone else to agree to work a bit in return for a bottle. For a bottle? Laura wonders in surprise. For an empty one or a full one? In the morning it's full but in the evening empty, Mīma explains.

Now he's arrived, that Arnolds, that White Negro. Laura likes the second name much better. Maybe Arnolds really is a Negro just faded in the sun? Maybe he comes from Africa where lions and elephants live? Maybe in fact he's an African king who's been deported to Latvia? Maybe Latvia for the White Negro is like Siberia? Laura would very much like the White Negro to be in fact the White Negro, not some kind of a common Arnolds. But Laura will probably have to be disappointed because the White Negro, no, Arnolds is cross.

"Not much that can be *sachinit*—patched up here, this shack can't be saved!"

He's calling Upītes farmhouse a shack! Laura immediately doesn't like Arnolds anymore. It's taken but a minute!

Arnolds is tearing off wood boards from the walls of the end room. Buka is going to live in that end room when she returns. The boards aren't new, but Arnolds will pull out the rusty nails from them, will turn the boards to the other side, plane them a bit and they'll do. Afterward he'll panel the walls.

"What is it, Ruski, why are you leering at me like Lenin at the bourgeoisie?"

"Laura isn't a Ruski!"

"Didn't you come from Russia? Where the devil are those pliers?"

"No, from Siberia!"

"Where is Siberia then? In England, is it? Where the devil are those pliers?"

"No, London is in England! Are you speaking to the devil?"

"Yes, the devil is my best friend! See, like this, with horns!" Arnolds makes a horrendous face.

Laura's heart skips a beat.

"Ho! Ho! What do you know—London! What do you, a Ruski, know about London!"

"Laura has a dress from London! And so what do you know?"

"You're asking to be slapped, Ruski!"

"Laura isn't a Ruski, you're the one asking for it!"

Laura now speaks and thinks about what she says only afterward. There are moments like this. Even when someone is friends with the devil.

Laura senses that she's gone too far, but—Ruski! It's such an insult! Ruski kids run around all summer barefoot and pick all the apples. Still green. The kind that have barely formed. The Ruskies steal carrots from other people's gardens. The Ruskies don't wash, the Ruskies don't know what a toothbrush is! The Ruskies have lice! Ruskies...

Mīma would know better what to say, how nasty the Ruskies are, Laura doesn't know so well.

Laura's indignation at this insult rises from the bottom of her heart so swiftly that it momentarily takes her breath away. Laura is not a Ruski! She's wearing sandals! From London, by the way! She doesn't steal carrots from other people's gardens! She brushes her teeth and she doesn't have lice!

Laura curls up into a fetal position and can't keep from sobbing. She curls into a ball, like a hedgehog does, when Ripsis the dog barks at it. No, she can't compare Arnolds to Ripsis, because Ripsis is a good and loveable doggy. He's not friends with the devil! It's a pity that Laura isn't a hedgehog, that Laura doesn't have quills with which to pierce Arnolds's repulsive mug. He's no White Negro king, no, he's not!

Her tears are so heartfelt and burning, as if exploding from a volcano. Laura never knew that she had a volcano inside. The lava pours down her cheeks and scalds the entire world. It would be good if that stream would reach Arnolds. Then he'd have to flee as quickly as his legs could carry him. His bowed, dirty legs! But if Arnolds didn't manage to escape, Laura wouldn't be at all sad, not at all.

"What is it? What did I say? I didn't know you were such a ninny. Why are you here getting underfoot anyway, why aren't you home with your mama?"

"Laura's home is here! And also with Mama! Laura has two homes!"

"People like you don't have a home! And shouldn't have! Your homes, you rich farmers the proletariat regime took away and it did right."

"The kalhoss gave it back to us!"

"What? Who?"

"Kalhoss!"

"Ruski! Ruski! Even such a word as kolkhoz you don't know how to say. It's not for sure yet how legally that farm was given back. It would be useful to check that out. To write to the district administration, for them to check it."

Arnolds takes a couple of nips from a bottle.

Laura doesn't answer. What if the farm really hasn't been given back legally? What then? Will they take it away again? She's afraid that she'll say something wrong again, that she'll be laughed at. And she's also worried about that devil who will hand Arnolds the pliers.

"You shouldn't have been allowed to return home from Siberia. All of you dragged back here! Bourgeois freaks! Two homes! Others have none! Where the devil have those pliers gone to?"

What can Laura do if others have none? That Arnolds has to live in a communal flat. She won't tell anything more to someone like Arnolds.

She won't tell him that Laura will live in Upītes farm until the grown-ups come to their senses.

Nor that Mama isn't home anyway during the day because Mama also has got work now. Liepa, man like an oak, has helped Mama get it. Mama is sitting in an office. Laura won't tell Arnolds what an office is, that it's the kind of house where everyone sits with their documents—their *bumagi*, doing calculations. They have to sit there all day and calculate nonstop.

She won't tell how Papa had wanted to take Laura back to Avoti farm, how stubborn he was, how he persisted that a child has to live with her parents. How Mama decided that she would ask the child herself. Would Laura like to stay at Upītes while Papa gets Avoti in order? During the summer, for a while, Laura will have two homes.

Yes, Laura wants two homes!

At Upītes there are cherries and plums, and hedgehogs. At Upītes there's an attic and also Grandpa. At Upītes there are horses and a white-tiled wood-burning stove. At Upītes there's a river!

At Avoti there are Mama and Papa and a spring! The spring flows almost between the two farmhouses. This spring is important.

Laura will have two homes!

She won't tell that Papa couldn't be convinced. That Mīma was angry then. How she told Papa off.

You should be ashamed of yourself! You make the child collect empty bottles from ditches! What will people think? God be merciful!

Let Mīma on the other hand not try to stuff the child's head full of church things and religion. There is no God, Papa has been given proof of this first hand! And Papa doesn't care what people think!

Laura too doesn't care what Arnolds thinks. It would be another matter altogether if he were the White Negro. But he's just a common Arnolds!

And Laura is no Ruski! When Arnold has turned his back to her, Laura quickly grabs the pliers and throws them far away in the grass. As far as she can. In the longest grass. Let the devil look for his friend Arnolds's pliers!

The Shortage and Francis

PAPA STILL HASN'T BEGUN work at a proper job. He had started, but then a shortage happened. Papa didn't have enough gasoline to take to the tractor drivers and couplers in the field.

That GSM, that fuel depot, one day was empty. Papa no longer had anything to transport. The boss turned up in his *bobik*—a Soviet restyled version of the American jeep. The boss who'd been nicknamed Jallopied Fatso. That can't be, he started to yell, there was a whole month's supply there, what has Papa done with the fuel? Papa has driven it to the tractor drivers and the couplers. As much as they asked for, he transported. Gas, oil, and lubricant. The boss should ask the tractor drivers what they did with it! Maybe the tractor drivers and the couplers inadvertently used more than necessary. No, the tractor drivers and couplers haven't used more than necessary, Papa must be the one who has peddled some on the sly. Kolkhoz's property!

Papa explained that he hadn't peddled anything on the sly, nor any other way. Papa had no need for the kolkhoz's property! At least not fuel. Does the boss think that Papa has a *Chaika*—a luxury car hidden in the bushes? Or a *Pobeda* car? No, the boss thinks that Papa drank that gas. Isn't drinking a common occurrence at the Avoti farm?

So, that's the story, says Mama.

Does the boss think that Papa drank the gas? That the visitors drank the gas? No, the boss is crazy! Papa and the visitors drank vodka, just the vodka that Francis brought! Who drinks gas after all? Laura knows and can go and tell the boss!

"Zip up that smart mouth of yours!" Papa interrupts Laura and continues to recount what's happened to Mama. Papa unburdens his heart. From it spill the new insult and old sorrows. Papa wants to show that he's a fighter but Laura can see

135

that the fighter has been wounded. Will Mama draw Papa back from the battlefield?

Let Papa write a resignation! Voluntarily.

Mama thinks that he'll have to write it. No, Papa won't do it because that would be admitting that he's guilty of something. Papa won't allow anyone to insult him like this! Almost called him a thief!

Then once more Jallopied Fatso pipes up. Papa shouldn't get his feathers all ruffled like a rooster, not to get in a tizzy, that's going to make it worse.

"If Liepa hadn't spoken for you, I wouldn't have taken someone like you on, you Siberian laggard! All of you are good-for-nothings! Such people have no place in an honest working people's collective, write your resignation!" That's what he screams, that boss. The fat ape! That Jallopied Fatso. He'll set up a court of comrades and there's no hope that anyone will be on Papa's side!

Would there really be no one, not one of the many visitors, the sincere Lamme village people? Papa doesn't think so.

"Write, Johnny, that crappy resignation, you must do it."

"But why? If I haven't taken even a drop of that gas? And I also know who took it, but I'm no ratfink. Who took it? Well, who took it, don't you see, everyone steals like the devil. No, they don't steal, just simply take. That's no longer called stealing, it isn't stealing, just taking. Only taking, given that all is held in common. At the kolkhoz all is ours. What's mine is ours, what's yours is ours." Papa doesn't know what to do. To tell the truth right in front of everyone, that the boss himself took it and now he's found a fool to blame? Papa is convinced of this, but he can't prove it. He's furious!

"Johnny, you're the most honest person in this world, but this time you have to give in. I love you so much. We'll manage."

"I love you too, Ance, even more."

Mama has dragged the wounded man out of the battlefield.

It's probable that Papa would have continued to fight with the boss, but then news arrives about Francis.

Francis has hung himself in the town of Tukums. Because of

unrequited love. The grown-ups are talking about some sort of letter. What is that—hung himself? Laura doesn't really know, no one explains anything to her, but Francis won't be coming to visit anymore. Mama abandons all her begun work. They must go to Tukums! Mama doesn't believe that Francis … No, it can't be Francis! Francis would never in his life do this! No, they must go to Tukums!

No, Mama won't go to Tukums to see Francis! Papa is yelling at Mama as if he's lost his mind. Papa will go but he won't take Mama along. Mama is the one to blame for everything!

"How can you say that? Would it be better if I had left you and gone with Francis? Would it be better if Francis and I had deceived you behind your back? Yes? That would be the solution? Who do you think I am?" Mama yells in response through her tears. Also Mama yells that she loves Papa not Francis! What is Mama guilty of—what?

"Johnny, don't you love me anymore?" Mama is totally crushed.

"How can you think I don't? Forgive me! But Francis!" Papa weeps. His broad shoulders are racked with sobs. "Why did you chase him away, why?"

"Don't blame me, please don't blame me! That's below the belt! That's so unfair!" Mama pounds Papa's chest with her fists. Papa clenches Mama's hands so tightly that she screams—ow, ow!

Ow, ow! Laura's heart breaks. Laura too has an unrequited love, when Papa and Mama quarrel like this. It's not a shallow quarrel like a tiny puddle. It's not an easily drained squabble like a pond, this quarrel is dangerous, very deep. Both their eyes are like wells. Laura's love is very unhappy at such a quarrel, because Laura, you see, Laura loves both equally! Laura doesn't know who is right and on whose side she is, doesn't want to know. Laura isn't on either side. But if a person doesn't side with someone, then a person is left alone. Alone in this wide world. Totally alone! Ow, ow!

Saint Peter

HAVING UNHOOKED FROM a shoulder-yoke pails full of water and placed them on the ground, Mīma is standing in the middle of the farmyard. Leaning on the yoke, she's gazing into the distance and wiping away tears with her apron. Today she's wearing the white apron, and that means it's Sunday. On weekdays Mīma has a checkered apron. Mīma likes the checks. Mīma doesn't like flowered aprons. The same goes for kerchiefs. Mīma has never in her life tied a flowered kerchief around her head and will never do so! Mīma won't dance along with the new fashion. This is why Mīma has skirts like no one else. They are thick and long, almost reaching to the ground. Mīma won't run around with her behind bared like the young ones. The same with the busy Russian house-dresses, which can now be bought in stores, she won't ever, ever wear such as long as she lives, may God help her! Mīma's life is long like the railway tracks.

"Look what I've got!"

Laura has a hedgehog in a basket. Mīma looks but doesn't really see the hedgehog.

"Be quiet. Better listen."

Laura listens with one ear.

"What's that? Who's playing there?"

"Saint Peter."

"Saint Peter?"

"Better listen."

Laura listens to the sounds, which are coming from the direction of the forest. That's over the railway tracks. No forest really, just a copse. The sounds break through the white light of birches, they wind through the green darkness of fir trees and come straight to Mīma, straight to Laura. They don't get lost. Laura puts down the basket with the hedgehog on the lawn and allows the sounds to enter. The melody is joyful and sad. At the same time. That's how it can be, Laura knows that songs are like that. Not all, but this is one of them about which you can't understand whether to be happy or to be sad, to laugh or to cry. If Mīma is crying then Laura will laugh.

"Be quiet child, don't laugh!"

Laura can cry if Mīma wants her to.

"Don't cry!"

Mīma doesn't say this to Laura for then she'd at least have to look at her. Mīma says it to herself, because tears are rolling down her wrinkled cheeks, hopping as if over a furrowed field.

"What did Saint Peter play?"

The melody has fallen silent. The silence no longer is as it was. Something has been added. Quite what really can't be determined immediately. Also the jasmine blossoms aren't the same as they were before. Now their fragrance is stronger. As if sweeter. As if more bitter. Also that can't be quite determined. But the world has changed. Laura senses it distinctly.

"A French horn. Peter once played that in an orchestra. In Riga."

"You know Saint Peter?"

Laura can't imagine that right here beyond the railway tracks, beyond the copse lives Saint Peter. Laura's heart fills with delight like a balloon with heady air, and it threatens to fly away! Saint Peter right here beyond the copse? Then God too must be right there! Doesn't Saint Peter work with God Himself? Played in an orchestra? In Riga? Doesn't Saint Peter have to guard the heavenly gates? Maybe he doesn't need to stand there all the time. Sometimes he can also descend to earth. To blow the French horn in the orchestra. Then back to heaven's gate.

"Why doesn't he play now in the orchestra?"

"He's turned odd in his old age."

"What is that—odd?"

"He lives on his own, doesn't talk to anyone, walks around in white clothes as if he had just come out of a washhouse, and on Sundays he plays hymns."

"What are hymns?"

"Church songs."

"Does Saint Peter live in a church?"

"What church! What kind of nonsense are you spewing! Where in Lamme is there a church? There's never been one. In Lestene, there's one of course. Peter lives in a washhouse."

Laura is disappointed. It would be better if Saint Peter lived in a church and the church would be right here across the railway tracks, beyond the copse. Laura has never been in a church.

"Let's hope they don't arrest him again."

"Why would he be arrested?"

"Help me! Lift the pail so I can hook it up to the yoke. Like so. I have to take the water inside."

"But you didn't tell me why Saint Peter needs to be arrested!"

"If you want to know everything, you'll soon get old."

Laura has heard this a hundred times already. Usually for Laura it's like water off a duck's back. Now, that it turns out Mīma knows Saint Peter, it's different. No longer is it like water to a duck. Laura would also like to play hymns like Saint Peter and also stand for a while at heaven's gate. Not for long. Just to feel what it's like—to be Saint Laura! Look, how she's standing at the heavenly gate, look, what a gold halo above her head, look how saintly! Not for long, no. To go by train for a long time, to stand for a long time at the heavenly gate. That's how one can really grow old soon. But that Laura doesn't want—to grow old soon. And odd. The kind who would have to be arrested.

Old age is a swinish thing. Grandpa says so. It's when your intestines want to crawl out of your stomach. That can't be allowed, what kind of a thing is that. That's why Grandpa wears a belt with a fist. The fist presses the intestines back. Grandpa can't carry anything heavy. That's why Mīma needs to carry the water. She places the yoke on her shoulders. Mīma carries all the heavy things, not only the water.

Laura remembers the hedgehog. The basket has tumbled over and is empty. The hedgehog hasn't wanted to listen for so long to the hymns. How long can a hedgehog listen to church songs? It's no fault of the hedgehog that he doesn't know a thing about Saint Peter. Never mind, Laura will tell the hedgehog about Saint

Peter. Also all the six hedgehog babies, whose quills haven't yet grown tough. What if the hedgehog also won't want to grow old fast?

The hedgehog babies when born have quills that are as soft, as light, as feathers.

Bread with Sugar

LAURA DUNKS A SLICE of rye bread in water and allows it to soak for a while. Can't soak it too long, then the slice can fall apart. Laura has learned how to do it. Her mouth waters at the thought. The fine sugar is once again not in its usual place! Where has Mīma hidden it? Only Mīma, who else.

Why does the fine sugar seem to Mīma like a thing to be hidden? It's from the seaside town of Melluži. Tilliņtante, Mīma's sister, will bring more sugar. At Tilliņtante's in Melluži there's tons of sugar. Mīma can't hope to hide the sugar from Laura! When she so desperately yearns for a slice of bread with sugar that her mouth waters all the time. It's surely not healthy to swallow so much saliva. It could even be harmful.

Laura begins to drag a wood stump toward the shelf. Mīma thinks that Laura isn't strong enough to do this. But she is! The sugar bowl has been hidden behind empty bottles. Laura reaches her hand in for the sugar bowl. With a crash the bottles fall. Laura's heart stops. In the adjacent room Mīma is having her afternoon nap. In the summer everybody has afternoon naps at Upītēs. Including Laura. At least, that's what Mīma thinks.

But Laura knows better, who's sleeping, who's not. The disturbed silence sets in once more. Only the flies glued to the flypaper buzz with their last bit of strength. They're probably not having a good time. Laura's heart calms down. She lifts the sugar bowl off the shelf. The sugar soaks into the moist bread slice easily like into swamp moss. Laura could devour ten such slices.

But now to the attic, because the attic is the best place. Mīma never goes up there. Because Mīma can't climb the ladder.

The ladder is missing several rungs, it's holding together on a wing and a prayer. The attic has been patched up sloppily. Any spot there can collapse at any moment. Mīma doesn't want to break her neck.

Grandpa won't climb in any case. Also Grandpa doesn't want to break his neck. No, his scruff. Papa says—scruff.

Laura doesn't know what that scruff is, just that Grandpa doesn't want to break it. Let the girl go up there, just as long as she doesn't touch the *kupars*. *Kupars*? What's that? The *kupars* is a big, green coffer under the sloped ceiling. That Laura shouldn't open! Grandpa doesn't want Laura to open it. Laura can't even open it. It's ornamented and ironbound. Lovely it is, but the forged decorations make the lid so heavy that it can't be lifted.

Here in the attic is the best place to eat her bread slice with sugar. Laura eats and gazes at the dust motes whirling in the sunbeams. The sunbeams that shine in through the gaps between the old wooden boards. The dust motes like the sun. Where the sun doesn't shine, dust doesn't go. Everyone wants the sun.

Laura settles down among old horse gear. Saddle-pads, horse-collars, bridles and old leather halters, which still smell of a live, warm horse. Laura feels the nearness of the horse. She offers the horse some bread with sugar. The horse doesn't want the bread with sugar. Laura knows that he does want it though. The horse is just refusing for Laura's sake. Just as Grandpa does. Laura licks her fingers.

She's going to do it today. She'll open that black door. Laura stands up and shakes off the sawdust clinging to her. The black door is soot-covered and smells of smoke. It's warped and stuck. It leads to a cubbyhole, which is stuck to the chimney like an enormous hornets' nest. What if it really is a hornets' nest, and not a former meat smoker, as Grandpa says?

A hornets' nest wouldn't be the most horrendous thing. But what if those doors lead to hell? Laura feels hot. Her knees buckle. Once more her mouth waters—that slice of bread with sugar hasn't helped.

What if the devil is squatting behind the door? What if it's a dog-faced monster?

Laura whips around and rushes back. She falls, sprawling full-length right on the horse's saddle. The horse under the saddle behaves calmly and reassuringly. Devils are only in fairytales.

But dog-faced monsters are for real! Yes, dog-faces do eat children but Laura is comforted by the thought that lately nothing has been heard along those lines. If some child had been eaten wouldn't Mīma have railed about it from morning to night? Laura wouldn't have been allowed to take a step outside.

In the black door a thumb-size chink appears. Through it darkness presses in. Seemingly presses in, but in fact draws in.

It's the darkest of dark that Laura has ever seen. What if a thief is hiding in that dark? What if a murderer? What if a German? What if a Russian? But what if a drowned man?

Laura won't be afraid of anything. How can a drowned man be there? Use your head! The black door must be opened, no matter what. While Mīma naps.

"Laura, where have you got off to again, you little rascal?"

Too late!

It's Mīma's voice. Only now Laura realizes that the sugar bowl was left on the table and the wood stump hasn't been put back in its place. Laura quickly steals down the ladder.

"Laura!"

"Yes, Mīma!"

Laura appears from the direction of the firewood shed. She wants Mīma to feel how kind, loveable, and obedient a girl Laura is.

"Did you have a good sleep? What did you see in your dreams? Did you take your medicine? Did the bugs bite you?"

Maybe she shouldn't have mentioned the bugs. Laura is worried that she maybe has overdone the sympathy. It may appear suspicious to Mīma.

"Take a jar and go pee in it."

"I don't want to pee!"

"Don't talk back!"

"Why do I have to pee in a jar?"

"Bilberry has got tangled up in barbed wire. Her udder is torn."

Laura doesn't have the courage to say that Mīma should pee herself. Bilberry is Mīma's cow.

"Why can't Grandpa pee in it?"

"God in heaven! Grandpa! Bilberry will die on the spot! Grandpa drinks and smokes. Poison he pisses not medicine!"

"Do I piss medicine?"

"Don't be vulgar! Aren't you at all sorry for Bilberry?"

Laura takes the jar and crawls under the lilacs. A child's pee supposedly is clean and good medicine. Phooey! It's not so easy to aim into a jar. The pee is yellow and transparent. Does it have to be like that? And how warm it is! Laura gets scared. Maybe she's ill? Maybe she's got a fever? The pee stream has created foam. What is that foam? Why does pee have foam? Maybe she's sick and will die?

"Mīma, Laura is sick. Will you cry when Laura dies?"

"What kind of drivel is that? I, an old person, could talk like that, not you, a young child. Come on, give me the jar. Now look, how lovely. Like amber. Bilberry will thank you. There, you see how well you did, what a spunky girl! Go and wash your hands! Go eat! You're as healthy as a horseradish."

Mīma hurries away. Laura sulks, she doesn't want to be a horseradish. Not like a horseradish, nor a turnip, nor a beet. She also doesn't want to be a spunky girl. Doesn't anyone understand that that's not said in praise? A piglet also can be spunky! Laura wants to be a refined and delicate girl. Pale with blue rings under her eyes. Like neighboring Lonia, whom everyone feels sorry for. No one feels sorry for Laura! Laura has to feel sorry for herself, but she hasn't got the time!

The sugar bowl is no longer on the table in the kitchen. The wood stump is sitting in its usual place. Laura has been caught. Why did Mīma not say anything? Why did she not scold her?

On a plate sit two thick slices of rye bread with sugar on them and also with cinnamon sprinkled on top. Mīma knows how much Laura likes cinnamon! That's Laura's plate. When she's eaten it clean, a piglet smiles back at her.

Grandpa

Mīma can't stop marveling, it's an absolute miracle how Laura has managed to get in Grandpa's good graces! Even Mīma hadn't dared enter Grandpa's dusky room when she wanted. For years now. Laura and Grandpa seemingly are a hugely compatible pair. It's not clear though whether Mīma isn't just jealous.

Yes, Laura is allowed to help Grandpa clean his pipe. To give another person his pipe to be cleaned—that's immense trust. In reality Grandpa has no means of refusing, Laura has earned the right to clean the pipe because she's precisely the one who found the pipe. Yes! Where? Where, where? Somewhere. Well fine, in the attic, where else. Laura doesn't lie by saying this, not at all. Isn't the *kupars* in the attic? *Kupars,* that enormously big, green chest that is ironbound and ornamented. Laura isn't allowed to open the *kupars's* lid, she's been strictly told. Laura shouldn't stick her nose in it! The heavy lid could fall on her, and then she'd die on the spot.

Laura needed several days to try every which way until she succeeded in lifting the heavy lid. What was of such importance in the *kupars?* Some sort of blankets, some old fur coats lined with sheep wool. They smelled like Shipley the sheep. Of course Shipley wasn't in the *kupars* because Shipley was running around in the pasture with the lambs. After so hard a job as the opening of the *kupars's* lid, Laura is disappointed. It's true of course that Laura for the time being has managed to look at only the top layer, but the *kupars* is as deep as a well. Well, and in one of the top fur coat pockets she's found a pipe and some sort of little sac. It turns out to be a tobacco pouch! Grandpa is very happy about this.

A person need not be ungrateful. That Grandpa has taken to heart. A truer word was never spoken. That's why Laura is allowed to clean the pipe. Grandpa had given up hope that his good old pipe could be found. With its tobacco pouch, no less! After all that's happened. Besides that, there's tobacco in it— Reinis, Grandpa's son had brought the tobacco from Riga—dry, fine, even shove-able in your ear, if need be! Can you believe it? After all that's happened.

After what?

Laura doesn't leave Grandpa in peace. Mīma is constantly working but Grandpa lies in bed and does nothing. Laura sits at the foot of Grandpa's bed along with his dog Ripsis and doesn't leave him alone. Talks and talks and fidgets. Questions and pesters Grandpa.

"What's lighter—a kilo of lead or a kilo of goose feathers?"

"It's clear that feathers are lighter," Grandpa is totally convinced.

"Not right, wrong! Both are equal in weight!" Laura rejoices. Giggle after giggle! Laura's giggles. Grandpa's shadowy room confuses Ripsis. It looks like Ripsis would like to laugh along, but is he allowed? Ripsis squints at Grandpa. Laura laughs until she gets hiccups. Grandpa smiles.

Can't be, he says. Yes, it can, Laura explains.

"Fine, but you girl tell me why there's salty water in the sea?" Grandpa wants to get even.

Laura thinks, but can't arrive at an answer, because she's never ever thought about this.

"Because salted herring live in the sea." This time Grandpa has won.

Ripsis no longer growls like he did initially. Grandpa no longer is as non-talkative as he was in the beginning. Slowly, bit by bit, Laura tries to piece together what Grandpa calls "all that's happened." Of course not absolutely all, nonetheless. Bits she gathers from Mama, bits from Mīma, bits from Grandpa himself.

Well, it happened like this.

The Russian dog-faced monster had arrived one night with a rifle and had taken away Grandpa's daughter Lilia. That's Buka.

And his granddaughter Anda. That's Mama.

And his grandson. That's Juris, Mama's little brother.

The dog-face had taken them away from Grandpa and, like cattle, had sent them in cattle cars to Siberia, to die there.

Then also the dog-faced Russian had shot Grandpa's son-in-law Edmunds. That's Mama's papa.

And he had starved his son-in-law's father. That's Mama's grandfather Jūlijs, the head of Lamme's civil parish, the old man Avots.

Laura has to clench her fist in concentration, so as not to mix up things, she can't mix this up because these are people after all, not some countable trees.

To continue.

Reinis, Grandpa's dear son.

Reinis, Reinis, a name that Grandpa mumbles, his back bent in sorrow.

Reinis right away had hardened his passionate heart aching for justice, and, without giving it further thought and burning with anger, had gone to wage war against the dog-faced monsters. Having sharpened his sword and put on his boots, he had left. Yes! To cleave the dog-faces in nine pieces! Having no wife, no children, why shouldn't he have gone? Reinis had volunteered to fight of his own free will, to get back from Siberia, to save from the paws of the dog-faced monsters his sister Lilia and her children Anda and Juris. His family! His dearest and closest people! And all the other people that the dog-faces have rent to pieces. Could Reinis have acted otherwise? No, Laura thinks that Reinis did right.

But the greatest misfortune was that Reinis had not been able to rescue them from the dog-faced monsters, no matter how he fought, no matter how he waged war. He couldn't do it, no matter how hard he tried. Reinis's last resting place it seems is by the Volkhov River. Laura really doesn't know what that Volkhov is and why Reinis has to rest by the Volkhov. But Laura will find out.

Then there's more.

The German dog-faced monster, without asking, had taken over their newly-built house. Mīma had to cook meals for him. Every day the German had shot at crows, just for fun, probably he didn't have anything else to do. He had raised two shot crows

on the flagpole. Mīma was passing by at that time and God
knows what kind of a devil had taken control of her tongue, for
Mīma had asked: "Is there a new flag in the Greater Germany,
Mr. Officer, Sir?" He had wanted to shoot Mīma on the spot
just like he did the crows but who would make meals for him
then? On leaving the German dog-face had burnt down the
new, beautiful house, which Grandpa had just built. A house
like a comb!

"Why a comb?" Laura can't connect a comb with the lovely
house.

"Like a beehive honeycomb, little dummy, yellow wax in a
honey comb, this is where the bees deposit their honey. Houses
like honey, like amber. A house that gleams and shines from
inside. There's no need for the sun. Of pine, the beams eight
meters long." Grandpa gets upset talking about it.

"Laura, leave Grandpa alone!" Mīma can ask as much as she
wants, but Laura has no intention of leaving Grandpa alone.

Mīma says, "Reinis fell."

"Why—fell?"

A Russian dog-faced monster shot and killed Reinis,
Grandpa's beloved son, although Grandpa still doesn't believe
it. Laura doesn't believe it either. Grandpa is waiting for the
day when Reinis, Grandpa's dear son, will be found. When he
no longer will rest by the Volkhov. Laura too thinks that he'll
return, will be found.

Laura sees that Grandpa finds it easier if someone else also
believes. Now in those moments when Grandpa no longer
believes, beside him is Laura who nonetheless still believes. The
pipe was found after all! Laura firmly believes, as firmly as she's
able to, because that helps Grandpa to believe and that unites
them and makes them feel closer.

However, Grandpa doesn't allow anyone to touch the pipe's
bowl, not even Laura, because one needs to have know-how, it's
a very tricky affair. Everything that's in the pipe's bowl mustn't
be scraped out. Some small bit needs to be left. Otherwise very
quickly the pipe can get a hole in it. Grandpa now and then rubs
honey into his chibouk, only afterward putting the tobacco in.

The pipe must be taken care of. Where would he get a new one? Grandpa loathes those rubbish cigarettes, those coffin nails. Laura is allowed to touch only the pipe's stem.

"Just be careful," Grandpa admonishes.

The pipe's stem is made from dark red amber, with a lighter stripe along its middle. Maybe once this stripe was white. Laura is allowed to clean the pipe's stem with a wooden pick. She can manage to do it with Mīma's pick, when there isn't anything better available. The cleaning must be done when the stem is still warm. Laura pokes into the stem carefully, and when the pick is pulled out it's black and sticky. That's the pipe's sweat. The sweat must be wiped off with a little rag and the stem probed again with the pick. Probed more.

"Laura, have you been sucking again on a pig?" Grandpa grinning teases her.

Laura no longer widens her eyes in shock as she did the first time when she heard this stupidity. And that's supposed to be a joke! It means that Laura's mouth is dirty. And so what?

"A spiral would come in handy," Grandpa says and relapses seemingly back into his illness, in which to tease is not proper and to joke is a betrayal.

Since Laura has been at the Upītes farm, Grandpa has come out of himself and then relapsed, occasionally becoming more talkative, but after a while resorting once more to being non-talkative. Now and then he laughs a little, just a bit. And then once more lapses into moroseness.

"What's a spiral?"

"A tiny brush, but the spiral is lost. Lost." Grandpa is sad about the spiral. Grandpa paces back and forth around the room as if he were caged, himself not realizing that he's moving, so great is his sadness about the spiral.

It's not true that smoking isn't healthy! When grandpa smokes, his shaking hands become calmer. His hands, holding the pipe, don't tremble as madly. The pipe is the one that keeps Grandpa's hands calm. All of Grandpa's thoughts are in the pipe smoke. He smokes the tobacco that Reinis has purchased and brought. The smoke rises like thoughts. It can be clearly seen that the thoughts are floating about the room. Only light thoughts come from the pipe. The heavy thoughts, drawn through the pipe, grow lighter, otherwise they couldn't float about like that. All those phantoms and nightmares that torment Grandpa to death at night, these wouldn't float about like dandelion fluff in the air, like goose down. These wouldn't float like small, white clouds. Maybe that black, sticky thing that Laura is scraping out, this isn't the pipe's sweat but Grandpa's heavy thoughts that the pipe keeps within itself? So black and sticky.

"Do it honestly, slowly, leave it, it'll be fine. Oh, oh, girl, you've really mucked yourself up like a chimney sweep. What will Mīma say?"

Both already know what Mīma will say. That a girl has no business fooling around with pipes! Does Grandpa also want to teach Laura to smoke? Ruin the child altogether? Mīma will scold both of them.

"Grandpa!"

"Well?"

"Let's go outside!"

"I don't want to go anywhere."

"Let's pull back the curtains! It's dark here. It's sunny outside!"

"No, no, my eyes."

"Let's open the window! So the fragrance of lilacs can come in. Mīma says that you can hang an axe in the air. How is that? In which place could the axe hang? Grandpa did you wash yourself this morning?"

"That's enough. I want to read the newspaper. Go play outside."

Read the newspaper! Grandpa just pretends to read. In reality he just looks at one point or—more likely—at one letter. Grandpa thinks that Laura can't see how old and bedraggled the newspaper is. Grandpa thinks he's hidden himself. Crawled into the bushes, fled into a bunker. Behind the newspaper no one will find him. Grandpa thinks that behind the newspaper he's safe. Laura can't understand who here really is the child, Grandpa or Laura.

"Grandpa?"

"Well?"

"Let's go outside!"

"I don't want to go anywhere."

"Let's pull back the curtains! It's dark here. It's sunny outside!"

Laura rattles off the same words again. How long can Grandpa bear this? One day Grandpa agrees.

The two of them sit on the sunny side of the house on a long bench. Ripsis is delirious with joy. Grandpa outside! In the sun!

The little dog tears along like the wind—from Grandpa to the oak tree!

From the oak tree to Grandpa!

From Grandpa to the well!

From the well to Grandpa!

From Grandpa to the woodshed!

From the woodshed to Grandpa!

And only to Grandpa. Once only Ripsis runs to Laura and licks her hand. Thanks for bringing Grandpa outside! Laura joins Ripsis—from Grandpa to the oak, from the oak to Grandpa, from Grandpa to the well, from the well to Grandpa, from Grandpa to the woodshed, from the woodshed to Grandpa.

Grandpa squints in the sun and shakes his head.

A dog's joy, a dog's joy, he every once in a while repeats. A dog's joy. Probably it's something given to everyone along with life, not only to dogs but also to humans. That probably is not just a bonus, not only a bonus. A human being should live with that inherent joy, one should.

Look now at the two of them—the girl and the dog.

Grandpa looks. No, joy is but a matchstick that burns down fast, just a matchstick. Grandpa wants to go back to his room!

"Grandpa, sit for a bit yet!"

The girl and the dog are both out of breath. Laura is all sweaty. Ripsis, who had collapsed without strength as if dead, has managed a couple more runs up to Laura's lap. Joy drips from Ripsis's lolling tongue. Joy turns like a carousel in Laura's eyes.

Fine, Grandpa will sit for a bit yet. Just a bit.

The Black Door

LAURA PERSISTS. The door to the attic's cubbyhole is open! Laura has managed it!

Her eyes slowly get used to the dark within. It's not so dark after all. Behind the door no horrendous or deep pit appears, no black hole as Laura had imagined. One that could lead to below, to God knows where, for example to hell itself. Hell is not there. Hell is below, but here, to get into the cubbyhole she must crawl upward.

The big hump that like an enormous black dog lies in front of the entrance is at Laura's shoulder height. No, it isn't a black dog with eyes the size of saucers! More likely the big pile is reminiscent of Aunt Maria's goat shed. That time when Aunt Maria's goat had fallen down from the manure pile and hung itself by its tether. Because the tether was short but the manure pile high, and Kolya, That Monkey, was too lazy to muck out the manure. Laura doesn't want to tumble down like Aunt Maria's goat. But she has to get up on top. Yuck! Phooey! Gross! But after all it's not dung. The big pile is made up of soil, sand, straw, and sawdust, and all sorts of rubbish. Laura leans her whole body on the hump and climbs. Her hands quickly become slimy and shiny. Yuck!

Her feet slip and slide. Laura holds on with the toes of her sandals, her chin, and her elbows. She's at the top! Suddenly she feels very hungry. Her mouth waters. There's a dizzying fragrance of smoked ham! And of a hunk of streaky bacon with cracklings! And of bread smeared with pork fat drippings! And with the tasty bits left after rendering fat!

Laura gazes upward. From black soot-covered poles hang enormous hooks. But they're empty. Probably there really was a smoking chamber here some time ago. This time the grown-ups have told the truth, really something to marvel about.

Laura sniffs her palms, licks them with her tongue. They smell of smoke and taste of salt. Laura's tummy contracts and croaks like a frog from hunger. Squirrels dance in Laura's stomach. The fragrance elicits dreams of a smoked sausage. Laura has eaten one only once in her life. How had such a sausage turned up at the Upītes farm, Laura doesn't know. Maybe from Riga. When Laura grows up, Laura will work in the Riga sausage factory and will eat sausages as much as she wants, that's what she had decided that one time.

Laura again yearns to work in a sausage factory. There's still time to decide, because Laura also wants to be an archaeologist. She falls down on her knees and with a stick, which as luck would have it has appeared from somewhere, pokes at the hump. She lies down on her tummy and digs. Digs and digs until she feels the joy of discovery. That arrives slowly. Excitement, joy, elation, jubilation. In that sequence. While continuing to dig. Now she can stop.

Drippings! Those are drippings of fat!

Soil, sand, sawdust, straw, dust, all sorts of rubbish which is held together firmly by the drippings. That's a hill of fat! That Laura has discovered! Almost like a miner discovering gold. For a thousand, maybe for as much as a hundred years people have smoked meat here. They've hung it on the big iron hooks. Since ancient times!

The meat has been smoked and the fat has dripped. The meat has continued to be smoked with the fat dripping. And for a hundred, maybe a thousand years, the meat has been smoked with the fat just dripping! Now there's a hill of drippings! A hill of fat! Laura has discovered it! No one else knows of it. Just Laura.

How sad that in Siberia there wasn't a hill of fat like this, how very sad that Laura hadn't discovered one like it in Siberia. Grandpa Jūlijs then wouldn't have died, nor would little Juris. For a while her sadness struggles with great joy. The great joy soon wins out. Mīma will no longer have to be afraid of starvation! That's what's most important. No one will have to die of starvation!

That rubbish and sawdust is really of no importance. And a bit of straw—that's really a small thing! Laura will try to figure out how to clean up the drippings. That could be done both before and after melting it down. Laura will try both ways. Laura will save Mīma and Grandpa, Mama and Papa! If a famine happens, Laura will save everyone. Laura will also save Aunt Maria. Even Kolya, That Monkey, who is a good person. If Mīma says so, then he's a very, very good person. And Aunt Maria is crazy about him. That monkey business Mīma thinks is only pretense because always when Aunt Maria talks like that, she's got honey in her eyes.

When Laura grows up she'll be an archaeologist. One who works part-time also at a sausage factory. Or else she'll be an opera singer, Laura still can't decide.

Snails

"Come, child, let's go gather snails." Mīma picks up an old milk pail, hands a dented metal bowl to Laura, and both wade into the garden's long grass.

They've already picked cherries, currants, and plums. Apples not yet, because they're not ready. Also the pears are to be picked later. All these new words Laura has learned. Now Laura knows almost everything that grows in the garden. But not yet the snails.

"Where do snails grow?"

"Look under your feet. There by the ditch you'll find the most."

Under Laura's sandals something cracks. Under Mīma too, something cracks.

"They've multiplied as if for the end of the world."

Mīma picks up a gray lump from the ground.

Stuck to it are some sort of slivers. Mīma throws the lump into her pail. She picks up another. That's a little stone, so pretty all wound up, look, it rattles on being thrown into the pail! Mīma now squats with knees bent. She picks up the little stones. Laura looks into Mīma's pail. The stones are moving!

"Mīma, what is that?" Laura is afraid, what if it's some kind of magic. "Stones that come to life?"

"Snails. Child, have you not seen a snail before?" Mīma realizes that probably the child has in fact never seen a snail.

Mīma doesn't know if she should laugh or cry. That child is seemingly from a different world. And so she is, she certainly is.

She mustn't forget that.

Dog-faces, dog-face monsters, they're the ones responsible for this!

It's only luck, only luck that the child is still alive!

Her thoughts have acquired sound.

"Mīma! Are you talking to me? No? To whom then?" Laura

asks and wonders, but Mīma waves her off. That gesture Laura knows. She senses its meaning. Grandpa reads a paper. Mīma waves her off. There's something in common in these two actions.

"Those are snails. They're not good. They devour the whole world, flowers, leaves, cabbage, lettuce. We'll gather them all and give them to the hens.

"What will the hens do with the snails?"

"The hens will eat them. For hens snails are a great delicacy. The hens then will lay more eggs for us." Mīma senses that Laura is upset.

"Why are they moving?"

"Well, they move because they're alive."

"Snails are alive?" Laura understands that she's stepped on a snail. A live snail!

"Now look there's one of their empty shells! Look! That's the snail's little house. It lives inside there. When it wants to hide, it draws itself inside, look, like these. But when it wants, it crawls out."

"Has this one crawled out?"

"No, that one's finished.

"How is that—finished?"

"Dead."

"Why?"

"God only knows! Keep collecting, little chatterbox, the hens want to eat!"

"Maybe that snail has just gone for a walk and will come back?"

"No, no, child, a snail can't live without his house. If you pull him out of his house, then he dies. Dead is dead. A snail is one lucky creature."

"Why lucky?"

"If only a human being could do this—carry their house along with them everywhere," Mīma sighs.

"But if a human being is pulled out of his house?" From Laura's question Mīma's lips start to tremble.

Mīma waves her off. Grandpa is reading his newspaper in his room.

Laura doesn't know if she'd like to be a lucky creature. No, Laura doesn't want to be instantly dead the minute she leaves the house. What if Grandpa doesn't want to go out of the house exactly because of this, because he's afraid of being dead?

No, Laura wouldn't like to lug her house everywhere with her.

"Do snails bite?"

"No, no, what would they bite with, having no teeth. A snail has horns. You have to say this: 'Snail, snail, show me your horns.' Look, immediately the horns are out! Don't be afraid! The snail has soft, tiny horns, see. With them he can't gore anyone. Fine, girl, with your mouth the work won't get done. We have to gather a pail full. The hens are waiting. Oh, my God, the place is full of them! Like this we'll kill two birds with one stone."

"How's that?"

"We'll save both the flowers and the lettuce as well as give the hens a treat. Look, this one was very chubby!" Mīma lifts another empty house. Laura takes it.

Its house is broken, but the snail is alive! It's moving. But it doesn't look at all like a lucky creature, not at all.

What does it look like? Like what? *Leposhka*! Laura remembers the word, which she thought she had long ago forgotten. *Leposhka* was flat bread made of grain husks, which was fried on top of the woodstove in Siberia. The snail looks like a gray *leposhka*, yes!

Laura examines Mīma's picked-up empty house. It's totally fine, better than the old one, still bigger. Laura knows what she must do! She needs to save the stepped-on snail. Laura will fix up that snail in a new house! She'll put in some moss, a feather or two so the snail can feel how good the new house is, so he doesn't feel sad about his old house. Everything will be fine, dear little snail.

Plaster

WHERE CAN MĪMA GET some plaster? Rats have infested the Upītes farm. While Grandpa does put out traps, they're useless. One and a half rats caught during the whole week. But there's a whole black cloud of rats, they're swarming and teeming all over the place, such a multitude has never before been experienced in life.

No wonder because a huge amount of *kombikorm*—a mish-mash of fodder—was brought into the barn and just left there in an open pile to be eaten by whomever wishes. Be they pigeons, or sparrows, or rats. Let them devour that kolkhoz's "delicacy," Mīma doesn't care. But for those damn rats, see, this doesn't suffice, they're invading the house! Nothing can be left in the pantry anymore.

And what kind of a pantry is it if nothing can be stored there nor added? The sack of flour has been gnawed into, the smoked meat contaminated, but in the grain bin there's been like a major feast! If they only ate, but rats do their thing. Mīma is so revolted by the rats, they bring on such nausea, that it can't even be expressed in words!

"Do their thing? What kind of thing do the rats do?"

"Do! Do—shit!"

"What kind of shit?" Laura wants to know.

"Rat shit! Rats pollute everything. Pigs!" Mīma is very angry. "We can't get any poison! There are two tomcats at home but will they catch rats, they sleep like hibernating bears."

Grandpa thinks that one rat should be caught live, soaked in *solyarka*—gasoline and set on fire. Then let go. It would flee to the other rats but the others would run away from it and all would be gone, just like that.

"So why just stand there, go catch one! Some catcher you are! Can't even tie your own boots! It's a good thing that you have the child to tie them for you! No! It's simpler with plaster! We must get some plaster, whatever the cost! Where to get this plaster?" Mīma rails.

When Laura is playing with the railway station's children on the train platform, Railway Annie comes out. She's the person on duty. If she comes out with flags and a megaphone, if she puts on a red hat, then everyone knows a train is coming.

Now Annie comes out just like that, to get some fresh air. It would have been better if she had stayed inside, because the station children instantly vanish, roll away like peas to all sides. Laura isn't convinced that she can continue what she's begun—to peel the colored paint off the station's dilapidated walls.

"How is the Upītes's mother doing?" Railway Annie, breathing in fresh air, asks Laura.

It sounds strange—Upītes's mother, but that's what other people call Mīma.

"Badly. Very badly," Laura replies and feels happy about how nicely the words—very badly—sound together, "very badly."

"Very badly, very badly, very badly!" Laura happily chants. To Railway Annie it doesn't seem like anything fine.

"Oh, heavens! What's the matter then? What ails her? Her heart?"

"No, plaster. Upītes's mother can't get plaster anywhere."

"What's Upītes's mother going to do with plaster?"

How should Laura know what Mīma will do with the plaster, because Laura doesn't even know what plaster is.

"Grandpa can't catch the rats. Poison can't be got. The tomcats are sleeping like bears in winter. Mīma desperately needs plaster. Otherwise the rats will eat all the eyes out of our faces and the hair from our heads."

Railway Annie has a compassionate heart. She looks around warily and draws Laura close to her.

"Tell Upītes's mother to come and see me. I have plaster. I'll give her some. Wait, hold on! Let's do it differently. Let her not come, I'll bring it to her myself. That'll be better. Upītes's mother need not come. And don't say anything to anyone!"

From Annie's voice it can clearly be understood that the plaster is something secret and threatening. Something dangerous and dreadful. Of course Laura won't tell anyone about the plaster. Laura herself is afraid of the plaster.

First Aid

"ANDA! ANDA! JĀNI!" Mīma yells from a distance, waving her arms.

Mama, hoeing the dill bed, sees her. Mīma has stopped, lacking strength because she's run all the way from the Upītes farm.

"Call an ambulance!" Mīma yells.

Mama throws down her hoe and runs toward Mīma, who is pressing her hand to her heart, her kerchief slipped down, gray hair disheveled.

"Call for an ambulance!"

"Is Grandpa bad?" Mama props up old, dear Mīma, who is on the point of collapsing, she herself looks as if she needs first aid.

"Laura!" Mīma gasps for breath and for a long while can't catch it.

"Laura?" Mama's heart leaps into her throat and freezes there.

"Laura's eaten plaster!"

"What plaster?" Mama doesn't understand anything.

"Call an ambulance! There's a telephone at the railway station! Otherwise the child will die!"

Mīma collapses like dead weight right there at the edge of the ditch.

"Johnny, Johnny! Where are you?" Mama at a run yells.

Papa appears at the door of the house.

"To the station! First aid! Laura's eaten plaster!"

"What are you raving about? What plaster?" Papa doesn't understand a thing.

Both race to the station. Where the only telephone in the neighborhood is located.

Railway Annie is sitting in her place behind a small window behind the door and is talking into a telephone receiver.

"Track two, third shunt. Collector. How long will it stand?

Fine. Information received," Railway Annie doesn't hurry, she can't interrupt her official duty conversation just because two people in front of her window are frantically waving their arms and yelling,

"Annie, please, call the ambulance! Please, please, quickly!"

Fine, fine but Anna first needs to know something before she phones. What's happened? What should she say to the first aid people?

"Laura has eaten plaster!" Mama yells, as if Annie were somewhere far away.

"Plaster?" Anna grows pale.

Papa can't stand it anymore that Annie's so slow to get it and not phoning. Why is she just goggling, biting her lip, and not saying a word? Papa himself would have phoned a hundred times over if he only knew what the number was in Latvia.

Annie places her hand firmly on the phone and moves it further away from the window. So no one can reach it. Annie can't call anywhere. No one can call anywhere. The line must not be engaged. That's categorically forbidden. She's waiting for instructions regarding the incoming train. In fact, they're orders. The railway is like an army. Annie must follow regulations. Very like in the military.

"Stop screwing with my brain! Call! Right now!"

"Annie, do you understand what we're saying? Our child has eaten plaster, she can die! Annie!" Mama pleads.

Papa wants to break down the door behind which Annie sits as if turned to stone, because the door is locked, those are the rules. Documents, money, state secrets after all. Annie won't open it. The railway station's duty officer's door must be locked. Annie slams the window shut and latches it from inside. Annie is sympathetic, but there's nothing she can do. She can't phone.

Papa slams against the window with all his strength, and the latch flies away in the air. Papa shoves his head through the window as far as it will reach.

"Phone, you *machka*—bitch!" He yells in a voice that now is unrecognizable. Annie has to phone or else Papa will strangle her.

At the Upītes farm Laura in the meantime doesn't understand

what she has done that is so horrendous. Where has Mīma taken off to, has she really gone to Mama and Papa to complain about Laura? About what? Is it about the fact that Laura has built a stove from four bricks behind the lilac bush, taken some matches, and lit it? Laura just wanted to cook up some rhubarb compote and that too in fun, because those weren't rhubarbs but thistle leaf stalks.

Laura hadn't thought of the smoke this would create.

Or is it about Laura's attempt again to tell fortunes with cards? This time for the station aunties and where Laura had forecast for Senta a bad end in a warm place. But for Zelma's sister Ruta—a long journey to the East. Laura just pretended to be Madalina, it's true, however, that she invented a few things so it wouldn't be boring. Or about the fact that . . .

Why are Grandpa's hands trembling so badly that he has trouble pouring out some drops of heart medicine on a sugar cube? Grandpa does pour these drops every day, but not always do his hands tremble so and Laura doesn't have to lie in bed like this every time.

Nothing hurts in Laura, how many times does she have to say so? What does everyone want from her? Why does Laura have to obediently lie in bed in broad daylight?

"Laura is thirsty!"

"You're not allowed to drink! And don't talk back!" Grandpa seemingly frightened is shuffling around the room, from one corner to the next.

Laura is truly thirsty, and who is she talking back to? Right now no one. "Laura's thirsty!"

"You're not allowed to drink right now!" Grandpa says.

What kind of thing is that, she's not allowed to have a drink anymore? Children shouldn't be punished like that! It can be done many ways—be scolded, told off, or be angry and not be talked to, be locked in the shed, even spanked, if something altogether crazy was done. All these punishments Laura in a way can accept, because they're just, but not to be given something to drink?

To keep a child thirsting? Until she dies of thirst? That's

tormenting a child! Pure torture!

Mīma has run off to complain about Laura! No, Laura herself will complain to Mama and Papa. How can one do that? And for what? For having eaten one bowl of flour? Mīma has a whole sack full of flour. Laura has just eaten one bowl full, a small bowl at that! If there hadn't been cream and sugar sprinkled on top, she wouldn't have even touched it.

Why such a fuss? Why was she asked in a nasty voice: "Did you eat it all?" Yes, Laura did eat it all, it was a lovely bowlful. Why did Mīma's eyes bulge and she immediately had to run somewhere?

"Grandpa, I won't do that anymore," Laura tries to make up.

"Laura, that's not what this is about."

"About what then?" Suddenly Laura breaks out in a sweat. Heat like a lightning bolt races through her. Have they really found out about Fredis's house? That Laura has been there? How she had prowled through it, knowing that Fredis wasn't home? A pigsty not a house! That she had seen a silver cup? That on it was written 'For Corporal Upītis, First Place." That's not Fredis's but Reinis's cup and Laura had wanted to take it, but hadn't taken it, because who doesn't know that you shouldn't take things that belong to others? But the cup is not a thing that belongs to someone else! She won't be such a wimp again, the next time she'll take it! If they found out about this, then there's no hope for Laura. Then Laura will have to suffer thirst until she dies.

"Does your tummy not hurt? First Aid will come soon," Grandpa strokes Laura's head, truly as if she was on her death bed.

"Who'll come?'

"First Aid. All will be fine."

"What is that?"

Grandpa doesn't have the time to answer, because suddenly the house is full. A *bobik* jeep or another American car adaptation—the one they call *vilitis*—Laura can't tell the difference, with a red cross in its window and Mīma, Mama, and Papa step out. Papa and who else—probably that's First Aid, who else can it be.

First Aid is an auntie in a white smock.

All of them rush to Laura. No, no, Laura can't get up! First

Aid makes her show her tongue, presses her stomach, Laura is ticklish. No, nothing hurts. No, she doesn't feel sick to her stomach. First Aid makes her look where she moves her hand. Laura looks up, down to the sides, as she's told. Where First Aid points, there Laura looks. Where she shows, there Laura looks. Laura wants to laugh.

"How old is the child?"

"Laura's five," she's not the one to be asked but she replies. Laura can speak for herself.

"Does the child attend kindergarten?"

"Laura doesn't go to kindergarten," she replies, clear as day.

"Why doesn't the child use first person singular pronouns?"

What doesn't Laura use? What pronoun? Which person? What is she doing again that she shouldn't be? This time she'll let someone else answer. Mama assumes the task.

She was taught in Russian at the nursery school in Siberia, and just very recently she's now in Latvia, and somehow she's got into the habit of saying it like this in Latvian—Mama says something like this.

"For all intents and purposes this child is healthy," First Aid pronounces.

"For all intents and purposes? How is that—for all intents and purposes?" Mama asks the question that is burning on everyone's tongue.

"There's nothing wrong with the child. It's odd, if it's like you told me," First Aid adds with suspicion.

"Where is that substance? Show it to me! For safety's sake I'll take it to the laboratory."

Good heavens, Laura has eaten it all, Mīma explains, no more is left of it, there's nothing to show. What a disaster, what a shame."

"Where did you buy it?" First Aid wants to know.

Mīma hasn't bought any of it, Railway Annie had given it to her for nothing, from the goodness of her heart, so what kind of a purchase could it be. They have to go and see Railway Annie. Laura has to come along, in order to have some tests done. What? Laura won't go anywhere! What do they want to do to her? Mama and Papa will come with her, so Laura need not be afraid. Easy to say!

"The child is thirsty. Can she drink now?" Grandpa asks.

"No way!" First Aid says sternly.

"Laura's thirsty," Laura whispers weakly.

"Until we clarify what the girl has really eaten, she's not allowed to have a drink!" First Aid sticks to her guns.

Railway Annie is sitting in her place behind the small window, from which the latch has been torn off. She has to show what she has given to comrade Upīte and what has led to the calling out of First Aid.

"Plaster," Railway Annie is shattered.

Railway Annie can't leave her post. Else she'll be fired from her job.

"Comrade Anna, you seem unaware of the seriousness of the situation, it's your obligation as a citizen. Show what you've given to Comrade Upīte and which due to parental negligence and irresponsibility the girl has eaten," First Aid urges, but Annie becomes even more agitated.

"I can't," Anna refuses to show the stuff.

"Annie, dear," Mama pleads.

"Listen, here!" Papa is indignant. "Are you going to show it willingly or else I'll phone the militia! What kind of poison are you peddling here, you speculator?" he threatens.

Annie takes a key from its peg, unlocks the door and, walking hesitantly, comes out into the narrow station's corridor. She unlocks the door with the sign "Red Corner." The keys are as heavy as chains. They drag Annie down. Annie stops.

"I'll rot in Siberia! I can't!" Annie falls to her knees on the threshold. Maybe because in front of her is Lenin's portrait? The red corner isn't at all like Laura had imagined it to be for a moment—a tiny corner, a lovely nook decorated with red rubies and radiating a red light like the star of Kremlin or like a semaphore, or like the Upītes farm verandah's single tiny red window when the sun shines into it. No, it's an ordinary room. The table is covered with a green tablecloth and in the corner stands a round, silvery wood-burning stove. Ah yes, on the table are newspapers—*Battle*, *Pravda*, and *Communism Morning*. They're not only bound, but also tied up with a string. Why should newspapers be tied up? The only thing red that's there are the many red triangular pennants hung on the walls.

"I'm to rot in Siberia! But I just wanted to do good!" Railway Annie repeats and doesn't stand up.

Everyone is uncomfortably silent. Railway Annie seems to have lost her mind. Gone mad as a hatter. Maybe she from the very start hadn't been quite right.

Annie gets up heavily. Behind the round stove there's a largish corner. Maybe that's where the red corner is? She draws back a curtain. On an old, dirt-encrusted table stands an enormous, yellowed bust. Around it scattered are some shards and a small hammer.

"Comrade Stalin! Josif Vissarionovich?" First Aid is stupefied.

There's no air in the room, it hasn't been aired for a long time. Clouds have covered the sun, suddenly turning everything completely dark. The long-unfired stove emits a smell of damp ashes and dust. Fear scampers among all present like rats. Fear and revulsion.

"Here it is, that plaster," Annie says, she has nothing to lose anymore.

She sees herself in Siberia, in its famine and its freezing cold, but she had only wanted to do good.

"Laura has eaten Stalin's bust? Ha, ha, ha! I would also like to eat it, Annie, can you give me some too? I would like to devour all of that vermin!" Papa laughs like mad.

It's too much for Laura.

Mīma and Grandpa are angry about the eaten flour.

First Aid wants to take Laura with her and do something or other to her.

Mama is wringing her hands.

Annie, it appears, will die in a minute.

Now Papa has become totally crazy. Laura has eaten something very bad, some sort of bust, but Papa is happy about it? Papa laughs but Laura is crying. Everyone around her is crazy.

"Laura is thirsty!" She yells but the madmen don't hear her. She wants to have a drink like never before in her life, to drink,

drink, to drink some water. Be it from a puddle.

And Papa just laughs and talks. This plaster, this so-called plaster, can be eaten until you're stuffed, it hasn't been plaster for ages, not plaster, oh, you women, you don't understand anything about chemistry, *yeibogu*—I swear to God, nothing. That plaster has become slaked, well, slaked, that's what the process is called, it's harmless, Annie, you can calm down now, your punishment has been canceled, better give the girl something to drink, thank God, everything is fine, that bust should be smashed to bits, I'll smash it, this dog-face, *yomayo*—fuck! What kind of an excuse for a hammer is that? Do you, Annie, not have a proper hammer, you don't? The soil is acid, with that damn bust you can lime the soil, why is it even standing here still ..."

Papa just rambles on and on, and slowly everyone unfreezes as if woken from the sleep of death, like conjured back from being stone, the sun again shines directly through the window.

"As a member of the party I'll have to report this incident," First Aid once more darkens the sky.

Papa is angry, Papa raves.

"Report what? Report where? Report to whom? Comrade Doctor! Why report? Has the party and the regime not sharply condemned the Stalin personality cult? Have you, comrade doctor, not heard that the party orders all upright citizens to free themselves ..."

Mama grabs Papa's hand but Papa is not to be restrained.

" ... to be freed from the attributes of the cult of Stalinism? From its manifestations? What are you going to report then? That Annie has done what the party demands and the regime orders? Better propose Annie for an award. Annie, calm down, you'll get a medal. But maybe you, Comrade Madam Doctor, you're against this? Maybe you don't even agree with the party's new policy?" Papa is firm with First Aid. Maybe even too much.

"How dare you, you who are from Siberia? Don't forget who you are! Stop your demagogy!"

"For you it's demagogy? The party's new line? Please answer, so we understand!"

Of course First Aid agrees with the party line! She only can't understand what right Papa, someone from Siberia, has to speak to her, First Aid, like this! She's speechless! Papa however has speech galore.

"Enough! Better give the girl something to drink," First Aid, seemingly mollified, pronounces and heads for the car.

"Thanks, Doctor! Thanks! Don't take this amiss!" Mama calls after her.

"Laura's thirsty!"

"Laura will drink pear lemonade as much as she wants! But Annie will drink some champagne!" Papa is ready to run to the store, which is nearby.

"Come now! I'm at work after all!" The mountain has dropped off Annie's shoulders.

A stone has rolled off Annie's heart. She's behaved like some sort of country bumpkin. Annie laughs shyly.

But now the telephone rings.

Annie will drink the champagne another time.

Laura doesn't have to work, she'll drink the pear lemonade right now.

Frogs

LAURA REALLY DOESN'T understand how anyone can be afraid of frogs. They have neither teeth nor stingers, neither fangs nor horns. But Rita flees from frogs yelling and shrieking. Also Rita is much bigger and older than Laura, she'll be attending second grade already. Frogs seemingly are slimy and revolting and, according to Rita, jump on her on purpose. In particular bull frogs. Whatever Laura tries to tell her friend doesn't help.

That frogs are beautiful.

"Phooey!" shrieks Rita.

That frogs are useful. They help scientists.

"Phooey! Don't talk rot!" Rita yells.

That frogs have a monument mounted to them in America!

"Phooey! Double phooey! What? What is that—mounted?"

"Like mounting a horse," Laura explains.

"How do you even know what's in America?" Rita becomes suspicious.

"My Papa knows," Laura responds.

"And how does he know?" Rita questions.

"Knows and that's all!"

"Your Papa knows nothing! Men generally don't know anything! All men are stupid! Only Lenin can have a monument! So he doesn't shit balls!" Rita is convinced.

"Lenin?" Laura only asks because she wants to hide her surprise about the word with the balls.

"Lenin has a monument in the town of Tukums and in Riga!"

"For Lenin—in Tukums and Riga, but for frogs—in America!" Laura doesn't like it that Rita doubts her Papa's knowledge.

"Frogs are necessary! They eat the bad bugs. Frogs are useful! In a pond, in a garden and in general!" Laura praises and defends the green hoppers. "They can even be eaten! If you don't have anything else, then you can eat frogs." This is the last good thing that Laura will proclaim about the frogs to Rita. She won't say anything else, that's enough. Papa has told her this and that more about frogs, but Laura doesn't want to get her Papa involved in this spat. As it is he has enough troubles.

"Eat? Phooey! Phooey! Phooey!"

Rita makes a big hullabaloo, trying to rub off with her hands the frogs from her thighs and her shoulders, while twitching her legs, as if she were covered from top to bottom with frogs. As if frogs were some kind of leeches that had attached themselves to Rita and were sucking out her blood.

No, Rita can't come along if Laura wants to play at the pond with the frogs.

Laura plays on her own.

She lies down on the warm gray plank-way, in order to be comfortable. It's possible that she'll have to lie there motionless for a long time. The water lily leaves need to be within reach.

While Laura settles herself in, the frogs who have been sunning themselves on the wide leaves, for safety's sake, jump into the water, but don't go very far. The frogs wait to see what will happen. Green tiny heads peek out from the water like mini-islets. Each islet has two observant eyes.

Now she has to lie there quietly and calmly until the frogs understand that Laura doesn't pose any danger, that Laura is the same as the gray plank-way, the same as the big rock at the edge of the pond, the same as the red-branched pussy willow bush, which, leaning over the rock, cools with its shadow.

The rock is very old, most definitely a hundred years old. It's not boring to lie here at all, although it seems so to Rita. The sweet flags, water lilies, blue and white forget-me-nots that grow profusely at the edge of the pond, the water mint and coltsfoot waft their perfume in the air.

The water exudes a light whiff of sludge. It's full of life, one just has to look. Snails, beetles, pond skaters, caterpillars—the pond is teeming. A dragonfly lands on Laura's shoulder. A shiver of wings, while it rubs its legs. Laura is being tickled, but she doesn't move. She can't trick the dragonfly. It already believes that Laura is the same as the gray plank-way, the same as the big rock, the same as the red-branched pussy willow bush, which, leaning over the rock, cools with its shadow.

Laura blows on the dragonfly, wants to blow it off, but the dragonfly thinks it's just a wisp of a wind. If the dragonfly wasn't on her shoulder, all would go as planned. You could take off, Laura thinks. The dragonfly, guessing what Laura is thinking, moves to a bulrush.

The frogs have understood that Laura is the same as the gray plank-way, the same as the big rock, the same as the red-branched pussy willow bush, and they return to their best-loved spots. On each of the widest water lily leaves once more sits a bright green frog. They stare like roebucks. When wet, they look as if they've been varnished. Laura senses the delight of the frogs. She feels the sun on her skin and a springy water lily leaf under her.

Laura could be transformed into a frog if she wanted to, simply it's not her intention this time. Laura chooses the nearest and the loveliest of the frogs. She looks directly at the frog. The frog raises itself on her front legs, and her white tummy with black dots is now visible. But it's a move of alarm, the frog senses something. She's suspicious.

"Dear little frog don't flee, please, don't flee! Don't be afraid! I won't do anything bad to you!" Laura with all the power of her thought attempts to instill in the frog calm and a feeling of security.

The frog does calm down and Laura's heart is jubilant—she understood, she did understand!

"Dear little frog, I'll pick you up now, alright? Don't be afraid, I just want to caress you. And to look you over properly! Is that alright?"

Laura patiently directs all her good feelings toward the creature.

She still hasn't moved an inch.

Laura wants to amend all of humanity's bad deeds against frogs, to prove that people can be the very best of friends to frogs. At the same time Laura wants to find out where frogs have the place through which they pee and poo. And she also wants to test if frogs eat boiled potatoes.

Laura shoots her arm forward! As swiftly as an arrow!

She's got it! Laura grasps in her palm the cool soft tiny body, which feels like it's made of rubber, and senses opposition. Laura expected this, she doesn't think that the frog would come to her like a lamb. Laura closes her fist tightly, as much as she can, the frog smells of cleanliness. It twitches and kicks, and looks for an exit between Laura's fingers.

Laura is saddened that the frog is fighting her. Was it not almost agreed? Where does the frog get such strength? It'll escape in a minute! Laura squeezes her in her fist out of anger.

"Stupid goose! Did I not say that I wouldn't do anything bad?" Laura now can talk in a loud voice.

All the other frogs have now jumped back into the water. Even their heads no longer show above water. The frog in Laura's palm has calmed down. She's come to her senses. Laura slowly and carefully opens her palm. The frog has stretched out oddly. How long it is! It doesn't move. Laura dunks and rinses the green frog in the water. Maybe she'll come to. The frog doesn't move. Laura shakes the frog by its hind legs.

"Well, what's happened to you? What's the matter?"

The frog has something in its mouth. A worm! The frog has choked on a worm! Laura will pull the worm out. Laura will save the little frog! Laura pulls the worm more forcefully, until it tears in two.

That's not a worm! Those are the frog's innards! Intestines or something like it! The frog is finished! What has Laura done? No, what has the frog done? It's died! She has rejected Laura's good heart! No, Laura has done something dreadful! The little frog trusted Laura! Laura doesn't know, doesn't know, doesn't know what to do, where to begin?

"Phooey!" A yell escapes from Laura when she's taken over by revulsion for the dead creature. "Phooey!" Laura discards the frog in the water.

It doesn't sink, and Laura feels a final hope like a sunbeam breaking through the red branches of the pussy willow. Maybe it will revive?

The frog without moving sways on the water's surface. The white tummy of the frog and the lovely water lily flower are very near to each other. From a distance they can't be even be told apart.

Laura stumbles and gets tangled up in the thick carpet of forget-me-nots, as she flees choking with sobs.

The forget-me-nots have fallen into her hair. Don't forget this soon! Don't forget that you killed a small, loveable, innocent frog, don't forget how you deceived and tricked it! A lovely, useful creature, don't forget this so soon! Don't forget it ever! The forget-me-nots wail after Laura.

The Bewitched Forest

LAURA GLANCES THROUGH the window and doesn't understand what Mīma is doing there in the bewitched forest. She's cut a lapful of flowers, broken off jasmine and oak branches and been in the meadow to gather daisies.

"Mīma, what are you doing?"

Lilies for Buka. Stocks for Grandpa Edmunds. He liked stocks. You can go mad with the fragrance, he used to say. Daisies for little Juris. For Grandpa Jūlijs and for Reinis, Mīma places oak branches. No, Mīma doesn't break them off right there. God protect us! Mīma breaks the oak branches from a totally different oak tree. It's further, at the end of the garden. Its trunk is as fat as one of the tanks, which the train transports along the railway, pulling them in an enormous chain. And every one of its forked branches is fatter than any tree. Ten times fatter. When one gazes upward, one can clearly see that along the more slender of the forked branches, which are the forked branches of forked branches, one could climb up to heaven. When she has a freer moment, Laura will climb up. But up these trees that Mīma, fallen on her knees, is right now caressing as if they were alive, Laura is not allowed to climb. Even though they would be exactly the ones that would suit Laura the best. Why is she not allowed? Well, just not allowed! Why wasn't she told right away that she wasn't permitted to even touch them with one finger? Why isn't this explained to a person right away? Laura had broken off some small branch that Laura needed. Laura had climbed up into one of the biggest of the linden trees. Laura wanted to do this.

Only then did Laura find out that these four oaks and two lindens were no ordinary trees. No, that cluster of trees makes up an enchanted forest. These trees, after the deportation to Siberia,

Mrs. Teacher with the school children had planted. With Mama's class of school children.

One of the lindens is Mama, the other is Buka. Mīma frets that Buka's linden has grown in the fifteen years much denser than Mama's linden. That Mama's linden doesn't grow so well. Mīma doesn't know what that could mean. Maybe it's a sign? What sign?

The oaks are Grandpa Edmunds, Great-Grandpa Jūlijs, Reinis, and little Juris, Mama's brother, who was five years old when the dog-faced monsters deported them. The same age as Laura? Yes. Laura thinks that she wouldn't let them deport her. Laura would get a big club. And, and, and! God knows how, but she wouldn't let them. Laura would rise up in the air, yes, Laura would fly away! But how could she... how could she alone fly away, while the others stayed? Laura would flee, but the others would be deported to Siberia to die there? How would that be? No.

"Mīma, what are you doing?"

"Why are you placing flowers under the trees?" Laura asks again.

"Today is June 14," Mīma replies. She won't say more, Laura senses.

Months and clocks aren't Laura's strong point, but she needn't show that. Laura will ask Grandpa, later, as something among other things.

What's June 14? Laura asks Grandpa, totally among other things. Grandpa hides behind his newspaper. The newspaper trembles like an aspen leaf. Laura has never understood why aspen leaves tremble, but aspen leaves do tremble. In the bewitched forest Mīma wanders among the trees. Her lips silently move. She's saying something. Maybe reciting "Our Father, who art in heaven"? Maybe she's trying to remove the spell from the trees?

Yes, how full and happy the house would be if Mīma was successful at this! As soon as he'd see Reinis Grandpa would immediately come out of his room, he'd laugh and talk. Buka would bake a cake! Mama would like the taste of Buka's cake tremendously. Grandpa Edmunds would carry the little round table into the garden. Grandpa Jūlijs would sit down, he is after all the oldest. Mīma wouldn't have to do anything, she could sit, her hands clasped in her lap. On her white apron, Mīma's hands would lie like baby Jesus in his manger. And Laura would be able to play with little Juris! Juris is five years old after all, the same as Laura. They would play like mad in the garden and at the end each bring five hedgehogs for everyone to see! And Papa! What about Papa? Everyone would ask Papa how his sisters are doing there in the region of Vidzeme, and Papa would say, fine, his sisters are very fine, and that all of them will have to once go to Vidzeme for a visit.

Laura sees a joyful, bustling crowd, she senses and rejoices about how large and happy her family is. But then little Juris has tired of playing and vanishes into the bewitched forest. Almost imperceptibly also the others have vanished among the oaks and the lindens. It doesn't matter, they've simply gone back into the trees and Laura hopes that no one has become lost.

A Lot You Know

PEOPLE TALK SOMEWHAT without making sense. Often the meaning of what is said is different. Even worse when they quote adages or folk sayings. Like never put all your eggs in one basket. Laura has to be careful all the time not to appear like an idiot.

A lot you know, Mīma tells her. Laura almost, almost is ready to believe her that this is praise, but now and then she senses that it's not. A lot you know means—you know nothing!

Laura gives Mīma heartburn with her probing. What kind of probing? Of all that is in this world! Does Mīma have the time to listen to a child's nonsensical trivia, when work and more work is chasing her?

Well, look now—Laura gives her heartburn! How can Laura give heartburn to Mīma if Laura herself doesn't have any? At least not at this moment when Mīma is raking hay, but Laura is playing with some large grasshoppers. And why—give? Doesn't Mīma have enough of her own heartburn that Laura has to give her more? And will Mīma give the heartburn back, when she herself gets enough of her own? That heartburn, which Laura has given, but in fact hasn't given, because Laura can't give what she doesn't have. Just the same as Liepa can no longer lend any money to Papa, because he doesn't have any more.

Grasshoppers. Grass hoppers. They're he-hoppers because they have horns. Grass hoppers because they hop on grass. Just he-hoppers. But where are the she-hoppers? In Siberia Laura at one point had a Doll. Not a doll, no. But a goat called Doll. She had just one horn. The billy goat or he-goat to whom at times the she-goat was led for a visit, he had two horns. The billy goat was very happy to see the she-goat.

In the meadow, Laura can't find any she-grasshoppers. Just he-hoppers with two horns. Never mind, Laura will just make

178

the she-hoppers. Laura pulls off one horn from a grasshopper, and a she-hopper is done and ready! Laura catches more he-grasshoppers and turns them into she-hoppers. Life with such she-hoppers will be much more fun for the he-hoppers. Laura is doing a good deed. It makes her happy to do good deeds. Laura is happy to correct the world's mishaps. Laura can give happiness to Mīma, see, that Laura can give to Mīma, because she has lots of happiness. Much more than the grasshoppers in the meadow, much, much more! One more she-hopper made!

"Laura, you little devil, what are you doing? Why are you torturing the grasshoppers?"

"Laura's not torturing. Laura's making she-grasshoppers."

Mīma doesn't understand. Mīma scolds. Living creatures! How would it be if someone would take you and tear off… Mīma realizes she can't say—a horn. She has to say something in its place. Mīma can't think of anything else.

Mīma smells sweetly of drying grass. She wilts more each day the same as the mown hay, dries up like bent grass. Her white kerchief is wiped full of perspiration. In doing the haying Kolya, That Monkey, has been very careless, thus four teeth of Mīma's good, light-as-down rake have been broken off, and she has to go ask Grandpa to put in new ones. Will Grandpa be wise enough to be able to put new teeth in the rake? What if rain comes—what then? Laura, a big girl, could help, but—no.

Mīma doesn't understand that for Laura it's more important to improve the world than to mow hay. As it is the sheep will just eat that hay!

"Don't ever do that again!" Mīma can't stop scolding. Laura senses the start of her heart burning. Mīma has given that heart burn to Laura! So that's how it happens.

"A lot you know," Laura exclaims.

The Well

Mīma and Grandpa are having an afternoon nap. It's dreadfully hot and muggy. The jasmine bush by the outside wall of the house has absolutely drooped, its leaves totally wilted, some already are crumpled up. Laura doesn't know what to do next. Her choices are many.

She could organize a snail race. She has a perfect place for it. Underneath the lilac tree there's a stone table. In days past it hadn't been just an ordinary bush but rather a bower. Why a bower? Because all around and above there were leaves.

What will the bower be called in the winter when there are no leaves? On the table Laura draws a circle with chalk. Laura usually colors the snails in different colors, so she can tell them apart. She places them in the middle of the circle, waits for a while, and the snails then start to crawl. The first to reach the outer boundary of the circle wins. Today she doesn't want to go and chase down the "racers." Besides she has to poke and thump the snails to convince them to move, oh no, Laura has gotten tired of doing this.

To the hedgehogs she has to go toward evening, that's when they're more likely to come out from the underbrush.

The clay has dried up. It will have to be soaked first to be pliable, so something can be made with it. Owls and monkeys, Mīma suggests.

A gadfly stings her, making Laura think of the horses.

Poor beasties, Laura wonders how they're doing. They're not doing well if the gadflies are biting. Laura will go and chase off the gadflies. She'll go as far as the Pichiņas farm, where the chained-up horses are grazing. Daira is small and old, but Wonder is enormously big and young. The kolkhoz had left the horses with Mīma, let her at her expense feed them those old hacks, as it is no one wants to use them as working horses, because Daira no longer has the strength for it. Wonder would still have the power but he's so big that none of the horse gear fits. Neither a breech band, nor a saddle pad, nor any other horse things. No halters fit, all are too small. Nor do the shafts for a cart or wagon fit—all are too short. That's why he's called Wonder because he's so wondrously big. Laura can go under Wonder's stomach almost without bending. Laura hopes that someday there will appear a person so big in Lamme, well, so big that he'll be just the right size for Wonder. No one like that has yet appeared.

Hopefully Daira won't be given away to make sausages, as Laura has heard the grown-ups say, hopefully they'll bring her back because Daira is Laura's riding horse. Grandpa calls Daira Laura's doggy. Usually Laura leads the horse to the wagon, first she climbs up on the stepping stool, then she makes the horse stand in such a way that she can clamber up on its back. Daira wordlessly stands, exactly as she needs to. Daira understands all. She has a bright mind and a good heart. Daira tries hard and she's very helpful. And now she's being eaten alive by gadflies! Laura has to go and save the horses from those blood suckers and vampires.

Laura crosses the field, now and then glancing back so as not to get lost on her return. It's better if the house remains to be seen. She breaks off a good-sized switch from an alder cluster, one whose leaves are thick, which makes a decent switch. By the time she reaches the horses, she herself has fought off the gadflies as if it were a dragon. Yes, a dragon with many, many heads! Each gadfly—one head! Take that! Take that! But new ones grow again!

The horses! They stand heads lowered. They shake their heads, how does that help? Around their eyes are still tons of gadflies. They're flicking and flicking their tails too, of course, but what good does it do? Just the same their tails can't reach everywhere they're being bitten. For this Laura has her switch! Get off! Off! The gadflies flee, but not all of them. Some are sucking so intensely that they've forgotten the world around them, intoxicated in their greediness, no switch will pull them off from their sweet sucking. Laura throws down the switch and begins to wage war with her bare hands.

The horses, knowing that help is on the way, lower their heads. All those fat hobgoblin flies must be crushed first around the eyes. The horses allow Laura to do this, they're grateful. Happy that Laura has come to help them. Laura squashes one after the other of the fat fiends. Squash, squish—blood dripping drips.

It doesn't even enter Laura's mind to feel sorry for the gad-flies, because it's not the gadfly blood but her dear horses' blood that the loathsome flies have sucked out! But that's not all that's wrong. Laura sees that the horses are dying of thirst, they want to drink. They've walked to the end of their chains as far as they'll go, both are stretching their heads to one and the same side. Laura looks at what the horses are reaching for. Is there water there?

Yes, what smart horses! A half-a-chain's length away is a well. How has a well appeared here in the middle of the field? Ah, yes, these are Pichiņas, their farm. No, no longer, but once it was their farm. The few old apple trees bear witness to that. Oh, no! Could it be maybe, maybe these are the same Pichiņas mentioned by Mrs. Teacher? On which during the war a bomb was dropped? Right on top of the farmhouse with Mrs. Teacher's mama still inside! Laura in fright falls to the ground. If she could, she'd dig down into the soil like a mole, but she can't. What if Mrs. Teacher's mama is still inside? Where— inside? Don't know, somewhere! Oh, oh! Mrs. Teacher's mama touches Laura's neck. Oh! Cold shivers! In such hot weather? But no, it's Daira, who is nuzzling at Laura's neck. If one thinks about it, would Mrs. Teacher's mama want to do something bad to Laura, even if she were here? Daira moves her head back and forth—no, wouldn't want to. Wonder softly neighs—don't b-b-be be afraid! It's good that no one else is here, Laura would feel ashamed of such foolish fear.

The farmhouse is no longer there, but a well remains. But its above-ground construction is almost gone. It used to be made of wood, which has totally rotted away.

As a general rule Laura is afraid of wells. Water sprites live in wells.

Laura is very afraid of the water sprite. The water sprite lives at the bottom of the well waiting for some child to want to even take just one look. The water sprite immediately pulls the child in! In the Upītes well one would be pulled in for sure! But the Upītes well is altogether different. It has a high, above-ground concrete surround, a turnable roller with a heavy chain attached with a pail at its end. The main thing is that the Upītis well is dreadfully deep. The water shines from below, from the dark, very far, far down. Laura once looked to see if it was really so fearful, and then Mīma told her about the water sprite, no, Laura never again would look in that well, never.

But this Pichiņas well maybe isn't even a well. The water isn't deep down, but totally near. The horses could drink easily if only their chains allowed them to do so. But the chains don't permit it. Laura tries to pull out the stakes to which the chains are attached, but she can't budge them. It's clay soil, hard as a rock.

The horses are dying of thirst, but the water is right here. See, even the pail is right here. Laura screws up her courage. The water is so close. That isn't a well for sure. Laura tries to scoop up the water into the pail. Now she can nearly, nearly reach it.

But nearly doesn't count. The horses are waiting. Laura is their only hope. Laura finds a plank of wood that's been tossed right there, and places it crosswise across the mouth of the well. That's altogether a different story! When she steps on the plank, she can reach the water. Laura dips in a hand.

The water is warm, having lain stagnant there. In it float last year's leaves and other rubbish, but that's nothing. Just wait, my horsies, Laura will get some water straight away, right now.

Laura dips the pail into the water and, when it's full, pulls it out. At that moment the plank breaks and the pail, no, the water sprite pulls Laura into the well.

Laura sinks under deeper and deeper. A dark eddy whirls around her eyes. The deeper, the colder, the deeper, the darker. Laura doesn't understand what's happening and Laura understands what's happening. The power of despair makes Laura struggle, she senses that the pail is still in her hands; she lets it go, because someone is pulling the pail with all their strength downward. The water sprite! Laura overcome with fear flails with both her arms and her legs, but she can't understand if it's upward or downward. The churned water becomes lighter. Laura has risen to the surface, but she feels that she'll sink right back right away, because she doesn't know how to swim, no one has the time to teach her how and she's only five years old!

Maybe she should allow herself to sink, maybe Laura will arrive in the underworld like the orphan girl of the fairytale, for whom a grain sheaf fell into a well? There then would be moss-covered old dodderers there, who'll want Laura to thrash them with a birch switch until they're rosy clean in an old fashioned wood-fired sauna. Laura won't thrash them with a bone of a corpse like mother's evil daughter. At the end Mother Fortune will give her... No, no Mother Fortune there, but the water sprite! No, no, Laura can't breathe, Laura's drowning! She doesn't know how but she again has arrived at the water's surface.

"Grab on to the plank!" someone yells, but Laura hears nothing, sees nothing.

She grabs for the well surround, but its inner surface has turned slimy green and slippery, Laura tries to grab on to a different spot, but there the surround disintegrates under her fingers like a piece of rotted wood or ashes. The water sprite pulls Laura back into the well. Suddenly she sees right by her nose the plank.

"Hang on to the board! Hold on to the board!" Now Laura hears and grabs the plank tightly, ever so tightly. "Now I'm going to pull you. Just don't let go!"

Laura obeys, rolls up on to the lowest part of the surround, so that now half of Laura is out.

"Give me your hand!" Laura marvels that the hand she's hanging on to is so slight and so thin.

"What are you doing here?" asks a girl in a light-colored dress and white stockings. The girl has dark hair and a pale face, she's just slightly older than Laura, a girl Laura doesn't know, a girl from the city, which immediately is clear. Laura isn't able to talk yet, and in general—she doesn't like such fancy girls who walk around in white stockings and with red nylon ribbons in their hair. Because Laura doesn't have white stockings nor does she have red nylon ribbons. Just brownish water still dripping from her hair, her clothes, from her mouth. Laura gulps back the water, the dirty, slimy water. She vomits and dribbles snot. Shame, that that fancy girl had to pull Laura out of the well. She's ashamed of the shame.

"Well, why are you shivering? Take off that wet dress! What's your name?"

No, Laura won't take her dress off, she's wearing old *trusiki*— underpants. Shame.

"Laura is called Laura! And what are you doing here?" Laura yells at her and right away feels that this doesn't sound like gratitude, not at all, more like reproach, as if the unknown girl had arrived totally at the wrong time, why come at all, what business of hers was it what Laura was doing in the well.

After all that's the way it is!

"I was told to get some fresh air. I'm visiting Lonia, she's my cousin. She's sick. Lonia and her mama are going to go live in Riga. There are better doctors in Riga. And Lonia and I, we'll be able to attend the same class. We'll be learning French. Where do you live?"

"At Upītes farm."

"Is it there?"

"Yes. Have you not been here before?"

"No. And I won't be here another time either. I don't like the country. These gadflies, how horrible!" The biggest of gadflies has landed just below the girl's ankle.

"Squash it!"

"No, I hate that. At home Lonia will take it off with some tweezers. Was it your grandma who beckoned to me?"

"Beckoned to you?"

"Yes, she waved to me. Like this. For me to come. There, by the apple tree. Otherwise I wouldn't have come here. I'm afraid of horses."

Laura doesn't know what to say. What grandma? Not Mīma. Mīma couldn't have waved. Who would have waved? Laura looks at the apple tree but there's no one there.

The water sprite has finally let go of Laura's heart, it can finally warm up to the unknown girl, but she's getting ready to leave with that gadfly still just below her ankle, she doesn't want to be in fresh air anymore.

"Don't go near the well again. Adieu, Laura!"

Laura doesn't answer. Adieu? What's this—adieu? Laura worries. What does it mean—adieu? Maybe Laura has been told off, insulted? Adieu? Regardless, she's probably being made fun of.

"Adieu yourself!" Laura says.

To be truthful, Laura wanted to say thank you. For what? For saving her. From what? Laura understands from what but she doesn't want to think about it, because terror has taken a hold of her, delayed terror. It moves along Laura's blood vessels like ice-cold iron. Who waved to and implored the girl to come and save Laura? And what if no one had waved, had implored? Nearby Wonder is worriedly neighing. Daira sighs in relief. Laura runs home without looking back. To forget the horses, to forget her wet hair that's full of green slime and black sludge. The wet dress is drying quickly on Laura's flesh like a drop of water on a hot stove. Home!

"Oh my God, child! Look at you! Where have you been?" Mīma is shocked.

"In a well," Laura replies and rushes up to the attic.

Mīma calls, scolds, begs, but Laura doesn't come down.

Laura is flying!

IN FRONT OF LAURA'S EYES stretch vast, level fields. Right up to the horizon. After all, that's the Zemgale region's flatlands! Like an enormous airfield. In a distance one can see Tīrelis—a moor with stretches and pools of water, the trees are small and offended, they don't want to grow bigger. It's good that Laura can see the moor from above because she's not allowed to cross to it by land. Not even go close to it. No one who has entered Tīrelis has returned, be it either a lost cow or a reckless human being. Just one boy had managed to scramble out at its edge, but he couldn't recount what had happened. The boy had been struck dumb in Tīrelis. Tīrelis doesn't want its secrets revealed.

The plowed fields below look like *pīrāgi*—golden turnovers, after they've been glazed with a beaten egg. For this purpose there's a rabbit's foot at the Upītes farm. Mīma makes Laura glaze the *pīrāgi* before they vanish into the hot mouth of the oven.

The fields are full of yellow and violet and all colors of flowers.

The fields of grain rise and fall in waves as if they were breathing. It seems to Laura that's it's her own breath.

Poppies, cornflowers, and daisies. One can see no beginning nor end to them. In places there's yellowed grass from the previous year, knolls and mole burrows. Laura is flying low. On purpose. So that her legs nearly touch the ground. Now and then they do, as Laura kicks at a knoll. It goes up in smoke like a puff-ball. She kicks at some mole hills, they're like small, black pyramids. Like in Egypt. There, the pyramids are only for rulers, but here in Latvia, each mole has a pyramid.

Laura pretends that she doesn't notice anything bad.

That everything is in the best order.

She lifts off higher, then once more kicks at a knoll. Her feet once more touch ground. Bird's-eye primroses! The loveliest of flowers! She could pick them and take some to Mīma, who very much likes flowers. Then Mīma will warm up, soften. In earlier times Mīma had a rose garden, a whole hectare's worth, but that was earlier. Now is not the right time to pick bird's-eye primroses.

Because a dog-faced monster is chasing Laura!

The dog-faced monster instead of a face has a ferocious dog's muzzle. Flat like a pancake, enormous fangs, sharp as daggers, hang over the edges. His tongue is long and flicks in and out like that of a snake.

His body is that of a human being, just short, squat, and hairy.

And the dog-faced monster has a beast's tail.

He's a horrendous monster, he eats human meat. He's grown fat like a pig.

A dog-faced monster knows how to hide, he's not easily visible. Just his intentions are clearly visible—to devour Laura, tear her into pieces, and swallow her.

The dog-faced monster is crazed with hate and the desire to wolf down Laura. The dog-faced monster has for a long time now had a grudge against Laura. About the fact that she managed to stay alive in Siberia. No one was supposed to stay alive, but Laura has. This makes the dog-faced monster crazy.

It's not as if she isn't afraid at all. She is afraid. She understands that she's playing with fire. To get involved with something like him is very dangerous. The dog-face is very close. Laura hears how he breaks through the willows. She hears how the dog-face pants, how he slobbers and wheezes. How the dog-faced monster smells. Dog-faces smell like carrion.

There! Now it's happening! With his smelly mouth the monster is getting ready to seize Laura's heel! He's already feeling beatific, grunting and growling. Imagining Laura clamped between his teeth.

How Laura is wriggling and kicking!

How Laura's soft bones are cracking, how tasty Laura's young blood is!

Now I've got you, you impudent girl! That's what the dog-faced monster thinks.

Fat, repulsive stinker!

And then, right then, the expected moment arrives. The moment, for which Laura is ready to put her life on the line.

A moment that stuns the dog-faced monster.

When the dog-face is already mid-leap, Laura suddenly pushes off from the ground and lifts off into the air! So simply. It's totally easy. She just needs to push off with great spiritual power. She can't just push off with her legs. Laura doesn't fall down to the ground, no. The dog-faced monster is just hoping for it. Not a chance! Laura is flying!

She changes the height of her flight without effort to annoy the dog-faced monster. Like a swallow teases a cat. You ca-a-aant catch me. Laura is not a swallow, she isn't getting ready to peck at the dog-face's ear, that would be too crazy. It's enough that the dog-face is frozen in shock! About the fact that Laura knows how to fly! How can such a little girl fly right past the monster's nose, here closer, here further, and the dog-faced monster can't do anything to her? How can that be?

The dog-faced monster squats in the bushes and blinks his stupid eyes. As large as saucers. That's also Laura's intention—to make a fool of this scoundrel. To make a fool of him. Leave him cross and sulking. Let him wonder. Let him paw the ground in anger. Let him brawl and go crazy! That's what he deserves. So he doesn't think himself to be God knows what.

Let him know that Laura knows how to fly.

It's hard for the dog-faced monster to grasp this. He's not all there upstairs. How can it be that such a little girl knows how to fly, while he, mighty dog-face, doesn't know how? The dog-faced monster has learned his lesson. Now he'll leave her alone. At least for a while.

The next time Laura senses that the dog-face monster is nearby, Laura will lure the loathsome creature to Tirelis. There the dog-face will fall into the marsh and perish.

He won't devour human beings anymore.

That'll be the next time. Now the weather is too lovely to spend any more time with the dog-face. Laura wants to fly just for her own pleasure. Just for fun.

A sense of great exultation and the joy of victory courses through her. Heavenly joy. The dog-faced monster can't do anything if Laura, a human being, knows how to fly!

Laura flies!

She feels her friend the warm wind, how it tickles. The wind has been her friend from the moment Laura stepped off the train, the wind met her already on the platform. Laura lies down in the wind like on a wave in the sea, like in safe arms.

The sun above is shining and the flowers waft their fragrance from below. The sun is loving. The flowers are dear. Laura flies between the sun and the flowers. Lightly! Joyfully! Beautifully!

The fields of grain breathe with Laura's breath. Tree tops breathe with Laura's breath. Laura forgets about the dog-faced monster, let him go to hell! The devil take him!

Laura flies!

That's a secret.

No one in this world is allowed to know that Laura can fly.

The Tar Pond

THE OLD TURKEY IS MAD. He's scolding.

That's nothing new. The turkey is often mad. Fit-to-be-tied mad.

Nothing pleases him. He spreads out his tail like a fan and begins to cackle. Nothing in this world is good enough for him. The world is coming to an end! The turkey's comb and beard turn more and more red. Now they're altogether blue. The turkey is blue with anger. At times like that Laura avoids him like the plague.

But what's going on now? All is not right also with the she-turkey.

Usually she's calm and lovable, but now she's racing around the farmyard as if on fire. And where are the turkey chicks? They're nowhere to be seen. Now it's clear why the turkey mama hasn't got a peaceful heart and why the old turkey is fit to be tied.

Their six tiny young have vanished. So why wouldn't they race in alarm around the farmyard? Now Laura too is running around. The turkey chicks are nowhere. Laura will go and look for them. The chicks can't be far. Laura doesn't want to get upset before she needs to.

But if the turkey chicks aren't home by evening then Laura will really get a scolding.

No, Laura doesn't always get a scolding when she's warned that she'll get one. But when Laura does get a scolding she hasn't always been warned that she'll get it. Laura contemplates which is better. Maybe the turkey chicks, the tiny rascals, have crept into the bushes by the stream.

She'll make sure that the chicks aren't by the stream.

Laura suddenly has a desire to paddle around in the stream. There's such nice shade there! The day is hot, a scorching sun. If it doesn't rain soon then everything will burn to a crisp. That's what Mīma thinks. Laura can't imagine how it will be if everything gets burned to a crisp. Everything. Absolutely everything? Also the water in the stream?

While Laura is thinking she hears weak cheeping sounds. They're coming from the direction of the railway tracks. The chirping gets louder and louder, so Laura must be heading in the right direction. Now she's running, as fast as her feet will carry her, because it's not just any kind of chirping. It's no joke! They're calls of despair, they're calls for help!

She's arrived at the railway tracks. The tracks are as hot as a tea kettle on a stove. Along the edges of the embankment there are many wild strawberries. Big, dark ones. The very biggest ones Laura can't bear to leave. It's a wonder that the neighbor boy Stasis hasn't yet picked them.

Fine, let those strawberries rot! Laura has to find the turkey chicks. They're still total little idiots, they've probably got tangled up in blackberry bushes or have got stuck somewhere.

Laura sees that the tiny birds are in the tar pond. It's the sort of pond that is full of tar instead of water. The railway workers use it to tar the railway ties. Children are not allowed to walk there. Why? Not allowed, and that's all! That's all Laura knows. But Laura also knows how lovely it is to walk on the tar pond. Like walking on ice. Just that the ice is black and shiny. Hard. And so smooth! There's no other place in this world that's so smooth where a person can walk.

The turkey chicks are clamoring pitifully and flailing their wings. Two of the six have lain down, probably tired out by their own squealing. Come, come, come! Laura calls out to them, but the turkey chicks don't move at all from their place. They stretch their tiny necks, gasping for air. Come, come on out! Come out! It doesn't look good. The turkey chicks don't listen to her. She can no longer bear the cries of the tiny birds!

Laura takes a step on to the black ice.

This time it's not hard. Her foot easily sinks into it. The tar is hot. It's good that Laura is wearing her new sandals. The turkey chicks aren't far away. Now Laura understands what the problem is. Those foolish rascals are stuck. Their tiny legs have sunk into the tar, feathers all glued together.

Laura reaches the first chick, grasps it and tries to lift it out.

The chick lets out such a holler that Laura unwittingly releases her hold of it. The chick is hurting. Also the rest now are screaming even more horrendously, except for those two. They've given up. Their tiny heads bent back, beaks open, eyes closed. Laura tries to pick up the sleeping chick. The black pond doesn't let the chick go. Her hands become smeared with soft, light gray feathers. The smell of the tar, which Laura has always liked, now is suffocating her.

Dear God, help, Laura whispers.

Her tears are almost cool, compared to the heat given off by the pond and the beams of the sun.

Laura is totally alone in this world with six dying turkey chicks.

No, Laura can't do anything here by herself, she has to find people to help her in a hurry. Laura is going to run and yell for help!

Suddenly Laura's heart almost stops. Laura can't move! Laura can't lift up her foot. Neither one or the other. The tar is burning her ankles. Laura wants to tear herself loose. She stumbles with her arms forward. The tar singes her knees and her palms.

Laura grows afraid. The evil spirit has led her here! He's lured a child here! Here she'll stay for ever and ever! Like a fly on flypaper, twitching for a while, and then it'll be the end. Or else she'll slowly sink under. In the beginning to her knees, after to her waist, but then ... She manages, however, to stand up. Laura wipes her hands on her chest. Her new dress! It's finished. Laura is finished!

Laura yells. Sometimes Laura is ashamed to yell, to call for help, but not now. No, no one hears, no one comes. The black pond sucks Laura ever deeper, Laura yells as if she's lost her senses.

"*Yobtvaimaty*! For fuck's sake! Stay still and don't move! Stop yelling!"

Kolya, That Monkey, half-naked, is standing on the embankment, tanned brown, just in his pants. Laura yells even louder. Only now she hears herself.

"I said, stand still and don't move! Otherwise you'll be in greater shit! Wait, I'm coming straight away!"

Laura doesn't believe Kolya, That Monkey, will come. He's a

drunkard! So let him be a drunkard, as long as he comes. Besides he's a Russian, even though a good person! No, he won't come! Why should he come? Aunt Maria's goat hung herself by her tether because of him, when she fell off the manure pile! Kolya, That Monkey, without a *polsh* of vodka, doesn't lift a finger. Laura doesn't have a *polsh*, he won't come. He's left Laura, so that that black hell's pitch will suck her under like a fly!

Laura screams.

"I said stop yelling! Are you missing a screw or something?"

Kolya, That Monkey, has brought a ladder and a plank. It's good that the ladder is long. He places the ladder like a path up to Laura, like a bridge, and throws the plank on top. That's how, crawling, he reaches Laura.

This is truly shit—he says. Laura grabs on to and clasps Kolya, That Monkey, around his neck. What the fuck is this here? He inspects if Laura's foot will come out. It doesn't. Inspects the other foot. That one, too, doesn't come out.

"Now then, girl. You'll have to part from your sandals. I'll unbuckle them, and you pull your foot out. *Davai! Davai!* Come on! Now! Pull! Put your foot on the plank! Like that. Good. *Umnica*—you're a smart one. Now the other one. *Davai!* Go on! Pull, pull! Stop bawling!"

Kolya, That Monkey, carries Laura to the pond's edge. The ladder remains sunk in the tar. Also the sandals remain in the tar.

But the turkey chicks? The chicks! Laura tries to tear away from Kolya's strong arms. The tiny turkeys!

"Stop wriggling! Don't slam my *pochkas*—kidneys. Does Grandpa have some *solyarka*—booze?"

Laura doesn't know if Grandpa has some *solyarka*, but wises up to what she must say.

"Mīma has a *polsh*."

"And what good does that do me?"

"Will you lift a finger and pull out the turkey chicks?"

"These ones won't make it. Never mind, new ones will hatch."

"If you lift a finger and pull out the chicks, then you'll get a *polsh*."

"Do you promise? *Zhelezno*—an iron-clad promise?"

"Yes. *Zhelezno.*"

"That's a totally different kettle of fish! It sure would help the *pohmelyas*—hangover! Then we have a deal after all."

Kolya, That Monkey, laughs, he's probably happy that he'll get a *polsh*. He carries Laura home. His stride is sure and smooth. No matter how she tries Laura can't keep her eyes open. Her head slides down on Kolya's, That Monkey's shoulder.

White Hares

Now and then, when the two of them are alone, Mīma begs Laura to tell her a word or two about Siberia. Could it really be that Laura doesn't remember anything, nothing at all? She was already quite a big girl there.

No, Laura doesn't remember anything.

It feels good to sit in Mīma's lap in front of an open wood-stove door and to gaze into the fire. It's so good that Mīma is for once calm and doesn't flit about like quicksilver.

Laura feels the heat of the dying coal embers on her chest and Mīma's soft warmth on her back.

It's true that Laura doesn't remember anything. As if someone had with an eraser removed Laura's memories. She just remembers the waiting for the time they'd be returning home to Latvia.

"When are we going?" Laura would ask and each time she was told, "Soon."

"When are we going?"

"Soon."

"When are we going?"

"Soon."

"When are we going?"

"Soon."

Sometimes it seemed to her that "soon" meant—right away, other times it meant—never.

Soon—meant something between right away and never.

Between a joyful flight toward the sun and a hopeless stay in eternal freezing.

That is truly impossible to explain.

In one breath.

In a few words.

Some sort of terrible hardship lay in their path. Like a dead horse lying across the road, that time by the Barrack. One could of course step over its neck. One could go around it, if one jumped across the ditch. Laura couldn't. Go around the dead horse, step over it, and thus continue onward. How can one? It's incomprehensible. Laura can't understand it.

The heat of the coal and Mīma's warmth—that's all she needs right now.

"Hares," Laura responds, when Mīma has already long ago forgotten that she asked about Siberia.

"Hares?" Mīma repeats.

"Many, many," Laura says and again falls silent.

"Were they running around in a field, those little hares?" Mīma kindly continues to question.

She's worried about Laura. The child is too withdrawn.

"No, they weren't running."

"What were they doing then?"

"Lying there."

That's all. Once more there's a hardship ahead. Laura doesn't say any more. Doesn't want to. Laura still doesn't know enough Latvian words to tell Mīma about the hares. Maybe that's it. No words in Russian either. Laura has almost forgotten them all. She's left them behind in Siberia.

One morning Laura had cleared a small spot on the Barrack's iced-over windowpane. She had blown out all the breath in her until she could see something. In the yard overnight a white hill had appeared. White, the same as everything else in the surroundings.

Where did such a hill come from? From where could something like this be created?

The whiteness, when you looked carefully at it, wasn't quite the whiteness of snow. What then? What kind of hill was it? Laura had to see for herself!

Wearing Mama's felt boots and quilted coat over her nightie, Laura went to have a look.

White hares! A whole hill of white hares? It was a miracle!

Airy and splendid snowflakes in a thousand colors sparkled on their thick, white fur coats. Coats shiny and with a soft down undercoat.

A red sun was dawning and the hill of hares looked as if it had been scattered with diamonds.

At the tip of every bit of fur there was a shimmering snow-flake. The wind lightly moved the soft hare fur. It seemed to Laura that the hares were alive and breathing. The entire world around her shone white and downy. Her heart clenched from the beauty of it. Tiny ears, paws, tummies, noses. The eyes were open. She touched the closest hare.

It was stiff, frozen solid. Laura jumped away. All the hares were stiff.

All the hares were dead! Thrown pell-mell one on top of the other. The hares seemed big to Laura, enormous. Then she noticed another color.

Red.

Seeped across the snow it was light pink, almost black where it had dried out on the tiny noses.

It wasn't the rosy sun of morning. That was blood. Tiny heads, underbellies. Here and there. Not immediately noticeable.

All the beauty suddenly disappeared. Where had it gone? It wasn't lovely anymore! No, it was! Laura with all her might wanted to get back that joy within herself that she had at the start. The snowflakes were just as splendid, and the diamonds glittered the same. She wanted to but couldn't manage it. Something had happened.

Sadness had found Laura's heart. Melancholy had woken in Laura's soul. Beauty, joy, beauty, sadness, beauty, melancholy. How can a five-year-old child describe all this to Mīma?

And the fact that Laura couldn't move, because she too had grown stiff and frozen. She had understood that she'd end up in one pile with the hares—dead.

And that only in freezing Siberia can one feel how burning hot are tears.

"Laura!" Mama yelled and in a flimsy housecoat and bare feet ran out to get Laura.

Mama's quilted coat long ago had been thrown on the ground. Why did Mama have bare feet? Ah, yes, Laura had her felt boots.

"Crazy child! Don't you know how many degrees it is this morning? Minus forty!"

Mama grabbed Laura and dragged her inside. Frozen and stiff like a hare.

Laura didn't care how many degrees it was?

Laura didn't care that she'd get pneumonia.

Laura didn't care that the Barrack's men had made a good catch in their hunt.

Laura didn't care that Papa alone had shot twelve hares.

That now for a good while there would be meat. That for dinner they'd have roasted rabbit, as long as Papa managed to skin it.

Laura didn't even know what that meant in Latvian or in Russian—to skin something.

"Mīma, what is that—to skin?" Laura speaks up.

The fire in the stove's belly has almost died down.

"Mīma!"

"My knees are totally stiff. Child, you're heavy. Let me stoke the fire. Remember that you always have to put the firewood in the stove with the fat end first."

"Why?"

"So that babies aren't born upside down," Mīma says as she leaves the room.

What babies? Does Mīma read thoughts?

Laura sits on the low stove stool. She forgets, or perhaps doesn't want to tell Mīma, what else Laura had seen.

Those tiny hare faces really weren't hare faces. Those were the faces of tiny babies, infant faces.

When Kima's, that big Russian girl Kima's baby died, because he was born upside down, they had to keep him frozen until spring, until the earth returned to its natural state. The earth returning is not like birds returning. When the earth returns—that's when the frozen soil unfreezes. It's just that the words used are the same in Latvian.

Kima gave thanks to the One who loves all mankind that her Vlady was now with Him. If he hadn't died, he wouldn't be with the One who loves all mankind. But now he is. That's good, Kima can be happy.

Laura didn't understand this.

The Barrack people didn't understand why the baby needed to be called Vlady.

Laura didn't understand why not.

As if from the depths Kima sang in a voice about the righteous souls of the ones sleeping. Oh, Redeemer, grant them rest. Those who are with Thee, Thou, who loveth all mankind. In Thy place of rest. Because Thou alone art the One who loves all mankind.

Laura didn't understand.

If the place of rest is with the One who loves all mankind then why is little Vlady lying in a little box, frozen like a hare?

Laura wants to ask Mīma. Mīma? Mīma is lifting a large steaming kettle from the stove, the vapor hits Mīma's tense face. With her bare hand she shifts the stove's hot cover plates. Once Laura just briefly touched one with a finger, and right away a blister formed! On Mīma's hand—nothing.

Laura doesn't understand.

The Spoon

ANIMATED AND EXCITED, Laura digs with a spoon. It makes the best small shovel. It's neither thin, nor light, nor does it bend, like those tin ones with which at Avoti they eat soup. This one is heavy, thick and strong, doesn't break at all, even if you have to pick up a stone. That is if it isn't too dreadfully big. Laura doesn't lift the big rocks, they're so enormous and heavy like hippopotami, doesn't even think of lifting them. For the moment there's no need, let the hippopotami sleep.

Mīma has taken it into her head to replant the rubber tree and has sent Laura to get new soil. New soil?

"Why new soil?"

"Because this is old. There's nothing in it anymore."

"What's not in it?"

"Nothing. That's why it's withering. Poor flower."

"Is a rubber tree a flower?"

"Stop chattering and bring me new soil. Take a pail. Beyond the maples there's a bit of a hill, which has very good black soil. There it's already begun."

"What's begun?"

"Begun to be dug. It's light soil, you're my plucky child. Don't carry a pail full! You can go a second time, if need be."

In vain Mīma waits for Laura's return.

Laura likes to be by the maples. Maples are good trees. The maples allow children to play with what they call "noses." In fact these are seeds with wings. Those can be pasted on noses. Then it seems as if a butterfly has perched on one's nose. Or an angel. The maple leaves are lovely. They've got five fingers like human beings do.

Laura likes the size and pride of the maple leaves. The trunks are thick and gnarled, because they're old. How can it be that maples are old, but soil under them new.

Beyond the maples there really is a little hill, yes, there's been some digging there. A shovel has also been left right there. It's a small sapper's shovel. There are several at the Upītes farm like that. Originally Laura had thought they were children's shovels but it turned out that they were field sapper's. Sappers, wrappers—something like that.

But what's behind the hillock? There are a lot of big rocks there. It looks like castle ruins. But beyond the rocks—aha, there's a pit! Laura sees an old bathtub and some other junk. Springs? Maybe it's not junk after all but valuable things?

The pit is overgrown with raspberry bushes and willows. Laura wants to see what's in that pit beside the old bathtub and the springs. How deep is the pit? Maybe it's an abyss.

Laura has to clamber over the rocks. Laura does get over them but then her foot gets caught and she falls. Laura grabs whatever she can reach. A raspberry shrub tears out of the soil with all its roots, Laura slips and slides on her behind for a moment. It turns out that there are also blackberries here and brambles. The raspberry bush has stopped her fall but, pulled out, it has left a large hole in the soil. Something is shining in that hole.

Laura climbs back up and finds a spoon.

But something else is glimmering there.

Laura pokes around with the spoon.

Laura's heart begins to skip and gambol like a yearling goat. It's a tiny vial! It's exactly like what she's wanted! Mīma has a similar one, but she can't give it away because it's not yet empty. Grandpa's vial isn't empty either. Of course Laura won't take the heart drops away from the old folks! No, now she can abandon such a thought because Laura already sees another bottle! This one even has a cork! Laura has found riches! Bottles! Brownish, green, transparent, even blue! Laura holds up each of the dug-up bottles against the sun. What lovely colors! Once Laura washes them, they'll be even lovelier. Laura will set up a drugstore.

At one time there was a drugstore here. It must have been so, because Laura finds a bottle of cough syrup. It's bigger than the rest, and Laura recognizes this bottle. In taking off the screw top she gets a whiff of how the cough medicine once smelled.

But her luck with bottles comes to an end.

Laura digs and scratches around with the spoon, but she doesn't find any more. Instead she finds an amazingly lovely shard of glass! It's white like snow, but in the snow there are small, red roses! Laura polishes up the shard against her sweater, rubs it with a strip of her skirt, and the shard lights up as if in a fairytale! Laura gazes at it as if enchanted. It's from some wondrous expensive dish.

Where is the dish itself?

The soil in the pit is in fact light, but new the soil is not! Mīma is mistaken about that. Laura's dug-up earth smells of decayed leaves. The old maples have scattered their leaves here in great abundance for many years. The leaves have turned into black earth. However, behind the fragrance of the leaves one senses others—profound, dark, sweetly bitter. As if rising from a dark cellar, as if from the brightly lit kitchen of a king's castle.

The old maples have hidden secrets here.

Is it not for naught that the old maples have gifted Laura with a tool—the big, strong spoon that they've put straight into her hands? In her heart Laura says thanks to the maples. For this entrusted task—to dig and to discover a secret.

Look, something round! Some sort of a ball, hard as a stone, but it's not a stone, her teeth feel that it's not a stone, can't understand, Laura pops it in her mouth, she'll suck on it, and then find out.

"Laura! Where are you? Laura!"

Mīma. Laura must answer so that Mīma doesn't worry, but she doesn't respond.

Here Mīma will never find Laura, so good is this place. Mīma's old legs won't get over the rocks!

"Laura, where, girl, have you again crawled into? At least answer, little devil! Laura! Oh, my God, such a child!"

Laura raises her head, but quickly lowers it again. Mīma's old, hurting legs! Moaning and huffing and puffing she's somehow managed to climb up on the hillock, picked up Laura's discarded pail and is looking all around.

Laura feels sorry for Mīma, but this time there's nothing to be done, absolutely nothing.

"Stop playing games. Where are you? You're asking for a spanking!"

Laura can be moved to pity but she can't be intimidated. Laura doesn't respond.

In her agitation, her tongue no longer finds the round don't-know-what, Laura spits out just soil, the round thing isn't there.

"Mīma!" Laura screeches.

"Thanks be to God!" Mīma responds.

Laura scrambles out of her hiding place, the brambles and nettles sting her bare shins and hands, she runs to Mīma, wraps her arms around her waist and bawls.

"God forbid! What were you doing in that jungle? All the rubbish that's there! There could be glass there! Did you get cut? What's the matter now?"

"Laura swallowed it!"

"What did you swallow?"

"Laura doesn't know. Something."

"What kind of something?" Mīma yells at her. "How big?"

"Like this." Laura shows her.

"Like a pea?"

"No, bigger."

"Like a plum?"

"Yes!"

"What did the plum look like? Did you bite into it?"

"No-o. Round. A bit longish. I couldn't bite through it."

"What was it like? Yellow, white, blue?"

"I don't know, it was dirty. Will I have to have my tummy cut open?" Laura can talk and bawl at the same time.

"Without doubt! The finest surgeon from Riga will have to be summoned for the duchess! Nothing will have to be cut for you, you naughty girl! You'll need Doctor Berzins, nothing else! Just castor oil down the hatch! You'll poo it out in the pot! It must have been a fatter glass bead or part of a necklace. Or some old broad bean! Why do you have to shove all sorts of rubbish in your mouth? What's this collection here?" Mīma points at the small bottles falling out of all of Laura's pockets.

"God help us, girl, you're been digging around in the old garbage dump? Have more sense, for heaven's sake! Yuck!"

Laura has been digging in the old garbage dump, in a rubbish bin, in a waste disposal, in a snake pit. Among slops, which have at one time, still before the war, been dumped there directly from a slop pail, phooey! Rotten cabbage, potatoes, and beets have been thrown there! Night piss pots have been poured out there, phooey! Dead cats thrown there! Old fish, carrion! Bacteria, all sorts of infectious diseases, poisons, phooey! And what if a grenade had exploded there? Mīma can't stop ranting.

Then Mīma sees what Laura is holding in her hand.

A spoon.

"Show me," Mīma says in a voice altogether different.

As if she was frightened. Is the spoon more important than Laura's swallowed round don't-know-what? What if it was poison?

Mīma looks over the spoon, rubs it against her hip, brings it close to her eyes.

"Laurie dear, there should be letters here. I can't see. Are they there?"

"They are."

"What letters are they?" Mīma's voice grows hoarse.

The letters are horrendously artfully convoluted, but Laura can decipher them.

"R and a U," Laura says.

Mīma takes the spoon and holds it in hands that are now trembling. Mīma gazes at the spoon until her chin also starts to tremble. She falls to her knees and starts to cry. Mīma sobs and moans.

Laura is scared silly.

Laura doesn't understand anything! There's rubbish, bacteria, poison, maybe even something explosive in Laura's tummy, but Mīma is crying about an old spoon?

No, about the fact that Laura is so nasty—that she doesn't listen, that she doesn't bring new soil for the rubber tree, that she doesn't answer from the pit, that she was digging around among bacteria, that's why Mīma is crying!

"Forgive me, dear, dear Mīma, please forgive me!"

The rest—I won't ever do it again—that Laura doesn't say. Laura wants to be an honorable person, one who doesn't idly throw words around.

"Thanks, my dear child."

Mīma says this? What's Mīma thanking Laura for, thanks, thank you, thanks. "Now let's go. Help me get up. R and U. Reinis Upītis. That's dear Reinis's christening spoon. It was lost. Thanks for finding it. Let's just not say anything to Grandpa, alright?"

"Why?"

"Grandpa will get very upset."

"Like you did?"

"More so."

Why more so? Reinis, Grandpa's dear son. That's what everyone says, that's how everyone talks. Feel sorry for Grandpa. But Reinis is also Mīma's dear son! Only now Laura realizes— Reinis is also Mīma's dear son! Everyone has forgotten that. Only Grandpa is pitied. And that new, lovely house, which was burned down, that was Mīma's too of course! And Lilia is also Mīma's daughter! And Anda and Juris are also Mīma's grandchildren! But everyone only feels sorry for Grandpa. Why do they not pity Mīma? That Laura can't understand. When Grandpa's pipe got found in the attic Grandpa began to believe that also Reinis would be found.

Reinis's spoon has been found!

"Mīma don't cry! Reinis too can be found!"

No child, Reinis isn't either a pipe or a spoon. No, dear child, no.

Mīma doesn't believe. For the first time Laura pities Mīma more than she pities Grandpa.

Wayside Leaves

WHEN LAURA, STUMBLING on a gravel path, has scraped and bloodied her knee, Mīma finds some plantain known as *ceļmallapiņas*—wayside leaves in Latvia.

When Laura gets her finger caught in a door, Mīma gets some wayside leaves.

When she cuts open her forehead on a rock, Mīma looks for wayside leaves.

Mīma gets out the heavy mortar and pestle. Pounds the leaves into a green gruel.

When Laura gets a splinter, a wasp sting, when a boil develops, when nettles have stung her, when a blister breaks on her heel from new sandals, when on humid evenings on Laura's knees again and again swell rosy peonies, out come the wayside leaves.

Mīma always has some wayside leaves on hand. Mīma tears off a long strip from a bed sheet and applies a compress on the ailing spot. The leaves, which in the evening are full with their juices, in the morning are dry as if they had been dry-cured, but the swelling has disappeared and the pain has vanished.

In the beginning the Latvian word *ceļmallapiņas*—wayside leaves seemed to Laura like the hardest word in the world. Totally senseless. A word that couldn't be either remembered or pronounced. A real tongue twister.

One day she gets another troublesome injury. A gooseberry bush for no particular reason to speak of has scraped and hurt Laura. Like a savage wild cat. On the palm of her hand is an angry red scratch. The ragged edges of the scratch slowly fill with blood. Mīma!

"Go, gather some wayside leaves."

"Where?" Laura isn't at all happy that she, a sick and injured person, has to go herself to God knows where.

"Everywhere, of course! Well, right there, at the edge of the path!" Mīma has to finish peeling potatoes.

Laura stands on the path and looks. Where? Kneels down and inspects. Where among the many grasses are those wayside leaves...

"Here! Here!" Some creeping leaves call out and move their seed stalks that look like tiny cudgels. "We're the ones you're looking for. We're the wayside leaves! Wherever there's a path or a road we're there! It's not important how narrow or wide the path or road, how far, how close. This same path to the well, see. It just seems that it's near. But, see, Mīma walks it three times a day and so she has her entire life. If you add up all those walks, then it can turn out that the path to the well is longer and goes further than the road to Riga. It could very well be that Mīma has gone three times around the world along this path."

"Really?"

"Yes."

"How is it that I've never seen you before?"

"We're not as noticeable as, for example, red poppies. As, for example, blue chicory. We're insignificant. We have to be like that, so not just anybody plucks us. So that only those do who have a real need of us. That's how it's intended," the leaves chatter.

Laura contemplates how it is—to intend? Who is the person who is the one who intends, who has intended it so?

"Maybe it seems to you that we grow just for fun? No, Laura. We grow especially."

"Especially?"

"That means—with purpose, with intent. We're full of all sorts of medicine like real drugstores. Yes, yes, and we're always open. All the time. We wait for the moments when we have to help. In the meantime all sorts of things can happen. What kind of a meantime would it be if nothing happened? What's happened to you now? Well, what are you waiting for? Pluck us! Don't worry, we regrow! Pluck boldly!"

"Pluck boldly!" Mīma comes up to her. The potatoes have been peeled, her hands have been washed. "The bed sheet is almost done for," Mīma says as she bandages Laura's hand.

Under the bandage Laura feels a slight tingling. The wayside leaves will chatter on for a while yet.

Oh, Sacred Lestene

LAURA IS WOKEN BY a door squeaking. It's the cupboard door that's squeaking.

Mīma?

The sun hasn't yet risen. Not the sun, but a bit of a pallid light shyly peeks through the window pane. Laura can calmly sleep on. What's sweeter than honey? Laura's sleep.

But nevertheless she must see what Mīma is doing at such a horrendously early hour. She always gets up early, but not this early. What's happening now? Mīma is getting all dressed up! Mīma dressed up? Where is she off to? Surely not to the barn nor to the hay field. With a black taffeta skirt? With her new silk blouse? What kerchief is that? Never has Mīma worn one like it. Is this a kerchief from the package? Yes, that really is from the package! How is that? Hasn't Mīma always firmly said that she'll never ever in her life put on her back anything from the package and will not allow anyone else to do so either? On her back? Mīma has said—on her back. About her head she hasn't said anything. Laura's sleep flutters away like a bird.

"Where are you going?" Laura has a bad premonition.

"Sleep, sleep, child. Shush! I'll be back soon. Grandpa too is sleeping."

"But where are you going?" Laura's voice sounds hurt. What kind of quiet and secretive skulking is this? To where? Can Laura, Grandpa, the farmhouse, and hens be left like that to run off to God knows where in the middle of the night? In the farmyard a horse is snorting. Ah, so! That means Mīma's not going to walk, she's going by horse and wagon! Could it be that Mīma's getting ready to go to the Melluži seaside town to her sister? Mīma has threatened to do so. She has threatened often enough that she'll once and for all go and live with her sister in Melluži.

"Are you going to Mell#i?" Laura is trying to control tears.

"What Mellu#i? Go back to bed! I've got to go to Lestene."

"Laura's going to come along!"

"No, she won't," Mīma cuts her short as if with a knife.

Laura can no longer hold back the tears. What if Mīma takes off? What if she gets lost forever? Something isn't right when an old person in the middle of the night gets dressed up and like a real criminal steals off in the half-dark. Something is dreadfully not alright!

"Laura's going to come along!" She has to yell loudly so that Grandpa wakes, let him get up and intercede. Grandpa doesn't wake.

"Don't wake Grandpa, quiet, please! Don't you know how hard it is for Grandpa to fall asleep?"

No, Laura won't let Mīma go anywhere! She wraps her arms around the taffeta skirt, which is cool and slippery and frighteningly strange.

"Fine. But quickly! Get dressed, wash your face, we'll braid your hair on the way."

On the way the braiding of Laura's hair is forgotten. A too slow and too calm Daira has to be urged on all the time, reins held taut, otherwise it looks as if Daira will fall asleep, will fall over the wagon shaft or will fall down full-length. Daira is cross, for where must they rush so in the middle of the night?

To Lestene.

Sacred Lestene! These words Laura has heard many times and not only from Mīma.

Oh, thou Sacred Lestene!—That's what people say when they marvel.

Ah, Sacred Lestene!—That's said in censure.

Sacred Lestene!—That's said to express joy.

That's said when one is angry, in shock, when one is exhilarated, for praise, and when scolding. That's said about impudence. It's said about generosity. Sacred Lestene suits every situation.

Laura's always thought that it's just a saying, like "God help us, such a child!" or "Good night, may the bed bugs not bite!", but it's not so.

It turns out that Lestene really exists. That Lestene is a place. That in Lestene there's a church. That it has been Mīma's church since the beginning of time.

Mīma tells Laura about it although Daira needs to be encouraged continually, and Mīma now and then must call out: "Daira, get a move on! Daira put your best foot forward! What now, she doesn't want to even drag herself! Giddy up! You won't get any oats of mine today! Totally spoiled!"

Mīma is unusually talkative. Mīma talks and talks. That Lestene's church is the most beautiful church in the entire region of Kurzeme.

Kurzeme is the same as Latvia, Laura knows. From the song "Blow Ye Winds."

Mīma recalls her confirmation and her wedding with Grandpa. Remembers her daughter Lilija's and her son Reinis's christenings. Lilia's and Reinis's confirmations, Lilia's and Edmunds's weddings, Anda's and Juris's christenings. Much has got mixed together in Mīma's mind, but all of it has been too wonderful to describe. Laura doesn't want Mīma to describe, as long as she continues talking about it.

She learns a lot about the church, but more about Mīma.

The church shone then in golden glory, because hundreds of candles had been lit. As the organ sounded, the sculpted figures carved from wood seemingly came to life. The angels blew their horns and beat their drums, and bees buzzed around the rose bushes.

"Came to life? For real?" Laura is overcome with delight.

Yes, the wings of the angels began to flutter, and the apostles turned to all sides. The church moved as if alive and God Himself was present, that Mīma can swear to. Laura is ready to believe it even without the swearing. Laura senses it through the mediation of Mīma's exalted and God-fearing heart.

"Did you see Him?" Laura whispers.

"Yes, child, in that beauty, in the wood fretwork and the stained glass window paintings, but those windows looked more like doors that would lead to the heavens. And those lanterns, and those organ sounds."

"Did you see Him?" Laura wants a direct answer.

"Yes, I saw Him in the words of the minister and in that air. His Holy Spirit."

"Holy Spirit?"

"In that mutually-drawn breath. When all the people breathe with one breath and cry from sacred joy. With hearts full of sorrow, but crying from joy. Daira, get a move on! Like this we won't get back home for breakfast!" Mīma swats Daira's tail with the reins. It's a good thing that Daira has the iron curb bit, that mouthpiece put on, otherwise she couldn't be urged onward and they, Mīma and Laura, would themselves have to pull the wagon.

"About the saying? It originated a very long time ago. When the church first opened its doors. Those star-studded arches! That starry firmament! Those gilded garlands of flowers and twining leaves, that altar, God help us! It flamed exactly like the sun. At that time people hadn't seen as much as they have today, all sorts of theaters and operas nowadays. Well and, yes, when suddenly wood-carved and painted sculptures come to life and the angels begin to flutter their wings, and the organ as well starts its wondrous sound, then people were unable to resist, they fell to their knees and called out: 'Oh, sacred Lestene!'"

Laura feels that she's together with those people of long ago who had fallen to their knees all as one with the angels and the sound of the organ. Laura has melted like a candle with all the other candles in that light that shone from the lanterns, she feels, that she's standing by the picturesque windows, which in reality are the doors to the heavens. Laura feels that she's breathing the great and mutual breath, that air. That Spirit. Laura is among those people who are at Mīma's christening, wedding and confirmation, and at Buka's wedding with Grandpa Edmunds, and again at Mama's christening by the silver christening font. Together with all the distant relatives. Laura is there with a heart full of sorrow and joy like all the rest. Like always. Oh, sacred Lestene!

"Let's stop now. Whoa, you lazy horse!"

Laura looks at Mīma as if she's seeing her for the first time. People change a lot when they put on a black taffeta skirt and a silk blouse and tie a kerchief on which they've said they never would wear.

"Why stop?" Laura wants to see the wondrous beauty faster.

"I have to say my good-byes."

"To what?" Laura feels suddenly afraid.

"To sacred Lestene," Mīma says.

"Why say good-bye?"

"Don't talk now, child. For five minutes, please. Don't ask anything. That's why I wanted to come on my own. Promise?"

Laura promises and looks to see how Mīma will say her good-byes for five minutes, but doesn't see anything. Just Mīma's bowed head with its new kerchief, from which the folding lines have not yet disappeared. It's already totally light, and a curious and too sprightly wagtail perches on the edge of the wagon. Laura isn't so sprightly. The unfinished sleep is asking to be finished.

When Laura raises her head, beside them a horse and wagon has stopped. On a fresh, just-mowed pile of hay sits an unfamiliar-to-Laura old man. Totally green. His clothing is drenched through with the juices of the green grass, his gray hair as if soaked with green ink. His hands green like the slime-covered atrophied and waterlogged pieces of wood fallen in a pond.

"Well, there you have it. Was it worth it to entomb a live human being inside the wall? Was it worth it to pierce out the eyes of that young man, that artist? Those are not idle tales, I know full well. If they hadn't pierced out his eyes, the man would have built another church like this one. But now it's the only one of its kind, and otherwise none else. It's too late, Alma, too late. There's nothing more to be seen there. Just turn around, Alma, turn that wagon around. Don't cause your heart more needless pain."

"Can it really be so bad?" Mīma asks in disbelief.

"It can't be worse."

"And nothing remains? Artur!"

"The walls. But they too have been demolished. The kolkhoz has set up a grain-drying kiln there. They've organized a real devil's threshing barn. A dog-faced monster's mill. The noise is such that you have to stuff your ears shut. They've torn out the floors, dug out the old baron's bones, like jackals tossed them willy-nilly. Pshaw!" Arturs spits green.

"But the organ?"

"It was the first to be wrecked and dismantled. I don't know what those dog-faces wanted from that organ. The pipes? What use are they to anyone? They're scattered here and there around the church's foundation, now overgrown by nettles."

"But the angels and all those wood carvings?"

"Overrun by a bulldozer! What can angels do against such a beast. Where the bulldozer couldn't reach, there the people themselves did. Smashed, hacked, sawed. Everyone, who wasn't lazy. Do people need firewood? Yes, they need it! Alma, here's some validol. Didn't you know any of this? Do the people in Lamme not talk?"

"There's no one left in Lamme village to talk. There's no one anymore whose heart hurts, nobody. A person or two has mentioned it, but I didn't believe it. Oh, sacred Lestene! Is only the saying now left?

"Don't say that. People came one night, a second night, and took the altar away somewhere. From the exposed decorative and splendid part of the organ also this and that. Where was all this taken to? Who drove it away? Don't ask me that. One really doesn't know if in the barns where the firewood is stored the angels aren't hiding somewhere among the logs," Green Arturs grins slyly.

"But the Spirit?" escapes from Laura. Only slowly has she understood what Mīma and Arturs are talking about.

"Spirit?" Arturs laughs. "There's spirit only in a sauna. Who's that plucky girl of yours, Alma?"

Mīma doesn't hear the question, and that's good, after all. What business is it of the green fellow?

"That's a horrendous crime," Mīma slumps as if in pain. Once more the soft folds of Mīma's kerchief can be seen.

"Where there's a crime, there's also punishment."

"I don't believe that anymore, Artur."

"Sooner or later, Avoti mother. I do know that. Look, the

one who sawed up the cross has already taken his life. God's mill grinds slowly, but well. It isn't the kolkhoz's mill!" The green man laughs in satisfaction.

Mīma turns the wagon around. This Arturs is too irreverent. Look what he's found to laugh about.

On the way back Mīma doesn't say a word. Daira's trot homeward is more lively.

The Fortune-Teller

IN THE MORNING LAURA has to eat at least a cuckoo's mouthful. Otherwise she can't go outside, because the cuckoo, that's the famine cuckoo, can coo-coo-cuckoo her away. If she'll be coo-cuckooed away, then next year there won't be any mouthfuls, neither a cuckoo's nor a non-cuckoo's. Nor a non-cuckoo's! Laura laughs—that's funny! Mīma is firm about this, laugh or don't laugh, and she herself eats a cuckoo's mouthful, breakfast she'll eat later. After she's finished her morning chores.

Grandpa wants to be left in peace. Grandpa won't go outside so he doesn't need such a mouthful, let that cuckoo hang himself. Grandpa isn't preparing for next year.

Laura will go and spend some time with Rita at Lejasupītes farm, alright? OK? Please, Mīma, please. She'll show Rita her new candy wrappers. One of these is from a candy called *Vāverīte*—that's a squirrel in Latvian and it's very valuable. It's gilded. It can be exchanged for three *Vēžu kakliņi*—crayfish necks, which are not gilded. Fine, OK, fine, Mīma gives her permission to go.

God knows where the kids have wandered off to, but Rita's mama doesn't know. She doesn't know where the kids, those skunks, are hanging out. They take after their fathers, the little parasites.

She doesn't pay attention to Laura anymore.

The Lejasupītes farmhouse is similar to Mīma's house. Only here the veranda's windows have been broken.

The large house has been divided into many small flats. At Upītes farmhouse there's only one door that leads to the yard, but here there are many. Each door is in a different color, each obtained from a different place. In Mīma's house there are curtains on every window, here old sheets have been hung, and rags have been stuffed in the broken, open panes. Laura has asked why that's so, but Mīma has responded that she doesn't want to either think or talk about it, why trouble her heart, let people live as they like. It's good that the previous owners of the farmhouse don't see all this, otherwise they'd turn over in their graves in Siberia.

Can one turn over in one's grave, Laura doubts it. Besides that Mīma doesn't know that people in the graves in Siberia are frozen stiff, because there in the depths of earth there is permafrost. Laura thinks that the owners of Lejasupītes can't after all turn over in their graves. No way they could. But let Mīma think they can.

Rita's mama has cards! She and two other aunties are playing a Latvian card game called pigs, while chewing on *semushkas*—sunflower seeds and fighting off flies. Shit-eating flies swarm around the game of pigs and even more around the real grunting and smelly pigs right there in the farmyard.

Laura can't peel her eyes away.

It's not the aunties that fascinate her, no, not at all. The aunties' armpits and feet stink, Laura doesn't like the Lejasupītes's aunties one bit.

It's the cards. Laura can't take her eyes off the cards.

The last time she saw some cards was in Siberia. In Madalina's hands.

Laura's heart suddenly aches, that's how much she misses Madalina. Madalina with the black curly hair and ever laughing eyes.

Madalina who was as pretty as the devil. It's just a pity that she didn't have legs.

The legs are with the devil's mother, Jukka, the Finnish guy had said, and had been ready to marry Madalina right on the spot. But she just laughed. The legs that had frozen in the deadly cold were *k chertovoy materi*—with the devil's mother—but, nonetheless she was the soul of the Barrack. It was that very Jukka who gave Madalina the nickname Ciganka Moldovanka—the Moldovian Gypsy, because she had cards and she knew how to tell fortunes. "Oi, Ciganka Moldovanka!"—howled Jukka, sang Jukka, whispered Jukka, cried Jukka, but Madalina just laughed. She had survived because of the cards, just because of the cards.

Strong and healthy people had died, but Madalina had not.

"Where is that God's justice?" she yelled, when she got to drink some *samogon*—booze, but no one answered.

Because no one knew where that God's justice was. Madalina continued to earn some money. For her fortune-telling she got a bit of milk, some potatoes, sauerkraut, and, now and then, also some lard. Yes, and *samogon*, that too. Even the wife of the *uchastkoviy*—the precinct boss—came to see her. She, who was a comrade. *Uchastkoviy* was a big boss, that's why Madalina always laid out only good cards for his wife. Just the very best. Cards that showed happiness and wealth, a faithful husband, beautiful and smart children, and a climb up the ladder in the upper echelons. The brighter a future Madalina forecast, the more generous the wife of the *uchastkoviy* and other female comrades would be. The comrades came and came, and brought groats and flour. Most of all the women comrades wanted to know about their husbands, that Laura couldn't miss.

Madalina shared with everyone. Madalina without legs, which had frozen totally off in the deadly cold, she was the one who helped the whole Barrack. Not vice versa. Because she had cards.

"Crush my soul, destroy it! Wreck my soul, wreck it, you viper's offspring! Destroy the purity of my heart, destroy it, you dog-faced monsters!" Madalina whispered and crossed herself several times, after she had lied like a horse. It's no honor for a horse, nor for a human being, and the cards have to be asked for forgiveness for the lies, not for the sake of the sack of flour, the bag of sugar, and bread but for the sake of the people of the Barrack. Ciganka Moldovanka was ready to sin a hundred times more and to be boiled in hell's deepest kettle. That's what she said, when Laura was allowed to look on, but when fortunes were told for real, then she couldn't be there.

Back at Lejasupītes farmhouse Manya has tired of the game, and besides—she has to go and check out where her old man has gone. Maybe again dragged himself off to Fredis to get rid of his hangover. Can't hear him sharpening a scythe anymore, nor mowing the grass. *Vot*, the bastard, she says. Manya knows quite well how to speak in Latvian.

Dusya doesn't have an old man and she doesn't know Latvian, the *semushkas*—sunflower seeds are finished and along with them, finished is her interest in life. The *semushkas* are a passion with her, an obsession, and because of them Dusya will have to go to the kolkhoz's granary to show her tits. For this the White Negro will give her a bit of the kolkhoz's *semushkas.* He can't give too much at one time, for after all it's the property of the kolkhoz, therefore Dusya needs to go there quite often. Just thinking about it makes Dusya laugh.

"It's a pity that no one knows how to tell fortunes," Rita's mama says as she gathers up the worn and greasy cards. "I'll have to get a move on," she sighs.

"Laura knows how."

Cards, Laura just wants to hold the cards.

"Put your money where your mouth is." Rita's mama doesn't believe her.

"Them that shits his pants them's gotta wash them." Manya adds and laughs, her big stomach jiggling. Will she have a baby? Laura suddenly feels sorry for that potential child of Manya's.

"This little skunk will tell our fortune! *Etot brat vrag naroda*! *Nedobitais!*—This midget 'enemy of the people'! Not killed off yet!" Dusya sniggers.

A feeling of being insulted overwhelms Laura as well as anger, yes, which rolls and rises in her like black smoke from hell, because the aunties are laughing at her. Stupid geese, Laura contemplates revenge.

"Laura knows how!"

"Well then lay them out. Who are you going to lay them out for?" Rita's mama asks.

"For Manya."

Laura will lay out the cards just so, lay them out just so!

"Better lay them out for me," Rita's mama throws the cards on the table.

Laura shuffles the cards, they're sticky and not so easy to separate and shuffle. Laura also needs time to push back the black turmoil.

"Well, *davai, davai,* don't drag it out!" Rita's mama won't spend the whole day fooling around with strange children.

"Everyone has to be serious and quiet. You're not allowed to laugh. Cards can't be laughed at and made fun of. Else the cards won't tell the truth. The cards can get angry and then during the night…" Laura darkens her voice.

"What at night?" Rita's mama feels some uneasiness. Such a toad, but just look at her talk, and hasn't it been said that now and then from a child's mouth God Himself chooses to say something.

Dusya laughs.

"Shut up!" Rita's mama exclaims.

"*Zatknis, dura derevennaya*—shut up you stupid country bumpkin!" Maya translates for Dusya.

Laura recognizes the power of cards over people. She remembers how in front of Madalina people used to grow silent. How the desire to know one's future made people shake and tremble as if in front of the greatest power. In front of Madalina, whose legs had frozen off in the deadly cold, the comrade wife of the *uchastkoviy* shivered in her skunk fur coat. Buka's fur coat, Laura's grandmother, which, as luck would have it, had been brought along from Latvia and exchanged for a sack of peas.

Laura brings to the table and applies Madalina's words and delivery.

"Cut the deck in half. Don't whatever you do raise the cards toward you! No!" Laura yells out in horrendous fright, because Rita's mama is ready to do precisely that. Rita's mama draws back her hand. She obeys, obeys Laura! "Pull out four cards."

Rita's mama pulls them out. It's just a joke.

"Now, four more. Just don't look at them! Do you want your eyes to rot away?" Laura screeches. "Place them on top of the first ones," Laura commands.

Manya looks on, Dusya falls silent. In Laura's hand the cards have been fanned out like a peacock's tail.

"Well, what is it now?" Rita's mama can't wait, as Laura studies the cards and knits her brow, forming deep wrinkles.

"You can still change your mind if you really want to know. Sometimes it's better not to know," Laura says with empathy, just as Ciganka Moldovanka used to say.

"Of course, I want to hear."

"Your husband will come back," Laura knows that Rita's papa has abandoned them.

"Ah, what did I tell you? Ah, what did I say? No need to tell fortunes for that!" Manya bubbles.

"You can't laugh at the cards! Do you want your tongue to dry up and shrivel?" Laura scares Manya.

"Let him come back, I'll show him! I'll tear out his balls by the roots!" Rita's mama is overjoyed at her husband's predicted return.

"But not to you. Jack of diamonds and the queen of spades. You're not the one. You've got blonde hair." Laura doesn't let Rita's mama be happy too soon.

"Oh my God. To whom then?"

"To the one whose hair is dark. You'll lose everything. You'll follow the wrong path. A new life will begin for you. The old one will end for you with the upper echelons because the queen of spades is saying bad things about you," Laura rattles this off like a handful of beans.

"Wait, wait! Can't you slow down?"

"What's that child saying?" Dusya senses that the business is becoming serious.

"The child isn't saying anything. The cards are talking," Laura answers in Russian.

"Oi, *nyemagu*—I can't—this is too much!" Dusya can't help but laugh at Laura, who's talking in Russian.

Just wait, Dusya, you just wait, soon you won't laugh anymore. Laura senses that the women are putty in her hands, just like the cards. The big, fat women with smelly armpits and feet. Laura senses the power she has. Power is pleasant, it's sweet and exhilarating. It spreads in Laura like a peacock's tail, expands like the dealt cards from the deck in her hand. Who owns the revenge? Laura does!

"Quiet, you old biddies! To whom will my husband return?"

"To Manya!" Laura announces. Laura will forecast this for Manya, take this!

"What bullshit are you, small asshole, spouting? I have

svoy—my own husband!"

"What kind of a husband is that? Have you been to the *zagss*—the registry office with him?" Rita's mama attacks Manya.

"Aha, how did the *zagss* help you? He left despite the *zagss*!" Manya doesn't give up.

"That's not all," Laura interrupts. "The ace of diamonds."

"Ah, *schto*—what's that?" Now also Manya wants to know.

"Nobody's telling you your fortune! What does it mean, Laurie?" Rita's mama has never really trusted Manya, now shortly her suspicions will be confirmed.

"By itself it doesn't mean anything. It has to be looked at together with other cards," Laura doesn't hide her great knowledge. "The six of spades!" Laura drags out lengthily what she has to say because she senses that her knowledge is slowly coming to an end.

"What does that mean?"

"The queen of hearts. That's you, and it means that there will be a great misfortune."

"What else now?" Rita's mama moans, she's totally crushed. Laura remembers little Ivars, and she suddenly feels a bit sorry for Rita's mama.

"But you can avoid it," Laura gives her hope.

"How?"

"From this moment on, keep all your thoughts to yourself, don't tell anyone anything, because close to you there's a terribly envious person," Laura warns her.

Rita's mama looks now at Manya, now at Dusya. Manya too looks at Dusya.

"What's that child saying?" Dusya asks worriedly. No one answers.

"If you'll keep quiet, the misfortune will pass you by," Laura adds.

"But the upper echelons? What about that? I won't be sent to Siberia, will I?" Rita's mama worries.

"Don't be afraid, only honest and upright people are sent there. Don't hope and don't feel sad! The jack of spades will want to marry the queen of hearts." She's the mother of her friend, after all.

"Me?"

"Yes, via the upper echelons."

"Dear God, via the office? There's only bosses there! Jack of spades? Who could be that jack of spades? The new agriculturist?"

"*Da ti shot razmechtalas*—you must be dreaming, the new *agronom*?"

"The cards don't say that. But the cards say that Manya will stand in your way. The queen of spades! That's a very evil card."

"*Da,* already tomorrow morning I'll drag *svojevo*—my old man to the *zagss*—the registry office! But *tvojevo*—yours I wouldn't take even for gold! Ah, and you're what? Ready to cheat on your husband with the new *agronom*?"

Rita's mama has already opened her mouth wide in rage, to finally say what she really thinks of Manya, but at the last minute, she remembers that she shouldn't reveal her thoughts to anyone.

"*Vsjo, da,* idiotic those cards, da, screw those cards, you, you louse, a skunk of a kid, stop, *da,* get lost, go to your babushka! *Vsjo*! Done and finished!"

"Don't swear at the cards, otherwise you'll burn in hell, in the deepest kettle you'll boil! You'll turn over and over in your grave!" Laura yells at Manya, sensing that Manya is not totally vanquished.

"Dusya." Laura quickly changes direction.

"What—Dusya?" Manya is cross.

Laura thinks. What could Dusya do?

"Dusya is going to steal your husband."

"Steal?" Dusya asks to make sure.

"What?" Manya's totally on fire now like a match put to discarded flax waste. "Dusya?"

"See, if that jack were on the right side, then something could miscarry, but when the jack is on the left…With the nine of spades on top yet. The outcome is totally certain. Later she'll give him back," Laura comforts her.

Laura wants to finish, because she senses that she has got

entangled and in too deep, has lied through her teeth and talked a lot of rot, and hasn't eaten breakfast. Just that cuckoo's mouthful. Laura anticipates her soul's destruction and wreckage.

"The cards no longer want to talk," she announces. "Do you want me to lay out some solitaire for you?"

Rita's mama doesn't want her to, she's got a lot to think over. But Manya does. How will Dusya steal and how will she give back her husband? Manya also says a couple of vulgar words about Dusya. Dusya doesn't understand anything, because that *sobachiy yazik*—dog's language she's certainly not going to learn, besides she doesn't have any *semushkas*, which could revive her spirit. Just indolent dreams are fluttering around Dusya. How she's going to go to the kolkhoz's granary. How she'll show her tits to the White Negro. How she'll again manage to get some *semushkas*.

"Well, *davai*—go on then!"

"Do you want the short or the long solitaire? The Chinese plait or Napoleon's grave?"

"What kind of a grave?" Manya's never heard of Solitaire, but she's suddenly afraid.

"I can lay out Klondike or the common solitaire. The common one is the best."

Laura stresses this, because she's afraid that Manya may choose the Chinese plait, or worse still—Napoleon's grave, which is a hard solitaire and which Laura hasn't managed to learn. Ciganka Moldovanka was teaching her, but didn't manage to get as far as Napoleon's grave. Madalina went back to her country, and Laura—to hers.

"Laura isn't going to lay out Solitaire for you. The cards are angry with you and I don't have the time now."

Laura throws the cards on the table! After all Laura is a busy person.

Laura wants to get away. She doesn't listen to what Manya calls after her. She's got to run. Has to flee! Save herself! It seems to Laura that her armpits also stink. Laura looks to see if they haven't got just as hairy as Manya's, Dusya's, and Rita's mama's. Not yet. But she's got to check again in the evening.

Five Fingers

LAURA DESPERATELY WISHES to have a tree house. Just like the one Stasis has. Stasis has made a home in a high ash tree after dragging old boards and roofing slate up there. The ash is enormous, and the house is horrendously, dreadfully high. That's in case the Old Russian should find it. But he won't find it, for the ash stands deep in the willows along the riverbank. Even if the Old Russian finds the tree house, he won't be able to climb up to it. Laura too won't be able to. If Stasis would help her, she could, but he doesn't help. His tree house is called the Headquarters. A funny name for a house, but everyone can call their house what they want.

The location, yes, the location of the house is important. The maple tree would be good, but it's too close to the windows. Mīma would see what Laura's doing. The chestnut tree is too far away, and from there Laura won't see what Mīma's doing. The tree house has to be where Laura can see everything but no one sees her. Nobody has any business spying on her.

Laura likes maples and chestnuts, because they're trees with leaves like fingers. One can shake hands with them because the leaves of maples and chestnuts are like human hands. It's not true that trees don't talk anymore like they did in ancient times. Maybe not as loudly as then, when trees had screamed and pleaded with human beings not to cut them down. And man, would you believe it, had gone off to God to complain. And God it seems had ordered the trees to be silent. Laura doesn't believe it and never will believe it. It can't be. Man himself has thought this up, but maybe Amelioration has thought it up. So that it would be easier to cut down the ancient lindens, to dynamite the oaks and to hew down the gray apple trees. But all the blame is laid on God.

Laura doesn't believe that God would support Amelioration. And trees do talk! The linden tree talks kindly and lovingly. Talks through the fragrance of its flowers. Through the buzzing of its bees. The linden displays its leaves like small green hearts. What else can the linden say, how else can the linden show its sincerity than by its many, many small, green, honeyed hearts? The maple is like a friend. She wants to play. Here, have my winged seed, take it, for your nose to have wings, paste it on! And then with its leaves! One morning the green maple has colored itself red or yellow. Hey! Hey you over there. Do you still recognize me?

Finally Laura perhaps has found the location for the tree house. In the garden there's an old apple tree. No, old apple trees are many, of course, but this one is special. It looks totally like an open hand. Exactly five fat branches have grown from a low, mossed-over trunk. Without much effort Laura can climb up into the apple tree's open hand. She can lean against all the five fingers of the hand. Gaze in all the five directions of the sky. Laura isn't going to call her house any kind of a headquarters. Laura will give her house a beautiful name. What could it be? It doesn't come to mind immediately.

There are all sorts of outgrowths on the branches, some nodes and gnarled bits begin to pinch and protrusions start to prick, if she sits for a longer time. Then Laura remembers the pillow in the attic.

Now that's better. The old pillow is as if made for Laura's tree house. It's just that white feathers are poking through the holes in the pillow. A mild breeze blows them all over the garden. That's good, because the birds will think that these are Laura's feathers and that Laura is a bird. They'll accept Laura in their flock. The jay won't of course. He'll cackle and screech. But let him!

Laura has her own house! Of course, also the Upītes farmhouse is her home, she hasn't forgotten that, may the Upītes farmhouse not be offended. The Upītes farmhouse is on the ground, but every person needs a home somewhere higher, above ground. Laura thinks about how to furnish it. She'll need a stove and dishes, what else? And what if it should rain? Once more to the attic!

The black umbrella with which Laura had wanted to jump

down through the narrow opening in the attic! Like the *shpions*—spies jump with parachutes. She didn't manage to make the umbrella a parachute, but it will do as a roof for her house! Laura's heart beats like a drum, joy makes it throb with happiness.

In the palm of the apple tree, on her pillow, Laura feels like she's in God's palm. God's hand has five fingers the same as a human being has. Laura is five years old, on each of God's fingers, and on each of the apple tree branches, one of her years.

No, she won't need a stove after all. It looks like Laura won't have the time to fry and cook. Laura has to look at the leafage. How the breezes play with the leaves. How they tickle, how they quiver. How they scold, how caress. How the breezes sniff at the tiny apples that still aren't edible, but, phooey, sour! Laura won't have the time to fry and cook, because through the leafage she'll have to look at the heavens. She has to study the blueness of the sky, no, blueness can only be in one's eye, Laura corrects herself—the depth, the depth of the heavens. Yes and the whiteness and non-whiteness of the clouds. She has to think thoughts. The ones that only Laura can think. Dream, dreams. The ones that only Laura can dream.

She still has to make certain that from here she'll be able to fly, if the branches don't interfere. Will she be able to land, after having flown enough. She should be able to.

She won't need a stove, Laura decides absolutely. But the house in the apple tree will be called Five Fingers. One can't grab a name for a house from blue air. Avoti are Avoti, because there's a spring there, and *avoti* in Latvian means springs. Upītes is Upītes because there's a small river there and *upītes* in Latvian means rivers. Five Fingers is the right name for Laura's tree house.

The Opera

SITTING IN THE FIVE FINGERS of the old apple tree, Laura starts to sing. First she remembers the melody, only afterward—the words.

That's Asya's melody, those are Asya's words. Laura has heard them a hundred times. Asya had sung this song for Laura as a lullaby. Mama sang *Aijā zūžū*—a Latvian lullaby—with these comforting sounds. So did Buka, who sang *Velc pelīte, saldu miegu*—*Draw in sweet sleep, mousekin.* Those Latvian songs were too short, Laura begged Mama and Buka to sing more, but that never happened. Sometimes they tried but then they fell asleep first.

Little one, I'm very sleepy, Mama murmured.

Laurie, I'm dreadfully tired, Buka excused herself.

Asya sang this. Where was this melody earlier? Where had the words been until now? Why does Laura remember them only now?

Be that as it may, Laura is singing. In the beginning more for herself, but when the melody and the words keep coming and coming, rise and swell God knows from where, she sings loudly from the heart. Laura sings to the old apple tree, the hedgehogs, the garden—she sings to the whole world. Laura's heart demands that she sing.

> Un bel di, vedremo
> levarsi un fil di fumo
> sull'estremo confin del mare.
> E poi la nave appare.
> Poi la nave Bianca ...

One lovely day a ship, a white ship arrives at the port. Laura has to wait a bit for the next words to come back.

Where were they during the time that Laura had forgotten them? But now they're here.

> Vedi? È venuto!
> Io non gli scendo incontro. Io no.
> Mi metto là sul ciglio del colle e aspetto,
> e aspetto gran tempo
> e non mi pesa,
> la lunga attesa.

Mīma, who's tending to the roses in the garden, starts to listen. The girl is singing! That's really good. Mīma is very pleased that Laura's singing, then there's hope that Laura feels at home here. Has adjusted to Upītes farm. What is it that the girl is singing there? At the top of her voice! Mīma listens, listens and then crosses herself.

Where's Grandpa? Grandpa has to hear this. Just so the girl doesn't fall silent while Mīma looks for Grandpa.

Grandpa doesn't understand what the issue is. Mīma hushes him, makes signs for Grandpa not to talk, for him just to come. Well, what is it, where do I have to go, there's no peace and none to be hoped for.

> E uscito dalla folla cittadina,
> un uomo, un picciol punto
> s'avvia per la collina.

Laura likes how that sounds—*dalla folla cittadina*—those words.

> Chi sarà? chi sarà?
> E come sarà giunto
> che dirà? che dirà?

As luck would have it the girl is still sitting in the apple tree and is still singing, even more loudly than before. Grandpa falls silent like Mīma. He doesn't believe his ears. Laura is singing in an opera voice. In Italian.

Chiamerà Butterfly dalla lontana.

What was next? Laura reconciles herself with la, la, la-a, la, la-a-a... The words soon are found again.

> *Piccina mogliettina,*
> *olezzo di verbena*
> *i nomi che mi dava al suo venire.*

In earlier times they had once in a while been to the Opera. When Reinis was studying at the University in Riga. Reinis liked operas, and at all costs he wanted that Grandpa and Mīma would see the White House, as the opera building was called by all, at night, he bought tickets, they had to drive there, had to go. To please Reinis. Mīma then put on her ermine collar. Grandpa put on his bow tie.

Laura sits in her Five Fingers and sings.

Both Grandpa and Mīma listen as if enchanted. The bow tie yes! Yes, Madame Butterfly, wasn't that what the opera was called? In Italian. A five-year-old child? That can't be. But it is, it is.

> *Tutto questo avverrà,*
> *te lo prometto.*
> *Tienti la tua paura,*
> *io con sicura fede l'aspetto.*

Laura falls silent. The song is finished.

Laura's experienced great joy and great sadness. Laura's been in Siberia, in the Barrack with Asya. The song has moved Laura, her feelings are surging high like a salty sea. The song has shaken Laura up like an earthquake, she feels tremors in her heart like underground aftershocks again and again.

An avalanche has slid off Laura, a heavy avalanche of ice from a mountain. The mountain is relieved, the mountain doesn't miss that avalanche, not at all.

Laura is all hyped, she is really cranked up, can't calm down, has to sing more. Not the same one a second time. For it in places has to be forced so that eyes almost pop out of one's head. Now Laura will sing "O, mio babbino caro." That's an easier piece. Yes, that one!

Applause sounds. In surprise Laura almost topples out of the apple tree. Mīma and Grandpa are clapping!

Laura feels confused and embarrassed. She gets angry. Rebellious. What kind of behavior is that—to spy on someone? It was as if Laura had been nude, and they looked! How are they allowed to do this—on the sly, from behind a corner to listen!

Laura's afraid that Grandpa will laugh. That Mīma will say … Don't know what but something irreparable. A song for Laura is something…Great. Important. Just for her. For her alone.

If Grandpa laughs right now, then Laura will hate Grandpa for all of eternity.

Mīma maybe will scold. Why is Laura hollering? If Mīma does that, then Laura will also hate Mīma for all of eternity. That's how it will be! Laura's afraid that it will be like that.

"Laurie, child, God help us, where did you learn such a song?"

It doesn't look as if Mīma was about to scold Laura. It looks like Mīma is confused. Laura doesn't climb down from the tree yet.

"Laurie, child …"

Grandpa just manages to say.

Can't understand what he's thinking. Why is Grandpa's cheek twitching? Grandpa is crying? Laura slides down the apple tree's trunk.

"Grandpa, what's the matter with you?"

"Nothing's the matter, nothing at all. Just some wind blown in my eyes."

"There's no wind!"

"No, no, you're wrong. Everything is fine. You sang beautifully."

"You liked it?" Laura snuggles up to Grandpa.

"If only Reinis could have heard it," Grandpa whispers to himself.

A trembling hand caresses Laura's plaited head. Mīma has again plaited her hair too tight.

"Very lovely, child, God help us, do help us," Mīma sobs.

Mīma draws Laura away from Grandpa and presses her to her apron. She kisses the back of Laura's head. Does Mīma see that Laura's hair is plaited too tightly?

"Where did you get to know Italian?" Mīma can't stop marveling.

"Italian?" Laura doesn't understand.

"You were singing in Italian of course. Where did you learn it?" Grandpa has to sit down on a tree stump.

"From Asya. Was that Italian?"

"Well, yes! What song is that?" Mīma asks.

"That's Asya's song."

"What does the song say?" Grandpa wants to know.

"It talks about Asya."

"About Asya? Asya is a Jewess of course," Grandpa and Mīma don't see any connection between the Italian language and Asya.

This and that they already know about Asya. Mama has talked about Asya and all of them had listened. That Asya had been so good, how much she had helped them in Siberia. That Laura had loved her very much.

That Asya has seven brothers in England, all of them musicians. That Asya had finally been allowed to write a letter to her brothers and that the first thing she had asked for was that they send some clothes for Laura. That the brothers had sent them and that Laura then could have strutted around in Siberia like England's princess, but hadn't done it, because other children didn't have such clothes, and it was better that no one should envy her. And the clothes could be sold for a lot. And so on, the story about Asya went. Mīma and Grandpa listened, but it seemed to Laura that they really didn't believe. Seven brothers. Sounds like a fairytale, it does. Seven yearling goats. Seven dwarfs. Seven wolf brothers.

But it's not a fairytale. See, it's not a fairytale! Laura had listened to what Mama was recounting and knew that she wasn't telling all, but she kept silent because one wasn't allowed to talk about Siberia.

"Asya is not a Jewess, she's a Hebrew woman!"

"It's the same thing," Grandpa comforts her.

"That's nothing bad," Mīma adds.

"Asya was an opera singer in London, but in Siberia Asya was a spy!" Laura wants Mīma and Grandpa to understand how notable a person Asya is.

"How did she suddenly get from London to Siberia?" Mīma doesn't understand.

"Mīma! Not really suddenly!" Laura reproaches.

"Child, then tell us two old idiots," Grandpa pleads. Well fine, while the song still sways in Laura's soul.

"Once Asya lived in London. One day a great white ship arrived in London. With that great beautiful ship arrived a Russian sailor."

"In what year?"

Laura doesn't know what year, a detail like that. Laura can't know absolutely everything in this world! Laura can also not tell them!

But now Laura herself wants to continue, in the telling to be together with Asya.

Well fine. Therefore.

The Russian sailor met Asya… Laura was too shy to say. Fine, she'll say it. Asya fell dreadfully in love, and the Russian sailor even more dreadfully. He went to all the operas in which Asya was singing. Went and went until he persuaded Asya to come with him to Saint Petersburg. In that Saint Petersburg there was a big, big theater, Asya could sing there. The Russian sailor promised. So they got married. Asya left her seven brothers, they were angry at Asya. They were dreadfully angry. They were seven wolf brothers! Not any kind of yearling goats.

So that was that. Asya and the Russian sailor then lived happily just that Asya didn't get to sing in that big, big theater. In the theater where they show movies, Asya got to see all the films. She got to see the one about Tarzan too.

Laura doesn't know how it happened but something did happen, something bad.

The Russian sailor was arrested by the dog-faced monsters and he was shot and killed.

Asya too was arrested by the dog-faces and they pierced and poked under her nails with needles. They broke her fingers. Five on her right hand and five on her left. They told Asya that she was an English spy and jailed her. She had a baby there, but it was born dead. Because they kicked Asya in the stomach.

"Are they human!" Mima interrupted to say.

"No, they were the dog-faced monsters who kicked."

"Who else can kick like that? A stomach in which there's a baby?"

Laura doesn't allow the thought that they could be human beings.

Such a thought could make Laura unhappy.

How could one live with such a thought at all?

Asya pitied her baby, never mind that it was dead. But the dog-faced monsters didn't give the baby to Asya, they took it away, and *vsjo*—that was that. Then, sometime later, they took Asya out of prison and brought her to the Barrack in Siberia. There with all the rest of them. And that's it. Well, almost.

Laura falls silent.

Grandpa and Mīma also don't speak. Laura senses how incomplete is her story about Asya. She shouldn't have even told it! Those are only words. Laura's story doesn't have a melody. You can tell so much more in a song.

Papa is right. No one should be told anything. Just the same no one will understand, no one will believe.

> *Amore, addio! Addio! Piccolo amor!*
> *Va. Gioca, gioca.*

Laura doesn't have the strength to sing more. Even if she did, Grandpa and Mīma don't have the strength to listen.

Horror Stories

LAURA HAS TO GO AND PLAY with the Lejasupītes's children. Mīma wants her to go. She thinks that Laura needs to be with other children. Laura doesn't think so, but goes if she has to go. She can go if Mīma wants her to. It's no skin off Laura's back because of it. Mīma's being sneaky. She's sending Laura to Lejasupītes because it's the closest neighboring farm. Mīma doesn't like it that Laura sneaks off to the railway station.

The station kids, some Russian boys, are great rascals. Mīma's hair stands on end thinking about what those little devils are up to. They prowl among the wagons, but those wagons, the great cisterns, can at any moment start to move! What all can't happen, arms, legs can be lost, and a head can be cut off by such a train as if with a knife!

Annie has complained that those station rascals apparently put all sorts of junk on the tracks.

"Not junk but five-kapeika coins!" Laura objects.

The five kapeikas have to be put on the tracks. When the train passes over them they turn into gold medals. Smooth and flat, one can't even tell that it was a five-kapeika coin. Laura doesn't see anything bad in this, but Mīma does.

If Mīma only knew that Laura had played "I dare you" with the station's Russian boys, God knows what she would have said?

That's when you first wait for the train to approach. The station's Russian boys know the schedule.

Laura doesn't know the schedule, but just the same feels a sweet excitement like the rest. The train is coming! It approaches like a storm! Ever closer!

Then you have to be ready to run over the tracks. The one who has stronger nerves is the last to cross. He's a hero.

At least until the next train. Laura usually runs first because she's the youngest and smallest and a girl besides. Girls don't have as strong nerves as boys. You'll run first or not at all! Viktor says this because he's the gang leader.

But to be first is still to be first, it's just important that your foot doesn't get caught. Laura likes the station's Russian boys.

At Lejasupītes one end of the farmhouse is full of Russians. Old Russian has a thick and long beard, everyone is afraid of him. He's killed his first wife. Accidentally, but dead and gone she is nonetheless. The five children of Old Russian are in an orphanage. His Russian woman has only one child—Stasis.

Stasis also knows Latvian and Old Russian is not allowed to hit him.

His own children, the rare times that they appear, he's allowed to hit as much as he wants but Stasis not, because then his Russian woman will pour sulfuric acid in his eyes.

Stasis is proud of his special status but just the same he sleeps in a different place each night. High on top of the hay in the barn or on the hayrack in the field. Because right now Old Russian is lost in a *zapoy*. What's that? That's when he's on a boozing binge. When the old man has got moonshine galore, don't you understand? Stasis wonders.

Laura understands. That hitting-the-moonshine is a horrendous illness. Like epilepsy or scarlet fever. Something like that. Mīma, if you think about it, is sending Laura directly into danger! What if this *zapoy* is infectious?

Laura goes to Lejasupītes.

She can't walk there so fast. An old, curved bridge traverses the little river. Made from round thin logs. Pretty. It takes time to examine it, see what's beneath, hop about on the rocks in the river.

Ivars is a pretty little boy, with white hair, and he's the same height as Laura. Laura likes Ivars, who's so quiet and loveable. But Ivars doesn't talk. He just sits and rocks. That's when someone sways back and forth, back and forth. He likes to sit and rock. Ivars wraps his arms around himself and rocks.

"Stop rocking!" Laura says and takes Ivars by the hand.

He obediently gets up and trustfully waits to see where Laura will lead him.

Laura doesn't know where to take Ivars. She's in a strange house, how should she know? Ivars doesn't let go of Laura's hand. He's very strong. Laura removes her hand by force. Ivars sits down in his old place and resumes his rocking.

"He's like that. Leave him be!" Rita yells.

"Do you want to see the dark stairs?"

Rita leads Laura into a dark hallway. When her eyes get accustomed to the dark, she sees the stairs. Stairs like any stairs. They lead to the attic, with the trap door closed.

"Here we tell horror stories! Do you know about the gold leg? No? But the one about the black coffin? How can you not know about the black coffin? But the one with the blue finger?"

"What finger?"

"The one found in meat patties! You don't know?" Rita is disappointed, but never mind.

She has to call Stasis. Then they'll be a threesome. For two girls alone it's too frightening. Stasis will come from his Headquarters, first making sure Old Russian is sleeping like the dead on top of the hay. He's not been killed yet, but Stasis will kill him, when he gets a bit bigger. He's made up his mind to do it and doesn't hide the fact. The door has to be closed and now the stairs are dark. They can start to be afraid. Rita tells the story about the gold leg.

"Give me back my gold leg!"

That's said by a corpse who has risen from his grave. It's actually Rita, but speaking in the corpse's voice. In her own voice Rita only shrieks from fear and squeals like a mouse caught in a mousetrap.

Stasis tells the story about the blue finger, which a housewife finds in the minced meat she's kneading to make meat patties. The situation is that her boy has disappeared and he had a finger exactly like this. And the rest can be imagined. Everyone has to tremble in horror.

Rita will still tell the story about the White Lady of Lake Lancenieks.

"Once long ago on a dark night…" Rita begins.

To Laura it seems that it would be better to say: "Once long ago on a dark, dark night." And it should be added that even the moon that night wasn't shining, as well as suddenly a dreadful wind began to blow, and it wasn't wind like the wind every day, but a horrendously cold wind that howled like a wolf and…

"Well then tell it yourself!" Rita is offended. How can Laura tell it, not knowing anything about the White Lady of Lake Lancenieks?

"You messed up my story!" Rita snivels. Stasis also thinks that Laura should tell the story. It's her turn.

What should Laura recount? Everyone is waiting. The dark stairs smell of cat piss. There are a lot of cats at Lejasupītes farm. Sounds can be heard of their chasing one another in the attic above. They're fighting and romping around. Suddenly one wails like a child. Laura will tell the story.

Once, long ago, on a dark, dark night, when even the moon wasn't shining, suddenly a dreadful wind rose, and it wasn't like an everyday wind, but a horrendously cold wind, which howled like a wolf…

"Well? What's next?" Rita is quite cross.

The dog-faced monsters catch people, shove them into cattle cars and drive them off. The people are like herring in a barrel, everyone is dreadfully thirsty, but the dog-faces don't give them anything. In that cattle car wagon is also Mrs. Austrums with her little boy. Everyone is sad, no one is laughing, only the little boy is happy and laughing. Mrs. Austrums does try to control the little boy, saying: "Don't laugh." But he doesn't understand, because he's young. He's just recently learned to run. Everyone else grows more sad, but the little boy just laughs and runs around, shaking his blond curly-haired head.

"Some sort of an abnormal one," decides Stasis.

"You're telling this too stretched out. What happens next? But make it short!" Ivars has fallen asleep leaning on Rita and is pinching her legs.

"In short it's that the little boy dies. That in itself is nothing because he's not the only one who dies in the wagon. The train doesn't stop for this. Whoever dies is thrown off the train. The little boy too must be thrown out.

"Mrs. Austrums, the little boy's mama, doesn't want to throw him out, but she has to. Finally the little boy is thrown out. But one night he returns once more. One dark, dark night, so dark, that even the moon doesn't shine, suddenly a dreadful wind rises, and that's not a wind like an everyday wind, but it's a horrendously cold wind, which howls like a wolf, and now Laughing Child is back.

"He once more runs and laughs. Just no one can catch him. Even Mrs. Austrums can't.

"When the train has reached its final destination and Mrs. Austrums is already living in the Barrack, Laughing Child is once more there. Mrs. Austrums is happy that he's arrived, but sad, because she can't catch him. Mrs. Austrums is beginning to think if she's the only one the child appears for, but, no, the Barrack people say: 'We all see him. Well, yes! He's laughing, running around, we see his blond, curly-haired head. Let him run around, let him laugh, just don't pay any attention.'"

"That's not interesting. You don't know how to tell a story," Rita stands up.

"That's not a real horror story. The story about the blue finger is real, about the gold leg is real, but this isn't," Stasis too isn't totally satisfied. His mind too isn't at rest. What if Old Russian has woken up? Stasis will steal some bread in the kitchen and will go back to his Headquarters.

Laura has totally disgraced herself. She should have said that she didn't know any real horror story, should have confessed it. That would have been better. Reality doesn't make a horror story. Reality is reality.

The White Ship

RITA IS SQUEALING LIKE a piglet. Soon she'll have to go to school but Rita hasn't done her summer homework. The school won't take Rita back! Rita will be sent back home! Rita won't get the warm school lunch! The teachers will kill Rita. Mama too will kill Rita, because Rita has forgotten to gather scrap metal. The October Child's star pin will be taken away from Rita! The lovely red five-rayed star with a golden Volodya like an angel in the middle. Rita's life is ruined forever. Rita will go and drown herself in the river!

Laura thinks that nothing will come of the drowning in the river. Even the deepest places in the river barely reach above one's knees. Well then, in your pond, where your idiot frogs are. Rita howls. Well, no, that Laura doesn't like at all. The pond will be contaminated if Rita drowns there. They must think of something else. What exactly has Rita really done?

That's exactly it, Rita hasn't done what she should have done. Rita hisses like a fly stuck on fly paper. What really? If she doesn't want to have the pond contaminated Laura will have to admit that she hasn't understood, she really has to admit it.

"I already told you! What end of yours do you listen with? During the summer I had to gather scrap metal!"

"What's that?"

It turns out that scrap metal is what looks old, long-ago already non-usable metal. But it only looks like that. In fact it's very useful.

"Who can use it?"

"You little twerp, just the same you don't understand anything!"

"Then tell me! If you want to drown yourself in my pond. Why does it have to be exactly you that needs to gather the what-cha-ma-call-its?"

"All the October Children need to gather it! Everyone else will have gathered it but not me!" Rita once more squeals like a piglet. "The scrap metal will be melted down and then a ship will be built."

"A ship?" Laura's breath catches.

"Yes, a ship! All the Lamme's school children are collecting. The whole summer all the children in all of Latvia have been gathering scrap metal, can you grasp it? And not only in Latvia but in all of the Soviet Union. All the Soviet children are collecting scrap metal. A lot is needed, a big pile, do you understand?"

"A big, white one? A big, white ship?"

"Yes! How many times do I have to say it before you get it!" Rita's nose is running and she wipes her nose on her sleeve.

"The kind that goes to Kurzeme in Latvia?" Laura remembers the big river in Siberia and the air that was full of tiny fish. So tiny that they couldn't be seen with the naked eye. A ship! Laura too wants a ship! Laura too wants to collect old metal. Laura too wants to take part! Laura can help Rita!

"Not to Kurzeme! To America!"

"To America?"

"That's what I'm telling you! But do you *tochna*—really want to help me?"

Yes, Laura can. Laura will also call Grandpa and Mīma, and Papa and Mama, and Rita will call her mama, yes, and Stasis!

"Stasis won't come, he's already collected all the best metal. That's why I have nothing to gather!" Rita wails once more.

Laura's enthusiasm and readiness to help loosens Rita's ability to speak, and she finally talks like a human being.

How beautifully the teacher had known to describe the strength that can't be seen in a drop but which becomes great and mighty when all the drops are combined!

Nearly all the children in her class had cried when the teacher recounted this.

That other children of the world don't have as happy a childhood as the Soviet children.

No, no, the children in America, for example, are very

unhappy. The bourgeoisie doesn't allow them to play. Makes them work from morning till night. In those grave-like countries. And the children, for example, in America, have nothing to eat. They're starving. Their parents have no money, because the bourgeoisie has taken it away from them.

Madness! How is it that Laura hasn't known this before?

Really? For real?

Well, yes. The teacher wouldn't lie.

Children could die!

That's why in a great hurry, a great, great hurry the scrap metal needs to be collected and the ship built, that big, white ship with which to transport some food to the children in America. Maybe potatoes or flour, or lard.

Laura has lard!

"Spread that lard, you know where! We need scrap metal!"

We! Rita says—we! A big, white ship! All the children will build it and Laura too! Laura's heart exults with joy when she imagines the ship full of food, docking on America's shore. How happy the American children will be!

Laura's heart wrenches when she thinks that it might be too late. What if some child, having waited in vain for the ship, dies? Laura feels a heavy burden of responsibility. She must act quickly! Laura has searched through all the Upītes farm surroundings. Now she has a large pile of scrap metal. There's a rusted wash basin, a tea kettle with a hole and bent, rusted pails. Four of them Papa had recently raised up from the depths of the well. The well hadn't been cleaned since before the war. That's what Mīma said and didn't very much want it to be touched. Let Papa leave it alone. Mīma was worried. There could be God only knows what in the well! There could be some mine or grenade, or even something worse.

"What could be worse?" Laura wanted to know but Mīma only waved her off. Nonetheless at the bottom of the well four rusted-out pails were found. Nothing worse was there. Laura would have liked something to be there.

Besides the four pails Laura has got some springs from an old mattress, spades, horseshoes, broken chains, a rusted-out

milk-separating machine with a lot of small funnels, a plough-
share, a sprocket-wheel and some other kind of scrap metals. A
mishmash. No one should expect Laura to be able to identify
absolutely all of that old junk. Laura collects whatever she can.
Mainly from the garbage dump. Even the rusted conserve tins.
Even those that are so rusted that they nearly fall apart in her
hands. Nonetheless they too could be of use. From one such tin
a couple of drops of iron could be made. If such a tin is melted
down, about a teaspoon of iron is obtained, Laura calculates.
Among other things, also teaspoons can be melted, why not?
Laura has taken three tea spoons from the buffet. The oldest and
the heaviest. Laura has a whole mountain of scrap metal! We,
children, have collected this, even though she hasn't seen Rita the
last few days. Rita is collecting scrap metal on her farm. Laura
is tired and proud.

Laura by herself has lifted, dragged, and lugged. All alone
because no one else has wanted to help her. Mīma doesn't have
the time, Grandpa can't lift heavy things. Mama and Papa are
busy. Laura suspects that they simply don't understand.

Rita's mama too doesn't understand how important the scrap
metal gathering is.

"Old fools!" Rita says. Laura agrees. Rita after all is Laura's
best friend.

Grandpa's Ring

LAURA IS THINKING ABOUT school. It's true, of course, that she'll be only in kindergarten and that also only because of Mama's pleading with the principal, but the kindergarten children will be in the school's building, and school is still school. On the first of September, she'll have to go. She'll have to bring a bunch of gladiolas. That'll be soon, because the gladiolas are already in bloom. Laura doesn't like gladiolas. They look cross and angry. They're shaped like a sword. Laura likes tiny and loveable flowers. Why does she have to bring gladiolas? Because that's what's done by everyone else. She won't be able to do what she wants. How is that going to be?

The Upītes farm potatoes have already been harvested. Today they're being gathered at the Avoti farm. Mīma has gone there to supervise. After Mama had asked if the harvested potatoes needed to be washed. A question like that has made Mīma worry.

Now Laura is alone with Grandpa.

Grandpa picks out from the big pile the plumpest tubers. Looks them over to see if any are damaged. The ones meant for winter have to be put aside. Laura has to pick out the small and tiny ones. Those will be given to the farm animals. To Pigsy and Oinky. But how about the sheep? Yes, also to the sheep. It's good that the sheep will get some. Laura picks for the sheep. For the sake of the sheep, it's worth it to do one's best.

The two of them pick in silence. They don't talk. It's fine that way.

Laura senses Grandpa's good-natured presence. Grandpa senses Laura's lively presence. Both sense the lovely and colorful world. The maples have colored their leaves like lips—red. The lindens and oaks are turning yellow more calmly and in a more restrained fashion. The oaks are full of acorns and full of

244

jays, who, chattering, peck off the acorns and carry them off in all directions. A flock of cranes in a V formation flies overhead. Laura could ask where are the cranes flying, but she doesn't. She doesn't want to disturb something great and good. The sun warms and warms, until it starts to beat down. Grandpa finds it too hot. He takes off his thick knitted sweater and smiles. You're my best helper, he pronounces. Laura likes being Grandpa's best helper. Likes it that they're just the two of them alone.

The earth is fragrant. The stalks of the old potato plants are burned in small bonfires. Smoke spurts wind up to the sky. Laura sees that Grandpa is leaning oddly to one side by the big potato pile. Grandpa? He doesn't answer. He's fallen sideways toward the pile. Laura grabs Grandpa's hand. A potato rolls out from it. Laura shakes Grandpa's shoulder. The shoulder is warm but unresponsive.

"Grandpa, Grandpa, what's the matter with you? Grandpa, get up! Please get up, Grandpa! Get up! Please, please!" Laura just repeats these words, over and over, as if she didn't know any others. She yells and yells. Swallowing tears, her voice breaking. Many, many times. Laura doesn't want to believe what at the bottom of her heart, with dread, she intuits. Laura shakes Grandpa's shoulder because she doesn't want Grandpa to guess what she intuits. And then suddenly Laura no longer can touch Grandpa, who is lying motionless among the potato tubers, and Laura is afraid, and Laura's ashamed of her fear, her fear of a Grandpa who has died.

At Avoti farm Laura's yells have been heard. The slight wind has been blowing toward Avoti, the wind has again helped.

Mīma brings a blanket. Papa has to work hard until he rolls Grandpa on to the blanket. Grandpa is heavy. Mama helps to pull Grandpa to the farm's closed-in verandah. Mīma doesn't allow them to enter the verandah first. Mīma apparently needs to go first. How will they get Grandpa in his bed now?

"Not in his bed! Grandpa has to stay on the ground," Mīma says, "Anda, you bring the straw! Jāni, bring water from the well."

Mīma doesn't make Laura do anything, but she herself leaves

and stays away for a long time. Laura's afraid to look directly at Grandpa. It's good that there's someone else there. The dog Ripsis. Ripsis is confused and whimpering he runs around Grandpa, licks his hands, now one, then the other, wants to lick Grandpa's face. Is that alright, should Laura allow Ripsis to lick Grandpa's face? While Laura thinks about it, Ripsis calms down. He lies down by Grandpa's head. The dog's breath moves Grandpa's white, still thick hair. Ripsis glances at Laura and makes her understand that he's going to lie there. In the future his place will be there. Here he'll stay and lie beside Grandpa, like it always has been. And let no one… Ripsis emits a growl.

Mīma returns with a bowl of water and a candle. She opens the window. Lights the candle. Now Grandpa's soul will be cleansed with water and fire and can fly out of the window up to heaven. Mama's brought straw, which Mīma places under Grandpa's head. Mama is crying. Papa wants to know if he can help in any way. Right now, no, while the flesh hasn't yet cooled off. Mama too wants to help.

"Go to the horse barn and the animal byre."

"Why?" Mama doesn't understand.

"Tell all the beasts that their master has died."

Mama starts to cry more loudly. Nonetheless she isn't sure that it really is necessary—to go to the barn and the byre. "Mīma, really, is it necessary?" Mama with a look asks for help from Papa. Papa lowers his gaze.

It's needed, of course it's needed! How can she not understand? Laura will go! Laura will tell them. Laura wants to move from her spot, from her frozen state, she feels cold, she runs to the horse barn.

"Daira, your master has died," Laura says. Great and important is the task Mīma has entrusted her with. Laura senses this with all her being, how sacred and solemn is her task—to tell and to announce, even though the news is sad.

Daira remains with her head hung. She understands. Now Daira will be able to remember how her master has raised her from a tiny colt to become a proper horse. How the two of them have ploughed and sowed, how they've driven to the Slokas village market with wagons full of plums and apples and how they've taken autumn goodies to their Melluži relatives. Precisely at this time of year. That was earlier. When the master was full of vim and vigor, when he didn't have to summon his strength just to live. Daira now will be able to remember her master's care and love.

"Wonder, your master has died," Laura says.

Wonder wiggles his ears. Probably doesn't believe it. Wonder will have to believe it after all and will have to celebrate in his memory the time when he was given his name. His master gave it to him, who else. Oh, how the master raved about Wonder, how he bragged about him, how happy they felt then, when Wonder grew, and grew, and grew! When they didn't know yet that Wonder would grow so big that no collar, no breech band and no saddle-pads would fit him he was so big. Wonder had grown too big. Too great had also grown his master's sorrow, otherwise the master would have ordered horse fittings for Wonder from Riga, which would have been custom-made for him, and he would have ordered a wagon with longer shafts.

"Bilberry, your master has died," Laura tells the cow in the byre.

Bilberry fans the air with her tail and gazes with sad eyes. Yes, yes. Bilberry understands and recognizes the master of the farm, but the mistress is dearer for her. In Bilberry's eyes for a moment fear appears for Mīma.

"Shipley, your master has died," Laura tells Shipley, because she's the oldest of the sheep and the leader of the flock. The sheep shove their heads together and think.

"Your master has died!" Laura tells Oinky, the pig. "Your master has died!" Laura yells to the chickens, so that all of them will hear.

Laura runs to the garden to the hedgehogs, the birds, and the snails.

"Your master has died!" Laura walks around the garden calling to the pear and plum trees, announces it to the cherry trees and the currant bushes.

When Laura returns to the closed porch, coins have been put on Grandpa's eyes. They're silver five-lati coins. That's the money of earlier times. Grandpa's hands have been crossed on his chest. Mīma wonders that Grandpa doesn't have his wedding ring on his finger. Yesterday he still had it. Mīma is convinced of this. That really is odd. Grandpa has never taken off his ring for more than fifty years. Papa comes out of Grandpa's room with a wide dark gold band in his hand.

On the table. Right in the middle.

The ring had been threaded on a string.

A small note is attached to it.

With an indelible pencil Grandpa has written: "Give it to Reinis when he returns."

Papa stretches out his hand, but neither Mama nor Mīma reach for the ring. They stand with lowered eyes.

Laura stretches her hand forward.

"I will. I'll give it to Reinis when he returns."

Did the girl say—I? Mama in amazement raises her weepy eyes. Not as she would have said—"Laura will give it." Has Laura really started to use the first person singular? Finally! After a couple of days she'll have to go to school, thank God, otherwise they'd think that the child is dim-witted, they'd say that her parents haven't taught her to talk properly. Papa hesitates.

"I. I'll give it to Reinis when he returns," Laura says again.

Papa looks at Mīma. What does she say about this?

Mīma nods in agreement. Five fingers close tightly around the ring.

Māra Zālīte was born in 1952 in Krasnoyarsk, Siberia, to a Latvian family deported to Siberia by the Soviet regime. A graduate of University of Latvia's Faculty of Philology, Zālīte has worked as poetry consultant for Latvia's Writers' Union, editor-in-chief of Latvia's literary magazine *Karogs*, director of the Young Writers' Studio and president of the Authors' Association. Zālīte has authored many volumes of poetry, numerous plays, lyrics for many Latvian choral and pop songs, several rock operas and musical librettos, and essays on Latvian culture and history.

Born in Riga, Latvia, poet and translator Margita Gailitis immigrated to Canada as a child. Gailitis returned to Riga in 1998 to work at the Translation and Terminology Center. Today Gailitis focuses her energy on literary translation and poetry, having translated some of Latvia's finest poetry, prose, and dramaturgy. Gailitis's own poetry has been widely published and has won her awards from both the Canada Council for the Arts and the Ontario Arts Council.

A Glossary of Terms in Russian and Languages Other than English*

amerikanskiy – American
amba – finished, the end, shit
avoti – springs
barohlo – junk
benzovozh – a gasoline transporter
betonameshalk – cement mixer
blyad – whore, bitch, slut
bobik – Bob – Soviet transformed American Jeep
brille – spectacles but here a nickname for outhouse toilet
bumagi– papers, documents
burzhuasniy – bourgeois
ceļmallapiņas – wayside leaves, plantain (Latvian)
chaika – a luxury car
"Chame, chame, deda genazvalos!" – "Eat, eat, little one!" (Georgian)
charka – a shot glass
cheremsha – wild garlic
chistiye – pure
cyberitalka
Da ti shto razmechtalas – you must be dreaming
davai – let's, sure, come on
diversantka – female saboteur
dofiga – I've had it up to here!, Enough is enough!
drandoleta – old, worn-out equipment
etagerska – *étagère* – a piece of light furniture
Etot brat vrag naroda! Nedobitiy! – This midget 'enemy of the people'! Not killed off yet!
furazhka – an army hat
gorodok – a town
goryuche smazochniye materiali – gasoline and motor oil materials

gruzchik – a loader, stevedore, dockhand
hana – end, finish
hlami – trash
imperialisticheskiy – imperialistic
k chertovoy materi – with the devil's mother
ķeme – apple sauce (Latvian)
kerzoviki – rubber boots
klyauza – complaint
klichka podpolnaya – code-name
kochegarka – a heating plant
kochiņi, polshiņi – quarter-liters and a half-liters of booze (Latvian)
kombikorm – a mishmash of fodder
kombinzhir – a mix of fats
komisyonka – commissary shop
konec filma – the film is over
kostyum – suit
krishka – end, finish
kupars – coffer, chest
lavka – a kiosk, a small store
Lejasupītes – Lower Rivers (Latvian)
leposhka – flat bread made of grain husks
liepa – linden (Latvian)
lomik – a crow bar
machka – bitch
maika – man's undershirt
nachalnik – commander
nafig– damn
naryadi – work order
navolam – full
nepolozheno – not planned
nyemagu– I can't
nye figa – no such thing!
ohranyiky – guards
ohuyetiy – fuck me!
partorg – party secretary
peresilkas – shunted from prison to prison

pilyit – to beef about something
pīrāgi – bacon filled turnovers
ploshka – a tiny candle
Pobeda – a make of a car
Pochkas – kidneys
Pohmelyas – hangover
Povidla – a brown, oily apple puree
polsh – a half-litre of liquor (Latvian)
prekratyity – to stop, discontinue
pribalti – the Balts
Pribaltika – the Baltics
prichom – why would they
pufaikas – quilted coats
raboche krestyanskiye – working man, farmer
sachinit – to be fixed, to be patched
samogon – booze
semushkas – sunflower seeds
shmons – a prisoner inspection
sin ribaka – fisherman's son
shpion – spy
shpionka – female spy
sobachiy yazik – dog's language
solyarka – diesel fuel
stroika – construction site
svolochi – scoundrels
svoyak – one's own
svoyevo – mine
tarataika – a large cart or similar contraption
tochna – really, for sure
trusiki – underpants
tumbochka – nightstand
tvoyevo – yours
uchastkoviy – precinct boss
umnica – a smart one
Upītes – rivers (Latvian)
uchastkoviy – precinct boss
uzvalks – man's suit (Latvian)

vedma – witch

V Moskvu. Da. Da. – To Moscow. Yes. Yes.

valenki – felt boots

vāvere – squirrel (Latvian)

vot – here now

vsyo – That's it! That's all!

yeibogu – I swear by God

yebitvayumaty – literally 'fuck your mother' – in text used 'fuck'

yobtvaimaty – literally 'I fuck my mother' in text used 'fuck'

yomayo – fuck

zagss – registry office

zakuskas – appetizers

zapoy – boozing binge

zatknis, dura derevennaya – shut up, you country bumpkin

zavals – absolute end

zeki – jailbirds

zhelezno – iron-strong

zrya – a waste, a shame

* The majority of the terms in the list are Russian. The language of all other foreign words is identified in brackets following their English explanation.

MICHAL AJVAZ, *The Golden Age.*
The Other City.
PIERRE ALBERT-BIROT, *Grabinoulor.*
YUZ ALESHKOVSKY, *Kangaroo.*
FELIPE ALFAU, *Chromos.*
Locos.
JOE AMATO, *Samuel Taylor's Last Night.*
IVAN ÂNGELO, *The Celebration.*
The Tower of Glass.
ANTÓNIO LOBO ANTUNES, *Knowledge of Hell.*
The Splendor of Portugal.
ALAIN ARIAS-MISSON, *Theatre of Incest.*
JOHN ASHBERY & JAMES SCHUYLER, *A Nest of Ninnies.*
ROBERT ASHLEY, *Perfect Lives.*
GABRIELA AVIGUR-ROTEM, *Heatwave and Crazy Birds.*
DJUNA BARNES, *Ladies Almanack.*
Ryder.
JOHN BARTH, *Letters.*
Sabbatical.
DONALD BARTHELME, *The King.*
Paradise.
SVETISLAV BASARA, *Chinese Letter.*
MIQUEL BAUÇÀ, *The Siege in the Room.*
RENÉ BELLETTO, *Dying.*
MAREK BIENCZYK, *Transparency.*
ANDREI BITOV, *Pushkin House.*
ANDREJ BLATNIK, *You Do Understand.*
Law of Desire.
LOUIS PAUL BOON, *Chapel Road.*
My Little War.
Summer in Termuren.
ROGER BOYLAN, *Killoyle.*
IGNÁCIO DE LOYOLA BRANDÃO, *Anonymous Celebrity.*
Zero.
BONNIE BREMSER, *Troia: Mexican Memoirs.*
CHRISTINE BROOKE-ROSE, *Amalgamemnon.*
BRIGID BROPHY, *In Transit.*
The Prancing Novelist.

GERALD L. BRUNS, *Modern Poetry and the Idea of Language.*
GABRIELLE BURTON, *Heartbreak Hotel.*
MICHEL BUTOR, *Degrees.*
Mobile.
G. CABRERA INFANTE, *Infante's Inferno.*
Three Trapped Tigers.
JULIETA CAMPOS, *The Fear of Losing Eurydice.*
ANNE CARSON, *Eros the Bittersweet.*
ORLY CASTEL-BLOOM, *Dolly City.*
LOUIS-FERDINAND CÉLINE, *North.*
Conversations with Professor Y.
London Bridge.
MARIE CHAIX, *The Laurels of Lake Constance.*
HUGO CHARTERIS, *The Tide Is Right.*
ERIC CHEVILLARD, *Demolishing Nisard.*
The Author and Me.
MARC CHOLODENKO, *Mordechai Schamz.*
JOSHUA COHEN, *Witz.*
EMILY HOLMES COLEMAN, *The Shutter of Snow.*
ERIC CHEVILLARD, *The Author and Me.*
ROBERT COOVER, *A Night at the Movies.*
STANLEY CRAWFORD, *Log of the S.S. The Mrs Unguentine.*
Some Instructions to My Wife.
RENÉ CREVEL, *Putting My Foot in It.*
RALPH CUSACK, *Cadenza.*
NICHOLAS DELBANCO, *Sherbrookes.*
The Count of Concord.
NIGEL DENNIS, *Cards of Identity.*
PETER DIMOCK, *A Short Rhetoric for Leaving the Family.*
ARIEL DORFMAN, *Konfidenz.*
COLEMAN DOWELL, *Island People.*
Too Much Flesh and Jabez.
ARKADII DRAGOMOSHCHENKO, *Dust.*
RIKKI DUCORNET, *Phosphor in Dreamland.*
The Complete Butcher's Tales.

RIKKI DUCORNET (cont.), *The Jade Cabinet.*
The Fountains of Neptune.
WILLIAM EASTLAKE, *The Bamboo Bed.*
Castle Keep.
Lyric of the Circle Heart.
JEAN ECHENOZ, *Chopin's Move.*
STANLEY ELKIN, *A Bad Man.*
Criers and Kibitzers, Kibitzers and Criers.
The Dick Gibson Show.
The Franchiser.
The Living End.
Mrs. Ted Bliss.
FRANÇOIS EMMANUEL, *Invitation to a Voyage.*
PAUL EMOND, *The Dance of a Sham.*
SALVADOR ESPRIU, *Ariadne in the Grotesque Labyrinth.*
LESLIE A. FIEDLER, *Love and Death in the American Novel.*
JUAN FILLOY, *Op Oloop.*
ANDY FITCH, *Pop Poetics.*
GUSTAVE FLAUBERT, *Bouvard and Pécuchet.*
KASS FLEISHER, *Talking out of School.*
JON FOSSE, *Aliss at the Fire.*
Melancholy.
FORD MADOX FORD, *The March of Literature.*
MAX FRISCH, *I'm Not Stiller.*
Man in the Holocene.
CARLOS FUENTES, *Christopher Unborn.*
Distant Relations.
Terra Nostra.
Where the Air Is Clear.
TAKEHIKO FUKUNAGA, *Flowers of Grass.*
WILLIAM GADDIS, JR., *The Recognitions.*
JANICE GALLOWAY, *Foreign Parts.*
The Trick Is to Keep Breathing.
WILLIAM H. GASS, *Life Sentences.*
The Tunnel.
The World Within the Word.
Willie Masters' Lonesome Wife.
GÉRARD GAVARRY, *Hoppla! 1 2 3.*

ETIENNE GILSON, *The Arts of the Beautiful.*
Forms and Substances in the Arts.
C. S. GISCOMBE, *Giscome Road.*
Here.
DOUGLAS GLOVER, *Bad News of the Heart.*
WITOLD GOMBROWICZ, *A Kind of Testament.*
PAULO EMÍLIO SALES GOMES, *P's Three Women.*
GEORGI GOSPODINOV, *Natural Novel.*
JUAN GOYTISOLO, *Count Julian.*
Juan the Landless.
Makbara.
Marks of Identity.
HENRY GREEN, *Blindness.*
Concluding.
Doting.
Nothing.
JACK GREEN, *Fire the Bastards!*
JIŘÍ GRUŠA, *The Questionnaire.*
MELA HARTWIG, *Am I a Redundant Human Being?*
JOHN HAWKES, *The Passion Artist.*
Whistlejacket.
ELIZABETH HEIGHWAY, ED., *Contemporary Georgian Fiction.*
AIDAN HIGGINS, *Balcony of Europe.*
Blind Man's Bluff.
Bornholm Night-Ferry.
Langrishe, Go Down.
Scenes from a Receding Past.
KEIZO HINO, *Isle of Dreams.*
KAZUSHI HOSAKA, *Plainsong.*
ALDOUS HUXLEY, *Antic Hay.*
Point Counter Point.
Those Barren Leaves.
Time Must Have a Stop.
NAOYUKI II, *The Shadow of a Blue Cat.*
DRAGO JANČAR, *The Tree with No Name.*
MIKHEIL JAVAKHISHVILI, *Kvachi.*
GERT JONKE, *The Distant Sound.*
Homage to Czerny.
The System of Vienna.

JACQUES JOUET, *Mountain R.*
Savage.
Upstaged.
MIEKO KANAI, *The Word Book.*
YORAM KANIUK, *Life on Sandpaper.*
ZURAB KARUMIDZE, *Dagny.*
JOHN KELLY, *From Out of the City.*
HUGH KENNER, *Flaubert, Joyce and Beckett: The Stoic Comedians.*
Joyce's Voices.
DANILO KIŠ, *The Attic.*
The Lute and the Scars.
Psalm 44.
A Tomb for Boris Davidovich.
ANITA KONKKA, *A Fool's Paradise.*
GEORGE KONRÁD, *The City Builder.*
TADEUSZ KONWICKI, *A Minor Apocalypse.*
The Polish Complex.
ANNA KORDZAIA-SAMADASHVILI, *Me, Margarita.*
MENIS KOUMANDAREAS, *Koula.*
ELAINE KRAF, *The Princess of 72nd Street.*
JIM KRUSOE, *Iceland.*
AYSE KULIN, *Farewell: A Mansion in Occupied Istanbul.*
EMILIO LASCANO TEGUI, *On Elegance While Sleeping.*
ERIC LAURRENT, *Do Not Touch.*
VIOLETTE LEDUC, *La Bâtarde.*
EDOUARD LEVÉ, *Autoportrait.*
Newspaper.
Suicide.
Works.
MARIO LEVI, *Istanbul Was a Fairy Tale.*
DEBORAH LEVY, *Billy and Girl.*
JOSÉ LEZAMA LIMA, *Paradiso.*
ROSA LIKSOM, *Dark Paradise.*
OSMAN LINS, *Avalovara.*
The Queen of the Prisons of Greece.
FLORIAN LIPUŠ, *The Errors of Young Tjaž.*
GORDON LISH, *Peru.*
ALF MACLOCHLAINN, *Out of Focus.*
Past Habitual.

The Corpus in the Library.
RON LOEWINSOHN, *Magnetic Field(s).*
YURI LOTMAN, *Non-Memoirs.*
D. KEITH MANO, *Take Five.*
MINA LOY, *Stories and Essays of Mina Loy.*
MICHELINE AHARONIAN MARCOM, *A Brief History of Yes.*
The Mirror in the Well.
BEN MARCUS, *The Age of Wire and String.*
WALLACE MARKFIELD, *Teitlebaum's Window.*
DAVID MARKSON, *Reader's Block.*
Wittgenstein's Mistress.
CAROLE MASO, *AVA.*
HISAKI MATSUURA, *Triangle.*
LADISLAV MATEJKA & KRYSTYNA POMORSKA, EDS., *Readings in Russian Poetics: Formalist & Structuralist Views.*
HARRY MATHEWS, *Cigarettes.*
The Conversions.
The Human Country.
The Journalist.
My Life in CIA.
Singular Pleasures.
The Sinking of the Odradek.
Stadium.
Tlooth.
HISAKI MATSUURA, *Triangle.*
DONAL MCLAUGHLIN, *beheading the virgin mary, and other stories.*
JOSEPH MCELROY, *Night Soul and Other Stories.*
ABDELWAHAB MEDDEB, *Talismano.*
GERHARD MEIER, *Isle of the Dead.*
HERMAN MELVILLE, *The Confidence-Man.*
AMANDA MICHALOPOULOU, *I'd Like.*
STEVEN MILLHAUSER, *The Barnum Museum.*
In the Penny Arcade.
RALPH J. MILLS, JR., *Essays on Poetry.*
MOMUS, *The Book of Jokes.*
CHRISTINE MONTALBETTI, *The Origin of Man.*
Western.

NICHOLAS MOSLEY, *Accident.*
 Assassins.
 Catastrophe Practice.
 A Garden of Trees.
 Hopeful Monsters.
 Imago Bird.
 Inventing God.
 Look at the Dark.
 Metamorphosis.
 Natalie Natalia.
 Serpent.
WARREN MOTTE, *Fables of the Novel:*
 French Fiction since 1990.
 Fiction Now: The French Novel in the
 21st Century.
 Mirror Gazing.
 Oulipo: A Primer of Potential Literature.
GERALD MURNANE, *Barley Patch.*
 Inland.
YVES NAVARRE, *Our Share of Time.*
 Sweet Tooth.
DOROTHY NELSON, *In Night's City.*
 Tar and Feathers.
ESHKOL NEVO, *Homesick.*
WILFRIDO D. NOLLEDO, *But for*
 the Lovers.
BORIS A. NOVAK, *The Master of*
 Insomnia.
FLANN O'BRIEN, *At Swim-Two-Birds.*
 The Best of Myles.
 The Dalkey Archive.
 The Hard Life.
 The Poor Mouth.
 The Third Policeman.
CLAUDE OLLIER, *The Mise-en-Scène.*
 Wert and the Life Without End.
PATRIK OUŘEDNÍK, *Europeana.*
 The Opportune Moment, 1855.
BORIS PAHOR, *Necropolis.*
FERNANDO DEL PASO, *News from*
 the Empire.
 Palinuro of Mexico.
ROBERT PINGET, *The Inquisitory.*
 Mahu or The Material.
 Trio.
MANUEL PUIG, *Betrayed by Rita*
 Hayworth.

 The Buenos Aires Affair.
 Heartbreak Tango.
RAYMOND QUENEAU, *The Last Days.*
 Odile.
 Pierrot Mon Ami.
 Saint Glinglin.
ANN QUIN, *Berg.*
 Passages.
 Three.
 Tripticks.
ISHMAEL REED, *The Free-Lance*
 Pallbearers.
 The Last Days of Louisiana Red.
 Ishmael Reed: The Plays.
 Juice!
 The Terrible Threes.
 The Terrible Twos.
 Yellow Back Radio Broke-Down.
JASIA REICHARDT, *15 Journeys Warsaw*
 to London.
JOÃO UBALDO RIBEIRO, *House of the*
 Fortunate Buddhas.
JEAN RICARDOU, *Place Names.*
RAINER MARIA RILKE,
 The Notebooks of Malte Laurids Brigge.
JULIÁN RÍOS, *The House of Ulysses.*
 Larva: A Midsummer Night's Babel.
 Poundemonium.
ALAIN ROBBE-GRILLET, *Project for a*
 Revolution in New York.
 A Sentimental Novel.
AUGUSTO ROA BASTOS, *I the Supreme.*
DANIËL ROBBERECHTS, *Arriving in*
 Avignon.
JEAN ROLIN, *The Explosion of the*
 Radiator Hose.
OLIVIER ROLIN, *Hotel Crystal.*
ALIX CLEO ROUBAUD, *Alix's Journal.*
JACQUES ROUBAUD, *The Form of*
 a City Changes Faster, Alas, Than the
 Human Heart.
 The Great Fire of London.
 Hortense in Exile.
 Hortense Is Abducted.
 Mathematics: The Plurality of Worlds of
 Lewis.
 Some Thing Black.

RAYMOND ROUSSEL, *Impressions of Africa.*

VEDRANA RUDAN, *Night.*

PABLO M. RUIZ, *Four Cold Chapters on the Possibility of Literature.*

GERMAN SADULAEV, *The Maya Pill.*

TOMAŽ ŠALAMUN, *Soy Realidad.*

LYDIE SALVAYRE, *The Company of Ghosts.*
The Lecture.
The Power of Flies.

LUIS RAFAEL SÁNCHEZ, *Macho Camacho's Beat.*

SEVERO SARDUY, *Cobra & Maitreya.*

NATHALIE SARRAUTE, *Do You Hear Them?*
Martereau.
The Planetarium.

STIG SÆTERBAKKEN, *Siamese.*
Self-Control.
Through the Night.

ARNO SCHMIDT, *Collected Novellas.*
Collected Stories.
Nobodaddy's Children.
Two Novels.

ASAF SCHURR, *Motti.*

GAIL SCOTT, *My Paris.*

DAMION SEARLS, *What We Were Doing and Where We Were Going.*

JUNE AKERS SEESE,
Is This What Other Women Feel Too?

BERNARD SHARE, *Inish.*
Transit.

VIKTOR SHKLOVSKY, *Bowstring.*
Literature and Cinematography.
Theory of Prose.
Third Factory.
Zoo, or Letters Not about Love.

PIERRE SINIAC, *The Collaborators.*

KJERSTI A. SKOMSVOLD,
The Faster I Walk, the Smaller I Am.

JOSEF ŠKVORECKÝ, *The Engineer of Human Souls.*

GILBERT SORRENTINO, *Aberration of Starlight.*
Blue Pastoral.
Crystal Vision.

Imaginative Qualities of Actual Things.
Mulligan Stew. Red the Fiend.
Steelwork.
Under the Shadow.

MARKO SOSIČ, *Ballerina, Ballerina.*

ANDRZEJ STASIUK, *Dukla.*
Fado.

GERTRUDE STEIN, *The Making of Americans.*
A Novel of Thank You.

LARS SVENDSEN, *A Philosophy of Evil.*

PIOTR SZEWC, *Annihilation.*

GONÇALO M. TAVARES, *A Man: Klaus Klump.*
Jerusalem.
Learning to Pray in the Age of Technique.

LUCIAN DAN TEODOROVICI,
Our Circus Presents...

NIKANOR TERATOLOGEN, *Assisted Living.*

STEFAN THEMERSON, *Hobson's Island.*
The Mystery of the Sardine.
Tom Harris.

TAEKO TOMIOKA, *Building Waves.*

JOHN TOOMEY, *Sleepwalker.*

DUMITRU TSEPENEAG, *Hotel Europa.*
The Necessary Marriage.
Pigeon Post.
Vain Art of the Fugue.

ESTHER TUSQUETS, *Stranded.*

DUBRAVKA UGRESIC, *Lend Me Your Character.*
Thank You for Not Reading.

TOR ULVEN, *Replacement.*

MATI UNT, *Brecht at Night.*
Diary of a Blood Donor.
Things in the Night.

ÁLVARO URIBE & OLIVIA SEARS, EDS.,
Best of Contemporary Mexican Fiction.

ELOY URROZ, *Friction.*
The Obstacles.

LUISA VALENZUELA, *Dark Desires and the Others.*
He Who Searches.

PAUL VERHAEGHEN, *Omega Minor.*

BORIS VIAN, *Heartsnatcher.*